DERAILLEUR

a cycling murder mystery

Greg Moody

VeloPress • Boulder, Colorado

International Standard Book Number: 1-884737-59-5

Library of Congress Cataloging-in Publication Data

Moody, Greg, 1952-
      Derailleur : a cycling murder mystery / Greg Moody.
        p.   cm.
      ISBN 1-884737-59-5
      I. Title.
      PS3563.05525D47   1999
      813' .54--dc21   99-13510
                                         CIP

Printed in the USA

Distributed in the United States and Canada
by Publishers Group West.

VeloPress
1830 North 55th Street
Boulder, Colorado 80301-2700 USA
303/440-0601; fax 303/444-6788; e-mail velopress@7dogs.com

To purchase additional copies of this book or other VeloPress books,
call 800/234-8356, or visit the Web at www.velogear.com.

Cover illustration: Matt Brownson
Book cover/interior design: Erin Johnson
Layout/Production: Paulette Livers-Lambert

Acknowledgments

Once again, my thanks to the staff of VeloPress, especially Amy Sorrells, and *VeloNews*. They are always ready with an insight and a chance to laugh. Also, my thanks to Steve Youngerman, Stephen White, and my readers, including Jim and Rhonda Hoyt, who are so generous with thoughts, encouragement, and a kick in the butt.

The generosity of the residents of Vail, Colorado—friends too numerous to mention—is also deeply appreciated.

But, as always, my greatest thanks go to Becky and Devon and Brynn. They bring me laughter and joy and hope, each and every day.

Thanks to them—and you—I am the luckiest man on the face of the earth.

For Becky
With thanks to those who read

CONTENTS

PROLOGUE

September

FORTY YEARS AGO

She was dancing inside a glass pressure-cooker.

September in northern Ohio usually carried with it the promise of fall, of cool days and crisp nights, an occasional day of warmth that naturally turned your face toward the sun and the sky, and the rising scent of oak leaves smoldering in the distance, curling into death, giving off a rare outdoor musk that cannot be captured anywhere else, by nothing else in the world. But this was not a usual September in Ohio. The heat of August carried over, pushing the promise of a new season off to a point no one could foresee, while imprisoning this corner of the world in a heatwave that made eyes sting and faces sweat and people grumpy as hell.

At the moment, Marjorie Stump was having a baby, which was among the worst things you could possibly do at a time like this, especially in a hospital without air-conditioning. She had never been good at timing, and now she was paying the price for a moment of carnal weakness and sin last December.

The labor was going on thirty hours. Marjorie Stump didn't even do things she *liked* for thirty hours.

Through the pain and the sweat she focused on the heavy, black-edged industrial clock hanging on the dirty, grey stucco wall over the door to her right, the crystal and face shattered in one corner, obviously by something thrown in anger or panic in the past. Inside, a large horsefly now sat defiantly, riding the sweep hand like a tiny Pecos Bill. Every now and then, the clock jerked spasmodically, as if a cog inside the works caught, fought with itself, then suddenly gave up the fight in a fit of disgust. Each time the clock shuddered, Marjorie Stump could swear she saw the weathered, water-stained stucco give, almost imperceptibly, as if the wall were ready to collapse, bringing the clock down to the floor, giving the horsefly one final, spectacular ride.

She turned her eyes as she gritted her teeth and bore down again, trying to find something new to focus on to lift her past her exhaustion and pain.

The nurse poked her head in the door.

"Anything?"

"Urrrrrrrrcccccckkkkkkk"

"All right, well, I'll be back."

"No, no," Marjorie whimpered, her silent, mental scream chasing down the tiled hallway after the woman in the starched white dress. "I need you. I can't feel my feet. You've got to stop the pain. Come back, come back."

She took a deep breath and cursed herself for her weakness. She didn't need the nurse's help. She didn't need anybody's help. She was in this alone, and she would deal with it alone. She raised her head off the pillow and felt a drop of sweat roll down the back of her neck.

The little off-white room, gone to grey, was stifling. They could at least open a window. Ah, but no. What if one of the new mothers screamed during delivery? What if someone showed an ounce of reality, an ounce of discomfort? What would happen to the sanctity of Youngstown, Ohio, if people screamed out the windows of the local hospital? You must be brave. You must be quiet. You must endure as all those brave little generations of women before you endured.

Don't embarrass the hospital.

Oh, my God. Oh, my God. Oh, my God.

She sank back onto her soggy pillow.

Oh, my God.

She pushed again, as much just to end it all as to bear her child. She suddenly didn't care, one way or another, how it all turned out. She hated the child, she hated the hospital, and more than anything, or anyone, she hated the man who had done this to her and now sat across the room, his ear close to a brown Bakelite radio, ignoring her, deeply involved in the Cleveland Indians and a late-season, meaningless contest with the Detroit Tigers.

Her head began to weave, back and forth, back and forth, in a fitful circle, as she began to repeat, over and over, "I hate you. I hate you all. I hate you. I hate you all. I hate you. I hate you all."

Marjorie Stump mumbled her mantra to the window, to the door, and back again, the repetition enough to make time finally move again and make the fly leave the sweep hand, fly through the hole in the crystal of the clock and out the door of the room. Beyond the glass, she saw movement in the trees as Mother Nature took pity on her servant Marjorie and sent a breeze blowing cool air off the petroleum foulness of Lake Erie. Now, if only the window would open.

"Elmo," she whispered hoarsely through dry, cracked lips. "Elmo?"

He paid her no mind.

"Elmo."

Elmo didn't move from his pose beside the radio.

Marjorie Stump turned to her side and saw a small silver tray, a hospital pan, of some sort, sitting on the edge of the table beside her. She reached for it, fingered it, and felt it nearly slip to the floor in her exhaustion.

With a surge of effort she clutched the lip of the pan and began to squeeze, tightly, her strength, nearly gone only the moment before, suddenly coursing through her as if driven by a sheer force of will. Tighter and tighter she clutched the metal pan, feeling a hot kernel of life begin to grow within her.

"Elmo," she said, in a stronger voice.

Nothing.

"Elmo?" she called, the anger and edge in her tone suddenly breaking through his mental fog, if only for a moment, causing him to wave at her with a sign of dismissal.

"EL-MO!" she cried, full voice, throwing herself to the side and flinging the tray toward the window.

He turned at both her cry and the shattering of the window, instinctively covering himself from the danger of flying glass that came nowhere near him. He stared, wide-eyed, at the window, then turned back to the radio. He didn't have time for her foolishness. The game was in the ninth. It was going to be close.

The temperature in the room suddenly dropped ten degrees as the breeze forced its way past the shards of glass and toward Marjorie Stump. As the first trembling of air crossed her brow, she felt a flutter of movement deep within her and began to bear down again on the baby that acted as if it finally wanted free of her womb.

"About time," she thought.

The breeze continued to surround her, caress her, fill her with a newfound power and strength that she had never experienced in her life. Mother Nature, she thought to herself, her eyes locked on a crack in a tree just outside her window, Mother Nature was the only one who cared, the only one who had come to her aid.

She closed her eyes for a moment and reveled in the cool of the breeze, the sensation taking her beyond the pain for a moment, for the first moment in more than thirty hours of moments.

The prim nurse stepped into the doorway and pushed her glasses back up on the bridge of her nose as her eyes grew wide at the obvious lack of respect for hospital property.

"Why is that window open?" she barked, putting the question directly to Elmo Stump.

Elmo drew himself away from the game for only a moment, despite the fact that his favorite beer was being advertised, and jerked a thumb toward the bed.

"Ask her. She broke it."

He turned back to the radio. The nurse stepped into the room and marched directly over to the side of the bed, mentally preparing the speech on how to act while having a baby, when she noticed that not only was Marjorie in a state of what appeared to be hypnosis, but that blood was soaking the sheets below her waist.

"Oh, my God ... God ... God. We've got to get you into delivery."

She scuttled to the door and screamed down the hallway toward a world that was outside the consciousness of Marjorie Stump. For herself, Marjorie felt only a vague sense of movement in her belly, while her mind drifted away on the cool edges of a late-summer breeze.

There were people around her now, a doctor off to one side, his voice flat at the end of a tunnel, and several nurses, trying to lift her up and away from the bed. Failing that, they began their work there, the moment being now at hand.

A nurse stepped to the left side of the bed, blocking Marjorie Stump's view of the paradise just outside the window. Without breaking her concentration,

Marjorie reached up and pushed to the side, throwing the nurse in a heap to the floor near the head of the bed.

"Hold her. Somebody hold her," the doctor shouted. A nurse stepped forward, again, into the path of the window, but was shoved away. The doctor, now with his hands full of water, mucous, and gore, turned to Elmo Stump, the game trapped in extra innings. The listener sat slumped in his chair, relaxed and satisfied in the chance of an Indians' win, casually smoking a Lucky.

"We need your help."

Elmo Stump took a drag and shrugged. "I've done my bit. This is your job."

Something washed over the doctor's hand and forced his attention back. He called over his shoulder, "This is an emergency. We need you up at the head of the bed to calm your wife."

Elmo blew the smoke through his nose, then popped a smoke ring.

"Don't see why." He glanced over. "She seems pretty calm to me. Besides, this is what I pay you for."

"Help us, please."

Elmo Stump rolled the butt of the Lucky in his fingers and pondered the plea.

"Fifty bucks."

"What?"

"Fifty bucks. Fifty bucks off the bill, no charge for the window, and I'll help."

The baby was starting to crown. Marjorie rose up in the bed and began to stretch herself toward the window.

"Push her down. Push her down," the doctor called. He cradled the baby's head for a moment, then cried out, "Yes, yes, all right. Fifty bucks. Fifty bucks."

Elmo Stump smiled and rose out of his chair. With all due deliberation, he ambled past the end of the bed where the doctor now held the top of his child's head and stood beside Marjorie's shoulder.

She didn't push him away, but not because he was Elmo, merely because he wasn't standing between her and the window like the two nurses before him.

Elmo took one last, deep, satisfying drag off the Lucky and blew the smoke down on Marjorie.

"Get rid of that goddamned thing," the doctor shouted, the baby, its head out, now caught by the width of its shoulders in the birth canal.

Elmo shrugged and turned, flicking the still-smoldering butt out the window, the cigarette leaving a trail of smoke as it crossed into, and then out of, Marjorie Stump's line of sight.

The assault through her window, her small passageway to the world outside, toward the one source that had given her comfort in all her pain and trial, sent a shock wave of hatred through Marjorie Stump.

The doctor, at the end of the bed, was suddenly holding a writhing, screaming baby that had left the birth canal as if shot from a cannon. Meanwhile, at the head of the bed, Elmo Stump rose up on his tip toes as something suddenly clutched his testicles in a vise-like grip. Elmo tried to writhe away, tried to scream, but the sudden viciousness of the attack on his manhood drove his breath completely out of him.

He looked down at Marjorie, who stared out the window in a state of blissful hypnosis, and slapped vainly, weakly, at her arm. He squeaked in protest at this violation of his most sacred spot. Elmo waved at the doctors and nurses at the foot of the bed, the doctor now collapsed in the chair next to the radio, his five minutes of effort having exhausted him, the nurses busy wrapping the latest addition to the Youngstown, Ohio, tax base.

"He's huge," one whispered.

"It must have been like trying to pass a watermelon."

Ignoring them all, Marjorie calmly stared out the window, the strength returning to her in great waves on the crest of every breeze, the pressure in her left hand continuing to build, and build, the natural force that lay outside the window growing within her, until she felt two small 'pops' and the clutch of clothing pull away in her hand.

Elmo fell to the floor, unable to breathe, unable to speak, unable to move, his hands grasping his crotch, a sack now filled with indefinable mush. His mind screamed for help while his voice remained silent except for a weak mewling and puking that carried under the bed and stayed there, alone and unheard.

An eleventh inning home run sank the Indians. The doctor shook his head and sighed as he rose up out of the chair, stepping over to the edge of the bed, now covered in blood, the afterbirth laying ignored between Marjorie Stump's legs.

He leaned over and slapped her heavy upper thigh.

"Nice job, Mrs…" he leaned back to check the name at the top of the chart at the end of the bed, "…Stump. Nice job. You were fast. Didn't even have time to get you to delivery."

He leaned back again and muttered to the nurses, "For God's sake, clean this up, will you? What the hell do we pay you for?"

The two nurses smiled blandly and turned their attention back to the baby.

The doctor turned back to Marjorie.

"Good job. Good job…" he reached down to check the chart, "…Marjorie. Nice job, Marge. You've got a lovely baby…" he turned once more to check, "…boy. A lovely baby boy."

He leaned over to slap her thigh again and noticed two feet sticking out from under the bed.

"What the…oh, my God," was all he could say. Slowly, as if in a trance, the doctor began to flail his left arm backward to the nurses, trying to get the attention of the two women to let them know that there was a man underneath the head of a bed in the maternity ward, desperately clutching himself and, judging by the rictus of pain that decorated his face, quite obviously dead.

Another great burst of noise and activity suddenly filled the room, but passed by the consciousness of Marjorie Stump without intrusion. A breeze washed across her and for the first time in more than nine months, Marjorie not only felt comfortable again, but suddenly in charge of her life, in control of who she was and where she was going.

She was going outside.

September

PRESENT DAY

Slowly, and with great deliberation, Fred Manfra drew the line across the bottom of the blueprint.

After 25 years as a draftsman, he still preferred to do the finish work on a print himself. He knew computers, he knew CAD programs from the first to the latest, but there was nothing in his mind to compare to the sense of doing at least some of it by hand, of leaving a bit of your own talent and creativity and sureness of hand on the final design, on the working print of a new development.

He sat back in his chair and reached to the side for the mug, carefully plucking it from a forest of mechanical pencils. He took a sip of the quickly cooling tea and pondered his latest creation.

Vail Mountain Terrace. Quite a name. Quite a location.

Manfra could see the Manfra/Skell Construction brochure now, with its "nestled in the heart of the Vail Valley" riff. He had to admit, this was going to be nice—nice and expensive. There wasn't much available with these amenities in this location at this altitude, or at this price. This was a whole new development on the mountain itself that reached up toward mid-Vail, the halfway mark on the peak. Even the filthy rich couldn't find places like this, unless, of course, they drove down the road to Aspen and opened a vein on their bank accounts.

"So, why can't they do their bleeding on me?" he whispered.

But the greed stirred up a reminder: of late loans and missed payments and construction schedules gone awry. They're probably not even working tonight. Somebody belches in Vail, and the crew takes the day off. This thing will never get done on time.

On budget was already shot.

Manfra tapped the mechanical pencil on the edge of the table for a long moment, wondering when, this time, he would see Skell again. His partner, the money man, was on the same schedule as the builders, it seemed. One day here, one lunch, one meeting, then off again for days at a time.

It was easier, Manfra thought, when he was just an architect. Here's some money, go draw something.

Now that the company was his, and Skell's, it got complicated and expensive. Everything he owned was in this project, every dime he had ever seen.

It wasn't going to be enough.

But it was, he had to admit, one hell of a project. He took one last look at the board and smiled, then crouched over his work to sign the corner with the chicken scratch he had been using as a signature since high school.

"Done," he said aloud to the empty room. "Done and done."

Manfra leaned back, slurped down the last of the tea, now tepid, and placed the empty cup on the far edge of his loose-plank table. With this, he thought, tapping the edge of the architectural design with the tip of his finger, he could finally afford real furniture. About damned time. He rose out of the chair, arched his back, and did a passable imitation of his cat.

"Damn," he said aloud to no one, for no reason in particular.

He stepped over toward the window, his eyes registering the dark silence of the Bonnie Brae neighborhood of Denver, an unusual situation, especially this close to University Boulevard.

He stood staring at his reflection in the glass, his eyes drifting down to the thickening around his waist that he hadn't been able to stop, despite a serious-ass diet for the past three years and a seemingly endless number of crunches in his basement gym. Next stop, he thought, liposuction.

Fred Manfra smiled.

He'd be able to afford that, as well.

His eyes drifted up the reflected outline of his body to his chest, also slowly going to fat. May have to have some breast work done as well, he thought. May as well. One-stop shopping.

As he stared at his own reflection, Fred Manfra noticed an odd trick of lighting, as if he were looking at a poorly tuned TV set and seeing a ghost image of himself, just inside the lines of his true reflection. The oddest thing about it was that the ghost image was wearing different clothing.

He dropped his head to the side as if to make the image shift, but it remained just inside his own outline.

Then, with a "pop-pop", "dink-dink", Manfra noticed two small holes appear in the middle of his reflection, just about chest level in the glass. He looked down at his shirt and noticed that the two holes corresponded, almost exactly, with the two holes that had suddenly appeared in his khaki shirt, just below his left nipple. He looked at them for a moment, then raised his head in a bobbing and exaggerated way. He looked at the holes in the window, then returned his gaze to the holes in his shirt, now seeping with blood.

Still staring, he fell backward in a straight-edge arc, catching the base of his skull on the edge of his wood-plank table-top, the force flipping the board and sending a shower of pens and pencils, notes and notebooks, and one empty tea mug in a reverse arc across the room toward the window.

The last sound that Fred Manfra heard was the sound of an empty tea cup shattering a window that contained two bullet holes and some much needed evidence for the Denver Police Department.

"Shit," he thought, expelling one final breath, "I broke a window."

✦

THE ROOT ROSE UP QUICKLY IN THE DIMMING LIGHT ON VAIL MOUNTAIN.

Harold Beaton, creator of the Beaton Bomber, leader of the BBs, the Beaton Bomber Bunch, and cult-figure of mountain biking, depending on who you talked to, cut his bike's line of descent sharply and clipped the edge of the root, shifting his weight to bring the bike back to the center of the treacherous single track.

This section of the course was abandoned after the World Mountain Bike Championships of 1994, and had generally fallen into disrepair, but Beaton still rode it every chance he could, the challenge of surviving the mountain and the shambles of a championship course breathing new life into his aging and creaking body.

God, this was ridiculous, he thought, fat, forty-five, and falling apart.

Beaton dropped down a ridge onto a service road and pedaled hard, picking up his speed going into the switchbacks across the face of Vail Mountain. He cut across the road and sailed cleanly through the ditch, picking up the trail to the first switchback without slackening his pace. He had altered his nightly excursion a bit, beginning the ride above mid-Vail to give him a better workout before tailing out into his condo near the Christiania Hotel. By this time next year, he'd have to go even higher on the mountain to get a decent workout before ending up at his new home in Vail Mountain Terrace.

Higher on the food chain, higher on the mountain, he thought. It's the price of fame, the privilege of money.

The Beaton Electronic Gearing responded beautifully under his touch, a new development from R & D, light years ahead of the old Zap! technology.

In combination with the latest Titanium Bomber frame, this was the culmination of three decades of bicycle development. It would be the starring feature in the Beaton booth at this weekend's Ishmael Coffee Race expo at the Dobson Ice Arena.

Beaton smiled. Then again, that's what he thought last year with the Beaton Carbon Fiber Bomber. It was the hit of the show. Got a lot of copy in the trade press. Even a *Denver Post* feature that was syndicated nationwide. Sold a lot of bikes. Too bad the joints were worthless. A few fold-ups at high speed made for some ugly lawsuits that only money could make go away before the media or some snoopy government agency got hold of them.

The thickening cloud cover made sunset come early. In the creeping gloom, Beaton stared ahead along the single track, trying to catch the mark where he knew he'd have to begin braking to safely make another hairpin turn. He didn't see it, but sensed the tree go by, close alongside his right eyelid. As he began to brake, he peered ahead for the turn, but at the last minute noticed a pile of rocks and logs blocking the turn itself. He was still going too fast to really do anything about it and resigned himself to the fact that he'd run off the end of the track at the turn and bury himself in the local flora for a few feet.

Such was life, such was the beauty, such was the reality of mountain biking. He had lived it and known it far too long to panic now.

Yet, in the split second as he crossed the line of the turn, he noticed, to his right, up above him on the mountain, a short and round figure holding a stick, a stick that flared and thundered in the still dusk of a Colorado night and scared the living hell out of Harold Beaton.

Reacting on prehistoric instinct alone, Beaton tore directly down the side of Vail Mountain, out of control and out of his head with fear. Blinded by panic he burst through the trees and shot across two switchbacks in a headlong rush.

He frantically braked, ignoring all his own, painfully learned rules about control at high speeds over uneven track. His arms ached from the battering of the suspension fork, a cheap knock-off that Beaton realized would never hold up and could cause him more legal grief down the road.

He threw a glance backward up the mountain and heard another "boom!" almost as if in answer to his look. He pedaled hard again, ignoring the brakes now. Looking backward had pulled him to the right and onto a line heading for another patch of trees, roots, rocks, and certain death.

Beaton considered bailing out for a second, but dismissed the idea, having never bailed out in his life. This was part of it all, he knew, and had been since that very first day on Mount Tamalpais, just across the Golden Gate Bridge from San Francisco, when he had driven up the mountain in his sports car with Susie Frenetti and had seen the bikes for the first time. He had stared and measured and committed the idea to memory, before racing back to the city, outlining the idea on paper and creating a fortune.

It hadn't been his idea. But, then again, it had. They were merely riders, he thought. It had taken him to make the most of the idea, he reasoned.

And now, he was in the thick of it.

Harold Beaton hunkered down on the bike and tried to pick a line through the foliage. One last peek of sunlight through a gap in a cloud gave him a clue, and he pitched the bike hard left toward a gap between a tree and a boulder. He caught the edge of his pedal on the rock but powered ahead, on line and just barely out of control. He caught himself suddenly in high grass and felt himself slowing naturally. He was going to make it. Harold Beaton would live to ride another day.

In his relief, he didn't notice the cliff that dropped straight down for five feet, rebuilding his speed before ending in a natural bowl that lifted him up into the air and sent him flying, pedaling madly through the air, between two trees and into a full-length, two-story, plate-glass window that shattered into a sea of crystal diamonds around the front wheel and then him, showering down around as the bike slammed onto the floor of the great room and skittered across the carpet into the central stone fireplace.

Beaton did a face plant into the rocks and felt his nose explode in a sea of blood and gristle, then fell backward, hard, against the floor, covering his face as the rain of plate-glass window pieces slowly subsided around him.

He pulled his arm away from his eyes with great deliberation, cringing once as a piece of glass broke noisily somewhere close by. He blinked, twice, then slowly took stock of his physical situation.

His toes still moved. His legs were sore, but didn't feel broken. His back—he shifted his pelvis—seemed intact. Slowly, painfully, he sat up, trying to catch his breath. He shook his head and felt his nose flop crazily to one side. He took a deep breath and blinked again, widening his eyes to clear his vision.

One broken nose. No other problems evident. Harold Beaton smiled.

Twenty-five years of putting his life on the line every time he rode a bike, and he had survived the worst that God had to throw at him.

Damn, he was good.

With deliberation, Harold Beaton rolled over on his side, then carefully balancing on his knees, rose to a kneeling position, took one last measure of his internal condition, then stood up.

He weaved for a moment, then caught himself, holding the edge of the fireplace for support. He took a breath, and then lifted his arms in triumph over his head. He had survived again.

"Beaton Bombers ... Rule," he shouted, the final word ringing maniacally off the shadowed rafters of the shattered room.

His arms high in the air, his triumph complete, Harold Beaton never saw the man with the collector's quality U.S. Army-issue Colt .45 step from the darkened hall and shout, "Die you two-bit son-of-a-bitch!" and fire six shots, tightly grouped, into the middle of the "t" in the word Beaton written across his jersey, the Spandex covering his chest doing little to stop or even slow the progress of the slugs going in or the blood coming out.

It was a rush into darkness, a flight toward a fiber and fabric barricade placed directly in the path of his face surrounded by a room highlighted by a colorful ski print wrapped in plastic just above a butternut leather couch that lay just beyond reach.

Harold Beaton grew still. He struggled to open his eyes again and did, his focus collapsing into an area closer and closer to his shattered body, his eyes staring for the last few seconds of his life at a piece of glass broken into the distinctive shape of Idaho.

Idaho, he thought.

I always liked Idaho.

THURSDAY

CHAPTER ONE:

WAY OUT WEST

THE .45 STUNG IN HIS HAND FROM THE RECOIL OF THE SHOTS, WHILE he realized that he couldn't hear anything other than a high pitched 'zing.' Leonard Romanowski stared across the floor, now covered with glass and blood, bicycle and dead body, and desperately tried to figure out who it was now expired on the carpet of the pilfered condo as he just as desperately tried to control his bowels.

Who would Bloody Angelo have sent?

He didn't look like the standard New York troglodyte Angelo sent around to the office. Those were merely enforcers, bone crushers, men without a conscience or lick of finesse who would break your fingers without a second thought and then hit a Coney stand for lunch on the way home.

No, anyone who would be after him now would be the top of the line, the kind of man who could blend into a crowd of Amish schoolteachers, step out suddenly, tap you twice behind the ear and then disappear back into the crowd without anyone the wiser.

Except, of course, you, as you died on the pavement from having your brains scrambled by a piece of lead smaller than the eraser on a pencil.

This was one of those, for sure, Romanowski thought: someone smooth and slick who could blend into the moneyed mountain playground of Vail, Colorado, on the weekend of some big bicycle race and, yet, daring enough to attack him full front through a plate-glass window.

Leonard fell backward against the wall and tried to control his breathing. They were on to him. Damn. And he had covered his tracks so well.

3

How the hell … shit. Something in the office. Something he hadn't noticed in his rush to get away from the City.

What? What was it?

Didn't matter. Didn't matter. He was here. They were here. He had to clear out.

Where? Where to now? There would, he knew, be more on the way.

Leonard's thoughts raced out of control, but there was enough sense left in the thunderstorm between his ears to realize that he had to get out of this house, he had to get to a place where he could be safe for a few hours and think this through.

He wanted to puke, but there was too much to do. Leonard rolled to his side and nearly fell down the hallway toward the one bedroom of the condo that did not have windows. He clutched the door jamb leading to the small white-and-blue room, stepped over to the bunk beds, the mattresses still in their protective plastic wrap, and zipped the blue gym bag shut. He was packed and ready to go.

You had to be ready to move, he thought, when you were trying to lift nearly five million dollars from the New York mob.

He slid the magazine from the Colt and reloaded.

Pick up your brass, he remembered. Pick up your brass. One last clue. Slow up the cops. Pick up your brass.

He slid the magazine home.

Leonard grabbed the bag and moved quickly back into the great room, finding four casings quickly, right beside where he had been standing, then, one under a couch and the sixth on the edge of the fireplace. He laughed, in a crazy, out-of-control sort of way that made him sound like Homer Simpson on a bender, grabbed his bag and strode quickly toward the door to the garage.

First things first, he thought. Find a new safe house. Find a safe place for the money. Get the hell out of Dodge, or Vail, or wherever the hell he was right now.

He pushed a button to open the garage door as he stepped carefully over the muddy floor to the car, which he had backed into the parking spot only last night. Then, he started the rented Chevrolet and pulled away from the condo-under-construction, scanning the area around him frantically for witnesses as he drove. Good. A midweek September night in the mountains and all the vacationers and homeowners were still down in Denver waiting for the week-end. Nobody had noticed anything, despite a sharpness in the air that must have carried the sound for miles.

He played with the gear shift and the accelerator as he rattled and swayed along the ruts of the tree-lined access road, overcompensating with each bump until he was bouncing in the cheap bucket seat like a rag doll in a washing machine.

He took a deep breath and tried to steady himself.

Not to worry, he thought, you've covered your tracks. There are no prints in the house. You haven't left any evidence for these mountain cops to nail you on. Besides, in two hours, after a drink, you can figure out where you want to go next, and just stay ahead of everybody.

"You are in control," he said, aloud, to no one in particular.

"You are in control."

The dual eyes of the headlights lunged frantically across the road and into the heavy pine, then back again, like a drunken man desperately running down an uneven hallway in the middle of the night.

Meanwhile, the single eye of the U.S. Army Issue Colt .45 stared from its perch on the fireplace hearth across a blandly cream carpet, now spotted with glass and grease and blood, toward the body of its latest victim.

The gun said nothing, but merely stared at its handiwork with an air of satisfaction from its still warm barrel.

✺

"ARE WE THERE YET?"

The man asking stared out the window as the last rays of sunlight began to disappear from the western sky behind what looked like an endless sea of mountains, each hill on the doorstep to a ridge, each ridge leading to a crag, each crag the gateway to a peak, the pattern repeated, from his perspective, into an odd sort of eternity. The sky went quickly from blue streaked with golden highlights to red to magenta to black, filled with more stars than he had seen since his last night ride through the fields of the Netherlands.

God, he thought, that was years ago. With Marie. And she had a blanket. He had never seen so many stars in the sky, even if he had to look around her bobbing head to see them.

He turned to the driver and asked again.

"Are we there yet?"

"You're worse than a four-year-old, you know that?" she answered with a mock anger. "No, we're not there yet, and if you ask me again I'll pull over to the side of the Interstate and kick you out. Got that?"

"I've got to go."

She laughed.

"Why didn't you go at Copper Mountain?"

"Because you wouldn't stop."

"We've got to get there tonight."

"Jesus. It's not like we've got to empty a tanker. I've gotta whiz. Thirty seconds, max."

"Can't take the time. I've got a schedule to keep."

"You better hope I brought extra pants. This is getting serious."

"I didn't tell you to buy that Big Gulp on the way out of Denver."

"The plane ride from Michigan dehydrated me," he whined.

"No, the two hours you slept with your mouth open dehydrated you. By the way," she said, turning toward him and poking his cheek with a finger, "the left side of your face is still flat from the window. You might want to do something about that."

Will Ross reached up and rubbed his cheek again, stretching his face while doing it. The feeling had slowly come back to his face during the long walk to the terminal and he had actually felt his eyeball shift back around to its proper position on the little train ride to baggage claim. He knew he was fine, but he stretched his face again for good measure.

Cheryl Crane pulled the roller-skate Ford rental to the side of I-70 and brought it quickly to a stop near a stand of trees.

"Okay. This is my gesture of pity. Thirty seconds from right—now. Better get going. The clock's running." She stared at her watch.

"I better not get anything caught in my zipper," he muttered, first fighting with the seat belt, then with the door lock and finally the handle. He wrestled his leg brace out into the crisp air of the mountains and stumbled down a short incline into a stand of what appeared to be mutated pine.

Just my luck, he thought, I'll start peeing and these will turn out to be Drug Enforcement Agency undercovers and I'll be busted for a bursting bladder. He smiled.

"Ten seconds," he heard her call from the car.

Just the first moment of release was a relief, the notion that after the discomfort, if not the actual pain, of a wave building behind the wall, letting that wall down for a few moments was sheer delight.

"Okay, that's it. Gotta go."

She revved the engine twice, the little four-cylinder wheezing in the thin air, then began to roll forward slowly.

Go, he thought. Just go ahead and go. This was something he had to finish. This was something he wanted to savor. He heard the crunch of gravel up on the Interstate, the rumble of the engine, now heavier and throatier in the thin air.

The stream fell to a trickle and he flexed his lower abs to squeeze the last drops out.

Thank you. Thank you. Thank you, God.

He dropped his head back and sighed.

Then the darkened area just off the highway lit up with alternating red and blue lights and Will felt his penis shrink into a button winkie, leaping back into his pants for protection. Wish I could hide in there with you, he thought, zipping himself quickly and turning back toward the road.

The officer was already out of the Colorado State Patrol cruiser and was walking toward Cheryl's car as Will hobbled from the stand of trees. Tripping over a rock, he muttered a sharp "Shit!" and was blinded by a sharp beam of light.

"All right." The tone was stiff and commanding. "What's going on? What's the trouble here?"

Will suddenly felt an urgent need to pee again.

"Nothing. Nothing, officer. I just had to stop for a minute."

The officer, stiffly at ease at the rear corner of the Ford, flicked the light back toward Cheryl and then again toward Will, who now scrambled unsteadily up the incline with his hands in the air.

"Peeing in the bushes? We frown on that around here."

"I'm sorry. I had one of those big drinks."

"He had one of those big drinks," Cheryl added helpfully from the driver's seat.

"You should have stopped in Copper—about fifteen miles back."

"She wouldn't stop."

The officer flicked the light over toward the steering wheel again. "You should have stopped."

"Yes, sir. I will next time."

"Where are you headed?"

"Vail."

He flipped open a citation book and quickly wrote down a series of notes, stepping, as he did, toward the open window on Cheryl's side of the car.

He glanced at Will.

"Get back in."

He glanced at Cheryl.

"License and rental agreement, please."

She scowled at Will as she dug around in her purse, trying to find both items.

"This is all your fault," she hissed.

"No, this is the fault of the 7-Eleven company and its franchisees, who created a drink bigger than the human bladder."

Cheryl turned and offered her license to the officer, followed by a crushed and crinkled yellow sheet of paper.

He quickly scanned them both, then handed them back to her, slapping his citation book closed.

He flashed the light in Will's eyes.

"You … should time your potty stops better. Vail is only a few miles away and you could have made it to the Amoco, easy."

He softened his voice, noticeably, when he turned to Cheryl.

"And you ... should have given him a stop at Copper, Miz Crane."

He smiled with recognition and then added, "Good luck this weekend. It's going to be a great race."

She shook her head as if emerging from a trance and stared at him.

"Do I," she asked, carefully, "do I know you?"

"No ma'am," he said, turning to return to his cruiser, "you don't, but I do."

As he walked, he ticked off Cheryl's recently acquired credits.

"Cheryl Crane, 28 years old, team leader of the Haven-TW racing team, newly formed, riding a new Colnago mountain bike frame with Manitou forks and Campagnolo rapid-fire shifting."

He stopped and turned back toward the car.

"Why didn't you take twist-shifting?"

"I like thumb shifters."

"Old fashioned, too. I like that." He smiled and turned back toward the cruiser.

"Good luck this weekend. The Ishmael can be a killer."

Cheryl and Will sat silently in the car until the flashing lights of the cruiser went off and the officer pulled back onto I-70, waving as he headed toward Vail.

"Feel better now?" she asked in a strained and sarcastic tone.

"Yes, quite," he answered quietly.

"Fine." She revved the engine and spun the wheels getting back onto the highway, gravel shooting behind giving way to a quick squeal as the tires dug into the asphalt.

As the car accelerated, she uttered a sharp, "Ha!"

Will turned to her and muttered, "I don't know what you're snotty about. At least he recognized you."

"Well," she said, rising in the seat as her pride lifted her into a smile, "I don't consider that snotty. I consider that pretty damned neat, don't you?"

"Well, only if you consider it neat," he continued, oblivious to her, "that he not only recognized you. He read off your stats like you played second base for the 56 Phillies."

"Yeah, he did, didn't he?"

"Well, yeah, but, I mean, for what?" He struggled for a point that was nothing more than the bark of a bruised ego. "You haven't even done anything yet."

The tone and tenor in his voice made her begin to deflate and she fell back a bit against the rump-sprung upholstery of the little rented Ford. The delicious feeling of glowing pride that enveloped her just the moment before began to slip away as she realized that, as biting and insensitive as his comment was, it was true. She hadn't done anything except type up a bio and get her picture taken in the bright yellow, blue and white Haven-TW jersey. Cheryl felt herself mentally pushing away the sudden and surprising, perhaps unwarranted, recognition that had just been offered up to her and the glorious feelings that had gone with it.

She sighed.

She checked the mirror and changed lanes, gunning the little engine to kick it around slower-moving traffic.

In the sound of her voice and the silence that followed, he didn't hear the quiet shift of her mood from a glowing warmth to a dark chill. In her own loss of spirit, she didn't hear the bitterness and loss of identity that had replaced the joy he once found in riding a bike, in being with her.

"He didn't have the slightest damned idea who I was ..." Will muttered, staring out the window, trying to find a reflection in the glass that might just tell him who he was on his way to becoming.

His voice trailed off and they continued the drive in silence, the only sounds in the car being the whistle of the traffic outside and the overworked gasps of the little heater in the car trying to wheeze its way toward a comfortable temperature that was, at the moment, completely outside its ability to achieve.

LEONARD ROMANOWSKI STARED AT THE PILE OF MONEY NOW LITTERING HIS bed, the stacks staring back at him like an eighth grader's geography project of the Italian Alps poorly rendered in green papier-mâché.

Four-and-a-half million bucks made a lot of papier-mâché.

Hauling it had taken him six trips up the back stairs to the second floor room of the hotel, the faux Tyrolean atmosphere of the lobby and the teenager managing the desk doing nothing for his mood that night.

Then again, he had been lucky it had been a teenager. Pulled away from what had been a phone call of seemingly international importance, the kid checked Leonard in, commented on how lucky he was to snag one of the few remaining rooms in the hotel, because of the damned bicycle race, no doubt, then went back to the phone conversation, solving the problems of the world while scratching his nuts and yanking at his crotch. He never noticed the agitation that surrounded Leonard like a fog or the sweat that beaded heavily on his forehead.

Lucky, too, that the room had been on the second floor, high enough to discourage impromptu visitors from the outside, especially since there were no balconies to climb, and low enough for a last-minute getaway leap into the night.

Things were finally breaking his way, Romanowski thought, collapsing into a padded chair in the corner of the room. He had fought off a tap man, walked away clean, found a new hiding place, second floor and everything, in the middle of a big and popular event, and knew, with a sudden inspiration, where he needed to put the money.

The bike race was a perfect cover for so much green.

"DIDN'T EXPECT THAT."

"What?"

"I thought roundabouts were European things," Cheryl said as she leaned between the car and the Amoco pump.

Will broke his concentrated stare at the glory that was Vail Mountain, the upper reaches vanishing in the gathering dust, and glanced over his left shoulder toward the highway entrance ramp and the new, European styled, roundabout that managed traffic at the intersection.

"It certainly shouldn't surprise you. You drove them constantly in Europe."

"Well, yes, I know. I just never expected one in the U.S."

"Maybe America is finally accepting some continental flair," he said, wistfully. "Now if they'd only accept the metric system."

"Oh, not that. It's the tool of the devil," she laughed. "Besides, how would it sound, 'Welcome to Denver—the one-point-six-kilometer-high city?'"

Will smiled at the nonsense.

The pump "dinged" and the handle jumped to a stop in the tank nozzle. Cheryl Crane slid it out and returned it to the pump.

"Don't you want to top it off?"

"What?" She turned back and looked across the low hood of the car toward Will.

"Don't you want to top off the tank?"

"Well, I suppose I could, but it's not like we're flying the Atlantic and need every precious drop. There are other stations in the country, the car is going to sit for the weekend, and at the moment, anyway, I'm paying cash and don't have all that much. And, besides, I'd always rather eat than drive."

"I always top off the tank," he said with a quietly snappish tone.

Cheryl sighed.

"If you want to top off the tank, then you come over here and do it. You come over here and drive. You come over here and wiggle your brace and your cast into this Contadina can of a driver's seat and get me where I want to go. But at the moment, I'm in charge and this is the way I do things. I don't let the tank get below half anyway, so squeezing in another six ounces doesn't mean the end of the world for me. I never could figure out why people were always spilling gas on their shoes to get a few more drops in."

Halfway through her rant, while the volume slowly grew and the edge took on the bitterness of the mountain night air, Will raised his hands in a gesture of surrender, his mind telling him to let it go and to find peace with her.

"Sorry. Sorry. Don't know what came over me. You're the driver."

"That's right, bud. I'm the driver."

"Hey, take it easy. I'm a friend, remember?"

"Yeah, I'm trying."

His ears perked up at her sarcasm and he leaned onto the roof of the car, staring at her hard.

"What's that supposed to mean?" he asked angrily.

"Look," she retreated, "We're both tired. We've been flying all day, had that construction delay in Denver, haven't had dinner, and have been driving for the past two-and-a-half hours."

"Don't forget your pal the cop."

"Jesus, Will, let it go, will you? I didn't know the guy. I'm not dating him. He was just a fan, for God's sake."

"Yeah, whatever...."

"Christ. Look. We're here. We're tired. Let's get some rest and find the team tomorrow. We'll both feel better. Let's just call a truce for now, shall we?"

She stared at him for a moment, hoping that he'd smile and break the mood that had descended upon him since Michigan, since the letter from the team in Europe saying that his services would no longer be needed in any way, shape or form. The promised coaching job, the managerial job, the chance to ride again, were all a pipe dream now, vaporizing around him like a puff of smoke in a gentle breeze. She understood both his anger and bitterness, as well as his need to be in a bad mood, but honestly, she didn't have the time to deal with it. She was taking over a team herself this weekend as both rider and team captain. A team captain for a team that didn't need a captain in a sport that didn't use them. But there was big European money here and they wanted a watchdog. Like it or not, she was that dog.

She was going to reenter mountain biking after losing her nerve two years ago thanks to tangling on single track and finding herself airborne over an Italian boulder field, planting the left side of her skull in what later looked like a miniscule break between two pointed boulders. It sheared her scalp and knocked her out, but saved her life. She didn't know who she was for ten days.

She shuddered at the memory and pushed it away.

She didn't have time for any of it.

"Look, I'm going to pay and get directions to the team hotel. Why don't you catch your mood and slide it back into the passenger's side. We're almost there."

"Thanks, Mom."

"Jesus. Just get in the damned car."

She turned her back on him and strode off to the brightly lit office of the station. She dug around in her pockets and pulled out a clump of bills, pondering, for a second as she walked, how many French francs made up a dollar and how much was she really paying for this gasoline?

Cheryl laughed and smoothed the wrinkles out of Abe Lincoln's face.

She had been in Europe too damned long.

Will watched her through the glass of the office, the fluorescent lights giving the dealings between her and the sullen man in the gas station shirt a pale green cast. Will wondered, idly, what the guy's name was. Bet it was "Bob." They're all named "Bob," he thought. Either that or ten zillion shirts were all printed up saying "Bob" on the little circle on the breast and were distributed free to gas stations around the country. Maybe they were really Merles and Earls and Bens and Jerrys, but when it came to pumping gas, everybody was "Bob."

Still staring at the glass, Will shifted his focus a bit, the interior of the station fading out, the reflection of the rental car taking hold. He stared at it for a second before realizing that while he could see the car, he could no longer see himself.

"Electric."

"Huh? What?" Will shook his head, while a sharp, sudden jolt of surprise ran down his spine. He snapped his head toward the front of the car, in the direction of the heavy, growling voice. What he saw was a heavy, growling little woman, built to the general specifications of a fire plug.

"Elec-tric," she said, dropping the shillelagh on the hood of the car and dragging its thick blackthorn head across the paint, leaving a trail of its passing on the cheap finish of the rental. "If you must drive a personal car—buy an electric. Otherwise, ride multipassenger transport."

Without thinking, Will replied, "What's it to you?"

With a snap of the wrist, the blackthorn cudgel whistled in the air and stopped with a sharp "pop" inside the right headlight. The sealed beam, off, but hot from the drive, hissed for a split second in the cold air, before the shattered glass rained down onto the ground.

"What's it to me—and what's it to GOD?" she replied, in a tone that made no attempt to disguise its sense of righteousness. "You would do yourself honor to get right with both."

Will nearly asked, "What's God got to do with my rental car?" but thought better of it. They still had to negotiate the streets of Vail tonight and would need the other headlight. He realized he was sweating and that this woman with the billy club who reminded him of his Aunt Maxine was giving him the creeps.

"You know," he squeaked, backpedaling frantically toward the back of the car, "I wanted to take a shuttle. I wanted to take one. But I didn't. I promise to do better next time."

By now he had skittered about the trunk of the car and had put a good eight feet between his head and her bat.

"See that you do, boy, see that you do," she muttered darkly, and waddled off into the night toward the roundabout. Will watched her go and despite his relief at her passing, nearly shouted out when she walked directly into traffic, sending three cars in the traffic lane skittering onto sidewalks or toward the center, honking madly, in an effort to avoid her and each other. She waved her stick in the air and brought it down, hard, on the hood of a passing car.

Will heard a sharp "honk" and a curse and the squeal of brakes as the driver jumped out of his Beemer and yelled at the figure that disappeared with a steady, deliberate tread into the night.

"Good God," Will whispered to no one in particular, "who the hell—what the hell—was that?"

As the traffic began to move again on the roundabout, Will quickly stumbled around the car to the passenger's door, opened it, jumped into the seat, dragging his manacled legs behind him, and pulled the door shut, locking it.

Cheryl left the gas station office laughing, opened her door and slid into the driver's seat.

"Got a joke for you later."

"Good, I could do with one," he said, realizing that a touch of fright had entered his tone of voice.

"You okay?"

"You bet. Couldn't be better," he said with an unconvincing smile.

She decided to let it go. As she started the car, she glanced over her shoulder toward the roundabout, where the BMW was still pulled up on the curb, the driver yelling off into a cold and empty night. "What's all that about?"

"No idea," Will said, staring straight ahead.

"Hmm," Cheryl turned back and put the little Ford in gear, flicking on the lights as the car rolled forward. Turning onto Vail Road, she began to pick her way through the darkness toward the hotel.

"Damn. We've lost a headlight."

Will leaned forward and stared down the road toward an approaching bridge, his attention immediately captured by the sight of two men in the distance, their presence only made known by the dim reflection of their bright Hawaiian shirts in the lone beam and the fact that their contrasting heights made them look like a walking pipe organ.

"Yep," he said, distantly, as this new image quickly replaced that of the human auto wrecker in his mind, "sure have."

CHAPTER TWO:

SNIPE HUNT

A S THE CAR WITH THE SINGLE HEADLIGHT TURNED OFF THE ROAD and into a parking lot, Stanley Szyclinski stumbled over a patch of uneven ground in the returning darkness and cursed quietly under his breath, the gun-metal-grey attaché case slapping at his side.

His partner, a short, round, bowling ball of a man, cranked his mouth to one side, without turning his head, and whispered, "Don't curse."

Stanley bent his tall frame in a number of odd directions to regain his balance and kept up with his partner. The pair looked like the symbols of the 1938 New York World's Fair moving quietly down a mountain street dressed in vibrantly colored Hawaiian print shirts.

"I'll curse if I want to. It's damned cold, I'm damned hungry, and it's pretty damned late. Let's go to the hotel."

"Angelo didn't send us here to go to the hotel when we got cold."

"Well, then, he should have sent us with some jackets."

Olverio Cangliosi—better known as Oliver Twist, the Owl and Old Cans, thanks to that piece-of-shit police reporter from *The Detroit News* he later beat the crap out of—looked at his partner and nodded. Angelo had sent them completely unprepared.

Not completely. They had a name, they had a picture and they had an address, but no idea of how to dress to fit in and absolutely no concept of how Colorado's climate in the month of September might affect said dress.

Other than one trip to California a few years back to whack the Bug, Ollie had never been out of the Detroit metroplex in his life. He had plenty of work there, along with a brother's family to raise. His love for just about everything in the gritty rust-belt town, the center of his own little universe, made wandering far and wide an empty thought.

What more was there to life than the corner of Michigan and Trumbull?

"Look," he muttered. "Cut the whining, let's find the place, make our visit and get the hell out. We can be in Denver by midnight and home by noon tomorrow."

"If the airport's working."

"If the airport's working."

They kept walking in the bitter silence of the night, stumbling occasionally over a rock, a step or a patch of uneven ground.

"I'm cold."

Ollie nodded. "I'm cold, too. But Angelo just didn't know."

He lied. Angelo Genna knew exactly what he was sending them into, for God's sake. The guy had a condo up here, somewhere. Bringing them the goddamned Hawaiian shirts was just some big damned joke on his part.

"It's a resort. You've got to dress like a resort," Angelo had said.

Well, there are resorts and there are resorts, Ollie thought. And this was no blessed Hawaiian print resort.

Now, their luggage was lost somewhere between Michigan and that Denver airport, and they were stuck with two bright Hawaiian shirts and no change of clothes. Bad omen, he thought.

Cattivo augurio.

And on top of that, he couldn't breathe.

Olverio Cangliosi was not a small man, but underneath what appeared to be a soft exterior, there was a will of iron and a stomach to match. He was tough. He was mean. He was surprisingly in shape. And yet, he couldn't breathe to save his life.

"Don't wheeze," Stanley said, taking another breath.

"Can't help it," Olverio gasped. "They built this town where there weren't no air."

"Man, you've just gone from six-hundred feet above sea level this morning to something like nine-thousand feet tonight. You ought to take some time to adjust. What that guy on Everest called 'acclimate.'"

"This isn't getting to you?"

"I feel it. I'm just not carrying the extra baggage."

Ollie stopped and stared at his business partner. Stanley immediately lost his smile. The chill of the night was nothing compared to the chill of Olverio's face.

Ollie turned and they struggled on up through the village toward the face of Vail Mountain.

The only thing that didn't stop him from dropping the contract right then and there was the idea that they could be done with it quickly. This guy had left a trail like a slug, and by this time tomorrow night Ollie could be safe at home in the comfort of his very own easy chair, at a mere six-hundred feet above sea level, watching his very own TV as his very own Detroit Tigers fell out of contention again, with a brand new, incredibly clean fifty grand sitting upstairs in grandma's trunk ready to be wisely invested.

He continued to trudge through the darkness along Vail Road, past the last of the hotels and along the front of the slopes on Vail Mountain. The darkness had become like a blanket now, smothering whatever light was bold enough to pierce this far into the wilderness. Stanley was right behind him, using Ollie's shirt as a beacon. He could hear the muffled clatter of the attaché case behind him.

"Shhh," he warned. "You sound like Antsie the peddler."

"Jesus. You remember him? I thought I was the only one who remembered him."

"I lived in the neighborhood, too. Just keep it down. Sound travels in this cold."

"Yeah, okay." Stanley paused for a moment. "Whatever happened to Antsie?"

"Buster No Knuckles happened."

"That's a shame."

"He shouldn't have kept the money he found. It was the Cavalier's money."

"Whose?"

"Tony the Cavalier."

"Oh, yeah. I forget him sometimes. Whatever happened to him?"

"Buster No Knuckles happened," Ollie said with quiet exasperation.

Stanley nodded with a sudden flash of memory.

"Oh, yeah. The forties. I just loved the forties in Dee-troit."

Quietly, they both smiled at the memory.

They passed a sign announcing the Vista Bahn Express, a chair lift up the mountain. The road suddenly backtracked across the slope and Ollie struck out into the darkness, stepping over an orange snow fence and into the heavily wooded terrain.

"Shouldn't we stay on the roads?" Stanley said, quietly, behind him. "I rattle more when I walk through this stuff."

"Hold it close," his partner answered, and Stanley responded, pulling the case tight across his chest like a man with a baby.

"I can't see shit."

"Don't curse." As soon as the words left his mouth, Olverio stepped in a hole and fell flat in the underbrush, cursing under his breath as he did so.

Stan smiled. "Don't curse."

"Shut up. Help me up and let's get on with it."

Stan lowered a hooked arm and Ollie grabbed it, pulling himself upright. He brushed himself off and peered through the darkness in Stanley's general direction.

"Thanks, pal."

"Don't mention it."

"There's a road up here, let's get on it and let's get this over with."

The pair cut through the yard of a condo, the back door of which seemed to empty out onto the ski slopes.

Must be nice, Ollie thought. Must be rich, Stanley thought. They both considered the investment possibilities as they stepped out of the yard and up onto Mill Creek Circle.

Ollie stood for a moment, almost sniffing the air, and turned up the mountain. "This way," he mumbled, and the pair resumed their upward trek.

"You okay?" Stanley asked.

"Yeah. I'm just getting used to the altitude," Ollie wheezed.

"Just don't have a heart attack on me, okay?"

Ollie turned with a grin. "Why, would you miss me?"

"No—if you crap out right here, I don't want to have to haul your ass down the mountainside."

The grin left Ollie's face as if it were ripped off.

"Look, Ollie, if you want me to do this, you just say so. I can do this one, easy."

"Don't worry about me," Olverio said, churlishly. "I'm here to do a job, I'll do the job."

"Hey, hey," Stan said, stepping back into a defensive posture. "Meant no disrespect. Meant no disrespect."

They continued, silently for a time, up the paved street to a cut-off, a newly plowed dirt road that cut into the trees higher up the mountain. A large white-and-red sign behind the road announced: VAIL MOUNTAIN TERRACE—AN MSC DEVELOPMENT—FROM THE MID-$2'S.

"Wow," Stanley said, adding a low whistle for emphasis, "the air ain't the only thing that's thin around here."

Olverio stopped and stared at his partner for a second in the darkness.

"What's that supposed to mean?"

"What?"

"The air isn't the only thing that's thin around here. What else is thin? The price? Is that what you meant? What about—the mountain isn't the only thing that's high around here. How about that?"

"I liked mine."

"Yours didn't make any sense."

Stanley lapsed into a sullen silence, punctuated only by a muttered, "What do you know?"

"I know how to make my allegories make sense for one thing. Watch out for the ruts."

At Ollie's warning, Stanley neatly sidestepped a deep rut in the road. He fell to the side, in another rut, forced his weight in another direction and threw himself back to the other side of the road and yet another rut. Ollie watched him frantically trying to regain his balance, the sight reminiscent of Pinocchio on amphetamines.

Finally, Stanley stopped at the side of the road, leaning up against a tree, wheezing to catch his breath in the mountain air.

"Thanks for your help."

"Anytime."

"By the way, it's not an allegory. It's a metaphor."

"Oh, for God's sake," Ollie barked under his breath. "Who gives a rat's ass?"

"Don't curse."

✸

WILL SIPPED THE BEER AND FELT THE ICY COLD SLIDE DOWN HIS THROAT, HIT the leading edge of his stomach and explode out around the sides. He loved that feeling. Doing it with a beer was even nicer, as it signaled the end of a long, hard day of traveling.

"I didn't know they were allowed to show movies that bad on airlines."

"Captive audience," Cheryl replied, with a smile, "although I think rows twenty-seven through thirty-one abandoned ship somewhere over Iowa."

"Could be, could be. How many cheesy sixties TV shows are they going to make into cheesy big-screen movies, anyway?"

She thought a minute, letting her eyes scan the rough-hewn woody interior of the pizza bar as she did, settling her eyes on a skinny, heavily dreadlocked guy sitting at the bar idly flipping through a race program. His appearance broke her train of thought for a moment, then she recaptured it, forcing herself to move on beyond the skinny, hairy vision.

"Probably, as long as there are junior studio executives who grew up in the sixties and never played outdoors or experienced life outside a TV tube," she answered, finally.

"You might be right," he said, nodding. "Rather sad, isn't it?"

"Oh, I dunno," she said, between sips, "there are only thirty-six original plot lines in the universe. It's up to Hollywood to retread them as slickly as possible."

"And these TV show things already have a built-in audience...."

"Sure, all the boomers who can't let their childhoods go."

"Will we be like that?" he asked, a quietly serious tone to his voice.

"Aww, don't worry sweetie," she smiled. "I'll smother you with a pillow before I let that happen."

"You're so sweet to me."

He had turned his back toward the wall in order to stretch out his legs and take some of the cramp out of the brace that ran along his left knee. For the first time in hours the walking cast on his right was no longer sweating, and he could actually feel the calf starting to loosen up.

The beer was doing its work.

Enough so that, when the man walked through the door of the bar, about 15 feet away, Will stopped in mid-thought to stare, the idea of finishing one thought before leaping onto something else gone with the blast of cold air from the outside.

Though it was dry outside, the man stomped his feet out of habit, as if he had just stepped in from snow and slush. He inched farther into the room, but surveyed the crowd carefully before committing and stepping too far away from the door.

Will stared harder, sure that he knew the fellow in the new, dark blue Columbia jacket. He knew him, but he was out of place, and being out of place, Will simply couldn't place him.

"I know him."

Cheryl glanced toward the man at the door.

"Who him?"

"Him him," Will said, nodding in the general direction of the door.

"Yeah, like I said," she answered, "who is he?"

"I can't be sure, because I never thought he'd leave New York City," Will whispered, as if talking to himself, "but I'd swear that's my agent, Leonard Romanowski."

On the "Romanowski," Will stood and walked quickly toward the door.

The man in the heavy coat leapt into the air as if electrified and turned to face him.

His hand was already moving toward the door knob.

"Hey, Leonard. Geeze, didn't mean to startle you, pal. Hi. Will. Will Ross?

Will Ross. Ross. Will. Twelve-and-a-half percent?"

Leonard Romanowski relaxed, but only partially, letting down his guard only enough to let Will in, for a moment.

"Oh, Will. Yeah, of course, Will. How are you. Howareyou? Fine? Good. Good. Good." He glanced down along the length of the bar, then back to Will, then outside, then back again.

"What are you doing here, Will?"

"Well, I was going to ask you the same thing, Leonard. I'm here for a race. Not racing, really, so don't be looking for a check ... are you okay? You look real pale. Here, come on over here and sit down. Have a beer."

"No, no. No beer. Not staying. Not now. Here? Why? Vacation. Vacation, Will. Yes. So, you're here for what? Bike race?"

"Yeah," he said, very slowly, "I'm not riding. She's riding." He pointed over his shoulder toward Cheryl, who smiled, waved and went back to her brew. "Cheryl Crane. She rides for Haven-Two Wheels."

"Haven? Oh, yeah. Didn't you ride for Haven?"

"Yeah, of course I did, Leonard. You cracked the contract. Got the checks. Kept fifteen instead of twelve-and-a-half."

"No. No. Not me, Will. Straight Arrow Romanowski. That's me. Always been me."

"Sure. Straight arrow."

"So, where are you staying? I can't stay now, but maybe later we can get together. So where are you staying?"

"Someplace called the Bavarian Haus or something like that. I think. Cheryl?"

She nodded and smiled. "That's right."

"Yeah, that's right. We'll be here until Sunday night, maybe Monday morning."

"Okay. Okay. We'll get together. I'll call. Love to see you. Love to talk to you."

"Yeah, love to talk to you, too," Will said, a natural suspicion growing in his voice.

Leonard turned to look outside, then back again.

"Don't, uh, don't tell anyone that you've seen me, okay?"

"What, yeah, okay, sure. Mum's the word."

"I'll explain it all to you. Really, I will. I'll explain it all to you, Bill."

"Will."

"Will. I'll explain it all to you later."

He nodded quickly, then turned, opened the door and stepped into the chill of the September night as if he were stepping into a raging blizzard. He drew the collar of the heavy coat around his head, then headed off in the direction from which he came only moments before. Will could see his mouth moving frantically, as if he were having an argument with himself over…over what?

Was it seeing Will? Getting caught? Caught how, Will wondered.

Will turned and looked around the bar for any unaccompanied women who might be waiting for the secret assignation of a lifetime with Leonard Romanowski. None fit the bill. He shook his head and walked back to his table.

Cheryl was ahead. He drained a quarter of the mug to catch up.

"What was all that about?" she asked, jerking her head toward the door.

"You know," he answered slowly, "I don't know. That was my agent…."

"He of the creative accounting?"

"One and the same. He walks in, sees me, turns nine different shades of white, then runs off, muttering to himself like Grandpa Ross when he thought he was on a mission for the government."

"Maybe he owes you money."

Will dug in his pocket and fished out a ten.

"No 'maybe' about it."

"Well, in that case," she answered with a smile, "I'd run."

Will laughed, a hearty, genuine laugh. He reached over and took her hand.

"You … you wouldn't run from anything."

He patted her hand and she pulled it away. Still smiling, she put both hands in her lap and knotted them together.

She stared at the beer, which hadn't helped her nerves at all.

There was something she would run from.

And this weekend was it.

❀

OLLIE TURNED AND LOOKED UP THE ROAD TO THE LONE FINISHED HOUSE INSIDE the development. "It's right up there." Ollie pointed and then walked past Stan deliberately, as if to say, "Enough of this foolishness." He headed for a single condominium about 75 yards up the hill.

"How do you know it's that one?"

"It's the spec house. Look at the sign on the front. That's the one they're using to sell all the other places in the development. You've got enough money in real estate. You should know this stuff."

"Yeah, I've got money in real estate. Doesn't mean I know anything about it. So it's the spec house. Why would our buddy hide out in a spec house?"

"Because it's the only one finished. Because it's the only one with heat. Because there looks to be one light on somewhere inside and the garage door is open. Because that place was on the brochure that Little Mike found in this guy's wastebasket in New York. Because that is where Angelo told us the guy would be, because the guy doodled the address down on a pad before he grabbed the money and ran."

Stanley nodded. "Good guess."

About 25 yards from the driveway, the pair stopped on the road and stepped into the underbrush facing the house. Working quietly, Stan opened the attaché case, and they both reached inside at the same time.

"After you," Olverio said.

"No, no," Stanley said, "I insist. After you."

They both hesitated and then reached in at the same time again.

Ollie plucked a small, triangular case out of the attaché before his hands could get jumbled up with Stanley's again.

"There," he said with smug satisfaction, "all yours."

"Thank you," Stanley said, not catching the tone.

As quietly as possible, Olverio unzipped the case, pulling the tiny Walther TPH out, followed by two magazines and a silencer. He loaded the gun quickly, moved the second magazine to his pocket and began to thread the silencer into the barrel. With his large hands, in the darkness, it would seem to be a problem, but decades of practice with the gun and its PPK sister made it routine. He was a surgeon, so adept at his specialty that he could do the operation in the dark.

Stanley, meanwhile, rooted around noisily in the case in the dark, searching for the spare magazine he was sure he had loaded and dropped into the case when he picked up the gun in Denver.

"Would you like me to turn on a light?"

"It would help."

"Maybe we should turn on some music, too. 'Music to Announce Your Presence By.'"

"Ha," Stan barked. "Ha, ha," punctuating each word in a whisper. He pulled the MP5K submachine gun out of its resting place and racked the slide as quietly as he could. "You know I like one in and one nearby."

"Have you ever needed more than the mag you've got in that thing?"

"No, but eleven is my lucky number."

"Eleven? You mean two."

"No, I mean eleven," Stanley whispered. "One and one—eleven."

"So, why don't you ever bet it?"

"I used to," Stanley said, finally finding the spare in the dark, fallen into the dying grass, "but I can't bring myself to do it in the Michigan Lottery."

"Why not?"

"Government should not be in the numbers game. That's ours. It has been for years, and now the good people of Lansing, with all their family values talk, make off with my living. It isn't proper."

"Agreed, but that's how they do everything." Olverio sat back on his haunches and then pushed his bulk upright.

"You ready?"

Stanley looked up at his business associate of the past forty-three years and reached for a small branch on a pine tree. He pulled himself up, cracking the branch as he did.

Ollie rolled his eyes. "Christ. Another calling card. Why don't we just wander up and ring the doorbell?"

Stanley smiled. "Yeah, why not?"

He stepped back onto the road and, walking about 20 feet back down the mountain, he found what he was looking for: an empty, discarded pizza box. Picking it up, he pushed a chunk of mud off the side and brought the submachine gun up underneath it.

"All set. Special delivery."

"Fifty-nine-year-old men don't deliver pizza," Ollie mumbled.

"Sure they do," Stanley answered. "I'm on a fixed income and nobody wants me despite my years of executive experience. It's the only way I can keep my condo."

He raised his eyebrows and gave Olverio a straight-lipped smile, the set smile that meant Stanley was ready for business. Ollie nodded and fell back, about four to five yards behind Stanley, now marching up toward the door.

Ollie cut across the darkened yard and silently, as silently as he could, worked his way across the construction debris toward the front of the house. He stood on an upturned bucket, released the safety and pointed the Walther, head high, at the edge of the door.

Stanley stepped up briskly and rang the doorbell, the MP5K balanced under the box. Ollie was amazed at how natural it all looked, with the exception, he thought, of the weaponry.

Stanley rang the doorbell again and waited. Both men listened carefully for any sound from inside, any indication that someone was moving or running or setting themselves up for a fire fight.

Neither heard anything.

Ollie caught Stan's eye and mouthed the word, "Garage."

Stan nodded, and Ollie moved off to his left, turning the corner into the open garage. He pressed himself up against the wall and moved again when he heard Stanley ring the doorbell and announce, "Pizza," in an old and tired voice not like his at all.

Ollie moved quickly to the door, his steps almost that of a dancer, despite his size, his gun never moving from high port. He paused for a second and reached out his left hand to try the door knob. It silently moved in his grip. As he pushed the door open, Olverio moved the gun down into a position level with the chest of anyone who might be standing behind it.

On the doorstep, Stan felt the hairs on the back of his neck begin to rise. He hated this part of the job, when he was the decoy and Ollie did the point work. He thought about ringing the doorbell one more time and then following his partner into the garage, but didn't. If this guy had any kind of brains, it would give away everything and they didn't want a mountain town gunfight. Small town cops didn't like that, even if it were between gangsters. That was the difference between the city and the country. Detroit cops loved it when the bad guys splattered each other. Made less work for them. The country cops said it disturbed their harmony.

Stanley shook off the thought and went back to the business at hand. Stay focused, he reminded himself. Stay focused.

He heard a creak on the flooring just behind the front door and tightened his pull on the trigger of the machine gun.

"Pizza," he called.

"It's me. It's me," Ollie said from the other side of the door. "Loosen up."

The door opened.

"Come on in. It's clear." He paused and thought for a moment. "Pretty much."

"He's not here?"

"No, our little pal isn't here."

"Somebody is?"

"After a fashion."

Stanley followed him down the hallway toward a well-lighted living room he could see just beyond his partner. For a finished home, he thought, the place was just as cold as outside.

Olverio stepped aside to reveal a beautiful room, lit by a shaft of moonlight, covered with what appeared to be broken glass, a bicycle, and a body that had been dead just long enough to stiffen up into a particularly ugly position.

"Who's he?" Stanley asked.

"Don't know. But it isn't Mr. Romanowski, that's for sure." Ollie scratched the edge of his temple with the silencer of the Walther.

Stanley looked up at the gaping hole in one of the plate-glass windows at the front of the condo, then back to the bicycle crashed into the wall, and then back to the bullet-riddled body that clutched at the carpet in a last grasp of life.

"Man," he whistled, "this guy had a really crappy evening."

"You know who he is?" Ollie asked with a sudden realization.

"No, who?"

"He's us."

"Jesus. You sure?" Stanley asked with shock. "Doesn't look like us."

"No. No. This guy. This Romanowski. He's so wired he thought it was us coming through the window at him. Bad luck for this guy. Too bad."

"Too bad for him. Too bad for us," Stanley said.

"Yeah," Ollie agreed. "He knows we're coming."

Stanley squinted into the darkness, then pointed at the hearth.

"At least he's not armed."

Ollie noticed the .45 Colt still keeping vigil over its kill. "Man, this guy is wound up," he said. "Best to take it slow."

"Well," Stanley said, absentmindedly. "We're just in the way here—let's make tracks."

"Yeah. He's not here. I suppose we can assume the money's not here either."

"We'll start again tomorrow."

"Should we go to the hotel?"

"Unless you want to sleep in the car."

The conversation continued in the same vein as they walked down the hall, past the bedroom with its single light still burning. Ollie turned back into the garage, wiping his prints off the doorknob. Stanley walked down the hall, doing the same to the front door and the doorbell. They picked up the conversation again at the front stoop, then crossed the rutted street to where they had left the briefcase. As they headed down the mountain road and back into the older and more populated sections of Vail, the town was turning off the last of its lights in anticipation of a busy weekend.

✺

WILL SLID BETWEEN THE COLD, FRESH SHEETS AND FELT THAT DELIGHTFUL change of temperature as his bare legs flashed back and forth, stirring up some friction and warming the little pocket near his feet.

"While you're at it, warm up my side, will you?" Cheryl called from the bathroom.

"No problem. Want me to warm up your pillow?"

"Leave my pillow alone."

"Naw, I think you need a warm pillow."

"Don't you be getting my pillow warm."

He could hear her gargle and spit.

"Don't you be touching my pillow."

"I've got your pillow. I'll just warm it up for you...."

She came charging out of the bathroom in a long, black Campagnolo T-shirt and threw herself on her side of the King-size bed.

"Give me my pillow, damn you."

"I was just trying to help. Besides, I didn't want you to smother me with it."

"No, I'll smother you with your pillow." She pulled hers away and fluffed it. "Getting it all warm. Nobody likes to start with a warm pillow and nobody likes to end with a cold one."

"I like to end with a cold one."

"A cold pillow."

"Oh." They were quiet for a moment as she arranged herself in bed. They stared at the ceiling.

"You left the light on," Will said, pointing toward the bathroom.

"Him that makes the most foul odors must turn it off."

"Oh! Oh! We are getting cruel in our old age, aren't we?"

"Old! Old! You little bastard! You were riding around when bicycles were still made out of wood!"

"Oh, damn ... well, Grandpa here...."

"Leave your teeth by the bed ... I brought you some ... yaaa ... water. Stop, stop, stop, stop."

They were wrestling now, in the bed, the smooth, crisp sheets bending, twisting and wrapping around them.

"Stop it. Stop it! No tickle! No tickle!" she screamed, breaking free of his clutches, rolling him onto his back, leaping astride him and pinning his arms back.

"No tickle!" she wheezed with a laugh.

"Okay, no tickle," Will nodded, smiling.

He gave up easily. He had her right where he wanted her.

"And no clothes, either," she said with a sigh.

"Ah, Sherlock," he whispered seductively, wrapping his lower legs around hers, locking her in place, "there's nothing better for tension."

She laughed.

"Will, I'm not really in the mood."

She tried to roll off him. He rolled her back on top.

"What if I talk like this?" he said, lowering his voice into what he thought was a sexy bass, but sounded more like one of the Budweiser frogs with a cold.

She laughed and felt him grow beneath her. Without a word, she began to rock, gently, back and forth.

Maybe it was good for tension. And maybe she could talk him into a back rub during intermission. And maybe they could go for a record. And maybe she could step outside her self for the first time since she had heard about this team, this job, this race, this weekend.

Slowly, very slowly, she reached down, took the edges of her shirt and pulled them up over her shoulders and over her head. She looked down at him with a knowing smile.

"Hey—you're not wearing anything, either."

"It was all part of my cunning plan."

"Your cunning plan to wha…."

She threw herself down upon him with a wild passion, kissing him hard and cutting off the end of his sentence. He didn't mind.

There was no conversation for some time.

Later, they both slept, better than they had in weeks.

FRIDAY

CHAPTER THREE:

REVEILLE

HOOTIE BOSCO ARCHED HIS LONG AND STRINGY BACK AND FELT TWO comforting snaps deep within his spine. He straightened up, swept his hair to one side, gathered it with his right hand and tied it off with an elastic band behind his shoulder, then adjusted his 80-percent dark, sea-blue sunglasses, all the while keeping his gaze locked on the mountain before him, now red and gold and a sharp green from the rising sun despite the blue panes of glass just before his eyes.

He looked at his watch.

6 a.m. Time to announce the arrival.

Despite the growing popularity of the sport and the growing professionalism of the teams and mechanics, he was still the first one in Margaritaville, the collection of tents and RVs and box vans holding the tools and bikes and effluvia of everyone competing in the Ishmael Coffee Race as well as those of the various companies and shops selling everything from bikes and suspension forks to bite-the-foil energy gels and knock-off T-shirts. He spit out the last mouthful of coffee and tossed the dregs in the bottom of the cup to the ground, watching them smoke in the chill and curl around the base of the heavy-duty tripod workstand his neighbors had stupidly left out the night before. He was amazed it made its way through the night in one piece. Bosco had been in the sport from day one and had learned early on to double lock and bolt everything, even if that didn't mean you'd find it there the next morning, no matter how much security was lurking on the premises.

Amazing how much stuff disappeared from a mountain bike race. Amazing how many people still felt that you could help yourself to whatever you wanted without a thought about asking.

He rooted around in his back pocket and found a set of keys, more keys, he thought, than any man could ever need, and found the master. He slipped it into the lock and released the bolt, threw the arm on the door and squatted down to shove it open.

With a roar and a final bang, the door hurled itself to the top of the van, a hollow "boom" rolling across the base of the mountain toward town and announcing that the first day of the race had officially started with the ceremonial opening of the van door by Hootie Bosco.

Bosco was a fixture on the racing circuit, that was certain, present at the birth on Mount Tam, then a second-rate rider, then a builder, then a first-rate crackpot and independent mechanic for one of the bicycle tool manufacturers. Hootie Bosco provided the best neutral service on the mountain, whatever or wherever that mountain was, and Hootie Bosco knew it. The indie had led to a squad, the squad had led to unemployment, and the unemployment had led to Stewart Kenally and Two Wheels.

Kenally was putting together a mountain bike squad and needed tech support. Bosco didn't have anything going and took the plunge. It was regional at first, just trying to get known against the big names, the bike company teams, but then Haven Pharmaceuticals, a French company, out of the blue, dropped a huge chunk of change into it, giving everyone a very nice little raise, and pushing the team itself into the front ranks, at least, in publicity and facilities, there being no results as yet to crow about.

In other words, everything and everybody were still in the formative stages, to the point where the new team leader was due in today.

And it was a girl. Bosco shuddered. He didn't have any problem with that, but Marshall Reed and Jeremy Jettman would certainly have a herd of cows over it all.

For a sport in which men and women competed on a near-equal basis, these guys were pure Flintstone as far as Hootie Bosco was concerned.

He ripped a sheet off Denver's *Rocky Mountain News* and tore it into fourths. Using a corner, he carefully rolled a morning doobie of epic proportions, reading the headline as he rolled, "Architect Murde..." The story disappeared as the wad of weed overtook it and buried it under a lingerie ad. He pulled the ancient blowtorch from the wall and fired it up with a bang and a hiss, turning down the flame to a usable burn that wouldn't remove his eyebrows. Hootie Bosco touched it to the end of the roll and watched with his daily dose of astonishment as the newsprint flared and curled around the weed. He sucked it in hungrily and fell back a step with a buzzard's delight.

He pulled a shop rag from a metal tie-down on the wall of the truck and shoved it in his back pocket as he boosted himself inside. He looked over the racks of bikes, mostly Diamondbacks, some Colnagos, and began to lift the frames out of the corral, little scraps of burning newspaper falling away from his mouth, their edges dotted with red diamonds of fire.

"Time to go to work, kids," he said, to no one bike in particular, then punched the power button on the deck, cranked the tenor down and let the bass line of Jethro Tull rattle dishes and blades of grass miles away.

Forty-seven, he thought, and still a child of the sixties.

He shook a forest of dark black dreadlocks out of his face and smiled as he watched the waves of sound move across the valley.

A LOW, BOOMING SOUND WOKE CHERYL CRANE UP WITH A START. SHE HAD JUST begun to lift the front wheel over a log that kept growing and changing and rising in front of her as it had all night. This time, as with each other time, she was sure she was going to make it over, but each time, she had collided with the side and been pushed back again. Then, like Sisyphus, she had risen up, after some commercial break in another dreamscape, to try the leap once more.

She had expended so much energy in that singular effort that she was more tired now than when she went to bed the night before. Will stuck his head out the bathroom door.

"What's that?"

"What's what?"

"That sound. Did you drop something in here?"

"Naw. Just something outside," she said, turning away from him, pulling her pillow into her chest and staring out the window at the upper reaches of Vail mountain, site of her short-term future.

Will resumed brushing his teeth, but kept watching her, not so much for what she might do, but how she was doing it. She was in a near-fetal position, with the pillow tucked in tight against her chest, a fiber-fill bullet-proof vest for whatever bullets life had loaded and aimed in her direction.

He spit out the toothpaste and leaned back into the room, wiping his mouth absentmindedly with a towel.

"You all right?" he asked, quietly.

She turned, almost with a start, and looked at him, first with fear haunting her eyes, then, with a smile.

"No, no. I'm just still waking up."

He nodded and started to turn back into the bathroom, when he stopped and looked at the floor.

"You know," he said, distantly, almost to an invisible third party in the room, "there's nothing wrong in being scared, especially in the situation you're in."

"I know," she answered, quietly.

"Remember your first day with Haven? The lone female soigneur in the ranks? You must have been scared then. You survived and won their respect."

She nodded, then, shook her head. "Yeah. Okay. But, but nobody relied on me, Will."

She buried her chin in the top of the pillow, her eyes lit up by a strand of early-morning sunshine.

"I just took orders. And—I knew a lot of the people on board when I joined up. I don't know anybody here. I haven't raced against any of these women in two years, if ever. I don't know team logistics or personnel."

She turned toward the window.

"I know," he said, quietly. "Stewart threw you in the deep end on your very first day. But use it. Get to know the people. Get to know the situation. Get through the day. Just one day. Then you'll have one down. Find somebody on the team who knows what's up. The mechanics, for instance. When I worked summers, my dad always told me—get to know the people who fix things first. So, since you don't have a janitor on the team, meet the mechanic. He'll tell you what's what. Stewart's handling all the travel arrangements and equipment. He'll show up sometime. As for the other riders, ask them up front what they need in support, then let them ride their race. It ain't like you're a den mother." He paused for a moment and watched her. "Just take it a day at a time."

"Like you did last January?"

Will ignored the sarcasm.

"I survived. Not by much, I'll admit," he laughed, tapping the toe of his walking cast on the edge of the bathroom door, "but I did survive. And how did I do it? I relied on my friends and I took it one day at a time."

"You sound like Ward Cleaver."

"Thank you, June. Me and Wally appreciate your kindness."

She smiled, with no conviction, her eyes lost in anticipation of the day to come.

"Look," he said, arms wide, "if all else fails, you've got me. I can't do any of the big stuff, and the decisions are yours, because you're the boss and I wouldn't know what to do anyway, but I'm a good sounding board and I'm one hell of a go-fer."

She looked at the plastic cast on his right leg and the half-moon ridge of scars around his left knee peeking out from a nylon and metal brace, one the result of a torn muscle on the side of a dead volcano in France, the other the result of a spectacular crash on a mountain descent.

"Yeah, I know," he nodded, glancing down at his legs, "I'm sort of a cross between Gabby Hayes and Hopalong Cassidy … but, hey … I'm here."

"I've got to do it alone."

"No, that's not true," he answered. "You've got to do it, but you don't have to do it alone. That's why so many people screw up the boss job they have. You don't do it alone. You rely on the people you work with to hold up their end and get the job done. This team doesn't rise or fall on your shoulders, kid."

"Maybe not," she said distantly, a bit of a grin crossing her face.

Will sighed, convinced, completely, that she hadn't listened to a thing he'd said. He wiped an errant bit of towel fluff off the end of his nose and stepped back into the bathroom, mentally preparing himself for the long and difficult job of getting her over this first race hump and making her believe that she had the knowledge and the guts to make the team work.

He took a look in the mirror and sighed, deeply. Much to do, he thought, far too much to do. And no time to do it. The person staring back at him sighed as well, the sound catching Will off guard. He looked into the eyes of the man in the mirror and tried to find his answers there. Who are you? What are you doing here? Where are you going? There was no answer. There was no spark. There wasn't the slightest glint of recognition between the two.

In the bedroom, Cheryl turned toward the window and sat on the edge of the bed, covering her nakedness with the pillow and holding it tight.

She took a deep breath of the thin mountain air and let it out slowly through her mouth and nose. She did it again, focusing on a point, high on the mountain, where a number of ski lifts crossed the ridge as if racing toward a terminus out of sight, higher on the wooded slopes.

One more breath and she realized that the knot in her stomach was not releasing.

She nodded her head, bouncing her chin on the top edge of the pillow.

"Good God," she whispered. "I'm scared."

THE 'BOOM' OUTSIDE HAD SOMEHOW FOUND ITS WAY INTO LEONARD romanowski's dream, grabbed him by the throat just as he was stepping over yet another mountain of money and yanked him partway back into reality. Only partway, it seemed, because as his eyes snapped open, he panicked, not knowing where he was, or who he was, or what in the hell he was doing as he began to fumble, terrified, around the room.

He raced to the door and then, wild eyed, turned toward the window and ran there, mouth open but silent, arms moving crazily, hoping to catch a look at something, anything, that might jog his memory and remind him where he was or why he was there.

He forced himself to stand, frozen at the window, while, slowly, his own sense of reality returned.

It was slow in returning.

First, as he stood there, he realized that he was Leonard Romanowski. He took a deep breath and remembered as well that he was a sports agent, and was safe in a hotel room in Vail, Colorado.

Slowly, like the movement of molasses in January, more short-term returned, such as the fact that in his room was nearly four-and-a-half million dollars that had belonged, at least at one time, to the scum of the earth, a second-rate hoodlum in New York who now realized that you can't bully Leonard Romanowski because Leonard Romanowski won't be bullied.

Or will demand payment for such bullying.

He smiled at his own success in pulling it off, then the chill returned to freeze his spine.

He had murdered a man the night before. He slapped his hands on the double-paned window, followed by his forehead. He had actually shot a man. Dead. Dead as a mackerel. He had shot him.

Leonard took a deep, rattling breath and stood up, trying to steady his nerves.

It was self-defense, any court in the world would see that. The guy had attacked him on a bicycle, intent on killing him. Besides, this was a murderer, an enforcer, a strong arm. This was the hit man from hell, he thought. Angelo had sent a killer to get the money back and teach him a lesson.

He stared out the window toward the banners and trucks and tents that marked the staging area for the Ishmael Bicycle Race and idly watched a rider hop over a stump, scoot up a nearly ninety-degree incline and leap into the air, suddenly knowing that maybe, just maybe, that hadn't been a hit man at all.

A moment of doubt suddenly crowded into his sleep-numbed brain, a moment when he just had to think, "Oh, my ... oh, my God," the thought taking voice against a pane-glass window.

"Oh, my God," he said to himself, the window reflecting the stench of too many cigars and too many Reubens and a night of sleeping in an armchair with his head back and his mouth open. The possibility of what he had done overwhelmed him and he began to sink to the floor, the scene outside his window beginning to smear and fog in his mind, the tents, the trucks, the bikes, the brightly colored banners, the early-morning walkers in their brightly colored shirts. The only noise in the room was the sound of a sigh and the squeal of his hands as they pressed against the glass, inching themselves down toward the pile that was him on the carpet.

They were still out there. Somewhere. And they were looking for him.

❋

OUTSIDE THE HOTEL, ONE OF THE TWO MEN LOOKING UP BLOCKED THE RISING sun with his right hand and stared at the photo in his hand.

"What do you think?" he asked, casually.

"He's small. He's ugly. He should be easy to find," replied his partner. He turned and looked at the riders and fans, young, in shape, most in bright jerseys or racing jackets. "Especially around here."

"So round, so firm, so fully packed—but he gave us the slip, didn't he?"

"Don't think so. I think he's still in town."

"Based on?"

"If he's freaked enough to blow an innocent away, he's freaked enough to bed down somewhere close until his brain stops banging."

The tall, thin man nodded as they continued their morning constitutional along the riverwalk.

"He's not going anywhere. Let's get breakfast."

"Famous last words."

"What's that supposed to mean?"

"Do you remember Mr. Acavado?"

"Which one was he?"

"He was the one who could wait until after breakfast."

"Well, he did."

"Yes, but it took nearly six weeks to find him again."

"He was no problem. He left a trail like a slug."

"That's not what you said at the time."

"What did I say at the time?"

"It was colorful, I'll give you that, it was more colorful than your shirt, that's for sure."

Their voices rose and fell in animated conversation as they went off in search of a morning meal, the Hawaiian shirts slowly beginning to fit in.

It was almost as if they belonged.

✳

MARJORIE STUMP WATCHED THE EGG DANCE AROUND IN THE PAN FOR EXACTLY three minutes, no more, no less, then grabbed the pan's handle and scuttled over to the sink, running cold water over her breakfast to stop the cooking process exactly where she wanted to stop it.

This had been her daily ritual for nearly sixty years, ever since her grandfather had introduced her to the beauty and simplicity of the soft-boiled egg.

She stepped over to the kitchen table and swept Abbey, the cat, off the top, sat down, and rolled back the sleeves of the camouflage-green, quilted housecoat. Kicking her feet twice, as if in a futile effort to reach the floor, she picked up the knife and brought it down, hard, on the egg, splitting the shell neatly and freeing the contents for her bowl.

As she scooped out the yolk and white from one side, a shadow fell across the table. She glanced up with a start to see a tall, blond hulk standing in front of her, very nearly filling the archway of the tiny mountain home. Her hand flew to her throat in fright, then, slowly, resettled on the cracked Formica table top.

She put down the egg and smiled.

"Good morning, Kelvin," she said with pride. "You scared me."

"Good morning, Mother," he said, his voice heavy with morning phlegm. He shuffled to the counter, his rough and scarred bare feet scraping the ancient hardwood floor as if he were wearing sandpaper slippers, and fumbled for a coffee cup.

"I missed you last night," she said, a trace of sadness in her voice. "Where were you?"

He collapsed into a chair across the table from her, his size, weight and the fury of his collapse causing it to squeak twice and groan with protest.

"I was distributing fliers."

"Which ones?" she asked sweetly, dipping a point of toast into the dark yellow of the egg.

"Anti-development number two. Stop Vail Mountain Terrace."

"Where?"

"East Vail. Developer's heaven. One of Jerry Ford's kids yelled at me."

"Which one?"

"One of the sons. The one with the big head."

"They all have big heads."

He snorted at the image.

It was clearly a case of the pot calling the kettle black, Marjorie realized, her son's head being the biggest, most out-of-proportion thing she had ever seen in her life. It sat like a prize-winning pumpkin on top of a tall filing cabinet. She stared down into her breakfast plate to dissolve the image.

"And you?" he asked, slurping his coffee.

"Me? I could have used your help, certainly," she said stiffly, coming back to the matter that was so clearly at hand. "I was on the mountain. I was in the village. I was preaching."

"What did you use," he asked, with a disinterested air, "the bacon rind shotgun or the shillelagh?"

"I used my Rachel Carson-autographed Louisville Slugger, of course," she smiled. "I'm no murderer," she laughed. "I refuse to kill one of God's creatures."

"I don't get it, Mother," he said, punctuating his words with another slurp of coffee. "You'll bash some boob's head in, but shooting bacon rind is a cardinal sin."

"All God's creatures all have a purpose. Even you, Kelvin," she said, sourly. "I needed your help last night."

"I was busy with the flier."

"The fliers are still in the trunk of the car, Kelvin. Where were you last night, son?"

"I was in East Vail," he said, the words straining out between his teeth and his hangover as his voice rose angrily, "handing out your goddamned fliers!"

The cane whistled through the air, slamming onto the table with such force that his now empty coffee cup leapt into the air, then fell back to the table top shearing off the handle. Kelvin Stump felt the air move sharply around him, the "bang" of the cane's impact rattling the dishes in the room and the few brain cells that had recovered from a night of nursing a bottle of scotch and small pile of cheap cigars at a locals' bar in Edwards.

He turned his aching and red-rimmed eyes toward his mother.

"In this house," she spat, "the Lord's name is not—not—taken in vain. Do you hear me?"

He nodded, warily, preparing to leap away in case the cane flew again.

"And in this house," she said, "you live by my rules and my schedule and my devotions. Do you understand?"

He nodded again, his head bobbing uncontrollably, like a plaster of Paris dog in the back window of a cheap car with bad shocks.

"You weren't with the fliers last night in East Vail," she said, her voice filled with a hateful disappointment. "You weren't arguing with one of Jerry Ford's sons. You weren't with me, defending the glory of the mountain against yet another mountain bike race that will bring yet again more congestion and investment and foul ideas to the town and to the ecosystem. You were engaging," her voice rose with righteous indignation, "in public drunkenness. I can smell it upon you."

She fell back into her chair, sweeping the cane across the table, pushing silverware and one small plate before it. Kelvin snatched up the plate as it reached the edge, the silverware falling to the floor in a discordant rhapsody.

"I am," she said, quietly, the anger passing from her face like a passing cloud, "disappointed in you, Kelvin."

He sighed heavily. "I know, mother. I'm sorry."

"There is a lot of your father in you."

He felt a sudden surge of shame well up inside him. He forced it back down like a burp that had picked up a hitchhiker and felt a burning in his chest, his eyes and his face. A thousand small thoughts filled his head, jumping connections, confusing him. He had been caught. There was too much at stake. He had to think fast.

"I'm sorry, mother," he whispered.

The stony grey visage of her face held for a moment, and then softened, almost as if the beam of mountain sunlight filtering into the window had melted her anger and restored her love for her son.

"I know," she said, quietly. "I know."

"Whatever you need, mother," he said, his eyes filling with tears, "whatever you need," he pointed out the window, "whatever she needs, I'll be here."

"You've said it before and you'll say it again, I suspect," Marjorie Stump said, softly. "But you are my son, and I will always give you another chance. Fight your demons, boy. Don't let them win out over the glory that is in your soul."

"The part of me that takes after you."

She nodded.

"Exactly."

He smiled, then looked at her with as much love and affection as he could muster through alcohol-benumbed eyelids.

"What is our plan for this weekend?" he wondered aloud, hoping to change the subject while picking a bit of cracked china off the surface of his quickly cooling coffee.

"We are going to," she said with quiet deliberation, "thoroughly ruin a goddamned mountain bike race."

She said it without thought, without realization, as she had for years. It made Kelvin Stump smile, as he reminded himself, yet again, that "do as I say, not as I do," had been the watchword in this home as long as he could remember.

He nodded in agreement with her, wondering through the facade how he could keep her happy, deal with her madness, and still walk away from the weekend free and happy and ungodly rich.

✹

LEONARD ROMANOWSKI HADN'T CRIED IN YEARS, BUT HE WAS CRYING NOW. Heavy sobs racked his chest and his cheeks were not tear-stained, but soaking wet, the water running down and staining the collar of his shirt.

He was lost. Lost in paradise, perhaps, but lost nonetheless.

His brain was racing on auto-pilot, with no direction, no rhyme, no point. He would have been hard pressed to tell you his mother's name.

He was lost. He was dead. It was merely a matter of time.

He continued to cry.

Leonard stared outside, from the creek to the bridge, the bridge to the courtyard, the courtyard to the people who crossed it, some rolling bicycles before them, some walking alone or in groups, all heading to a central point beyond his range of vision, somewhere up along the deep green and gold that was Vail Mountain, somewhere high up into the sky, where they would ride and ride and ride and ride....

He sat up, pushed himself away from the wall of the hotel room and jumped to his feet.

The riders. Holy shit. That was it. The riders.

This was ... he struggled not to lose his thought in the muck that was his head this morning ... a race. The Ishmael Coffee Race. And he was in the thick of it. He turned again toward the window and looked out. He had seen something as he had checked into the hotel. Something that might work. Two minutes at the window and he saw one again, two people struggling to roll it up the street. Yeah. Something like that. Something like that would be perfect.

The entire scenario fell into place.

Will. The final piece. Wasn't that Will he saw last night? Will Ross. One of his clients. Where? Where did he say he was staying? He struggled with a reluctant memory.

Oh, what an idea.

What a great idea.

He danced around the room, humming to himself and returned to stare out the window once more. A great idea that includes Will Ross and one of those things filled with money.

A brilliant idea.

A brilliant idea that would save his life.

And it was Rachel. His mother's name was Rachel.

CHAPTER FOUR:

STARTING LINE

"HOW DO I LOOK?"

"You look fine," Cheryl said, "why do you care, anyway?"

"We're meeting your team. I wanted to make a good impression." Cheryl laughed and shook her head as she stepped through the doorway of the Pancake City Restaurant, keeping the door open with one hand for Will, then stepping away. Will, who had been busy examining his reflection in a pane of glass, missed the opening and stepped into the edge of the door, with a resounding "thunk."

"Smooth, very smooth," she said, as he hurried up behind her at the "Please Wait to Be Seated" sign.

"Thank you, very much." He paused, glancing in the mirrored wall and said, "So, what do you think? Am I gaining weight?"

"What?" She asked without stopping her scan of the restaurant.

"Am I gaining weight?" he asked with mock seriousness. "You know, we have a tendency to pack it on."

"Who we?" she asked.

"My family. The Rosses."

"Well, no, I didn't know that," she said. "Your mother is thin, your sisters are thin, your brother works out. Your dad has a little pot belly, but...."

"See? It's there. It's genetic."

"It's breakfast."

"What?"

"You're still eating like you have to ride 250 kilometers this afternoon. All you have to do today and yesterday and tomorrow is sit with your feet up and watch the races. Drink a beer. Have some peanuts. Of course you're going to put a bit on."

Her eyes caught a pale cloud of blue-white smoke in the corner of the room. Without knowing for sure, she stepped toward it, somehow drawn to the notion that this was her team.

Will followed quietly, the torn muscle in his right calf singing, the tightness due to the edge of cold that sat on the morning. He should have stretched. He'd catch that later.

"You know," he said, bumping the back of a blue-haired bouffant with his elbow, "you can burn calories just by sitting. And the bigger the TV screen, the bigger the calorie burn."

Without pausing as she worked through the crowd, Cheryl whispered back over her shoulder, "You just tell yourself that, okay?"

Will shrugged. It hadn't worked. It always worked for him, talking about something, anything else, serious to nonsense, always got his mind off the problem at hand, gave him a breather, and then allowed him to step back into it with at least some sense of perspective. It wasn't working for Cheryl. She was focused on the job, the day and the team, not to mention the races of the weekend. Nonsense about his waistline wasn't about to change that.

He ran his hand along the top of his jeans.

Was he getting thicker? There was no roll, but the skin seemed heavier, as if someone had just installed a cheap pad underneath the carpet of life.

He gave it a quick pinch. Better get back on the bike, he thought.

"Hi," Cheryl said, stepping up to the table. Four sets of eyes slowly turned from their conversations and stared at her. The eyes belonged to two men, both in riding gear, a pert and very young woman, wearing a parachute-cloth jumpsuit, and an older man, of no determinate age, with a head of exploding dreadlocks. The same man, Cheryl remembered, from the bar the night before. They all turned and peered at Cheryl and Will through a cloud of blue smoke.

"Yeah?"

"Need something?"

The two male riders worked almost in tandem, immediately throwing a wall up between themselves and the interlopers. The young woman visibly retreated, the interruption causing a bothersome loss of attention. The bleary-eyed Rastafarian had no reaction at all, but merely stared, shifting his focus slowly from Cheryl's face to her chest, to her hips, then across to Will's knee, the left, still in a removable brace, over to the plastic walking cast on his right leg, then up to Will's black-and-red Team Haven windbreaker, then to his face, spending the last few milliseconds of the gaze trying to peer through the dark cover of Will's sunglasses.

"Yes, as a matter of fact, I do need something. I'm Cheryl Crane and I need my team."

The table was silent for a moment, save for another cloud of blue smoke shot skyward and into a vent by the dreadlocked man in the corner.

Will could feel the men at the table slowly retreat into a defensive posture, while the woman rose imperceptibly in her seat. The human chimney smiled and waved off a small belch before saying, with a laugh, "Well, Cheryl Crane. Big Momma. We be your team right 'cheer. Indeed."

Will smiled in return, realizing quickly that these would be tough nuts to crack and only the humor of the man with the grease-stained hands would make it any easier.

Without an invitation, Cheryl turned and reached behind her, pulling up a chair to the edge of the half-moon table. Will did the same, turning the chair at an odd angle to accommodate his leg brace.

The six sat, silently, staring at each other for what appeared to be the half-life of radium, until Will finally broke the silence, addressing the young woman and offering a handshake.

"Hi, Will Ross. I'm a roadie just in from Europe."

"Hi," she said, not offering any other information.

Will's eyebrows rose in a bit of surprise before he plowed on. "Look, I can guess who you are, but then we'll be here all day." He paused for a moment, then offered his hand again. "Frannie?"

She caught herself and looked up from the menu she had so thoroughly focused on.

"Uh, yeah. Frannie. I'm Frannie Draa."

"D-r-a-y?"

"No. D-r-a-a. English. Contraction of Drake."

"Really? You don't usually contract English names." Will leaned forward and looked into her eyes. She warmed immediately to the attention.

"Don't know how. Just did. Least for the past 100 years."

"Really? Fascinating," Will said, quietly, drawing her into his confidence. "Any relation to Sir Francis Drake?"

"Excuse me," the dark-haired man next to Frannie in the booth said with a biting tone, "I'm not here to discuss genealogy. I'm here to ride and win. So, you're the team captain?"

The tone was edged, but not sharply derisive, and aimed at Cheryl.

"Right. I'm Cheryl Crane. I've worked with Haven for the past two years and with Stewart Kenally for the past 14."

"I don't really care about your job résumé," the dark-haired man stabbed. "I care about your riding experience and I care about this idea of a team captain." The thin, blond-haired man beside him nodded, then turned to look at Cheryl.

She sighed. This was going to be worse than she imagined.

"Two years with Rapido Consegna in Italy, riding downhill and supporting Paola Melzi in the cross-country. Four years with TW in Michigan. Two years at U of M trying to convince the school to field a team."

"And how long since you've been on a bike?"

"Two years. Accident."

"That's comforting."

"I don't believe I know you," she said, extending her hand.

He did not reciprocate. Her hand hung in the air for a moment before she slowly pulled it back.

"I don't believe you ever will," he said, finally. "Second question: what's this team captain shit? Mountain bike teams don't have team captains."

Cheryl stared at him without anger, though the man's tone made Will lean forward in a clearly defensive posture. Cheryl pinched him under the table. Slowly, he sat back. This was her game.

She ignored the slur, said, simply, "Haven's money. Haven's model. It's a

French 'thang.' They wanted somebody eyeballing the operation." She smiled again and turned to the blond rider next to her heckler. "Hi. Cheryl Crane."

He hesitated for a moment, then extended his hand. "Hi. Jeremy Jettman. The Jettman. Downhill and slalom."

"Great," she said with a smile, "how long have you been in the game?"

"Two seasons as a pro. One out of work. Did a lot of BMX riding growing up."

"Great. That's great experience. Where do you come from?"

"Wyoming. Near Jackson."

"Great. Great riding there."

"Yes, indeed," the voice intruded harshly. "Oh, my. Isn't it all just great. Just goddamned fucking great?" The venom dripped heavily in the tone.

All eyes at the table shifted.

"My name is Reed. Marshall Reed. Me?" he said, his tone rising into a childish falsetto, "Why, teacher, I hail from Tennessee and I ride my bike every day, like I have for the last ten years. Pro? Three years pro, but passed over for this team captain 'thang' because management prefers a slice with connections. Oooooh. But me. I'm ready to ride. And I ride downhill and cross-country. Just stay outta my way and we'll be fine."

Cheryl tried, but couldn't stop her face from reddening at the insult. Frannie Draa lowered her eyes and smiled into the palm of her hand.

"Great, Reed."

"Yes, it is, it is great, isn't it?" he said, sarcastically. He turned to face Will. "And if you've got any thoughts about teaching me a lesson for insulting your squeeze here, let me tell you, Galahad," he pointed a crooked, obviously broken finger toward Will, "I'll gladly kick your Tour dee France ass any goddamned time you want."

He smiled, almost a grimace, then went back to drinking his coffee, obviously lost in an egotistical funk.

Cheryl slowly swallowed a desire to pick up the coffee pot and slam it against Marshall Reed's temple, possibly rendering him senseless. She turned slowly and faced the chain smoker at the end of the table who was quietly, without hurry, squeezing out a small flame that threatened the end of a dreadlock.

"And you, I take it, are Hootie?"

"Yes, ma'am. Hootie Bosco at your service."

Will cocked his head and stared at Bosco. "Your mother had a real future-telling flair, didn't she? How'd she know that Hootie would be in about now?"

"She didn't," Bosco explained, slowly rubbing the end of the tight braid between his fingers, "she named me George. George Taylor."

"So, is Bosco a nickname?"

"Nope. Bosco's my legal name. Had it changed."

"Along with the Hootie?"

"Naw. The first name comes and goes. Bosco is forever."

"Why do you change your first name?"

"I do it in honor of whatever group throttles my monkey at the moment, man. For a while I was REM Bosco. For a while I was Dead Bosco. There was even a sad period of my life where I was Bonnie Bosco. But now, for the moment anyway, I'm Hootie."

"They haven't had an album in a while. Isn't it about time to change again?"

"Yeah, I'd do it too, pal, but there just aren't any groups that are staying around for more than one or two tunes at a time. I need long-distance bands. This name-change shit ain't cheap once you get a lawyer involved."

"No doubt."

Fascinated by it all as she was, Cheryl interrupted Will and Hootie to ask about his background and training.

"Do it all, always have. Since 1970-shit-somethin'. Can fix anything. You name it."

"Where and when?"

"Where doesn't matter. It's been everywhere. When—whenever you need it, ma'am."

Cheryl began to feel the knot release in her gut. Finally, she thought, somebody I can work with. He may be weird, but there was an element of trust already there, as if what he said was also what he believed was also what he would deliver.

She smiled and nodded.

"And … Frannie?" She asked almost tenuously, as if coming on too strong or too harsh would drive this small, possibly frightened animal back to ground. "Where have you been? How did you get here?"

She smiled sheepishly, and glanced, first at Marshall Reed, then at Jettman and finally at Will. Then, and only then, did she turn to Cheryl.

"I rode a lot of Colorado amateur stuff. NORBA races. Two years at CU-Boulder, too, on their road team, before I got out to turn pro."

"How long?"

"How long what?"

"How long have you been a pro?" Cheryl asked quietly, with as much gentleness as she could muster. This whole group was like a batch of dental patients waiting angrily for root-canal surgery.

Frannie paused and looked down at her plate. The eggs had grown cold. She stared for a moment, seemingly embarrassed by her answer.

"How long, Frannie?" Marshall Reed barked, "how long? Tell our fearless leader."

"Two weeks," she mumbled. "Only two weeks."

Cheryl smiled. Only a babe.

"Don't worry, Frannie," she said, with a tone of comfort in her voice, "two weeks lead to a month which leads to a season which leads to a year. You've got to start someplace. Just stick with it. I'll help you wherever I can. So will Will, here," Will nodded, acknowledging Frannie's smile, "and so will—Hootie—and Jeremy and even Marshall."

Reed piped up sarcastically, "You bet I will sweetcheeks. Anything you need and we'll get right out there and win one for the gipper!"

The mood was immediately and irrevocably broken. Frannie Draa immediately slid back into her silence, while Marshall Reed took a long slurp of coffee and began to rise.

"Move it, Jeremy, some of us have some riding to do."

"Sit down," Cheryl said, almost under her breath.

Jeremy Jettman heard her, as did Will and Frannie and Hootie. All stopped and watched Reed's reaction. It was obvious that he either hadn't heard or simply didn't care.

"Move, man, I've got to walk the course before practice…"

"Sit down, Marshall."

"...begins, and then I've got to hammer out a few laps before the amateur shit makes it life-threatening out there."

He shoved against Jettman trying to clear an exit. If he got to the floor, Cheryl knew, he'd be gone, no matter what she said.

She stood and reached over, grasping Reed's earlobe between her thumb and index finger and pinching hard. He yelped, leaping up onto the padded leatherette seat in an effort to get away. Though it pulled her at an odd angle, Cheryl Crane hung on as if that single lobe was her lifeline between safety and disaster.

Reed finally found his voice again. "Ack. Ack. Ack. Acccrrrrrck."

"Sit down, Mr. Reed, we are not finished." She released her grip on his ear and watched as he fell, heavily, into the seat. He stared at her angrily and then pushed hard against Jeremy Jettman, trying to break free of the table.

Jettman didn't move, frozen by the sight of what he had just seen.

"Jeremy, let me out, goddamn it," Reed hissed.

"Bullshit, Jettman," Cheryl hissed back. "Don't you move a goddamned inch."

Marshall Reed gave one more shove and then fell back into the seat.

"What about practice, fearless leader," he snarled. "Can't I practice like all the good little boys and girls?"

"You can practice all you want ten minutes from now, when the team meeting is over. We'll set a practice schedule and we can all practice. But don't you dare try to ignore or upstart me again, punk. I've been working with European pros for the past two years in a grunt job doing grunt work. I've been bullied, battered, fondled, insulted, ignored and pushed around like nobody's business. There have been two attempts on my life and God knows how many butt pinches. I've put up with the biggest assholes on the Continent, most of which make you look like Dennis the Menace. So, unless you want me to rip your legs out of their sockets and beat you to a bloody death with them all the while whistling 'Night Train' out of my asshole, then you'd better get with the program and stop being such a complete and total, egotistical son of a bitch!"

Her voice had slowly risen through the soliloquy until the entire restaurant had become a part of the event. With her final word, silence reigned supreme. Will noticed that over at a nearby table, a coffee cup now held approximately two-and-a-half times its legal limit.

Will desperately wanted to laugh, the speech and tone both so completely out of character for Cheryl. It had created a curtain of tension that hung over the room like an asbestos fire wall. He turned his poker face back toward Marshall Reed waiting for the reaction. This, he knew, would be telling. Here, he realized, Cheryl had played the big cards, in order to hold the team together and find out what kind of bully Marshall Reed really was: the kind that would back down in the face of a challenge, or, the kind who would rise up and spit back in the challenger's face.

Reed's face, stark white with anger, showed no reaction. He slumped back into the booth and stared angrily at Cheryl.

Will's eyes smiled. The back-down kind. The kind to watch because they'll stab you in the back as soon as they get half the chance, through lies and rumors and general crap.

"All right," Cheryl said, "wrap up breakfast and then we'll meet at the box van. I've still got to register. One hour. It is a box van, right ... Hootie?"

"Yes, ma'am. Big box van with a big damned Haven-TW logo on the side. Looks like a moving truck if you ask me. And you don't need to register. I handled it for the entire team. Knew you'd be in late."

"Great. Thank you. We'll have a secondary meeting there, at the truck. Then, you're free to practice. I have no regimen. You know you. You know what you have to do...."

A thin, fortyish man with greying hair that was slowly moving backward across the top of his head, stepped up beside Cheryl.

"Do we have a problem here?" he asked, officiously.

"Well, let's see. Do we have a problem here, Marshall?" She turned and stared squarely at Marshall Reed. "Do we?"

Between white, hard-pressed lips, he pushed out, "No, no problem."

"Nope," Cheryl turned to the restaurant manager, suddenly taking on the tone of the preacher's wife at a Sunday social, "not a problem in the world."

"Well, let's keep it that way, all right, miss? I will not tolerate disruptive behavior or cursing in my restaurant."

"Understood. And I agree with you completely."

Taken aback by her calm and acquiescence, the manager shook his head and stepped back.

"Well, well, see that you do."

"Of course, sir, sorry for the problem," she said, in her best bowing and scraping tone.

"Okay, then," he muttered. Turning, he stopped and stared at Hootie Bosco. "There is no smoking."

"Where?"

"Here. In this restaurant."

"It's not posted. By law, it must be posted."

"It's posted at the front door. This is a No Smoking restaurant."

"Since when?"

"For about the past seven years, my friend."

"Well, my friend, I wasn't here when you created the law and when you decided that a little sign on the front door was enough to handle the problem. My mistake and my apologies."

In a flash, so quickly that Will couldn't be sure what happened, Hootie Bosco's arm had moved and the burning cigarette had disappeared into his mouth. One, small, final puff of smoke escaped from his nose.

"I've seen that trick," the manager snorted. "It's in your mouth and you'll pop it out as soon as I leave."

Hootie Bosco smiled and opened his mouth wide. Whatever was there wasn't there any more.

The manager stared for a second, then broke his gaze with a shake of his head and walked away, calling over his shoulder, "your check is on the way."

All eyes turned back to Hootie Bosco.

He smiled, pulled his hand from under the table and replaced the burning Marlboro in the middle of his smiling mug.

"One hour. Box van." The check came and Cheryl snapped it out of the waitress's hand. "I'll catch the check." She eyed the bill and handed the waitress thirty dollars that seemed to appear out of nowhere. "Keep the change."

"Thank you. Thank you. You have a nice day, now. By the way, there's no smoking."

Hootie smiled and put the cigarette out in his eggs, making everyone at the table slightly nauseous. "Thank you. Sorry. One of those hideous, unconscious habits we all have."

"Aw, sweetie, don't worry. I ain't gonna charge you with grand theft. I just don't want you to have to put up with Hooper again."

"Well, thank you, dahlin'," Hootie said, smiling.

The waitress stepped away, turned, and stepped back.

"By the way, really nice hair."

"Thank you. You've made my day, you most certainly have."

MARJORIE STUMP MADE HER WAY THROUGH THE COLLECTION OF BICYCLES AND biking gear and cycling aficionados that littered the base of her beloved mountain.

Each day, the crisp air was a bit more befouled with fumes and exhaust, the land itself cluttered with growth and the sprawl of ticky-tacky houses everywhere, her mountain, her mountain degraded just a bit with another lift, another event, another battering by man.

She doesn't have time to recover, Marjorie thought, she doesn't have time to recover.

As she plunged through the crowd, without showing her deepening sadness and anger, she smiled and had a kind word for everyone she passed, encouraging the riders, welcoming the spectators, wishing the vendors a profitable day. In her wake, with his long arms, Kelvin quietly snipped spokes with a pair of professional wire cutters that would snake out of a sleeve, do their work and disappear back up the sleeve in a single, quick and fluid motion.

"Welcome to Vail, everyone, welcome to Vail," she'd call. The riders, still groggy from pre-race activities, both official and unofficial, the night before, gave her a rheumy-eyed glance before going back to their business of trying to wake up and look competitive for this, the first day of practice.

Marjorie Stump ambled up to the Haven van and banged her cane loudly on the side.

"Jesus!" came the shout from inside.

"No, it's someone else."

Hootie Bosco stepped into the sun from the depths of the step van and shook his head. For one, brief, stunning moment, Marjorie Stump could swear that smoke rose from the man's dreadlocks.

"Umm. Oh. You—you are European, aren't you?" she said, pointing the knurled end of the shillelagh at the blue, yellow and white Haven-TW logo.

"Huh? No, ma'am," Hootie said, rubbing an imaginary stain off his hands with a shop rag. "I'm from Oregon."

"No," she said, with a tone of exasperation creeping into her voice, "no … your people, your people here."

"No, ma'am," Hootie said, as politely as he could muster, since he knew he still had two bikes he had to set up in the next twenty minutes, "my people come from Hawaii and Indianapolis, Indiana. I don't know where before there."

"No, no, no!" she shouted, trying to put an end to his end of the conversation by banging the cane against the side of the truck in a staccato beat. "Your company. Your sponsor. They come from Europe. It's not a question. It's a statement. Haven. It's a European company. You're a European team."

"No, ma'am," Hootie said, with a generous tone, leaning around the edge of the truck, pointing at the logo while subtly checking for pock marks and damage to the finish. "TW, see that TW? Two Wheels. It's a bike shop out of Detroit. Or, someplace near Detroit. Someplace in Michigan, anyway. We're an American team."

"Haven is a huge corporation," Marjorie Stump intoned, the bit now in her teeth. "There is no way that a major corporation is going to play second fiddle to a bike shop out of Detroit.…"

"It's not Detroit. It's near Detroit. Romeolopolis, or something like.…"

"Haven is your sponsor. This is a European team."

"Well, that will surprise all the Americans who are on the team, that's for sure. Even the captain is American. But she just got here from Europe, if that makes you feel any better."

Suddenly, Hootie Bosco felt like he was in the middle of a "Flintstones" cartoon.

Bam-bam! Bam-bam-bam!

The woman had stepped into the van and the entire thing rattled like a metal can of BBs.

"Jesus, lady!"

"Do not! Do not," she preached, "take the name of my Lord in vain!" She raised the cudgel on high and brought it down with a "bang!" on the floor of the step van again. "You are a European 'sponsored' team," she said slowly, trying to get her point across, finally, to the Hawaiian Hoosier who stood before her. "Because of that, you should be aware that the Green movement began in Europe and that it has spread to this country, and as a team with a European connection, you should be holding to European eco-values and refusing to take part in a sport like this that decimates the delicate, top layers of the ecosystem and increases the risk of erosion on the mountainside—my mountainside—God's mountainside."

She paused and took a breath. She hadn't been planning a lecture this morning, but the opportunity to inveigh before this member of the great unwashed was simply too good to pass up.

She pulled herself up to her full and magnificent 4 feet 6 inches.

"European eco-values?" Hootie asked, raising an eyebrow as he did. "Like the eco-values of all those East German and Polish and Romanian and Russian companies that indiscriminately buried heavy metals and toxic waste and mercury and turned huge tracts of land into dead zones for the next ten thousand years?"

Now it was Marjorie Stump's turn to raise an eyebrow. She deflated just a bit, down to at least 4 feet 5-1/4 inches.

"Uh, yes," she sputtered, "but those were corporate aberrations." She was not used to being questioned or debated.

"Aberrations my Aunt Fanny," Hootie smirked. "Those were government-sponsored companies. Government-controlled. The will of the people. The whole communist spiel. Don't give me this aberrations crap. The Greens barked like hell, but never did anything about it. That's the problem. They still wanted their radios and batteries and cars and electricity, too. Just like everybody else."

"Governments, not Greens."

"No, of course not. Not the Greens," Hootie said with mounting sarcasm.

"And what's this about God? God's mountainside? If he didn't want us to ride it, he wouldn't have invented...."

Marjorie Stump swung her walking stick at Hootie's thigh. He saw it coming and deftly jumped aside.

"Watch the stick," was all he said.

Their eyes locked in a battle of wills, before Hootie broke his gaze, Marjorie mistakenly claiming a mental victory. Hootie looked up past the hulk that stood behind and to the side of this woman, near a row of bikes, to see Cheryl and Will approach.

"You want to talk to someone about it," he said, "talk to her, she's the team captain, manager, grand poobah. She's the one to argue with. I've got work to do." He started to turn back into the step van, but before he did, he locked eyes with the golem that was Kelvin Stump and said, in a voice of pointed determination, "Hey, Fred, I see the snips snaking out of your sleeve. Anything of mine or my neighbors comes up cut in the next few hours and, by God, I'll track you down, tie you up and pull your nuts out through your eye sockets. You hear me?"

Marjorie turned and stared at Kelvin, then rapped the knuckles of his right hand through the long sleeved-windbreaker. He yelped and dropped the wire cutters. Using the cane for balance, Marjorie reached down and picked them up, then threw them on the floor of the step van.

"I do apologize for my son."

"I appreciate your doing that, ma'am. Especially since you disagree with our riding. He starts clipping cables or spokes and somebody could get seriously hurt."

Marjorie nodded and then turned to face the woman in the Haven team jersey as she approached the van. Marjorie wasn't upset about cables being cut. She was upset about Kelvin being caught.

She sighed heavily. As clumsy as his father, she thought.

"Hi. What's up?"

Cheryl stepped up to the strange grouping around the Haven-TW truck, grateful for something that might take her mind off her quickly approaching first run of the day.

"Are you in charge here?" Marjorie Stump asked in a sharp and urgent voice.

Cheryl shot a glance toward Hootie Bosco, who simply raised both hands in a gesture of resignation and disappeared into the back of the step van, but not without first shooting one last warning glance toward Kelvin Stump.

"Yeah," Cheryl answered. "I suppose I am."

"Well, then," Marjorie said, the confidence returning to her voice, "you should not be here."

Immediately, Cheryl felt her defenses and her hackles rise. "Oh, really? Any particular reason why?"

"Any number of reasons, young lady. You are in charge of a European team. Europe leads the way in Green politics and thought…."

"Since when?"

"Since the 1970s, Miss. Beyond that, you are a woman. You should be more concerned with the saving of another woman. Your mother."

"Are you threatening my mother?"

"No. You are."

"I'm threatening my mother?"

"Yes."

"How do you figure?"

"You are threatening her by your indiscriminate riding upon her."

"My what … wait. Wait. We are talking about different mothers here, aren't we? You're not talking about Rose Cangliosi of Detroit, Michigan, here, you're talking about…."

"Mother Earth."

"Yeah, that one."

Marjorie Stump reached across a bike and grabbed Cheryl in a pale and liver-spotted, vise-like grip, pulling her in close to her. Cheryl reacted, falling back while trying to twist her left arm free, only succeeding in brushing her leg against a chain and smearing her leg with grease.

"Goddamn it."

Marjorie Stump drew her in sharply, "Don't you ever take the name of the Lord in vain."

Cheryl twisted her arm down, against Marjorie's thumb, and broke the grip. As she pulled her arm away, she noticed a pale red shadow of a small and gnarled hand on her arm.

"Sorry," she said, rubbing the mark vigorously, "I'll watch my mouth."

"Your mother would want that."

"The one here?" she asked, pointing at the mountain.

"No," Marjorie answered.

"The one in Michigan," they said together, Cheryl with a tone of heavy resignation.

"Well, I'm sorry, Mrs....." she paused, looking for some help.

"Stump. Mrs. Marjorie Stump."

"Mrs. Stump. But this is what I do. I ride. I ride on marked trails and stay to them. I don't disturb the surroundings. I only ride on private land when I have permission, and I try to restore whatever damage I may cause. Most of us do," she said, waving her arm in an unfocused arc behind her. "I think that's pretty good. It might not be up to your environmental standards, but it's a step above what other sports do."

"You shouldn't be riding on your Mother."

"Hey, sorry. Gotta dance."

"Well, I just think...."

"I'm sorry, Mrs. Stump, I don't mean to be rude, but this could go on forever and I've got to get to work. I need more practice than the average bear. Sorry. Maybe we can continue this later or some other time or perhaps you can talk to the promoters of the race—they're in that tent over there," she said, pointing in the distance, "the Ishmael Coffee Race tent, or, you could even talk to the developers of Vail itself, they've got an office around here someplace, I'm sure...."

"They do, and they don't listen anymore."

"Ah, I see you've already tried some of my ideas," Cheryl said with a smile that was a cross between understanding and passing the point of giving a damn. "Well, I'm sorry. But ... that's the way it goes. You've got to change with the big guys. Working on the peons like me doesn't do a damned bit of good."

"Don't sell yourself short, dearie," Marjorie Stump huffed, "you'd be amazed what can happen at the grass roots between you and your Mother and God."

"I'm sure. But not at this grass roots. I've got too much to do."

Marjorie Stump nodded, as if in agreement, but more to simply end the conversation. Cheryl was grateful when the small Michelin man of a woman turned and looked down the grassy, tent- and van-edged lane to the main race tent.

"That is where the bosses will be?" she asked.

"Sure as shit," Cheryl replied without thinking. "Maybe even old Mr. Ishmael himself, or, whatever his name is."

Marjorie Stump turned and stared at the young woman for a long, hard, and uncomfortable moment.

"You shouldn't curse. It makes you ugly."

"Sorry."

"And you're such an attractive young woman."

"Thank you."

"What would your mother think?"

"She'd think it was none of your business, even if she did agree with you, but, then again, that's my mother."

The two women stared at each other for another long, uncomfortable moment, before Marjorie Stump broke the gaze and turned sharply away.

"Kelvin," she called out behind her, never glancing back, "come along now!"

And Kelvin did, moving away at a lumbering pace, revealing Will Ross trapped between a heavy metal tripod workstand and three fully suspended mountain bikes.

Cheryl stared for a moment after the shadow of Kelvin Stump passed across her like last spring's lunar eclipse, and smiled.

"You were a big damned help."

Will nodded, almost sarcastically, and finished extricating the outer bar of his brace from one of the bikes.

"Excuse me. Besides, I couldn't run to your aid and help vanquish," he looked beyond her to watch Marjorie Stump and her large offspring turn a corner behind the Ishmael Coffee tent, "whatever that was. I was trapped behind the human Maginot Line. Every time I moved, he moved. Every time I shifted, he shifted. That's how I got hung up on the bike."

"I don't want to know."

"In fact, I think you may be right. You don't want to know."

She smiled and shook her head in mock exasperation and turned to the mechanic who had stepped back to the edge of the Haven team van.

"Is it gone?"

"Yes, she's gone," Cheryl said. "What was that all about, Hootie?"

"Don't ask me, ma'am. She just wandered up and started ragging to me about saving Vail Mountain for God and how, since we're a European team, we ought to be Greens. But she sure as hell didn't know much about European environmental impact."

"And you do?"

"Yes, ma'am. I'm a veritable storehouse of completely worthless information."

"Fascinating."

Hootie smiled and wiped his hands.

"Yep, it's an amazing talent," he said, turning back into the van, where he stepped into the darkness and his voice lowered to a mumble, "I can remember all kinds of worthless shit, but I can't remember where I put my keys to the van...."

"Oh, by the way," he said, suddenly reappearing. "You might want to mention something to other team leaders or riders—I'll talk to mechanics—but that big asshole who was with her was clipping spokes."

"What?" Will rose up in shock to something approximating his full height. The effort, at altitude, was getting to him.

"Wha.... I'm sorry," Cheryl said, "what was he doing?"

"He was clipping spokes," Will answered. "Most'll catch it right away, all the clanking and shit, but it's a pain in the ass. Just what you need before a run or a race, pull off the wheels and toss 'em to the mechanic. It's a nuisance. Breaks your rhythm. Damned nuisance for everybody."

Cheryl turned back to Hootie who now sat on the edge of the step van, shaking the last of the morning from his hair.

"How do you know?"

"Caught him. Dead to rights." He leaned over and picked up the wire cutters and tossed them across to Cheryl, who caught them smoothly, once more impressing Will with the range of her physical talents. He would have taken them in the forehead.

"He was slipping these out of his sleeve and going for the Colnago." He nodded in the direction of a bright yellow bike plastered with new Haven-TW logos. "Your bike as a matter of fact."

She stepped quickly over to her ride and ran a hand lovingly along the top tube, crouching down next to the front fork.

"Any damage?"

"Don't think so," Hootie replied, "I'll check later, but I think I caught him just before he got to snippin'." He looked back down the line of vans toward the village. "Thing is he had that stupid-assed smug look people get when they think they can get away with anything and have been, so I'd best wander down the way here and check with other teams to make sure they didn't get hit."

He slid himself off the van and stood up, his hair moving independently of his head. It caught the chill of the breeze and moved, first away, then in the direction that he was going to move. Will watched, fascinated, as the pair of them walked away. It was as if Hootie Bosco lived with an animal on his head.

"You with me?" Cheryl asked, tapping him on the shoulder.

"Huh? Oh, yeah," Will replied. "It's just … where did you get him?" He motioned in the general direction of Hootie Bosco and his hair, both stepping into a team area just down the lane.

"I? I didn't get him. Stewart got him. You can complain to him on Monday if you want."

"No. No complaints. Stewart knows people who know their jobs. I was just wondering."

Cheryl smiled as she watched Hootie in the distance.

"Quite a character."

"Quite."

Will laughed. "And he's all ours."

Cheryl turned and gave him an evil grin.

"What do you mean, 'ours,' roadie?"

Will froze as if he had been shot.

"Oh. Oh. That … that … was low. That was low."

She laughed, a sound that finally relaxed Will from the tensions of the morning and the meeting with Reed and Jettman.

X

MARJORIE STUMP MARCHED, LOCK STEP, ALONG THE BACK OF THE TEAM AND promoter tents, the anger quickly building in her like a summer thunderhead over Colorado's Front Range. She could hear Kelvin galumping behind her, making no attempt at silence.

In a moment of fury, she turned and, in a move so fast that her short arm and the heavy shillelagh looked like the blur of a single line, rapped Kelvin, hard, along the side of his right knee.

He yelped and fell into the back of a tent, then rolled down to the ground in pain.

He crumbled into a fetal position, his mouth open in a swallowed scream of agony, his mind desperately trying to find a means of expression. He barked, twice, then inhaled sharply, looking to his mother with teared and pleading eyes, his mouth moving, but silent, the word forming but never coming out.

Why?

"Because," she said in answer to the unvoiced question, "it is one thing to monkey wrench. It is another thing to get caught. We are the Guardians of the Domain, Kelvin. GOD never, never, gets caught. Now, come with me. We have tires to deal with."

She turned on her heel and tramped away, leaving Kelvin alone in his anguish in the tall grass, energy-bar wrappers and an empty energy-drink can decorating the area around his head.

Kelvin said nothing.

His mouth remained open, but the pain remained stuck in his throat behind a white hot ball of shame and anger.

CHAPTER FIVE:

THE DEEP END OF THE POOL

THE VISTA BAHN LIFT WHIRRED AND CLANKED, EACH SHUDDER making Will whistle through his teeth.

It wasn't so high. After all, the people didn't look like "HO" train figures. Not yet, anyway. Maybe "O" gauge. It just all seemed so tenuous, all this weight from all these open cars held up and carried by a series of pylons and one, well-used steel thread.

Will examined it carefully on the fly for damage: the errant split, the wild hair, the loose connector, but couldn't find anything.

He settled in to white knuckle the ride all the way to a place called mid-Vail.

Cheryl, on the other hand, loved it all: the openness, the sense of flying, the small voice inside her that said she could kick Peter Pan's ass. She gazed over the expanse of the White River National Forest that kept opening up before her, almost as a gift from God, and smiled in excitement and awe. She twisted back and looked down the mountainside, the village already laid out before her like a picture postcard view of heaven, tiny, delicate, serene.

She looked down between her feet and watched the gigantic pines cruise by silently beneath, while being amazed by the size of the boulders that lined the groomed ski runs.

No wonder these were called the Rockies, she thought. Hate to pull a Bono and wrap myself around one, though.

Everything was so rich. Everything was so green. Everything was so big and free and forever. Everything about it screamed Colorado. John Denver didn't sing the half of it.

I could live here, she thought.

She turned her face to the sun and felt the warm work its way through the very slight chill that sat just on the top of her skin.

I could live here. I could live here forever.

She didn't know how long she had her eyes closed. She opened them as the chair hit a separator on the final pylon before the turnaround and Will squeaked again.

"You okay?" she asked, shocked by the ashen tone of his complexion.

"Yeah, fine." He looked ahead to the turnaround. "How do you get off this thing?"

"Bar lifts, you walk away. Simple as that, guy. You, uh," she chuckled, "never really did anything like this before, did you? Didn't you tell me you used to ski in Michigan?"

"Did. But it was all rope tows and poma lifts."

"Well, geeze, those are more dangerous than these. People falling off, sliding down, getting hung up."

"Yeah, okay, I agree," he wheezed, feeling the change in altitude every few feet, "and I did run into one once, did a great endo. But at least it was on the ground."

"You sound like Daffy Duck on skis."

"Well, maybe I wasn't graceful, but I did have fun."

"So why'd you quit?"

"I kissed two trees in one day and decided that God was trying to tell me something."

"Two trees? Man." She shook her head. "So, what do you figure the big guy was trying to tell you?"

"Well, of course … be safe. Ride bikes."

She looked, blankly, at his face, covered with scars from a high-speed impact into the back window of a Peugeot, then, glanced down at his left leg, still in a brace from an accident on a mountain road in the Tour de France, then, up to his left arm, still discolored from the gravel and cinders that had been ground into it during the same crash, and, finally, down to his right leg, the calf of which had been split from knee to heel on the side of a spent volcano while carrying a collapsed teammate to safety.

She nodded.

"Sure that was God?"

Before he could answer, there was a clank and a whir and they were there, the bar leaping up in front of them, Cheryl stepping out and away, Will jumping off and losing his balance on the angled platform, the heel of his brace catching on a break in the wood and forcing him to fall and roll down the slight incline. Cheryl clumped up beside him. As he lay there in the dirt, he carefully examined her new riding shoes, refusing to look up at her face.

"This isn't skydiving, you know. You don't have to 'hit and roll.'"

"Thank you."

"Here."

She offered him a hand, but he refused to take it, twisting himself around and up into a sitting position. Now that he was back, quite literally, on terra firma, he could enjoy the view.

"Mighty pretty country around here, Rompers."

"What?"

"You know, I've loved you since I was in rompers," he said with a grin.

"Are you okay," she asked, suddenly concerned, "or did you bump your head again?"

"Not me, not me," he said, sad to know that the woman he loved didn't have the slightest idea what classic Groucho meant in the great grand scheme of the universe. He worked his way upright, as she retrieved the bike from the guy who had pulled it off the Vista Bahn lift.

"First-class travel," she said as she rolled the bike past him.

He brushed off the ass of his jeans.

"First class—Slovenian Airlines."

"You grump too much."

"Yeah, maybe I do. But I am alive."

She stopped and looked him over carefully.

"Not by much."

"Granted. But what's the thing about hand grenades and horse shoes?"

"In your case, stay away from both."

He stopped, looking up toward a small chalet perched back in a clearing. From the second floor of the chalet, ran a long ramp leading down to a service road.

"What's that?"

"Launching pad, I suppose," she replied, feeling her hands grow clammy inside her gloves.

"Really, which course?"

She stared at him for a second with pure exasperation.

"The downhill course," she said slowly, as one might speak to a walking rock. "The downhill starts at the top and goes down. The cross-country starts at the bottom and goes up."

"Well, yeah. That I know. I'm not a complete doofus," he said, suddenly realizing the stupidity of the question. "You're … uhh … going to ride on that?"

"You bet." She tried to keep the knot in her stomach from finding voice.

"It's narrow."

"It's all bike handling. Nothing to it."

"But how much bike handling have you done in the past few months, or, even years, kiddo? You've been watching other people do it, but you haven't been doing it yourself."

"Thanks for your vote of confidence."

"Jesus. It's not that, it's just—hell, I'm just worried."

"Don't," she said softly. "It's just like riding a bike."

He stared at her for a long moment, then simply shrugged.

"See you at the bottom of the hill."

"How are you getting there?" she asked, cocking her head back toward the Vista Bahn.

He caught the move and made an exaggerated counter in the other direction. "Thought I'd walk."

She nodded, smiling.

"Thought I'd ride."

✗

SHE STARED DOWN THE 80-FOOT RAMP FROM THE SECOND FLOOR OF THE CHALET, the ribbon of plywood suddenly looking narrow and dangerous, the brown, mottled wood snaking off into the distance in a strange form of forced perspective, the end thin line that merely connected with another strip of brown, a service road that was much wider, but just as dangerous. This was, essentially, no different from throwing herself into the deep end, she realized, hoping, beyond hope that it really was true that you never did forget how to ride a bike.

But this was to riding a bike like heart surgery was to dissecting a frog.

Oh, mother, father, every adult known to man, if you were lying to me all those years, I'm going to track each one of you down and paint you the most horrible death, she thought, trying to keep her mind on any subject other than the one at hand.

"You want a time on this?" the guy at the gate in the NORBA sweatshirt asked.

She took a deep breath. No. Time was not the issue here. Getting to know the course was the issue. Survival was the issue.

"No. No time. Thanks."

Her communication skills were reduced to single-word responses.

"Okay," he nodded. "Anytime."

He swept his hand to the side, like a maître d' lifting the red velvet rope and leading the way to the table in a bad William Powell movie.

Cheryl shifted slightly on her seat, rose up, and brought her weight down on the pedals.

Commitment.

The first push was the worst, for as she brought her right foot down, her stronger side, she felt the bike tack a bit to the right as if she was compensating with the front fork.

Cheryl brought herself back on line and realized that she was perilously close to the edge of the plywood ramp and quickly gaining speed. If she braked, or panicked, she knew she'd lose it on the edge. There was only one way to survive the drop to the service road.

She sped up.

She hit the angle between the service road and the plywood ramp with a lurch and felt her head snap up. The Manitou suspension up front took the majority of the impact, but she was so far out of training that her weight was poorly positioned on the bike and she felt a resultant shudder run through her from her ass to both other ends.

Instinctively, she began to pedal, hard, toward the first turn off the service road, perhaps 200 yards ahead. Left turn. Sharp drop. The amateurs would walk their bikes the six feet down the cliff. Professional downhill racers, of course, would not.

What was she, she wondered, as the orange barricade fencing was coming up quickly. What was she?

She braked hard, swept left and took the drop, which went hard right at the bottom. This was it, the test, the initiation, the breaking point for herself, her bike, her weekend. If she could ride this, she could pick up time, she thought. If she walked it, she would lose. The back wheel skidded to her left and she slid, rode, fell down the embankment all at once, hit bottom, gasped and pedaled on.

Cheryl snapped a smile to herself and drove forward. Memories of a near death experience on an Italian trail falling quickly behind her as she rode.

She powered along the narrow ribbon through the trees, convinced that she could hear a thup-thup-thup as she passed each one. Her senses were heightened to the point that colors seemed almost hypnotic when she realized, out of the lower third of her vision that she was approaching a large and nasty root that ran along, then across the trail at a difficult angle. She braked hard, threw her rear wheel to the left, then pedaled hard again, hitting the thing straight on in the narrow confines of the forest cut.

This time, she hit and timed the impact correctly, allowing the rear suspension of the custom Colnago frame and the Manitou fork up front to absorb the shock, while her elbows and knees compensated for whatever was left over.

She barely felt it.

It made her smile.

It really was just like riding a bike.

A woolly bag loomed up suddenly, marking a turn in the trail. She began to brake, realizing that gravity and her own excitement had built up a lot of speed through the trees. The woolly bag was to prevent those who hadn't been paying attention to their speed from sailing into the trees and across a ditch and to the cliff that led to a service road six feet below.

Insurance mandated safety, she thought.

She slowed and took the hard-right turn, shifting gears to pedal up to the top of the rise. She pushed hard at the top, again, feeling her front wheel carp a bit toward the left.

Bad idea, she thought, bringing the wheel back on line and flying down the single track to the dip in the ditch and the service road just beyond. The story at the bar last night was that some TV reporter goof had done the same thing at the top of the same ridge on Wednesday and had rolled off the cliff, dropping the 20 feet to the service road below, bouncing real good, cracking some ribs, knocking the wind out of himself, and winding up with a TV story the next day.

That's reporter involvement.

Officially, that spot in the universe was called the Latte Grande Launch, but, unofficially, it now carried the title of Brody's Launch in the reporter's honor. It was said that in his embarrassment, he didn't see the humor in it.

Cheryl smiled at the thought, then clamped her lips closed. A passing truck on the service road threw up a cloud of dust and pebbles that threatened years of Clearasil and orthodontia. Still, as she picked up her pace, the dirt road was a shot of confidence after the drop through the trees. Ahead, another band of orange plastic barricade bent her back into the trees and across the rake of the ski slopes.

First she was in the trees and then, bang, she was in the midst of the slope, racing a ribbon that seemed cut perilously into the hill, then, bang, into the trees again, having a bit more room on each side for mistakes, but encountering roots and rocks left over from the close crop grooming of the slope. A drop, a hairpin, and she headed back across again, noticing, out of the corner of her eye, that another rider was following up closely behind her.

Had she really taken that much time? Had she really been that slow? What would happen tomorrow when this one was for real?

Her mental wandering had drawn her away from the task at hand, staying controlled and focused on the ribbon of single track. Into the woods again, she faced a hard left turn, followed by a sharp right and a drop, 3 to 5 feet, nothing major, but very nearly straight down. The turns she anticipated, but the drop caught her off guard, her front wheel going airborne, then slamming down, hard, on the packed clay of the mountain side. The suspension took a lot of the impact, but again, she felt the explosion run up through her arms and down to the small of the back, then slap her tailbone down on the gel seat. She would feel that one tomorrow, for sure.

She rose up out of the seat and began to pedal hard, pumping the bike to regain what she had lost through inattention. Across the Riva Ridge ski run, Cheryl shot back into the woods and hit a bermed turn that dropped her to the side, unexpectedly, then threw her into a speed trap.

Knowing that it was here that she'd make up her time, Cheryl cranked it up in the big gears, hitting at least 45, maybe 50, on the 750 meters of wide open double track. This, she knew, was as close to heaven as she'd ever get and reveled in the sense, the experience, the pure joy of it all.

Then, once again, reality closed in around her.

She braked hard and turned the bike into the first of the switchbacks across the lower Tourist Trap, feeling the first of the real chop in the course, the front end of the Colnago bouncing and whipping unnaturally along the washboard. The dry summer in Vail had powdered the course as well, leaving her rear wheel grabbing futilely for anything resembling purchase.

She slid through another turn and into yet another high-speed zone across Golden Peak. She survived the top of the mountain and now had only about a kilometer, five switchbacks and an off-camber jump at the end of the run to deal with to survive.

Lost in her thoughts of survival, the first switchback came up fast, too fast. She slid hard in the turn and felt her back wheel slam into a woolly bag along the course edge.

Damn it, she thought, pay attention to yourself.

She was prepared for the next switchback to the left, and then, quickly on, the turn to the right again. She crossed back and forth across the face of Golden Peak, giving whatever spectators there might be this early in the game a clear look at her style, her speed and her bike-handling abilities.

Somewhere, inside her head, sat the notion that they were less than impressed by it all.

She hit the jump cleanly, feeling very smug and pleased with herself. As she passed under the finish banner, she noticed one little girl, perhaps nine years old, applauding, while her father eyed Cheryl suspiciously. She pulled up quickly, about 8 feet from them.

"You were good, Cheryl Crane, you were good," the little girl shouted with a burst of enthusiasm.

"Thanks," Cheryl said, not quite as sincerely as she had intended.

"Who the hell are you?" the father asked, his eyes dropping from Cheryl's face to the logo on her chest to a slick-back program for the weekend race.

"I'm Cheryl Crane. I'm with Haven."

"Haven? What the hell is Haven?"

She pushed the bike to the side of the course, moving down and away from man and daughter, while trying to compose herself mentally. The ride had been survivable, but the ride had been hideous as well. Will had been right. She had been away too long, far too long, to take on something like this. She had grabbed for the brass ring without realizing that the damned thing was glued into the chute and she wasn't on the horse correctly. She was destined for a fall.

"Hey, you."

And the last thing she needed right now, as she desperately tried to reorder her head after such a disastrous downhill, was some asshole with a program and an attitude trying to make her name and place in the universe jibe with his own sense of self worth.

"Hey, you."

"Hey, what?" she answered angrily, turning on her heel and punching her chin out.

The man backed up quickly, taking two steps backward before even realizing he was retreating. The little girl, however, moved ahead and stood at the back of the bike, smiling proudly up at Cheryl.

"You did good."

"Thank you."

"No, really. You did good. You're all upset right now, because you think you didn't do very good, but you did. You took the turns better than just about anybody and you kept your pace high during the rough stuff. You did good."

"How could you see the technical stuff?"

She turned quickly and pointed toward a red telescope about 30 feet away, pointed up the mountain.

"Usually I use it to look at the moon, but I brought it up here and pointed it at the turns. I've got a lens that makes everything right side up, otherwise it's upside down and you can't watch a race like that, even though I look at the moon that way sometimes."

"Really?"

"Really. So I watched you. And you did really good."

The girl's father stood quietly in the background, not moving from the position he had retreated to just moments before. Cheryl glanced at him for a moment, realizing that her anger had been soothed by a little girl with a machine-gun patter and a kind word.

"That's a nice jersey," the girl said.

"Thank you."

"Is Haven new on the circuit? I don't remember it from some of the earlier races."

"Yeah," Cheryl answered, dropping into a crouch to be more on an eye level with the young fan. "Yeah, it is new. TW here, in blue, is for Two Wheels, a bike shop in Michigan. Haven is a big vitamin company in France. They put in the money that really made the team a possibility. I knew the owner of the bike shop and used to work for Haven in Europe, so I got a chance to ride."

"Did you ride a lot before?" the father asked, almost apologetically, from the background.

Cheryl answered without taking her eyes off the little girl's face, as if frightened of breaking the connection with her. "I didn't ride much here, that's for sure, but I did ride in Europe a lot, especially Italy. I ran against Pezzo a few times. And some others."

"Melzi?" the girl asked.

"I met her, but never rode against her."

"Fentini? Abrusco? Andolini?"

Cheryl laughed. "Yes. Yes. No. You know your Italians."

"I read."

"What? It's not like the Denver papers write much about mountain biking."

"No. I live near The Tattered Cover, in Cherry Creek, in Denver. I go there and buy racing magazines. Even the Italian ones. I can read some Italian. Well, not read it, but I can figure it out. Sometimes. Sometimes I can. With the pictures."

"Amazing."

"No, you're amazing," the girl said, with a huge grin. "You ride."

Cheryl felt a pulse of heat shoot through her, almost a hot flash, that made her gasp and her face flush. It was a twinge of embarrassment, to be sure, but also a sense of pride in who she was and what she did, a sense that she hadn't felt in years.

"Thank you."

"No, thank you. It was really fun watching you, Ms. Crane."

"Cheryl. I'm Cheryl to my friends."

Now, it was the girl's turn to blush.

"I'm Devon."

"Devon, it's a pleasure," Cheryl smiled, putting out her hand. The girl took it happily and shook it madly.

"Here," Cheryl said, standing up and suddenly giddy from the altitude, activity and accolades, "take this." She unsnapped her helmet and swung it across the seat of the bike, and quickly pulled the Haven-TW jersey over her head.

"It needs a wash, but it's yours if you want it."

"Do I? Do I?" the girl squeaked in delight. "Thank-you, thank-you."

"Drop over by our truck later and I'll sign it with a permanent marker for you. We've also got some giveaway goodies and I'll fill a bag for you, Devon."

"Thank you, Cheryl."

"You here for the whole weekend?"

"You bet."

"Great. Stop by."

"You riding again today?"

Cheryl paused a moment, then glanced up the mountainside. The fear and disappointment of the past few moments were gone, replaced by the desire to do it again, do it better, do it faster. She looked back at the girl, for a moment, almost able to catch her reflection in the glow of her eyes. Maybe her mother had been right all along, she thought. Women, she had said, relied on each other, while men, she found their support inside their own past and what they've done with it.

Cheryl Crane smiled, both inside and out.

"You know," she said, rubbing her hand across her bare belly, just below the line of the grey sports bra, "I might just do that. Although," she said, looking down at her midriff, "I better put on a shirt, first, don't you think, Devon?"

"I do. I'll watch. Go ride."

Cheryl laughed at the burst of chatter.

"I will," she said in the same rhythm, tousling the girl's hair as she did. "I will."

She turned and gathered up the bike, pushing it off toward the Haven-TW van.

There was a reason to do this, she realized, a reason bigger than any she even carried within herself. It was simply—the reason to be.

Role model.

Damn. You never know where you're going to find them.

She pushed off toward the van and glanced backward. The girl was clutching the jersey close to her and watching Cheryl go. She smiled and waved.

Cheryl smiled and nodded, realizing that she felt better and more at peace with herself than she had in years.

Life is good, she thought.

Riding is better.

LEONARD ROMANOWSKI FINISHED HIS FLASH PACKING OF THE ROOM, SLIPPED his arms through the handles of the gym bag, wearing it like a backpack, and put all his effort behind moving the weight of the large, black case. It had been easy to steal it from the lobby. After all, no one watches their bags when they're empty. Now, the bike case was full of cash and on its way to safety, with, one would hope, him directly beside it.

He had come to realize, with a shock, that the gun was lost, but it was a street purchase with no tie to him. And after what had happened last night, it was probably better that he didn't have it with him anyway. He was no gunslinger. He was a sports agent, a far deadlier breed.

With another heavy push, he felt the catch give way and the box slide easily across the carpet. The wheels were working now, torn free of the tiny cut in the carpet, which was no longer so tiny and could no longer be described as merely a cut. Turning back to look at that, he didn't notice the paste board wall and what a protruding hook slicing into it could do.

He bumped and wiggled his way toward the door, opened it carefully, took a glance outside, and sighed deeply in relief. Life or death could have been standing outside waiting for him, and this time, luckily, it was at least another few minutes of life. He quickly scanned the hall and made a snap decision that, while taking only a split second in reality, seemed like a UN debate in the firestorm that was his mind.

Take the main elevator to his right, or head down the hall, to his left and take the freight elevator to the lower parking lot, right near his car? They'd expect him to take the freight elevator. That's for sure. That's the wise move. Stay out of the main traffic patterns. So take the main elevator, throw him off. Or, would it? He might think Leonard had figured out the old freight elevator scam, so, cover the main elevator and catch him by surprise. But, then again, maybe not. What if there were two or more sent after him? They could cover both the mains and the freight. Not the stairs. But he couldn't take the stairs, because of the damned box. What should he take, where should he go, what should he do?

With barely a pause at the door, Leonard turned and began to roll the heavy case along the carpet toward the freight elevator. Death likely awaited him inside, but at the moment it was the only option.

Now sweating heavily from both fear and exertion, he turned the corner and slapped the "DOWN" button on the elevator. Deep within the building he heard the machinery begin to whine as the cabin climbed up to meet him. A bell rang, dully, somewhere inside the works and Leonard Romanowski once again took a deep breath.

The door slid open and the carriage was empty.

Not a particularly religious man, he lifted his eyes to heaven anyway, thanking whoever or whatever had kept him alive for another few minutes. He slid the box into the freight elevator and pushed the button for Parking 1. Somewhere, near the delivery entrance for the hotel, there was a car, which led to safety, which led to ... his plan.

His glorious and magnificent plan.

Again, it all passed through his mind in the time it took the carriage to pass through one floor, but seemed an eternity between his ears. And, quite frankly, Leonard Romanowski was amazed. The plan was perfect. He rarely thought in such detail. He rarely thought in such minutiae. Then again, he rarely thought.

The bell rang again, once more, dully, somewhere within the works and the doors slid open. Again, he was alone. The breaks were falling in his favor.

He slid the case to the delivery door, cracked it open and took a glance. It was clear. Quickly, he rolled the case to the back of the rental car, opened the trunk and wrestled it in. The back seats popped down, giving him the extra few inches he needed. The car settled visibly in the rear as the heavy black bike case, filled now with four million dollars in stolen mob cash, dropped the last few inches to the floor of the boot.

He slammed the lid shut, smiled to himself, and stepped quickly around to the driver's side door. One quick stop and he, along with a gym bag filled with five hundred thousand dollars, cash, American, was off on a magical mystery tour of the Colorado mountains.

"Go ahead, assholes," he thought to himself, "find me there."

He put the car in gear, pulled back smoothly, and drove quickly out of the parking lot, ready to surprise a friend with the greatest gift known to man, in return for the greatest favor any man has ever done for another.

Watch my money.

And Leonard Romanowski knew, as the nose of the car peeked into the Colorado sunshine, that Will Ross would be happy to do it for his old buddy, his old pal, his never say I-can't-get-you-a-job agent, Leonard Romanowski.

The car pulled up onto the road and was quickly caught up in the crowds gathering for a weekend of professional mountain bike racing. Leonard's senses were alert, but he remained calm. After all, there is safety in numbers.

As the quiet returned to the loading area, two figures emerged from between two cars, and quietly went back to work monkey wrenching what they found parked there.

A Beemer—an ice pick in the Michelins. A Ford Escort—a shot of quick drying insulating foam up the tailpipe. The sole electric car in the bunch was left untouched.

Marjorie Stump moved quickly, if not quietly, between the cars, checking, thinking, gauging their worthiness, pondering, all the while, the man in the cheap rental who had just pulled out.

"Kelvin," she whispered, as much to herself as to him, "what do you think that was?"

"What, Momma? What do I think what was?" Kelvin asked, full voice, as he shuffled up noisily beside her.

"What do you think was in that box?"

"What box?"

She turned with a look of both sorrow and pity toward her son, so big, so full of life, so committed to the cause, so damned dumb. Marjorie Stump sighed heavily. Despite the fact that he was Elmo's son, she loved him so, and reminded herself to remain patient with him.

"That big black box the man had to drag out to his car. What do you think was in it?"

"Bike," he replied simply. "It was a bike box."

"No, love. Too heavy," she said, playing with the three little white hairs that she had been cultivating on her chin. "No, it was too heavy to hold a bike."

"How do you know?"

She sighed with exasperation, "The trunk. The trunk of the car dropped, quite a bit, when he put the case in his trunk. That tells me that it was not a bike, but something heavy. What does it tell you?"

"I dunno," he shrugged.

"Frankly, I don't know either," Marjorie said, stroking one hair as if it were a small cat sitting on the leading edge of her neck, "but I certainly would like to know."

She turned and looked at all the possibilities for mayhem that sat quietly in the garage before her and made a quick decision.

"Kelvin," she turned to the tree trunk of a son who stood in a stupor beside her, "I want you to follow that car...."

"How am I supposed to do that," he asked with quiet astonishment, "I'm on foot. He's on wheels."

"Yes, yes, indeed, but that bicycle race I so deplore might just be our salvation. He can't travel fast in Vail today. So ... follow him. See where he goes, If he stays in town. Where he rents a room. But, most of all, what he does with that box."

"Then what?"

"Then, find me and tell me."

"Why?'

She moved far too quickly for a woman her size and age, snapping the shillelagh out and catching the nerve bundle at the base of his wrist before Kelvin Stump had any chance to defend himself. His mouth popped opened in a bellow of pain and emotional hurt that he quickly swallowed before he turned behind a car and threw up on the expensive, if flat, steel belted radial.

"Because," she hissed, "I want to know."

In the moment he looked at her, Marjorie could swear she saw a flicker, a quick burst of hatred, then his eyes cooled to their usual dullness, as he nodded and turned, loping down the aisle and up the ramp into the sunshine, cradling his wrist as if it were broken.

She felt a moment of shame for herself, at her anger and her abuse, a moment of compassion for him for the same, before putting it all aside and turning back to the job at hand. She stood next to the dull red Ford Explorer, the back seat filled with the travel toys and general scrap of children, and passed it by.

Maybe she was losing the steely heart and toughness of spirit she needed for this sort of thing.

As she walked toward the stairs, she stopped at the Mercedes and drove the ice pick home into what appeared to be a brand new set of Pirellis.

Then again, maybe not.

✦

MEANWHILE, IN THE ROOM VACATED JUST MOMENTS BEFORE BY LEONARD Romanowski, two men, both dressed in Hawaiian print shirts, looked over the tear in the carpet and the thin line tracks that led down toward the freight elevator.

"I knew it was too easy. Two phone calls and a solid guess is just too easy. Are we skunked?"

"Now?"

"Yeah."

"Hmm, maybe. But we know he's got it with him. And we know he's got most of it in one box."

"Silly."

"Stupid."

"On the run?"

"Maybe."

"What you thinking?"

"He split it out and is going to dump the big one until we give up."

"What if we catch him?"

"He uses it as a chip."

"Bargaining?"

"Yep."

"Where'd he go?"

"Dunno. He got any friends around here?"

"Hafta check."

"Check on a rental car, too."

"Indeed."

"He won't go far. That case is pretty damned heavy from the looks of it and pretty damned thin. About yea by yea."

He held out his short, but muscular arms in a rough approximation of the box size.

"Keep an eye out."

"Keep an eye out."

"Anything else?"

"Yeah."

He pulled the door of the now empty hotel room closed behind him.

"You ready for lunch?"

CHAPTER SIX:

SECOND CHANCES

WILL STUMBLED BACK TO THE BASE OF THE VISTA BAHN LIFT JUST in time to see Cheryl lift off for a second round on the mountain. The machinery roared and squealed behind her, lifting her with a jerk and shooting her skyward, but she was oblivious to the sheer mechanical desperation of it all. She was beaming, lost in another world, and never saw him. He nodded and smiled at the figure as she disappeared into the sunshine over the first line of trees. He knew what she was feeling.

She had been offered an opportunity, and in return had delivered a magnificent morning ride.

He had felt the same things, yet in a different place, at a different moment in time.

He sighed.

The sun was up, but there remained a decided chill in the air. Will gathered the thin Haven windbreaker around him. Damn, he thought, didn't it ever warm up around here?

Will looked down at the tangle of credentials that littered his chest, some from today, some for tomorrow, some generic ones that covered races and dreams gone by in places thousands of miles away. They always got him in and made him a part of anything.

Until now.

Despite the badges of honor worn upon his chest, which he thumped in a way only Mighty Joe Young would truly understand, he was outside this community of riders. He walked into the pit area and was among them. He caught snatches of conversations filled with words and phrases he had used himself, regularly, over the past sixteen years.

He walked between bike stands and tables and corrugated boxes, and people glanced and nodded and smiled in his direction, but, Will knew, as he approached the Haven-TW box van, that he was no longer a part of any of this. He would never be a part of this day in particular, this place, or this race, and he would never again be a part of cycle sport; for now, most certainly, he stood outside the realm of the chosen.

He was the winner of Paris-Roubaix a mere five months ago. Two months ago he had been riding in, and been mangled by, the Tour de France, the greatest race in the world. He was a team lieutenant. He was a champion. He was watched and photographed and adored by old ladies, pre-teen girls and people with green teeth. But now, he stood outside a box van in Vail, Colorado, unrecognized and alone, without prospects, nursing legs still battered and torn and bruised and shackled, all for the greater glory of a team that had already forgotten him. And he was being stared at by a man with enormous Rastafarian dreadlocks, who looked right through him as if he were a plate-glass window that had just finished a date with a bottle of Windex.

Hootie Bosco stared, then shook his head, making his hair dance in a bright and befuddled way, then smiled.

"Hey, hey, it's the boyfriend. Right? Our fearless leader's boyfriend dude. Cool. Come on up, man, join the party."

He moved a box of errant gears, straps, cables, and a few Necco wafers to the side and patted the wood floor beside him, offering a seat.

"Thanks. I appreciate it, but I'm gonna wander around."

"Naw, naw, stick. Stick here for a while. Take a load off. I could use your mood. I'm feelin' too light today. Besides, you might get arrested out there lookin' like you do. Naw, really. This is Cheeryville, today, man. Everybody around here is too damned happy for my blood."

"It's the off-season. They're happy you're here to spend money."

"Really, think so? Damn, I was hoping they just liked me for who I am." Hootie Bosco laughed and shook his head again, making his hair shimmy like a Jell-O ring that had lived in the back of the refrigerator way too long. "Come on, join me. My hair don't bite. Anybody but me, anyway."

Will couldn't suppress a chuckle, no matter how much his self pity commanded him to, and maneuvered the brace over to the edge of the box van. He turned, balanced his weight, and hopped, which was completely unnecessary, his butt clearing the bottom lip of the box van by inches, then coming down, hard, on the rough wooden flooring.

"Must be tough to get around in those things."

"Yeah. They make life interesting."

"Now, where'd you get that one?" Hootie Bosco pointed at the short, plastic walking cast with the Velcro straps that encased the lower third of Will Ross's right leg.

"The cast—I got on a volcano."

"No shit?"

Will smiled. "No shit. Tore my calf muscle right down the middle. The cast is to help it heal long. Cuts rehab time."

"How long ago did that happen?"

"About six weeks."

Hootie Bosco smiled. "Doesn't sound like it cut nothin', man."

Will shrugged.

Hootie Bosco pointed at the brace that surrounded Will's left leg. "And that one?"

"That one…."

"Don't tell me. That leg, if we take off the brace and your pants, will show, quite vividly, the dangers of falling off a bike at sixty miles an hour on a narrow mountain road, then bouncing off a guard rail. Right?"

Will involuntarily shuddered at the memory.

"Right. Good guess."

"No guess. I only asked you about the other one to see how you'd tell me. Speaking of that, tell me, pal, what was that guy ahead of you on? From the video I saw, he shot off that road and into the air like he had found the secret of flight."

"Bad shit. Synthetic steroids."

"Bad load, huh? Well, just proves what I always say."

"And what's that?"

"Know your pharmacist." Hootie turned and smiled, but it was empty, a smile that showed the memory of too many friends lost at the feet of the demon god medicamentum. He shook his head again, watched a few hairs float free for a few moments of independence on their flight to the ground, and looked back at Will Ross. Seeing Will's distance, he dropped his normal tone of voice two octaves and tried to sound like his father.

"Don't worry. You'll be okay. You'll ride again."

Will started, and turned to stare at Hootie Bosco. It was as if there was another person in the box van with them.

"Don't worry about that, either, my friend," Hootie said with a smile. "I am many people in one body. I am Hootie. I am all the lessons that Hootie has learned. I am one hell of a mechanic, able to adjust a derailleur at fifty miles an hour on a straight line descent, not unlike the one that claimed the top layer of your hip and all the little hairs that once lived there. I am a writer, a lover, and a reader. Despite the fact that I haven't written shit for three years, haven't loved for four, and am determined to fight my way through 'Moby Dick' before I move on to anything else. And, so, I haven't read anything else, aside from bike magazines and the occasional *Playboy*, which I read merely for the articles, mind you, the pictures only serving to stir me up in unconventional ways, since I started Mr. Moby nearly eight months ago. I am all those things."

He paused and took a deep, almost comical, breath.

Will canted his head a bit and asked, "Why 'Moby Dick'?"

"Because you're supposed to read it. Because nobody in this town, other than the head librarian, has ever read more than the 'Classic Comics' version. And because," he paused, staring up at the mountain, his face going slack and pale, "because that mountain took my future—it took my life. It took my love. I will have my revenge on it someday. I will by all that is holy!"

He said the last, standing, in a loud, defiant chant, before dropping back to a sitting position on the floor of the step van. Will stared at him in shock and disbelief.

"Jesus, is that true?"

"Naw. Except for the stuff about the librarian. I just wanted to read it. She'll be around here this weekend. You ought to meet her."

"Who?"

"Moby Dick. No, the librarian. Sheila Webster. Friend of mine. She's gonna be here and complain what a Pazeekaville we've made out of her hometown."

He smiled, a 200-watter that lit up the surrounding area.

"And you?" He spread his arms, offering Will the floor.

Will returned the smile, but then looked toward his feet, which barely brushed the top of the dirt and grass at the base of the ski mountain. And what about him? What could he tell this guy? What could he tell himself? What was going on inside his head? What the hell had happened to the lower half of his body? Most of this stuff would heal, that's for sure, but would it ever be able to survive the punishment of a race again? Would he ever be able to ride? And if so, where, and for whom, and for how much, and....

"Pain in the ass, isn't it?"

"Huh, what?" Will shook himself out of his reverie and brought himself back to the base of the mountain in the back of a box van at the start of a race weekend.

"Pain in the ass wondering about your future, isn't it?" Hootie asked with a gentle smile. "Look, I've been there, man. That day when you ain't sure you can do it anymore, and nobody wants you, and your body is saying it ain't in the legs and it ain't in the head."

"Yeah."

"Been there. Done that. But it was easier for me. After all, I was just a rider. You were a winner. A champeen. Indeed. Won the big one. Lots of big names never won that race. Lots of big names refuse to ride that race. And they were shooting at you, weren't they? I think you get degree-of-difficulty points for that. Wouldn't you say?"

Will looked at Hootie Bosco and couldn't suppress a grin, not only of amusement, with the man's hair a pure force of nature, but of gratitude, because Hootie Bosco, for all his outrageousness, had cut directly to the chase in Will's head.

William Edward Ross had been a champion, a champion who had risen out of nowhere, claimed a huge prize, and then settled back until he stood....

"At the crossroads," Hootie Bosco said, staring up the mountain, "at the crossroads. And it's a bitch."

"It sure is."

"Well, if I could, a little bit of advice: Don't live through her, man," he said, pointed in a vague way up the mountain. Will knew without asking that he was referring to Cheryl.

"Don't live through her. You'll put pressure on both her and you until the whole damned thing, whatever it is you have, breaks apart in a million pieces." Hootie Bosco turned and smiled again, this time, though, it was a smile of sadness and loss. "I've done that one, too, man. Great lady. Bummer city."

"It is."

"You know, then?"

"Yeah. Came close to losing her a couple of times. Ego. Bitterness. Picky shit." Will kicked the walking cast at one of the fully suspended mountain bikes. "And this—I don't understand this sport, man."

"Same as the road. It's just a daily dose of the worst of Roubaix without the smooth spots in between. It's bouncing and puking and hanging on for dear life and hoping to god that your tires, your frame, and your guts all hold out until the finish line. So what's so different?"

"Different kind of riding, man," Will said, distantly, "different kind of riding all together."

"Bullshit. Myths, legends and lies. All created by roadies and gravel grinders, little ego pukes just trying to keep each other out of the mix. But look at it, man, Furtado, Tomac, Overend, they crossed back and forth, no problems at all. All kinds of Eurotrash do it. Why can't you?"

"Frankly, I wasn't all that good a road rider."

"You were when you had to be."

"Maybe."

"No maybe. Shit," Hootie barked, throwing what appeared to be a hand-rolled and hearty medicinal dose of weed, still burning, into the grass beside the truck. He glanced down at the cast on Will's right leg.

"How long has that been on?"

"About six weeks."

"Time for it to come off."

"I dunno."

"Shit, man. You go any longer with that thing on there, and it's going to become a permanent part of your leg."

He reached down and grabbed the end of one of the Velcro straps wrapped around the cast. "When did the plaster come off?"

"About two weeks in."

"You should have never put this on. There was plenty of healing by that time." He tugged at the straps again, sizing up the cast. "So you've been in this an extra four weeks without a doctor's slip on it?"

"He said it wouldn't hurt anything."

"Except livin'. Time for freedom, my man. You game?"

Will realized, suddenly, that he was sweating, that he was afraid to take the cast off. Why, he didn't know.

"Can't hide behind it forever, dude."

Which, Will knew, was the why. As long as that cast was on, he'd never have to ride again, he'd never have to prove anything. He'd never have to succeed or fail on two wheels.

He'd just be.

Empty. Alone. Dead to the world. But, with an excuse.

"Take it off." Will heard his own voice from far away.

"Sure now?"

"You bet. Take it off."

"That, my friend, is what I like to hear. A person coming to life again."

"What?"

Two Velcro straps ripped free before he answered. "A person, like you, coming to life again. Alive. Know the concept? Coming to life. Getting back into it. You've got to grab life by both hands and hang on for dear life. Otherwise, they might as well put you in a home and feed you that canned liquid food they serve to the veggies. Honest. They sell that shit now, can you believe that? To people with their own teeth. Like it's gonna help them go scuba diving or something."

The cast slipped free of his foot, and Will wiggled his toes. The cool air felt wonderful.

"Free at last. Free ... at ... last." Hootie Bosco threw the plastic-and-foam cast in a high arc that sailed behind the truck and landed, with a crash, in the bottom of a community dumpster some 25 feet away.

A guy standing next to the dumpster jumped and threw a vague and damning curse Hootie's way.

"Don't worry, pal, it missed you," Hootie shouted back, "this time."

"Hey, man," Will said with a squeak, "that's 200 dollars of walking cast there."

"Shit. You'll never need it again," Hootie replied. "What are you going to save it for? Your kids? A garage sale?"

"You never know."

"You never know what—that you're going to do that again? Maybe so. Maybe not. Don't live your life on the maybes."

"Maybe you're right."

"Shit, there you go again."

Will dropped the few inches to the ground and began to walk gingerly around Hootie's work area in front of the van. The calf felt good. Weak, tight, but good.

"What about that other one?" Hootie asked, pointing at the brace.

"Naw. Let's just do one at a time. I'm not ready for full-flight freedom yet," Will answered. And yet, deep down, he thought, maybe he was. He eyed the bright yellow and blue Colnago set up for Marshall Reed.

Maybe he was.

"Go ahead. It's not going to bite you."

Will shook his head.

"Naw. It's another man's bike. You never ride another man's bike."

"Where in hell did you get that shit? Is that European shit? A bike's a bike until a rider knows that bike. And Reed hasn't even gotten the saddle sweaty on that one. Take it. Ride it." He flipped a helmet to Will. "Be the bike, Ross."

"What about the brace?"

Bosco looked at Will's left leg.

"Yep. That is a problem. But it's not an excuse. It bends in the middle. Now put the helmet on and ride around."

"I don't have shoes."

Hootie reached into a wooden box near the lip of the truck and produced a pair of deck shoes that looked like they had been retrieved from a dump. Twice. He tossed them to Will who dropped both to the ground without really touching them, kicked off the slipper on his left foot and and wiggled his feet inside. A strap from the brace curled dangerously around his left foot.

"Now, Christ on Kari-oke, Ross—ride the goddamned bike!"

Will didn't know what else to say. "Yes, sir," was all that came out as he slung his free leg over the saddle, settled himself in, balanced his left foot on the top of the clipless pedal and rode away, slowly, on the goddamned bike.

✺

IT WAS LIKE FLYING, WHEN YOU REALLY STOPPED TO THINK ABOUT IT. FLYING in turbulence, of course, the washboard and graupel giving you a shaking like a Radio Flyer on the school steps; but it was flying, nonetheless.

Her hair, pulled into a tight pony tail, flew behind her, a brunette streamer like jet exhaust on the flats, snapping to the side on each turn, lifting up behind, again, as her speed and confidence grew on the bike.

Cheryl Crane shot out of the last bermed turn and poured it on, catching the jump just before the finish banner off stride, resetting herself in the air, and dropping down to the finish like the pro she had become again.

The little girl with the dark brown eyes and the bright white teeth smiled from behind the bottled water banner and threw Cheryl a high and tight thumbs up.

Cheryl smiled and waved in return.

That, she thought, was the daughter she would someday have.

Without a second thought, she rode to the base of the Vista Bahn, stepped off her bike, waited a little impatiently in line, dropped her bike on a rack behind the lift chair, stepped up and into the seat, and flew to the top of the hill again. She was looking for another moment of freedom and joy that marked her release from the box she had spent the last few years building for herself.

She took a deep breath and smiled.

We all build boxes for ourselves, she thought, some becoming velvet-lined traps for our dreams. Today, she was climbing outside hers.

And she didn't know what was out there.

Or, she thought, thinking of the faces that crowded her life at the moment, who might be out there with her.

❀

IT WAS BASIC RIDING, LITTLE MORE THAN SIMPLY STAYING UPRIGHT ON THE bike and keeping your feet up on the pedals. That, it seemed, was the most difficult part of all this, the pedal part. Toe clips, little baskets on the front end of the pedal would basically accommodate any shoe in a pinch, but they were not to be found on racing bikes anymore. Technology and gizmos had outstripped them and moved onto clipless pedals, those meant for shoes with a cleat, along the line of a ski binding. Trying to pedal around in deck shoes and a leg brace, without cleats, wide as they might be, just wasn't getting the job done.

Will could balance and shift his right foot on the pedal easily, especially now that the walking cast was gone, but the brace on his left leg was unforgiving. It fought and squeaked and pulled each time he tried to readjust his foot position to the point that he could only make the most minor adjustments without the angle of the brace thrusting his foot forward or back or left or off the pedal completely.

Worse still, he kept looking at his feet and trying to visually readjust, which was proving to be something other than a wise idea in the middle of a crowded downtown Vail on the first morning of a race weekend. As the front wheel rose up onto the bridge over Gore Creek, Will, his head down, felt, more than heard, a shout ahead.

"Heads up!"

Will's head shot up as if spring loaded, and, rather than seeing a street in front of him, saw nothing more than a wall: a wall comprised of a man, a small gap, then a woman—a short, thick woman brandishing a cane, a cane that appeared about the size of a lamp post.

Without thinking, Will made himself as thin as he could on the bike, touched the handlebars a bit to the right and threaded the needle between the two. As he passed, he could feel the heat radiating off the wall of human-ity, and hear the "swoosh" of the shillelagh as it broke the air in the vicinity of the back of his head.

"Sorry," he called back over his shoulder. "Sorry."

He picked up his pace and avoided the next turn on Meadow Drive, riding up to the frontage road and taking a right. In a few moments, he'd be out of traf-fic and away from pedestrians. At least then he could figure this machine out.

He shifted, suddenly aware that he was no longer worrying about foot placement on the left. Glancing down, he realized that in avoiding the pair on the bridge he had accidentally caught the loose strap of the brace in a por-tion of the pedal. It was secure now. He'd be in great shape.

As long as he didn't stop riding.

That, he knew, could create a whole new set of problems.

✱

MARJORIE STUMP WATCHED THE RIDER DISAPPEAR UP VAIL ROAD TOWARD THE roundabout and cracked her cane atop the crossbeam of the bridge.

"Damn them. They think they own our town."

She turned and looked at Kelvin.

"Why didn't you stop him?"

"What?"

"Why didn't you stop him?"

"How? How was I supposed to stop him?"

"Pushing him over would have been enough."

"He was moving too quickly."

"He nearly assaulted your mother."

"Yes, mother."

"You should think a little bit more about her."

"I think about her all the time."

"You should show it, then."

"Yes, mother."

She sighed with a certain measure of frustration. "Oh, just go. You have a job to do, just—just go do it."

"What about protecting you?"

The knob of the cane caught him right beside the left knee, and he paused for a moment to wait for the pain to begin. It was sooner than normal. The bruise that was already there from an earlier bashing hurt almost immediately, while the deep and sickening pain from the bone came later, deeper, harder.

He stared at a stand of aspens and tried to meditate, waiting for the pain to rise and peak and subside. He felt his eyes tear and his mouth open in a cry of pain, but he made no sound. He hadn't made a sound since the promise he made to himself the day of his fourteenth birthday. Then, he had passed the peak of the pain and stood up to his full height for the first time, towering over his mother and realizing something profound about his life.

He was not his mother's son.

His breath came out in a ragged blast. He shook his head and returned to a Friday afternoon on a bridge over Gore Creek in the middle of Vail.

"There. Are you ready now to continue? Fine. I'm going for lunch, but you, Kelvin, I want you to find out more about that heavy bike box. Find out where he took that box and what's in it. And don't return home for lunch until you do."

"But what if he doesn't...."

"Don't return for lunch until you do...."

"Yes, mother."

Kelvin nodded and loped away, favoring his left knee. He checked the change in his pocket—nope, not enough to buy lunch in this town on a heavy tourist day. So he continued his search for the small, white Chevrolet rental car, low at the tail. His initial search revealed that it had left the hotel in such a hurry this morning only to park a few blocks away in the Transportation Center parking lot. When he discovered that, he went to tell mother. She wanted to know and never waited to know. But he couldn't be certain that the car and driver were still there. Actually, he didn't much care about that. For the sake of his future, he had his own worries.

One of those worries being his mother.

Another being the answer he might find at the other end of a phone call.

His future could be riding on both.

"WHERE'S MY BIKE?" MARSHALL REED SHOUTED INTO THE DARKNESS OF THE step van.

Though the van wasn't that deep, Hootie Bosco still emerged as a wraith from the blackness, forcing Reed to step back suddenly with a start.

"Jesus, man. You're too damned weird for words."

"So you say."

"Where's my bike?" Reed asked with a touch of impatience in his tone, sweeping his arm across the Haven-TW playground.

"Which one?"

"The Colnago, asshole."

"Loaned it out."

"What? That bike was set up for me."

"That bike was way beyond you, Reed. You should be grateful it didn't toss you and kill you in those things you described as runs today."

"Don't get in my face, you freak. I want my fucking bike here, and I want it here now."

"Problem is, it ain't here. It will be soon, I can promise you that. But I'm not sure I'm going to give it to you then. Until I decide your equipment needs, why don't you ride the Diamondback and let it go at that?"

"I don't want to ride the Diamondback."

"Well, given what they're paying you to do just that, I'd ride the Diamond-back. There are little problems with contracts and commitments, and things like that you should really pay attention to ... you know—no bucks, no Buck Rogers, that sort of thing? Diamondback is your sponsor. You ride Diamondback."

"Is it all done but the shouting?" Cheryl Crane said with a smile as she wheeled her Colnago up to the side of the step van.

"Plenty of that, I can tell you."

Reed turned on her.

"Look—I'm number two on this team and I deserve a new ride. The Col-nago's are here and one is set up for me."

"Sorry. I wasn't aware you were number two on this team."

"Seems to fit," Hootie muttered.

"But which bike are you missing?" Cheryl asked, concerned. "Which one? I don't see another."

"The one he loaned out. And who'd you loan it out to, anyway?"

"Friend of hers," Hootie said, proudly, tossing his thumb in a backhanded manner toward Cheryl, who started, visibly.

"What—the boyfriend? The gimp? Jesus, I want my ride back, now, you fucker."

Hootie shrugged. Cheryl composed herself quickly and turned to Reed.

"Look. Diamondback sponsors Two Wheels. The TW side. Which, incidentally, hired you. Colnago is only supplying some trial bikes for the Haven side of the equation. And that Haven side is me. Your sponsor is Diamondback. They're paying you. You ride the Diamondback."

"Meanwhile, your boyfriend rides away on a top-flight bike that by all rights should be mine. Man, I don't know who's signing the checks for this piece-of-shit team, but I'll promise you something: I'm gonna find 'em, I'm gonna raise holy hell with 'em, and I'm going to be in charge of this team next season."

"Hey, help yourself," was all Cheryl said in reply.

Hootie added, "Just don't piss off your sponsors. You do, and you'll be riding Huffy's you picked up on sale at Kmart."

"You two don't know what the hell you're talking about," Reed said, angrily, grabbing the Diamondback and pushing it toward the Vista Bahn for the ride up Vail Mountain, "and you don't know who in the hell you're messing with. I want the Colnago back," Reed shouted over his shoulder.

"And you'll get it, I assure you, my young buckaroo," Hootie shouted after him.

He smiled and pushed his fingers through the forest of dreadlocks that was his head.

"That is—if I deem it so."

Cheryl and Hootie silently watched Reed push his Diamondback toward the chair lift, anger radiating from him like shimmers of heat from an Arizona highway.

"That boy should drink decaffeinated," Hootie said aloud.

"Either that, or let his ego apply for statehood," Cheryl replied with a smile. She paused for a second, then turned toward him, "So ... you're loaning out team equipment to boyfriends with battered legs?"

"Battered egos, actually," he answered, picking up a red shop rag and turning back to the workstand.

"You actually got him on it?"

"I didn't get him on nothing. He got himself on it all by himself."

"What about his legs?"

Hootie nodded his head toward the dumpster. "That plastic cast of his is now sleeping with the fishes, and he can ride with a brace. So, I sent him off."

"Marshall does have an argument—that bike was set up for him."

"I believe in commitments. The little bastard made a commitment to Diamondback and so did the team before you and the big money came on ... so ... to my way of thinking ... he's supposed to ride Diamondbacks. Hey, it's not like we're making him ride flea market material. He's riding top-of-the-line merchandise. If I changed the logo, he'd never know the difference."

"So, where'd he go?" Cheryl asked, kicking vaguely at the dirt at her feet.

"Reed or your little friend?"

"Will," she answered, quietly.

"I dunno. He rode off happy as a clam. Don't know where. Don't care where. That's his bike as far as I'm concerned now, and he can go anywhere he likes with it. Hell in a handbasket, for all I care."

"Sponsors won't like that."

"Shit, sponsors don't know where 90 percent of this stuff goes," Hootie said with a smile, tossing a smashed derailleur into a junk box, "they just want to see the logo on ESPN and Outdoor Life."

"I've got to account for all of this."

"Naw. Stewart's got to account for all of this. And all he's got to say is, 'What? Where are your bikes? In the warehouse. In Dee-troit. Hope to hell it don't get broken into ... or they're in Cheryl Crane's garage. In Dee-troit. Hope to hell it don't get broken into....'"

"I get the idea." She smiled and turned, looking toward the town, most of it blocked by vans and people and condos and sponsors' banners.

"Don't worry," Hootie said, quietly. "He'll be fine."

"Oh, I'm not worried."

"Sure you are. Watching somebody come back to life again is always a scary thing."

She nodded. After a long moment, she whispered, almost afraid to hear the reply, "Any idea of why?"

Hootie stopped wiping the cable he held and smiled at her.

"Because he might be fixin' to fly away? Don't worry. He's not the flyin' kind. Especially when he's got somebody like you."

"Maybe I should wait for him."

"Maybe you should practice. You're timing right now for a top-ten finish. Draa is doing well, and Jettmann and Reed are okay. No worries. As for Ross—let him surprise you."

She shook her head and hung the bike on a workstand.

"Yeah, I should practice. But, I've got two under my belt. Get a third or a cross-country this afternoon. The altitude is getting to me a bit. Maybe I'll just ... go for a walk."

"Yeah. You do that."

She flipped her helmet up in the air and caught it with the top of her head.

Hootie Bosco watched her go and smiled. Very slick. Very slick move. Very slick lady.

He sighed. Damn it all. I can talk to them. I can laugh with them. I can be the father confessor of them all, but I sure as shit can't find one for myself and can't figure out why.

He shook the dreadlocks again, a small cloud of smoke, dust and dandruff flying off in a number of new and interesting directions, sighed heavily, and went back to threading the brake cable.

CHAPTER SEVEN

ANOTHER FINE MESS

OLVERIO STUCK HIS NOSE DEEP INTO THE HEAVY CHINA MUG AND LET the steam of the incredibly hot coffee rise through his nostrils and up into his aching sinuses.

"This is killing me."

"What? Or, should I ask, what now?"

"This altitude. It's so dry, my sinuses are killing me."

Stanley shoved another bite of thick bread slathered with apple butter into his mouth. When he spoke, small bits threatened to escape and fly across the table, and yet none ever did.

"You should use that saline stuff."

"What saline stuff?"

"That nasal spray I bought down in Denver when we picked up the tools."

"Do you have it with you?" Ollie asked hopefully, pulling his nose out of the cup.

"Sure."

"Can I use it?" he asked expectantly, reaching his hand across the table and dragging a cuff in the apple butter. "Shoot."

"Sure, I have it and, sure, you can't use it. I don't know what planet you're from, bub, but we don't share Chapstick or nasal spray in Detroit. You must be from Cleveland."

"It's just one shot."

"No," Stanley said, firmly, with a tone of righteous indignation. "Get it through your thick head. I don't want to share nose goo with you."

"Some friend. It's not like I've got a cold."

"That's exactly what I am. And don't you forget it."

Ollie's disappointment made him dive his nose toward the quickly cooling liquid in his cup, but now the cup was doing nothing more for him than simply obscuring his face.

He burrowed his nose deeper into the mug, searching for relief from pain and pressure just above his eyelids. As the door to the small restaurant closed, Ollie lifted his eyes and froze.

He needed confirmation from Stanley, but it seemed pretty clear to him, even as he sat quietly in a corner chair at a corner table with a coffee cup wrapped around his beak and a heavy French Roast blend working its way up his nostrils, that he had seen this man before, in a photo, in a photo in his pocket.

Unless he missed his guess, they were now sharing a restaurant with none other than Leonard Romanowski, newly minted millionaire, minted with someone else's money.

"DAMN! GODDAMN IT!"

He slammed the phone into the cradle, once, then again, and again, hard, just to make sure he had broken the connection.

The secretary at the MSC construction office had been crying, crying to the point that she was useless for any and all information.

You could ask her about loan approval, construction starts, wells drilled, foundations poured, or the capital of Peru, and all you got in return was sobs. Sobs about Mr. Manfra. Sobs about Mr. Skell. Sobs about the Denver police wanting to chat with Mr. Skell. Sobs to the point that Kelvin Stump got nowhere close to the information he needed.

And so, he slammed down the phone and stomped off in the most recent direction of the man with the car, down Bridge, toward the clocktower.

He had too many balls in play to continue the hide-and-seek game, but until he saw an avenue of escape, he had to work the flippers. Then again, he smiled, it took a man with balls to play a game like this—a multimillion dollar game of charades.

✤

THE MAN AT THE DOOR HAD STOPPED HIS GAZE AT THE PAIR. AT FIRST HE almost stared at the Hawaiian shirts. Then, he found himself wondering why the man in the bright yellow one was gluing coffee to his face. Sensing no threat, and out of politeness, he glanced away.

Olverio quietly placed the coffee mug before him, then picked up a napkin and dabbed the Starbucks from his nose.

"Bingo," he said under his breath.

"Hmm?" Stan raised an eyebrow.

Ollie leaned forward and smiled, picking up a map of Vail that sat on the table between them. He pointed at a parking structure as if it were a seriously impressive point of interest for the town, and tried to keep the tone and rhythm of what he was saying touristy in nature.

"Now, look at this," he said aloud, "right here near the, let's see, the Hubcap." He dropped his voice a notch. "Right behind you, I think, is our missing friend."

Stan smiled with a thin and shallow grin.

"You see," he said calmly, "there's always time for a hearty lunch."

Ollie sat back expansively. "Well, now I do," he said, adding quietly, "I've never really had a fish jump into my boat before."

"You sure? Did you make our friend? Or, are we going blotto, chasing some Vail local with a taste for cheesy sports agent clothes?"

"99 and 44."

"That sure. Hmm. Did he make us?"

"We got a glance, but he didn't pick up on it."

"Why should he?"

"No reason. Never seen us."

"We be from Dee-troit. He be from New Yawk."

"Exactly."

Stan reached up and scratched the top of his head, leaving a tuft of sandy brown hair in a Kewpie doll peak on his forehead.

Ollie rolled his eyes. "Classy. And something that no one will ever notice."

"What?"

"Never mind." He quickly licked his hand, reached over and pushed down the hirsute pyramid.

"Jesus," Stanley said, "don't do that. God. That's worse than you using my nasal spray."

"Don't curse."

The little man across the restaurant watched the conversation with bemused interest, then went back to his menu.

"Good …" Stanley was about to say "God," but then switched in midstream, "… gophers."

"What does that mean?"

"No idea, but it's big in Minnesota." Stanley smiled, then glanced quickly behind him as if checking the weather outside and marked Leonard Romanowski's position at his table in relation to them, the exits and other diners.

"Is he worried?"

"Doesn't seem to be. We got another glance, but he smiled."

"We're a damned comedy act."

Olverio sighed.

A young couple at a front table finished paying, argued for a moment over the proper tip, then stepped outside, leaving the place empty except for them, Leonard and a waiter who glanced at both tables then stepped out quickly for a smoke.

"Shall we?" Stanley said, turning back to his own table.

"Yes. Let's," Ollie said with a pointed flourish.

The pair rose and Ollie dropped $22 on the table next to his plate. He had no idea what the bill might be, but this certainly had to cover it. He didn't like over-tipping, but he'd cover it later in the expenses.

"Ready?" he asked aloud.

"Certainly am," Stanley said, and they stepped toward the door.

Out of the corner of his eye, Stanley could see the shoulders of Leonard Romanowski stiffen and then relax as the restaurant began to empty. Two steps forward and the pair, moving almost as one, slid silently beside the small man in the ill-fitting but obviously expensive sweater, pulling chairs from adjacent tables tight beside him and effectively pinning him in.

"Good morning, Leonard."

"Yes, indeed. Good morning, Leonard."

The man froze in mid-sigh, a tiny drop of fear hanging in the air for but a moment, before dropping silently and falling to its death on the table so very far below.

There was a pause, too long a pause, Ollie felt, before the denials began.

"Uhhh, excuse me," Leonard Romanowski choked, almost in a kind of basso profundo squeak, "do I know you, uhh, gentlemen?"

"No, actually, Mr. Romanowski, you don't," Ollie said.

"No, you certainly don't," said Stanley with a flourish.

"Then, uhh, can I help you?" Leonard tried to smile, but it came out more as a death mask grin. "I'm trying to eat here."

"Yes, we know you are."

"We know that."

"But we feel," said Stanley, "that it's really not nice to try and stiff someone else with the bill."

"Oh, no," Leonard said, shaking his head with eyes that were wildly scanning the room for another face, an exit, some miracle to appear. "No, I'm paying … I'm paying." He reached for his carry bag on the floor beside him, and Ollie grabbed his wrist in a vise grip.

"Ahh … no, I'm afraid you don't understand, Leonard. First, even if you do have money in there, it's not your money. It's Angelo Genna's money. So, you see, you're making Mr. Genna pay for breakfast and that's just not fair. Secondly, if you were thinking that there was something else in that bag that might get you out of this fix, like a 1910 model Colt Army Issue .45, I really do hate to tell you this…."

"Hate to tell you this…." Ollie echoed sadly, shaking his head back and forth.

"… but you left it on the hearth of a fireplace up on the hill after you used some poor schnook for target practice."

"Poor schnook," Ollie mumbled.

"I hope, for your sake, that it wasn't registered in your name," Stanley added.

"Me, too."

It took time, but Leonard Romanowski finally got a grip again on his mind. When he spoke, he tried to make his voice sound as calm as the voice a man just explaining how he wanted his lawn cut by the new service.

"Gentle ... men," he said, his voice shaking just a bit until he swallowed hard, "I ... think, oh, Christ, I think that you have ... um, found me. And that's to your, uh, credit, gentlemen. I, uh, appreciate your concern about my weapon, certainly. But, I uh, did not register the gun and uh, that is, I suppose, in my favor."

"It is, I think, in your favor," Stanley agreed. The waiter stepped back into the room, and Leonard looked at him suddenly with wild and pleading eyes.

"Can I get something for you gentlemen?"

"No, I don't think so," Ollie said. He glanced quickly at the plastic nametag. "Are you Bobby?"

"Yes," the waiter said, obnoxiously flashing the tag at Ollie, "see, says right here ... Bobby."

Ollie nodded with a smile, hiding the fact that he wanted to see what a set of nucks could do to this asshole's nose in a split second.

Leonard Romanowski started to rise out of his chair. Stanley put his thumb and forefinger at Leonard's hip and squeezed, the sudden pressure and pain dropping him back into the seat.

"Well, Bob," Ollie said, as pleasantly as he could muster.

"Bobby," the young man corrected.

"Yes, Bobby. Anyway, 'Bobby,' a police officer was just looking for you this moment. Something about towing a car?" Ollie raised his hands in a mock question, as if to ask the importance of the information he had just passed on.

Bobby the Waiter's face went blank, then stark white.

"Shit," he shouted, ripping off his apron, name tag and all, and sprinting toward the front door. "Damn fucking small town cops," he shouted as he threw the door open.

Ollie, Stan, and Leonard Romanowski could hear a steady stream of cursing aimed toward mountain town law enforcement disturb the peace of the street and recede in the distance. Leonard visibly deflated, his last chance for salvation, at least for now, disappearing in a huff down Bridge Street.

"Now, Leonard," Ollie said quietly.

"Yes, Leonard," Stanley mimicked. "Now, Leonard."

"Where is the money, my friend?"

Stanley nodded. "Yes, the money?"

⁂

WHAT HE WAS DOING AT THE MOMENT WAS VERY LIKELY HIGHLY ILLEGAL.
There had been a sign back there, something about no vehicles and foot traffic only, he thought, maybe it was no motorized vehicles and he was okay, but, whatever it had said, he had been too busy trying to replace his right foot on the pedal to really focus any attention on it.

Will threaded his way through the pedestrian traffic on the creek trail and smiled at the bike's response. He wasn't sure what it was, the size of the tires, the weight distribution, the physics of it all, but this thing handled beautifully.

If he could just get a pair of riding shoes for this thing, he'd be set. Well, that and get rid of the brace, then he'd be set. That and some proper riding shorts, then, he'd be … and some gloves, some gloves, and GripShifts … then he'd be set.

He laughed aloud to himself as he rose up to a patch of open pavement and picked up his pace, concentrating on keeping the right deck shoe on the right pedal. God, he thought, I always have been and always will be a techno dweeb.

It all started with that light on the Schwinn and the rear-wheel generator that made you feel like you were riding up Everest, and it has progressed to this: a bike with every bell and whistle imaginable that he now thought needed some streamers for the handlebars.

Will pulled onto the street and made the turn toward the base of the mountain, just as a young man, cursing a rich stream and radiating steam heat raced past him toward the village parking structure.

Will watched him go, then stepped off the bike and walked it through the crowds toward Hootie and the truck, unconsciously falling into a marching rhythm behind a tall, blond man.

"OH, I CAN'T. I CAN'T," LEONARD SAID, FRANTICALLY, "I CAN'T," AS HE TRIED TO quietly and surreptitiously find any possible avenue of escape. "I can't. After all, how would that look, with me being dead and Angelo getting his blood money back?"

"It would look exactly the way it's supposed to look. Mr. Genna trusted you, Leonard."

"No, no, no, no, no, no, no," he said, rapidly, "that's not the way it's supposed to happen! This is hell. This is hell."

"Exactly," Stan answered, "that's exactly where I came from, Leonard. Now, why don't you calm down and let's talk about this?"

Leonard Romanowski collapsed like a jack-o-lantern three weeks after the main event. His breathing became shallow, his eyes unfocused, his mind became a blank. A natural reaction to staring death in the face.

"Don't pee in the restaurant, Leonard. Keep control of your bladder," Stanley said.

"You're going to kill me," he whimpered.

"Oh, relax, Leonard. We aren't going to kill you."

"Whaaa?"

Ollie sighed and patted Leonard Romanowski on the hand. "We aren't going to kill you, Leonard. So just calm down."

"We don't kill people, Leonard, we reason with them."

"That's right, pal. We're the angels of the second chance."

"Buster No-Knuckles ... now he ... he already would have you stuffed in a coffee pot."

"You'll ... you'll...."

"We'll what, Leonard?"

"You'll ... the money ... the money."

"You need some verbs in there, pal. That's something to think about in the future. You'll need some verbs."

"I ... I...."

"You think as soon as we've got the money—we'll kill you. That's not right, Leonard. You see, Leonard, we're not killers. We're businessmen."

"Businessmen," Stanley added.

"Like middle management. Upper management wants to dispatch you for screwing up."

"Screwing up, big time," Stanley added.

"But we believe that you've learned your lesson. Now, you can't work for the company again and you've got to abandon all your salary and benefits."

"What ... wha ... benefits?"

"Verbs, Leonard, find the verbs. That four-and-a-half million dollars in benefits you've wandered off with ... and ... you'll have to stay on this side of the Mississippi River for the rest of your life."

"Rest of your life," Stanley added.

"With a new name."

"New name."

"But," Ollie continued, "you'll be alive. Alive and well and happy and breathing the air."

"Wha ... wha ... why? Why?"

"Aw, Leonard, hell, we don't like Angelo any more than you do."

Stanley nodded.

"Bu—bu—bu...."

"Oh, you're backing up, Leonard, that's not good. You need to move forward in your language skills. Let's go talk, okay? Some place you feel safe. And calm."

"We're not going to scramble your brains, Leonard," Stanley said, in a sing-song, comforting manner, "we just want the money back."

"I ... I ... don't have...."

"We figured that. You don't have. But you know, don't you?"

✺

THE BLOND MAN THAT HAD BEEN THE ADVANCE GUARD IN FRONT OF HIM stepped off to the side and stared intently into a shop window across the street from the clocktower. Will continued on, his progress slowed by people with what could only be described as "the thousand-yard stare," walking blindly into his path as he tried to maneuver the bike down the street. He found himself moving sideways until he finally drew up next to a set of steps leading up to a restaurant. About twenty yards away, he could see Cheryl moving through the crowd toward him. He smiled and waved.

❋

LEONARD ROMANOWSKI STARED AT THE TABLE, WONDERING, AS ONLY A MAN IN his situation could, how the hell he ever got into this mess and how such a beautiful plan had gone so absolutely and completely into the shitcan of life. The three men rose, as one, and began to move toward the door.

✳

THE COOL AIR OF THE MOUNTAIN WAS WORKING ITS WAY OVER, UNDER, AROUND and through the mesh and steel of the removable knee brace. It tickled. Will reached down and tugged at one of the Velcro straps, loosening the top edge of the brace around his middle thigh, immediately feeling the release and the cool air on the already damp patch of his jeans where the brace had bit into him. Cheryl stepped up to him, reached over and, with one hand, pulled the strap tight again.

"One more week. You've got to wear it full time one more week."

"It's healed, I tell you. The stitches are out, the skin is strong, and I'm ready to go. This is just for show right now. Show and sympathy, and I'm not getting much of either." He paused for a moment and found himself smiling at her smile.

"So, how'd it go?"

"Frankly," she couldn't help but grin, "it went great. The first run scared the crap out of me, and the second was like riding a rocket. It was just plain wonderful."

"Any news of the children?"

She squinted at him for a moment, then, understanding the question, nodded.

"Hootie says they're doing fine. I figured as much. Jettman's a toady. Frannie's a kid. And Reed. Reed's still a prick. You know, he's one of those guys who is never happy with who he is or what he's got because somebody's always cheated him out of his birthright. If he'd put all that energy into riding," she stopped for a second, realizing she was ranting, "then he'd be a champion and he'd get the things he wants out of life. But he doesn't. He bitches and moans like a nasty little old man, and the world just finally gets tired of it and passes him by, making him more bitter than he ever was before."

Will just smiled. "And he's all yours."

She laughed and turned, her eye caught for a moment by a glimpse of a gauzy cotton peasant dress in a shop window, partially blocked by a blond man staring past them toward the restaurant.

"So, what do you think?" she asked, working her eyes around the man to get a view of the dress, before following his eyes to the door of the clocktower.

"About?"

"I still haven't had anything to eat. Wanna catch this place for lunch?"

"We should have stayed at Pancake City. This place looks like it might serve real food."

Cheryl shook her head and moved quickly to the top of the stairs leading to the door. She turned and watched as Will looked around him for a place to safely store a high-end mountain bike that could and would do a disappearing act if left unattended. Finally, he shrugged, looped the bike over his shoulder and began to carry it up the step.

"You can't bring that in here," Cheryl said.

"Well, I ain't leavin' it out here, that's for sure," he answered, as the door began to open behind her.

Cheryl felt a blast of warm air and heard the sound of voices, strained, but in easy conversation, rise up behind her. She reached her right hand out for Will, then turned to face the three men leaving the restaurant.

"Jesus," was the word that leapt, completely unawares, from her mouth.

"Don't curse," came the immediate reply, followed by "Jesus."

"What the...."

"Why...."

"Jesus."

"How'd you...."

"Oh, my...."

"Jesus."

"Jesus, Cheryl," said Stan.

"Stanley."

"Cheryl."

"What are you…."

"Will!"

"Leonard."

"… doing here?"

"Cheryl."

"Ollie."

"Who're you?"

"What?"

"Cheryl…."

"Oh, my…."

"Leonard, what the…."

"… God."

"Will…."

"Cheryl…."

"… you're a lifesaver."

"What?"

"Stanley, what are…."

"Cheryl…."

"Ollie…."

"Will…."

Leonard grabbed Will's hand in the confusion and pressed their palms together, hard. Instinctively, Will closed his hand around the small item stuck to his sweating palm.

"… a lifesaver, man."

"Leonard!"

Will screeched as his agent, Leonard Romanowski, late of New York City, currently of no place in particular, grabbed him by the collar and twisted him down toward the steps. The flexible, removable leg brace didn't flex like it was designed to, and Will felt a hideous strain on the ridge of scars that circled his left knee. As he fell to the steps, he felt Leonard Romanowski bound over him and the bike that had now become an exoskeleton on top of him. He was trapped, as were the two men with Leonard, one pushed back into a corner near the door, Cheryl collapsed against him, while the other took a step and went into the spokes on the front wheel.

Will heard a slap on the pavement of the street, followed immediately by a quick and panicked bounding away. He turned his head to see Leonard running faster than anyone would ever give him credit for, a gym bag dangling off his arm, a solitary blond man keeping pace not far behind.

Will turned to see Leonard's two companions, both in fluorescent Hawaiian shirts, curse silently at both Will and his fleeing sports agent. Stanley grunted and pulled his foot, sharply, from the spokes with a "twang" and stepped quickly around. He immediately bounded to the third step, then jumped down to the street. Ollie, moving with a balletic grace, stepped this way and that, almost floating down to the street beside his partner.

Olverio sighed, then turned to Stanley.

"Shall we?"

"I suppose," Stanley said, making a disgusted face at Will before turning to Cheryl with a smile.

"Excuse me, ma'am." He tipped an imaginary bowler.

"Yes, excuse us," Ollie said. "We'll see you around town then." He smiled. "Come along, Stanley, tools to get, work to do."

They both smiled at Cheryl, glanced at Will, then moved quickly down the street with a practiced and deliberate tread. Cheryl moved next to Will, watched them walk down Bridge, and felt her world collapse around her.

She sank into a crouch as Will was making slow moves in an effort to push the bike off himself and twist his left leg back into the proper position.

"Shit," she said aloud, to no one in particular.

"What?" Will asked, sighing with relief as the leg finally came full forward again.

"Just what I need," she said, again speaking to no one in her vicinity.

"What?"

She looked off toward the mountain, with an air of sad detachment.

"A family reunion."

CHAPTER EIGHT:

WE ARE FAMILY

WHAT? WILL POINTED OFF AFTER THE DISAPPEARING PAIR. THEM? Cheryl nodded, slowly. "Yeah, them."

Will turned in shock as the pair, one tall and thin, one short and round, walked down the street, with measured tread, into the distance. As they turned the corner near the parking structure, determined, certainly, but not hurried, he turned back to Cheryl and visibly quailed at the color of her complexion. In just moments it had gone from rich and full, the picture of vibrant and robust outdoor health, to a pale grey, two shades lighter than death. She slumped to a spot on the corner of the steps leading to the restaurant.

"Holy smokes, are you okay?"

The words jumped from his mouth with genuine concern, then, in her silence, rattled around the narrow street before disappearing up toward the mountainside.

A man in a white apron with the name tag of "Bobby," ran up from the opposite direction and stopped, panting, at the base of the steps.

"Good Christ," Bobby said, wheezing, "are-you-all-right?"

"Yeah, thanks," Cheryl answered. "I think I'm fine."

"Good. Then get the fuck off the front steps of my restaurant before you puke."

"Bobby" pushed the bike with the bent front spokes to the street, then loped quickly up the steps with nothing more than a quick glance toward Will and Cheryl and made for the door of the restaurant. As he threw it open, a heavyset man appeared, as if by magic, his white shirt splattered with bits of the day's lunch set-up and unleashed a torrent of invective toward "Bobby," the main concept behind it being that this someone obviously didn't think that "Bobby" should go jogging down the street in the middle of his shift. The door closed, blessedly, leaving Will and Cheryl alone, sitting quietly on "Bobby's" steps.

"Come on," he said, sliding his arm under hers and lifting, "let's get you moving around. You've had a hell of a shock."

She fought him for a moment, dividing her attention between him and a bubble of stress-induced nausea that was working its way toward the back of her teeth, then allowed him to pull her to her feet.

"Let's get to the truck," she whispered, sounding something like a four-day flu victim.

Will nodded dumbly, having no idea at all where the Haven-TW box van was parked at the moment. He helped her find her balance, then reached down and picked up the bike. Rolling the bike between them, with a regular squeal of protest from the front rim, the two began walking toward the mountain, toward the peace, serenity, and life on a bike that she had left carefree, less than an hour before.

Around them, the icy blue Colorado sky and the deep green of the trees blended perfectly with the village itself to create a picture-postcard mountain world, the kind of place most people only dreamed of ever finding. The three of them, man, woman and bike, pushed up the slight incline, through the crowds and past the shops that, even now, two months before it got serious, were beginning to gear up for ski season.

Cheryl dragged her feet at first, leaning heavily on the bike, making the squeal of the rim on the brake pad all the more pronounced with each revolution. Slowly, she began to regain her footing and stepped along with Will, until the corner of Gore Creek, where she pulled her arm free and stepped off on her own. Her color was a dingy yellowish pink; but the pink, Will noticed, was finally beginning to win the battle for her face.

"Are you okay?" he whispered, anxiously.

"Yeah. Yeah. I think I'm getting there," she mumbled. She stood in the middle of the street, then suddenly bent over at the waist as if to retch, bounced twice, took a deep breath and stood upright again.

"You're okay?"

"Yeah, I'm sorry."

"That's okay. I understand."

She shook her head. "Oh, if you only did."

"Okay. So, I don't. So tell me. What did you mean when you said Laurel and Hardy there were a family reunion?"

She turned on him and snapped, "Don't say that. Don't you ever say that."

"Jesus, what?"

"Don't every call them Laurel and Hardy."

He stood and stared at her, a look of genuine concern and question in his eyes. He spread his arms, palm up, as if to ask, "Why?"—but no sound came out. He stood silently, a man at the end of the hall, a dead-end, unless she opened the door to her life from her side.

She could see it in him. The questions. The fears. The inability to move beyond her last sentence. After a moment of tense silence, Cheryl Crane began to relax, seeing that with him, more than anyone else, perhaps, in the world, her story was safe.

She sighed deeply, glanced at the ground as if to find some secondary measure of assurance there, took a breath and looked up at him.

And so she began.

"These guys are the reason I changed my name. These guys are the reason I got the hell out of Detroit. These guys are the reason I've run away for the past six years."

"From where you live...."

"Yeah, and from who I am."

"They really threw the fear of God into you."

"Who was the guy you knew back there?"

"Leonard Romanowski. He's my agent."

"Well, Leonard Romanowski, your agent, is the one with the fear of God in him, right now. And if he's not quick, he's a dead man."

Will laughed with disbelief.

"You think I'm kidding, don't you?"

Will's laughter sputtered, then ground to a halt.

"You are, aren't you?"

"No," she said, raising her eyebrows, "I'm not. Those men," she lowered her voice, "are not pro wrestlers your buddy is trying to sign up. They're killers."

Will stared at her silently, his face blank, his mouth slightly opened in a dull, empty look.

"Enforcers, Will. They're muscle. Strong arm. Hit men."

"Hit men? Like mob guys, hit men? No shit?" he asked with a surprised and excited smile.

"No shit, Will. And they're my uncles."

"Your uncles?"

"My uncles. My family. I am a mob baby, pure and simple."

"Jesus. I'm sleeping with Connie Corleone."

"Don't make fun, goddamn it. It's not like the movies. It's not anything like the movies, Will. It's not some big warm family of 'The Godfather' that everybody wants to be a part of—ooo, let's go cook with Clemenza in the kitchen. That's so much crap."

Will stifled the little-boy excitement of having met, for the first time in his life, real, live gangsters. He could see, in her eyes, that she was deadly serious about it all.

"You want to know what it's like, Will? It's like any corporation where the guy at the top gets a lot of money and the schmoes at the bottom are scraping by, breaking into pop machines to make the payments on their Cadillacs between jobs. The big job? The big score? It's like hitting the lottery for them. And then, after they hit it, they lay awake nights worried that somebody's gonna put two in the back of their heads to shut them up or take it from them."

"Jesus."

"Exactly. Stan and Ollie, they're smart. They saved and invested...."

"Invested?"

"Invested. They bought Polaroid at six. They had little companies. They bought houses. Paid taxes. Invested. Made money. Went legit. As legit as you, can, I suppose, when you work like they do … but it was enough to support those around them." She paused and took the bike with the broken and bent spokes from Will, slinging it onto her back. "We owed them a lot, Will."

"So, what's the family connection?"

"Uncle Ollie, Olverio Cangliosi, is my father's older brother. He's a second-generation American. Raised my father, pretty much alone, from a boy in one of the worst neighborhoods in Detroit. Sent him to the University of Michigan. Pushed him into financial law. Securities. Investments. Somebody that Uncle Ollie could use."

"You make it sound like that's important."

"If you've outlived your usefulness with them," she said, distantly, "you've outlived … your life."

"Was your father into this?"

She shrugged. "Had to be. This was his life, in a way, his family, certainly. He was legitimate. He just had some screwy clients. I dunno. I like to think … that he tried to stay above it all."

She smiled. "A daughter. Defending her dad."

"I didn't know him all that well," Will said quietly.

"He was something," she said with a deep and lasting sorrow. "He worked hard, really hard, and there were times when I just plain never saw him, just always heard him, the creak of the door, the thump of his shoes in the hall, when he came home and I was upstairs in bed. He always looked in on us. He always smiled, kissed a finger and pushed it toward us. No matter how late it was, no matter whether we were awake or not."

She grew quiet and distant.

"When he was home, though, when he could be with us, the whole world opened up, Will. There was laughter and there was music, there was food, Mama sang in the kitchen, there was life, god, was there life."

"Sounds nice."

"It was, but it wasn't very often. He spent a lot of time sweeping up after messy people."

"When was all this?"

"Before you knew us. When you knew us. He kept it pretty quiet, from us, from Mom. As if we were all safe if we didn't get involved. The less we knew, the better."

Cheryl looked at her feet for a moment, then continued as she walked up the street toward the base of the mountain.

"My mother—well, she's Polish. Her brother was Stanley Szyclinski. The tall one. She met my father through her brother's partnership with Uncle Ollie. So—you see, I'm all mobbed up. Mobbed up. Screwed up. Big time."

"Look, though," he said, "a lot of people have crappy families. People you want to forget, ignore, run away from. But that's not you. It doesn't have anything to do with you. That's what your dad did. Your uncles. Not you. You've got nothing to do with it."

"God," she cried, a bubble of emotion passing her lips, "if that were true, love, if that were only true."

He stepped forward to say something, to soothe her obvious pain at what he had just stirred, then paused, the man who had lit the fuse, wondering whether to spit on it and put it out, run like hell, or stand fast and watch the emotional blast.

"So tell me the truth."

"Can you handle it?"

Will was taken aback by the question, his quick, off-the-top-of-his-head response was "of course," but something in her tone made him pause and ponder the thought for a moment. Would knowing this change him or her or them? Quite possibly. But would not knowing be even worse in the long run?

"Yeah," he said finally. "I can handle it."

She sighed, thinking the exact same things that had crowded his mind only moments before. "We'll see."

She put the bike down between them. She stretched out her arms and leaned across it, one hand on the handlebar stem, one on the seat. It was as much for protection as it was for support.

"Remember that driver, that farmer, who killed Raymond? Ran the barricades and killed my brother in that race?"

"Yeah, I remember. I was there."

"You were there, weren't you? Ever wonder why my parents didn't sue him for doing that?"

"No. I really don't . I was pretty screwed up after that for a while."

"For a long while. We all were. Ever wonder what happened to that farmer?"

"No, frankly, I don't."

Will's voice grew distant as his mind carried itself over the years, back to a Michigan road at the height of an August heat wave, the corn creating its own wall of humidity you had to cut through as you rode. Raymond Cangliosi, just ahead, the lead rider in a two-person breakaway, dropping low into a turn as they both heard the screech of tires and the screams of surprise as the truck drove through the barricade. The green, rusted, puke pale green of the truck box was all Will could remember, except for a shout of defiance from the driver and the pain that rose up from parts of his body he had never felt before. Will took a deep breath and shook the image away. It hadn't haunted him for years, but now it was back. And it hurt all over again.

"For a long time," he said, slowly, "I dreamed of revenge, of getting back at that asshole somehow, of making him feel the pain that I felt—I guess—both inside and out."

"He paid for your college."

"What?"

"He paid for your college. That farmer. He paid for your college education, such as it was. Well, he didn't. His estate did. My father made sure of that."

"His estate."

"Yep. Stan and Ollie paid him a visit. My father sued the estate for Raymond's death and your accident and won big."

"Look, something is telling me not to ask this, but what happened to the farmer?"

"Stan and Ollie happened. Seems for some reason he climbed up the tallest point in his barn and did a swan dive into the working end of a manure spreader. Did quite a number on him."

"Like…."

"Don't ask. They found pieces of him all over the place. See? That's my family. It's great. Whenever they get together it's like a reunion of anybody whose picture you've ever seen on the wall of the post office."

She said the last words with infinite sadness, then turned and took a few quick steps toward the mountain again, swinging the bike up on her shoulders and starting to put as much distance between her and her last revelation as she possibly could.

Will didn't move, but just looked after her for a moment before he said, quietly, "That doesn't explain it."

Cheryl turned back, the bike riding her back, the wheels sticking out like a pair of wings, one, perfectly round, the other, bent and mangled in the center as if in the fall from heaven.

"What?"

"That doesn't explain it," Will said. "A farmer is killed. Revenge. Your father cleans out his estate for wrongful death. Retribution. Some nasty uncles pay for a lot of things in your life. Restitution. But that's not it. That doesn't explain it. Why are you so afraid of them—even hate them—so much? Why did you run? Why did you change your name?"

"Spelling."

"Oh, cut the shit, Cheryl," Will roared, causing people to stop in their blind hikes toward nowhere and focus on the burst of emotion in the middle of the street. "Why? Tell me. If you don't, this is going to fester inside us as long as we're together. It will eat us alive. I don't need to know everything. I don't need to know who your first boyfriend was or the day you had your first period—but—Jesus. This is personal history. This is the kind of stuff that drives you. This is baggage. And we're both going to have to carry it ... just ... just like you've been carrying mine this season. Yeah. Just like you've been carrying mine with Kim and Haven and the win and the crash. Yeah."

"Yeah?" she asked, dropping her voice to a stage whisper, "you've drawn an audience."

She looked around and smiled, an embarrassed, but "screw you" smile to those who were eavesdropping.

Will's tension exploded into anger. "Jesus, don't you people have anything better to do with your lives? Get the fuck out of here!"

They turned and walked away, embarrassed about being caught.

"Yeah," he whispered harshly, trying to contain his raging emotions, "sorry. But, please, tell me. Let's get it out, and let's go home."

"It's not that easy."

"Just do it, Cheryl, and let's deal with it."

"It's not that easy!"

Cheryl had turned her face away, then back, as if considering what she said. Now, he saw that her eyes were full of tears.

"This could destroy us," she said, her voice hollow. "Us. You and me."

"Yeah. It could. No doubt about that," he said, his voice fearful. "But it would anyway if it wasn't said. If it didn't happen. This is the kind of stuff that festers in a relationship. This is the kind of stuff that eats away at the foundation."

"Until ..."

"Until there's nothing left."

"Nothing."

"I understand that," he said, quietly, reaching for her hand. "But this one is killing you. It's made you run. It's made you hide. It's made you hurt. It's made you."

"They...."

"They what?"

"They made me."

"How? I don't follow."

"Those two—are—the—ones. Who—killed ... my father."

"What?"

The word shot out of him in a blast, pulling his hand away in its violence, his shout rattling off the walls and causing people to turn again, to see who was causing the commotion, before slipping back into their own lives.

Cheryl hadn't heard him at all, the pressure of the blood in her ears drowning out any other sound. The words she spoke were distant as if coming from a dream.

"I saw it. I saw them. I was nineteen. Two weeks away from my high school graduation. It was the first time my mother had ever let me drive downtown on my own. I went to my father's office. I don't know why. I don't remember. Maybe Daddy needed a ride. I just ... it was in an old bungalow. I remember that. His office was in an old bungalow. I used to play in the backyard sometimes. Really small. Unpretentious. But I drove there. I drove there, and

I walked in, and there they were … Uncle Stanley and Uncle Olverio. Something must have gone wrong. Daddy. They were … bending over my father. And there was blood. And it was everywhere. And … it was … everywhere. And they looked at me. And they didn't look shocked and they didn't look hurt and they didn't look angry. Their eyes, Will, their eyes were—dead. And I turned. And I ran out, and I got in my car. And I could hear them calling my name. Cherylann. Cherylann Cangliosi. And I locked the door and I drove home. I wouldn't tell my mother what happened. She found out later. She found out later. Not about them. They kept their skirts clean. Stayed right beside me at the funeral. Holding me and my mother up, they did. Standing right beside me in case I intended to freak and start screaming to everyone there that I knew what had happened. And, the problem is, I did. I did know. I knew that if I stayed around, I was as dead as my father. Because I had seen them, Will. I had seen them."

"And then…."

"And, then, I ran. The next day I applied for my passport. And I went to Stewart Kenally at Two Wheels and asked him for a letter of introduction to anybody, any team, he knew in Europe. He gave it to me—even called—got me my first ride in Italy. Mountain bike team. When I took off from Detroit Metro I was Cheryl Cangliosi. When I arrived in Europe, I was Cheryl Crane. And with everybody but the IRS—that's who I have been ever since."

"So why'd you come back? Why didn't you stay in Europe?"

"It's been years. I missed my mom. Detroit, strangely enough. Besides, I had learned to live with it. I can hide it away and ignore it now. But, more than anything else, I just hoped they'd figure that since I hadn't talked, I wouldn't talk. Silence is golden. And, I was sick of Europe. I wasn't riding there. I was picking up guys' underwear and wiping their noses for Haven. Who wants to do that for the rest of their lives? So … I figured—I hoped—that I could hide out just as well here as there. I could see my mama as Cheryl Cangliosi, tell Stewart my stage name, and keep one pedal stroke ahead of them right here in the U.S.

"Satisfied?"

Will shook himself out of his silence and stepped toward her. Cheryl took a step back and he stopped. He reached a hand out toward her. She took it and he squeezed.

"I had no idea," he murmured.

"Yeah," she said with a sad laugh. She could feel that her face was puffy and drawn. "That was the point."

"To keep things from the people who love you?"

It wasn't a laugh as much as a snort that followed Will's question. "No. It wasn't the point to keep things from you. It was the point to keep you alive. Do you realize—how often—when I scream in the night—I want to tell you? Do you know how many times when I clutch you so hard after making love that I want to shout it all into your ear and cry—for my father, for what I've lost, for what might happen to you—for who I am? I've wanted to tell you—my mother—my priest—someone—for years. Every night. Every day. It haunts me, Will. When you catch me mumbling when I drive, I'm talking to someone— an imaginary friend, maybe—about that. It's there. It's me."

"You've got to tell someone. It's making you nuts. It's killing you."

"If I don't—it kills me figuratively. If I do—it kills me literally. Some choice."

Will stood silently for a moment, began to wave his arms as if he were about to say something, stopped, waved his arms again, and stopped.

"I don't know what to say."

"There's nothing to say, Will."

"No. There's, there's got to be something. Something that I can say that will make this all right, that will take all this away...."

"... that will make it all better?"

"Yeah, that," he said, his arms still moving. "I feel helpless here, Cheryl. You've seen horror and faced death and felt it's cold hand on you, and I'm standing here and I'm supposed to be protecting you and...."

"I don't need you to protect me."

"Yeah, I know," Will said, pointedly. "Look—I know you don't need me. You do just fine without me. But I can't help but feel," he slowed his words down even more, "that I should be able to do something for you. To make the hurt go away. To make you feel better. I've got it stuck in my head that I've got to protect you."

He paused, frustrated with himself. He wasn't getting anywhere and was simply repeating himself.

"So. Never mind," he finally said. "You don't need me. I'm here if you do, but I know you don't."

He reached over and picked up the bicycle from where she had dropped it.

He smiled at her feebly, completely at a loss for anything else to say, his mind filled with revelations and emotions that he couldn't express and couldn't safely contain. For a moment he returned her steady gaze, then realized that his eyes were scuttling back and forth, searching for an escape from her pointed stare. He snapped her a grin and started to walk past, back up the road toward the noise, confusion, and safety of the race day crowd and the box van at the base of the mountain.

Two steps beyond her, he heard her say, almost in a whisper, "You're wrong."

"What?"

Will turned back, suddenly afraid of where they might be going, what she might be saying, and, all right, selfishly, where it would all lead, for him. Without her, he was alone, unemployed, with no prospects, no future, no chance. Without her, he was alone, at a new starting line in his life, the road ahead obscured in grey, the fog this year having parted, only for a moment, to show him a flash of light, a flash of success and possibility. To show him her.

Without her, he was will ross. Lower case.

He took a deep breath.

"You're wrong," she said again. Without another word, she walked past him toward the van.

"What do you mean?" he croaked.

She laughed, openly and honestly through her tears, then smiled crookedly at him.

"Yeah, Will. I've seen horrors. I've run scared. I've been brutalized in some ways. But—oddly enough—I'm okay. At this moment in time, it's okay. And it's okay because I've got you. You're wrong when you say I don't need you, because, friend, I do. I need you because you listen. Most times. I need you because you're cute. I need you because you make me laugh. I need you because you try. You never give up. I need that in my life. Somebody who keeps trying with his life and the lives around him. Even if he fails, he rises up again and tries again. You don't walk away, Will. There's always another thing to try. And—I need you because, unlike just about anybody else I knew on that team in Europe, you understood who I was and what I was trying to do. Don't ever think for a second that I don't need you."

Will smiled and dropped his head a bit.

"Besides," Cheryl said, with a sparkle in her eyes, "you're great in the kip."

Will's head shot up in surprise and he blushed a deep, deep crimson. He smiled, sheepishly.

"Gee, thanks."

Cheryl laughed out loud, her mind quickly and quietly repacking the emotions she had spilled out over the floor of her soul and returning them to their hiding places; there being, strangely, fewer to put away this time, as if some had disappeared with exposure to light and love and the person in her life.

She stepped with a new energy and up the incline and through the crowds that were gathering around the village shops for lunch. She turned and looked over her shoulder at Will, who stood, silently, watching her, unblinking, for the next cue as to how or what he could do or say.

"Come on, let's see what magic Hootie Bosco can work on your bike."

"My bike?" he brightened.

"Yeah, your bike. What the hell, I'm the boss, and if I can't spread the freebies around to my family, who can?"

They smiled at each other and bounded up together toward the street and the noise and the life that lay just beyond, the thought of the three who had brought them to this point to endure these revelations pushed out of their minds for the moment by the golden brush of the day and the gentle thought of each other.

As they rounded the corner, in the distance, he turned and smiled at the strength of her profile and said to himself, "Family? That's not a bad idea."

CHAPTER NINE

WINDFALL

I T WAS A STRANGE FEELING FOR MARJORIE STUMP. SHE NORMALLY didn't feel anxious. Normally, she made those around her feel anxious. But now, at this moment in time, she felt anxious. For some reason, unknown to her, she felt a sense of death and danger in the air, a warning for her rustling through the trees above her on the mountainside, as if Mother Nature, herself, was trying to warn Marjorie Stump to run, escape, to fly, rather than to stand and fight.

It was that notion that made Marjorie Stump so uncomfortable. For more than thirty-five years, the notion, the sense had always been to stay and fight. What she felt, when she stepped outside into the Colorado sun, was the will, the desire, if not the need itself, to fight the developers, to fight the growth, to fight The Company in her precious valley, the valley that she had embraced before any of them. If she needed to fight society at large, if she had to rage and burn and sabotage to get what she wanted, to achieve what she demanded, to protect the valley, then, by God, she would do it.

She chuckled. Make that by G.O.D.

That was the nature of her. That was the reason behind G.O.D., the Guardians Of the Domain.

There's no doubt The Company had been here first, but they were so small then, it didn't really seem to matter. Then skiing caught on, and Denver grew, and suddenly, for no apparent reason, Vail became chic, an upper-middle-class Aspen, while Aspen became a high-end Vail, destination resorts for people with money who were determined to spend it and ruin her mountains while doing so.

She had fought to preserve it as she had found it, then, as the growth became overwhelming, to turn back the clock to the point where there were no ex-presidents in the east valley and there were no more plans to enclose the highway in a tunnel and cover the tunnel with even more condos and apartments and expensive housing and no more plans for trains to Denver and a bigger airport and no more, just no more.

No more.

She looked around her quickly, as if caught napping on a park bench. Despite the crowd in the Village, here, in Lionshead, just beyond the ice arena, it was fairly quiet. She could count herself alone.

Kelvin.

In her nervousness, in her dialogue with the world around her, she had forgotten about her son. She looked down, past the arena, toward town. A bus rumbled past a clump of walkers in the distance. But there was still no sign of Kelvin. It added to her anxiety.

It was a simple thing, she thought: follow the man with the sagging car and see what makes him so panicked and his trunk so low. If he left town, so be it. But if he stuck around, see what he was so jealously, carefully and nervously protecting.

Weight that could drop the shocks on a rental car that low had to be something heavy. And something heavy in a bike box like that could be a lot of things, but a lot of things didn't make people sweat like that. Money—money made people sweat like that. And, if it was money, then, so be it.

She just wanted to know.

She just wanted to know … so … she could borrow it.

From her place on the bench she stared up into the woods that climbed up the side of Vail Mountain. She would borrow it. For a lifetime, perhaps, but the man should think of it as an investment in his world. Saving that world was an expensive proposition, especially when you realized that you were fighting people every day who had strip-mined money from the American public with cheap films and legal briefs and ticky tacky housing developments only to spend it here in her valley on cars that were never driven and clothes that were never worn and houses that were never lived in, other than a week in the summer and two around Christmas.

Disuse, misuse and outrage, she screamed, mentally, slapping the tip of the heavy wooden stick sharply on a rock next to her bench.

A couple, walking behind her, jumped at the sound, looked at her, and hurried along, not wanting to be drawn into the obvious wall of anger that surrounded the small, blunt woman.

She hadn't heard them. She hadn't seen them. She was lost in a trance, gazing up the side of her mountain, lost in her dream of what the valley could become again, pristine, inviolate, natural.

Don't dream. Don't reach. Don't plan.

Don't let your imagination run, she thought, there is no room for imagination in this world.

Marjorie Stump closed her eyes and leaned back slightly, taking a deep breath, filling her lungs with the freshness of the day, revitalizing, invigorating, crisp and clean, if, of course, you could filter out that very slight tang of diesel from the highway above and behind her.

The anxiety was lessening. She took another breath. The tension was wafting away on a breeze. Her sense of fear and danger was gone, now, as she wrapped herself in the beauty and majesty of her mountains.

Her mountains. Her valley. Her life.

She drifted away....

"Mother!" Kelvin said sharply, his voice and the slap of his feet against the pavement a thick, off-rhythm drum beat charging up behind her.

She spun, angrily, the thick wooden head of the shillelagh whooshing through the air and catching him just at the front right corner of his right knee. He dropped, with a roar, that blended into a low and frightened squeak, onto his knees, onto the curb, just behind the bench.

He clutched an edge of it, bending his head down, wanting desperately to retch. The blow against his knee had dropped him, filling his eyes with tears, but the drop to the curb, concrete on kneecaps, had disabled him. He felt the wind rush out of his lungs and hatred, once more, fill his heart. There was so much to say, so much to do, and yet, this woman, this harridan from hell, could only think of beating those around her.

He should simply let her have it, right between the eyes....

"What?" she asked, sharply. "Why are you looking at me like that?"

"Like what?" he wheezed, suddenly trying to change his inflection and manner into one of gentle conciliation. Not yet, he thought. Not yet.

"Like that. Don't you look at me like that," she raised her hand, "or I'll slap the look right off your face, Kelvin. I am not to be trifled with, I am not to be surprised, I am not to be spooked by someone sneaking up on me! I will not have it. I will not put up with it."

Kelvin Stump took a deep breath and nodded. "Yes, mother. My apologies for scaring you."

She softened a bit, the bitch in Birkenstocks smiling, reaching out to her son as if to make amends.

"You were always such a noisy clod, Kelvin. Good for heavy lifting. Good as a threat to those who didn't know your gentle and stupid nature, Kelvin. But so noisy. So clumsy. I thought, so many times, you understood. The stick, the punishments, the favors and treats, nothing ever did work with you, did it, son?"

He stared at her, his eyes those of a large, obedient dog.

"No," she whispered, stroking his face, "nothing ever really did."

The gentle touch along his face lasted only a moment before Marjorie Stump snapped her hand away and changed her tone completely.

"So—what did you find out about our friend?"

"Our friend?"

"The man," she said, with no little exasperation, "the man with the car with the trunk with the case. The man you were following. Did you see him, did you find him, did you learn anything, anything at all, about him?"

"Yes," he whispered, not only trying to conceal what he felt was important information, but also trying to keep his emotions in check. He didn't want any more of that cane. He didn't want to reveal himself in his excitement. "Yes. He parked at the transportation center and I lost him. I went and couldn't find him, but I heard those noisy metal doors open and I ran out on top and then I saw him—with that case—and I saw him go into the Bavarian Haus. With the case."

"Where'd he go?"

"I don't know. By the time I got to the lobby, he wasn't there, so I waited. And then, he came down. And he left and walked up Bridge Street with this gym bag he had. Nothing else. No case. He went to the clocktower. I think for lunch."

"What did he have?"

"I don't know."

"I was joking, Kelvin."

"But, Mama," he rattled on, ignoring her sarcasm, "there were these two men. Inside. Two men. Big guys. Mean looking. Both big guys. Muscles. When he went in he was alone, when he came out, they were with him and they were taking him somewhere."

"Where?"

"I don't know. I ... woof," he took a breath and blew it out quickly, as if catching his breath again.

"You have grown up here, Kelvin—you shouldn't be out of breath," she admonished.

"Yes, I know, mother," he said, simply, leaning heavily on the back of the bench, trying to steady himself after the excitement of the past hour. "But as they came out of the restaurant, they ran into some people, bike riders, I mean, really, ran into them, and the little guy I was following broke away and jumped down the steps and ran away. So, I followed him...."

"Who are they?"

"I don't know. But he was afraid of them. He certainly was. And, I chased him and I helped him."

"You helped him escape?"

"Yeah, pretty cool, huh? Just as he was running into the parking structure, you know, the big one...."

"I know," she said, peevishly.

"He was lost and I yelled, what level? And he said, number three, and I yelled, 'This way!' And he followed me and we went right through the short-cuts I know and found his car."

"What's that?" she said, pointing the tip of the cane toward the blue gym satchel he held behind him.

"That's what I've got to tell you about. This is marvelous," Kelvin said, with almost breathless excitement. "Okay. Okay. So, I see this guy run from the other two guys, the big, mean guys, right?"

"Hurry up."

"Okay, okay, mama. So, I help this guy find his car and all the way the guy is saying, 'You saved me, you saved my ass.' That's what he was saying. I would-n't say that. And we get to his car, and even though those guys were right behind us, he opens this bag," he shook the blue gym back at her for empha-sis, "and grabs a stack of bills and throws it in the car, for him, I guess, okay, then he says to me, he says, 'You saved my ass, pal, here,' and he shoves this bag into my hands and says, 'Keep it, it's yours, 'cuz there's plenty more where this came from,' and he gives me this bag and then he jumps in the car and he backs out and drives away, just leaving me there, and I yell, 'Thanks,' and he yells, 'Thanks and I'll be back' because he's got more stashed here somewhere I think with a friend of his, and it was just great. It was just great."

"Give me the bag," she said, quietly, putting out her hand.

"Oh, mama, you won't believe this."

"Just give me the bag, Kelvin."

He studied her for a moment, a smile crossing his face that seemed open and honest and completely insincere all at once. He paused, handed her the bag, pulled it back, then thrust it at her as she flicked the cane, again, in the direc-tion of his right knee.

"I can't believe, Kelvin, how difficult you are becoming. I should have left you in Ohio with your father."

"My father's dead."

"Exactl…."

The word froze in Marjorie Stump's throat, held there by the sight of a portrait of Benjamin Franklin staring back at her from inside the blue satchel. In fact, it was not merely one portrait of Benjamin Franklin that held her in thrall, but many, many, many portraits of Benjamin Franklin staring back at her, happily printed in green, as if the great inventor was having a huge family reunion with himself in the ballroom of the Blue Satchel Hotel.

"Oh, my," was all that was able to work itself past the lump that had set up housekeeping in Marjorie Stump's chest.

"Oh, my, indeed," Kelvin answered, his smile a genuine look of appreciation now, now that he had finally, for the first time in his life, made his mother speechless.

"Oh, oh, oh, my god, Kelvin," Marjorie rasped, her breath coming in short, shattered bursts. "How, how, how much, how much?"

"I'm not sure, yet. I think about four-hundred thousand dollars, mother." A smile covering his face, as he, too, couldn't believe their good fortune or the fact that $50,000 was carefully stuffed in the back of his shirt.

"This—this is ours?" she asked, incredulously. "This is ours?"

"Yeah, can you believe it? This is a gift. He gave it to me for saving his life. He kept saying I saved his life."

"And you give it to me…."

"Yes. I … give it … to you, mother."

"Bless you, Kelvin," Marjorie Stump said, quietly, "for you are a good boy. A very good boy."

"Thank you, mother."

"And then—when he gave this to you—what did he say?"

"He said, 'There's plenty more where this came from.'"

She scratched her chin, playing with one of the small white hairs that grew wild along the jaw line.

"Plenty more. Plenty more. Did he say where?"

"Where what?"

The cane flicked again, the heavy knob brushing the top of Kelvin's right knee, causing him to flinch, jump back and curse silently.

"I know what you said in your mind, Kelvin. Don't say it. Don't curse. Even silently. Where did he say the rest was?" she asked.

"He didn't. He didn't say. He just gave this to me as a reward and jumped in his car and started to drive. He wanted to get out of the public parking lot before those big guys got him. Blocked him in. They were coming, mama."

"Too much information, Kelvin, just answer the question," she said, tartly.

"He didn't say."

"And he ran."

"And he ran. Yes. He ran."

"That means," she said, quietly, taking one last look at the lovely, comforting face of Benjamin Franklin in the satchel before zipping it up and turning to her son, "that somewhere, out there, there is more money. Enough money so that he was willing to give you half-a-million dollars in cash as a reward.

There is enough money out there, somewhere, for me to truly do battle with the desecrators of this mountain and restore it to what it was and what it deserves to be."

"But, mama. Aren't you happy…."

"Oh, of course, Kelvin," she said soothingly, stroking his cheek in reward for the good fortune he had brought their way. "Of course I'm happy with this. But this wouldn't buy a two-week time share in Vail anymore. It's chicken feed. But we will use it wisely. And, find the rest."

"Why, mama, why not be happy…."

"Because, dear son," Marjorie Stump said, simply, "I have a plan. And my plan requires this ten times over. Come along, now, Kelvin. We have work to do."

She turned without another word and began to walk toward the center of Vail Village. As one of the city buses passed, she rapped it sharply along the side with the heavy blackthorn head of the shillelagh, frightening the tourists on board.

"Goddamn it, Marjorie!" came a shout from the driver.

"Electric, Henry! Electric! When will you learn?" She said the last over her shoulder as she marched, with a light heart, toward town. Kelvin dropped in close behind her.

"Tell me again, Kelvin. Carefully, this time, everything you saw. Everything you did. Everything he said."

"Everything?"

"Everything, son. The money is in town somewhere. With a friend, I'd suspect. Or some kind of safe place. Maybe a friend's safe place. Who knows. But that's why I say, tell me everything."

"I'll try."

"Good," she smiled, hefting the bag. "You're a good son."

The bag felt heavy in her hands, as if filled with hopes and dreams and possibilities.

"Did he mention any names?"

"Angelo somebody."

"Last name?"

"No last name. Just 'the bastard' would never get this back."

"Oooh," she nodded, "sounds like stolen money. Maybe criminals. Makes me happy to keep it. Anyone else?"

"Yeah, yeah, as a matter of fact," Kelvin said, brightening, as if an errant power surge had broken a memory free from the back of his head and pulled him from his steady gaze at the satchel, which was no longer his property. "Yeah. He mentioned another name."

"What? What was it, Kelvin?"

"Ross. He said the name, Ross."

She nodded again, her head bouncing happily like that of a spring-loaded dog in the back window of a cheap car on a bad road.

"Ross."

She walked quicker now, the satchel swinging back and forth maniacally, her next step as clear to her as a morning on the mountain top.

"Ross," she said, simply. "We start with him."

✦

THE MAN THEY WERE GOING TO START WITH SAT CALMLY NOW BESIDE THE Haven-TW step van, basking in the mountain sun, staring up at the mountain greenery, filling his lungs with mountain air.

And wishing he had a cigarette.

There was really no need, as he didn't smoke, and the first inhalation, he knew, would bend him over at the waist, barfing up a lung as if he were trying to find the penny he swallowed when he was three. But Big Tobacco's advertising had been so prevalent, so omnipresent throughout his life that there were times that simply called for a smoke. He realized that this urge was a marketer's dream come true, but he felt a need for those cool, rich, Virginia tobaccos, skillfully blended, that would nail him back against the van and make him pass out at altitude from lack of oxygen to the brain.

Maybe he didn't want a cigarette after all. Maybe gum. Or a blade of grass. Or a beer. Or some Jameson on ice with a splash of water.

Maybe. Maybe. Maybe, maybe, maybe.

Something to do with his hands while he waited to find out the fate of the bicycle, the top-of-the-line full-suspension Colnago mountain bike that had its front spokes mangled by an errant foot. At this very moment, Dr. Hootie Bosco of the Universitatum Velocipedia E Pluribus Unum was busy working his magic upon the rim, hoping to restore it to at least some measure of its earlier glory.

It's not like the bike belonged to him or anything. Despite Cheryl's statement, it was a team bike. A much-desired team bike, if Marshall Reed's current tantrum upon seeing it on the operating table meant anything. Will tried to shut his ears to it all, but it kept intruding into the beauty of the day, his psychic determination to relax after Cheryl's familial revelation.

"What the … what the … what the…." Reed barked.

"Hell," Hootie answered, "the word you're looking for is hell."

"Hell. Damn it! What the hell happened to my bike?"

"Not your bike," Cheryl answered quietly, not even looking up from the race bible she studied, "a team bike that was loaned out. Such things happen. Get used to it. Most of the bikes we've got will be in pieces by Sunday night."

"Yeah, but this was my bike," Reed screamed, his face a patchwork of blue veins throbbing on a red background. "This was my ride. I had dibs, given my position here on the team."

"Dibs?" Hootie barked a laugh, never taking his eyes off the front end of the frame. "I didn't know dibs worked here. I call dibs on that condo over there."

"Can it, Marshall," Cheryl said, without volume, but certainly with a power to her words. "This bike belongs to the team, and whoever I say gets it, gets it. We've been over all this before."

At that moment, Reed's teammate and underling, Jeremy Jettman, decided to weigh in with his opinion.

"It's not fair," was all he said.

Cheryl Crane flipped the sunglasses up on her forehead and squinted at both of them.

"Jesus, you two are a piece of work. Do you come in the set or did we buy you individually?"

Neither said a word.

"Well, let's get something straight right here and now. Life's not fair. You know? Life's not one goddamned bit fair. You either learn to live with that fact and get on with it, or you get yourself a new plane of existence. Which will it be, boys? Because I haven't got time to fuck with you today on top of everything else."

They both stared for a second, then backed off. There was an underlying power and sense of threat in the tone of Cheryl Crane that made them both realize that this was not a time to confront, this was a time to back away quietly and complain bitterly at a distance.

Jettman muttered and sulked, then brightened tremendously as Frannie Draa approached the pit and smiled at him. Jeremy slid gracefully to her side, talked for a moment, before the two then turned and walked toward the center of town.

Reed watched them go in disgust.

Hootie Bosco caught Reed's angry glance, stuck his head out of the darker reaches of the back of the van and shook his hair, the dreadlocks bobbing and weaving like the bantam weight champ. He followed Reed's look and watched Jettman and Draa disappear into the town together. He wiped his hands on a red shop rag and looked at Marshall Reed as if he were a surgeon who had just let Grandpa sail off to that great velodrome in the sky.

"Marshall, I'm sorry."

"About what, you freak?" Reed replied with a sneer, his courage to belittle returning.

"Two things. First, sorry about your toady, there. The possibility of sex does that to a person. And," he lowered his voice, "the bike, the bike, man," Hootie said, his head rolling back and forth slowly, deliberately, in the manner of great Elizabethan tragedy.

"Aw, shit. What about the bike?" Reed whined. "I thought it was just the front wheel."

Bosco stepped back into the shadows and ran his finger along a black line at the base of the headset up to the top tube.

"See that? Crack. Weird torque split the metal on the headset. Haven't you ever seen that before? This bike is toast. It's hardly good for parts."

"Aw, goddamn it," Reed continued to whine, staring into the darkness of the van then turning on Cheryl, "and it's all your fault—because you let your piece of shit roadie boyfriend take a bike that wasn't meant for him. Promise. This is a promise. Hear me?"

Cheryl looked at him and nodded. "Promise, gotcha."

"The promise is—I'm going to Haven, I'm going to Two Wheels, I'm going to Colnago, if I have to, and you, you will be slammed for this—I promise. Dumped. They will hear about it and, by god, we'll finally do something about how you're running the team."

"Fine."

"That's it? Fine? Well, then, fine," he said, flustered, her tone and attitude throwing him off a perfectly good rage. "I'm going to get on a phone right now. Right this very goddamned second, and we'll see what happens. We'll see."

His finger was pointed in her general direction, wiggling with anger and frustration. He dropped it to his side, nodded angrily, and marched off in the direction of the hotel.

Cheryl watched him go, before turning to Hootie Bosco.

"What's the prognosis on the bike?"

Hootie pulled the workstand forward into the sunlight and ran his finger up along the black-line crack, then wiped it down with the red shop rag. The crack, the line, the damage to the bike disappeared.

"Just fine, once I check out the fork."

"What about the crack?"

"Ah, the only thing cracked around here is Mister Reed. This bike is indestructible. Damned near bulletproof. It'll still be standing long after Mr. Elegance there," he said, pointing around the corner of the step van toward Will, "is dead and buried, ground into so much landfill on the cross-country course."

"I heard that," Will said, sleepily.

"I hoped you would," Hootie replied.

Will pulled himself up slowly and walked around the back of the step van, running his hand along Cheryl's shoulders as he moved past her. He felt her stiffen, if just for a moment, and then relax, the tension running across her upper torso letting go under his touch, as the skirmish with Marshall Reed disappeared into the distance.

"Hey," Hootie called, "the important stuff is up here."

"Huh? Yeah," Will nodded, his mind suddenly split between thoughts of Cheryl and the conversation at hand.

Hootie reached back into the darkness, threw a restraining bolt and lifted the bike off the workstand. Swinging to his left, he turned the bike into the sun, the light of the day reflecting brightly off the yellow, blue and black frame, the silvered components, the restored front wheel.

"Man, that's beautiful," was all that Will could say.

"Hey, Dr. Bosco, plastic surgeon to the stars. Nothing much, really, three new spokes and a spin. Bigfoot didn't do as much as you thought."

"Can I ride it?"

"Sure, but let me tell you something, pal," Bosco said, lifting the bike over the lip of the step van and setting it gently on the ground. "The first thing you want to do is get some shoes. Real shoes for mountain bike riding. There's gotta be a store in town that sells them. Then, you've got to get more ride time, even on some trails around here."

"I get the bike again?"

"It's no good to me. It's been stepped on. I have no idea if there is any collateral damage."

Cheryl smiled. "You've been watching too many war movies. Look, Will, use the bike. Quite frankly, I like the idea that you'll be putting your cute little buns on it rather than Reed with his fat and hairy ass."

Both Hootie and Will grimaced at that image, then mutually smiled at the thought of Marshall Reed going ballistic seeing Will on the bike, his temper leading to a blood pressure level that might just pop his head.

"Go get the shoes, go ride the bike," she said with a grin, turning back to her paperwork. She stared at it for a minute, the race bible, the extraneous sheets of schedules and logs and expenses, threw it all into a greasy box just recently emptied of parts, and stood up. "Speaking of which, I think I will."

"You think you will what?"

"I think I will go ride. I think I will go ride the cross-country course, if only to get some time in the cleats and my blood moving again."

"Drink water, you're at altitude."

"Thank you, Mother Hootie."

"Yeah, and...." Will tried to think of something wise to say.

"And?"

He paused for a second, reset himself, leaned forward and kissed her lightly on the cheek.

"Yeah, and have a good ride," was all he finally said, his voice betraying the concern he still felt for her.

She turned away from Hootie and looked at the start-finish line, then up the tracks and the ski runs toward the top of the mountain, hidden by a cloud.

"Look," she said, muting her voice unnecessarily, as Hootie had, once more, disappeared into the bowels of the truck, that, oddly enough, had nothing even approaching the general definition of bowels, "I'm okay. No, really, I'm fine, Will. I've dealt with this stuff off and on for years. I'm thrown that they're here. I'm worried about what is going on. I hate their guts for what they did. But I'm safe, pretty sure, anyway, and I'm dealing with it. I've put it away for now. It's okay. Time tends to throw sand on stuff like this, no matter how hard you try to keep your hatred alive. I'm fine."

She ran her hand over his face and turned, sweeping up her helmet. She mounted the bike and began riding toward the cross-country course.

"Isn't the start of the course in town?" Will wondered aloud.

"I'll pick up the Lionshead loop just outside town. There'll be some traffic. Shouldn't be much, though. I'll see you later."

Will watched her go, then called after her impulsively, "I love you."

She stopped, turned, and smiled.

"Thanks, that means a lot."

She rode away, Will left standing near the van, waving to a figure receding in the distance. He suddenly felt like June Cleaver waving good-bye to Ward before another hard day at the office.

Will turned and began to walk toward town, saying good-bye to Hootie as he passed the rear of the truck and hearing only a gentle snoring from the darkness in return. As he walked toward Hanson Ranch Road and the first of the village shops, he checked for his wallet and wished he still carried the American Express Gold card he had stolen from the Haven Team manager in France a few months before. He had given it back.

Honesty.

What a bitch.

He marched off in search of riding shoes, his hands dug deep into his pockets, his right mindlessly fingering a key to a bike box that in the confusion on the steps of the restaurant, Leonard Romanowski had forced on him not two hours earlier, a key that in the high emotion of that moment and those that came immediately after, Will Ross had already forgotten, along with Leonard Romanowski.

※

LEONARD ROMANOWSKI HAD NOT FORGOTTEN.

As he desperately tried to breathe, the problem being two small knife wounds high and left on his chest as well as the fact that he was bent in two in the trunk of a cheap rental car, Leonard Romanowski thought about the men who were chasing him and the man who had helped him and the client, in whose closet, he had left his entire life savings, gathered together over the last ten days.

The muffled voices outside the trunk moved closer again and he heard a click and a rattle just above his head; there was a heavy snap and the trunk lid lifted open and Leonard Romanowski fell backward, cracking his spine on the edge of the trunk.

The impact drove the wind out of his lungs and blood across the floor of the Chevy.

He was a mess. And he knew it. He was also dying. And Leonard Romanowski knew that, too. He sat for a moment staring straight ahead, looking at the blood on his pant legs, the blood from his chest that should never have traveled that far down, and thought about the missed chances, the days spent in worry, the times he had been given a chance and had failed to take it, the loves he had squandered, the life that had passed him by, and yet, he still did not feel sad about it. It hadn't been a good life, necessarily, but it had been his life. Sometimes, he figured, that's enough.

He took a deep breath that stopped about midway from the pain in his chest. His feet were getting cold. Shutdown. He had heard about this. Shutdown. The body shuts down to protect the heart and the brain.

He chuckled at the thought, a bubble of blood forming at his lips. Protecting the two things he had never really used in his life.

He wanted to turn and face the two men who had been given the job of bringing him to this place in time and this state of being. He smiled, unable to control the drool, knowing the drool was his own blood, spread out over his own teeth and lips. But he couldn't help it.

Despite what they had done to him, despite the fix he was now in, he couldn't help but smile. He had made their life a mess. There was money out there, somewhere, somewhere for all of them to find.

And only he knew where it was. Only he knew where it was. Only he knew … only he … knew.

As he mouthed the words "Screw you" to the man standing behind him, Leonard Romanowski's head dropped slowly to his chest. A deep rattle, released from somewhere within him, shook his entire body for a moment, before he grew still. He suddenly seemed smaller, as if his very spirit, his life force, had been holding him up.

And he was quiet.

Stanley Szyclinski scratched his head, forcing the hair to stand straight up. He turned to Olverio Cangliosi and shrugged.

"Well, what do we do now?"

"What do you mean, what do we do?" Ollie said, gently bending Leonard Romanowski forward and carefully shutting the lid of the trunk, making sure to wipe off any areas he might have touched with a cream handkerchief. "We do our job, that's what we do."

"I thought that was our job," Stanley said in an angry whisper, thumbing back toward the trunk before carefully wiping the rear side panel and door handle he had touched.

They stepped away from the car and walked quickly and quietly toward their own car, parked one level below. Without a word, they got in. Ollie started the car, backed it up, and drove slowly toward the exit.

They were both lost, in questions now. How and who and where was the money?

Ollie spoke finally, as the car pulled up onto South Frontage Road, turning toward the highway and the parking structure near Lionshead, their hotel, and a moment of relative peace in what had become, quite quickly, a three-acre mess on a one-acre lot. He said to Stanley, "The money. The job always was, and always is, to find the money. To recover the money."

"And," Stanley said, his finger in the air like a professor adding a point, "to teach a lesson."

"The lesson has been taught. Now it's time to find the money."

The car stopped at the European roundabout and made its way around the obstruction and onward toward Lionshead.

"I hate those things," Ollie said bitterly.

"No shit."

"Don't curse."

"Yeah, yeah," Stanley answered, the fatigue clearly sounding in his voice. He was tired of this job, tired of the running, tired of the town and the village and the altitude, tired of his niece popping up at the most inopportune times, tired of the direction of this entire weekend.

But Ollie was right. They still had a job to do. He sighed, turned and said, "Okay. So what's next?"

"What's next is figuring out who the major players are in this sordid mess."

"Sordid? Where'd you pick that one up?"

"Build-your-vocabulary tapes. Play 'em in the car."

"So who do you figure?"

"Don't know. Did you see the guy who ran down the street behind him? Who was he? Was he following or just running? That guy with Cherylann at the restaurant this morning. We've got a whole town full of athletes, and he was a sports agent...."

"Not much of one."

"I don't know."

They pulled into the Lionshead parking structure, took a few silent turns about the facility and parked close to the exit. They stepped out of the car and both slumped against it, as if the day had drawn the majority of their energy from them.

"I'm getting too old for this," Stanley mumbled.

"You never know," Ollie said, with a tone of resignation.

"How's that?" Stanley asked.

Olverio leaned up against the roof of the car, the momentary respite taking the weight off his right foot that was being pinched into a pulpy mess by a pair of new, narrow loafers.

"You never know who it might be, who might be Romanowski's safety, his safe house, the one person he could trust in this town."

"Plenty of possibilities," Stanley said, looking across at the mountain, still clearly busy with riding, training, and general activity.

"Well, we can run ourselves ragged around Vail and check them all, or we can make one call to New York, have a lovely dinner on Angelo Genna's money and wait for an answer that can either take care of all this tonight or by the end of the weekend at the latest."

"What call?"

"Call Angelo. Have somebody with some sense check out Romanowski's client list."

"From what I've heard, can't be all that many," Stanley said.

Ollie nodded and began to walk toward the stairway to the street. "Focus on cyclists," he said, over his shoulder, "and then take those names into the streets of Vail to see if such a person exists."

A cloud crossed Stanley's face and he furrowed his brow. He walked quickly after Ollie and wagged a finger in his general direction, "What if he just dumped it? Found a safe place and just dumped it?"

"No place is that safe. You don't just dump four-and-a-half million dollars. Nobody would. Greed and worry wouldn't let'cha. No. He stashed it with somebody. Somebody safe."

"How can you be so sure?"

"Because that's what I'd do. I'd stash it with somebody safe."

"Like who?"

"Like you."

Stanley smiled at the compliment.

"Likewise, I'm sure."

"You bet," Ollie said, spying a pay phone at the corner of the ice arena, "somebody safe."

WILL ROSS PUSHED THE DOOR OF THE HOTEL ROOM OPEN AND JUMPED BACK into the warm hallway. Somebody had cranked the air conditioner up to the point where ice was forming on the front of the TV set. Will walked cautiously in, blew out a stream of air to check if he could see his breath, and tossed the bags on the bed. The new shoes, complete with the proper cleats, had set him back a tidy sum, helped by the sports bag, helmet water bottle, and gloves. He couldn't afford this life for long. Even survive the weekend and he'd need to find a job.

His mother's voice was in his ear.

"In a factory! You'll have to work in a factory!"

He should have gotten the teaching certificate. At least it would have shut her up.

He pulled the shoes out of the box and stuffed them in the bottom of the bag, along with the gloves and helmet, pulling tags and little plastic wires from it all as he went. It was a shock, in a way, to the depths of his very system. He hadn't paid for cycling gear in years. The various teams, good, bad or indifferent, had always just given him more than he could ever use. His father's garage in Michigan was filled with frames and gearsets and jerseys and gloves and shoes and cleats....

But that was then. This was now. He stood up and pulled off his shirt, then undid the brace on his left leg before unbuckling his pants and stripping out of them as well. Wearing only a pair of half socks he walked across the room, bent over, and dug in the bottom of his Haven duffel bag. God, what an image, he thought to himself; let's hope nobody wanders in the door at this moment and comes face to face with his hairy, one-eyed monster. Deep inside the duffel, wadded into a corner, he found what he was looking for: a pair of Haven riding shorts that he had worn to absolutely no distinction in the Tour de France. He stared at them and sighed, rubbing the fabric in his fingers and feeling the magic slowly, ever so slowly, drifting away.

Jesus, get a grip, he said aloud to the empty room, pulling the shorts quickly, over his nakedness and realizing that he had pulled them over a little roll of, not fat, necessarily, but softness, hovering around his belt line. He now understood his grandfather. Each time Will saw him in Kansas, his pants were a little higher. What were they hiding then? What was he hiding now?

He stood and stared in the mirror for a moment, pinching his waist. His eyes rose until he was staring at himself again in the mirror. Who was he now? Who was he becoming? He shook the image away.

He picked a pair of sunglasses off the TV set and stepped to the closet, opened it, and reached in to grab a long-sleeved shirt. The late-afternoon sun was going to be cool quickly, and there was no need to be stupid about this trail riding. Brambles and shit were everywhere.

He reached in, and, through the darkness of the sunglasses, couldn't quite see anything other than the crushed tops of all his shirts. There was a black maw just below the shoulder line of everything on his side. He couldn't quite make it out. Lifting the sunglasses to the top of his head, he stared at the bike case, propped up on its narrow end. It was the only way it could fit into the closet. And in fitting it into the closet, it had crushed and wrinkled all the clothes on his side of the closet. Not that there was anything much different about that, as he pretty much wore everything crushed and wrinkled, anyway, but there was a principle to consider here.

"Christ, Cheryl, goddamn it," he barked, "this fucking case goes in the truck. You don't put it in the...."

He pulled on the case to free up his clothes and realized, quite suddenly and without warning, that it was not only heavier than he had ever imagined it to be, but the contents had shifted in his quick and angry yank, which pulled the case over the top of its balance point and over on top of him. Caught by surprise, Will stumbled backward underneath the case, and tried to get a foot in a brace position behind him. His foot caught the nap of the carpet at an odd angle and threw him off balance. The heavy bicycle case pushed him over, trapping him between the edge of the bed and the floor.

With his arm wedged between the case and his chest, he was still able to breathe, but the angle didn't allow him any leverage on the case itself. He took a breath to steady himself and slowly began to wiggle out. The weight of the case—which at one point slipped back and pinched one of his fingers—made it difficult, but within a few moments he had worked himself down to the point where he could move freely into the open triangle between the floor, the case, and the bed rail.

He lay there for what seemed a very long time just breathing and wiggling his toes in embarrassment, thinking of nothing other than how he could explain this moment of extreme clumsiness to Cheryl if she happened to walk in at this very moment, which was, of course, what she did.

"Hey, you here? I just stopped by to pee," she said aloud into a room that could have very easily been empty.

She poked her head around a corner and stared, her eyes growing wide with the question on her face.

"Don't say a word," he said, his finger shooting up in the air to silence her surprise.

"So what's with you?"

He made a face.

"I've fallen—and I can't get up."

CHAPTER TEN:

WE'RE IN
THE MONEY

WILL STARED AT CHERYL FROM UNDERNEATH THE MAKESHIFT
pup tent and raised a hand.

"Pull me out," he whimpered.

"Honest, I'd love to help you, love, but I've gotta pee."

She turned with a quick, nasty smile and darted into the bathroom, turning on the exhaust fan to hide the sounds of what she was doing. The fan rattled to life like the engine of a poorly tuned P-51 Mustang. She had to shout to be heard over the din, which was a moot point as Will wasn't listening anyway.

"So, what are you doing buying a bike? The Colnago's your's as far as Hootie and I are concerned. And why buy unassembled?"

Will, still flat on his back and staring at the ceiling, heard only a buzz of conversation from the bathroom, lost in the mechanical squeal of the exhaust fan.

"Jesus," he muttered, rolling on his stomach and pushing himself up just enough to crawl out of the hard-shell camp site, "I can't hear you."

"What?"

"I can't hear you!"

"What?"

"I can't hear you. Damn," he whispered and sat down on the end of the bed. In a moment, the toilet flushed, the water ran, and the exhaust fan came to a clanking, grateful halt. The door opened and Cheryl stood before him.

"I couldn't hear you in there."

"And I couldn't hear you," he replied.

"In a way, that's good," she laughed and pointed at the black bicycle case which was weighing down her side of the bed.

"So what's with the bike?"

"Don't ask me. That's yours, isn't it?"

"No. My case and my bike are down at the truck. My bike is there in case I need to ride it," she said, sweetly.

"Smart ass."

"Wait a minute, that's not yours, Mister buy-out-the-sporting-goods-store?" she asked, laughing, looking at the bags and boxes littering the bed.

"No," he said, now genuinely puzzled, "it's not mine. I just figured that you were storing something here."

"Well, whatever it is, I don't particularly care for it sitting on my side of the bed," she said, stepping over to the case, grabbing the end handle with one hand and lifting. The weight caught her off guard.

"Good Lord," she barked, turning to Will, "what the hell did you put in here, scrap iron?"

"I'm telling you—I didn't put anything in there."

She braced herself and pushed it, lost control as the weight of the contents shifted again, and dropped it, hard, against Will's clothes and the back of the closet. A "boom" rumbled through the wall.

"Jesus. Thanks a whole hell of a lot. My laundry appreciates that."

"Sorry. God, what do you think is in this thing?"

"Frankly, my dear, I have no idea."

"But you give a damn?"

"Of course I give a damn, especially given the rest of my year so far."

"What do you mean?"

"I've had a little too much experience with plastique and corporate conspiracy to let something unknown sit in my closet next to my bed."

"Our bed. And my side," she said, still staring at the black case crushing his wardrobe.

"Same thing," he said, pushing his knees and rising from the edge of the bed. "Let's see what we've got here."

"Sure?" she questioned, backing away half a step.

"No, I'm not sure, frankly, but I figure we've got to know, and there's only one way to find out for sure."

"You're not going to open it, are you?" she said, trying to take another half step back but blocked by the bed.

"No, I'm going to get it into a position where using my X-ray vision won't irradiate my clothes or the stash of Zagnuts I've got hidden in a bag in the closet."

She paused and looked at him with a pained expression.

"You've got Zagnuts and you weren't sharing?"

"I've got three and, no, I wasn't."

"Some friend."

Will reached into the closet and grabbed the top handle, pulling the box.

"I'm not your friend. I'm family."

"In my case," she said, sadly, "that's not a point in your favor."

"Sorry," he sighed. The contents shifted again, but he was ready for it this time, bracing himself against the closet. Still, the damned thing was heavy.

"Some assistance," he wheezed.

"Yeah, yeah, sure," Cheryl said, stepping over the bed and coming up beside the case directly opposite Will. "What do you want me to do?"

"Well, we can't open it here. Let's get it over there near the TV set. I think we can drop it down there."

"Okay. Let's go turn it over, onto its wheels."

"Right. On three."

"Right. On three. One-two-three."

They were off the beat, but, working together, the case went over easily and dropped, heavily, onto its wheels.

"Heavy little bastard, isn't he?"

"Unwieldy, too," Will answered.

Together, they manhandled the case around the edge of the bed and toward the one spot in the room with any sort of open space available. They lowered the case lengthwise, keeping the logo and the locks pointed up.

Cheryl wiped her forehead, somewhat disgusted with herself. She was sweating more now, from moving a case eight feet, than she had all day on the downhill and championship courses.

"So, what now, Brainiac? You got a key?"

Will sat back, a little frustrated with her sarcasm.

"No, I don't. And I don't have any tools, either."

"Great, so now we've got a big case of rocks in the middle of the bedroom floor, which, I'm sure, you'll stub your toe on every night as you amble to the pissoir at 3 a.m."

"Ease up. Ease up," he said, staring at the locks of the case and the shard of paper stuffed in the seam of the case. "I'm thinking …" he put up his hand "… and don't say 'don't strain yourself.'"

"Oops. The relationship is over. You know all my lines."

He leaned forward and studied the paper stuffed into the seam. "You got a comb?"

"Yeah, but I don't think a comb is going to open that—unless, of course, you're Jimmy Valentine."

"Just give me a comb, Ma Barker." He put out his hand and held it there as she walked into the bathroom and stepped out a moment later with a hot pink oversized comb. She put it in his hand and stepped back.

"This, quite honestly, I've got to see."

"Stand back and be amazed," he said, leaning forward dramatically toward the case. He turned the comb over to the thicker tines and picked at a closed loop at one end of the sheet of paper. It pulled, caught, then pulled again, slowly rolling out like a sheet of paper caught in a player piano. One edge caught and tore, but the rest pulled out cleanly. In one move, Will pulled the paper toward him and tossed the comb back to Cheryl. Surprised, she caught it with her chest.

"I'm impressed."

"Frankly, so am I," he said, sheepishly. "I didn't expect it to come out that easily."

"What's it say?"

"It's from Leonard, Leonard Romanowski," Will said, quietly, "my agent, the guy you said was in so much trouble. Listen: 'Watch this for me, Will. Should be back Sunday night. Keep it quiet and please don't open it.'"

"Well, that's tells me something," Cheryl said.

"What does it tell you?"

"It tells me we should open it."

"But he said, 'Don't open it.'"

"Look, Will," Cheryl said forcefully, "I'm not about to hold something for somebody, somebody on the run, without knowing what it is—especially if he goes out of his way to say, 'Don't let anybody know you have it.' That sucks big time."

"Look," Will argued, "Leonard is not the kind of guy who would screw you...."

"No," Cheryl answered quickly, "he'd screw you. And us. Me, alone, he wouldn't screw because I wouldn't let him."

"Come on, Cheryl," Will whined, "this is something ... this...."

"Come on, Will, I want to hear this argument of yours. This guy has spent your entire contract with him screwing you and taking ten percent for the honor."

"Twelve-and-a-half."

"You know you want to open it as much as I do."

Will sat back on his haunches against the side of the bed, all the while staring at the locks of the case.

"Yeah. Yeah. I want to open it as much as you do," he said finally. "There is the problem of the locks, you know."

"Hootie would know how to get them open."

"Yeah, but do you really want to tell him?"

"No, just tell him you've got a locked case that you need to get open. How would he do it?"

"Maybe. Maybe," Will whispered, lost in thought. His mind was working on something and taking him someplace, but leaving him no idea as to where that might be. He continued to stare, first at the ochre shag carpet, then at the locks, then at the blank black-green of the TV screen, then at the locks, then at his pants, piled onto a chair in the corner, then at the locks, then at his pants, then at the locks, then at his pants. His pants. He stared at his pants as if they might talk back to him and unscramble the thought that refused to come to the front of his brain.

"Christ in a Chrysler!" Will shouted, jumping to his feet, losing his balance in a wobbly leap to the chair. He grabbed his pants and scrambled to push his hands into the pockets, first the left, then the right, looking for a specific memory amid the nickels, dimes, and scraps of paper that lived there.

"What the...."

"This—this—this ..." Will screamed, yanking his right hand free and pushing the key into her face.

"Take it easy, for god's sake," Cheryl soothed. "What are you talking about?"

"Leonard. Leonard," Will wheezed in his excitement. "On the stairs. When he was being hauled down the stairs by your uncles. In the confusion, he pushed this into my hand. He gave me this."

"What did he say?"

"Christ," Will whispered, eyes wide, "I don't remember. Jesus. I don't remember. But this key. This case key. This bike case key. Man. Do you ... what do you ... it's gotta."

"Only one way...."

"To find out," he said, finishing her sentence.

They nodded at each other silently. Will stepped over to the case and knelt beside Cheryl in front of it. He reached out his hand and fit the key into the case lock. He took a breath, let it out and turned. Nothing. He made a face, then turned in the opposite direction and felt the lock begin to turn under his hand, releasing the draw on the latch. He worked his way down the locks on the case, then turned to Cheryl.

"Ready?"

She nodded. "Ready."

Will reached for the center latch.

"Ready?"

"I dunno," she answered, a catch in her voice. "What if we find something dead in here?"

"You read too much cheap fiction," he responded, his voice without a shred of confidence. "There's nothing dead in here by any stretch of the imagination. It's probably dirty clothes."

"Pretty heavy dirty clothes."

"Really dirty. Maybe. But nothing dead."

"Nothing dead. You're sure?"

"Nothing dead. I'm sure," he nodded frantically, the bouncing of his head nothing more than an overtly physical attempt to convince himself of something he had no idea to be true.

"Okay."

Will reached again toward the center butterfly latch and gave it a turn. The case lid popped up, then stopped, caught by the two outer latches. Will and Cheryl leaned down and freed the two butterflies. As they leaned back the lid popped up perhaps a third of the way. Will pushed it all the way up and into the screen of the TV set.

They had been wrong.

Dead wrong.

There was, indeed, something dead in the case.

Ben Franklin.

Lots and lots of little Ben Franklins.

And he had been dead one damned long time.

Will and Cheryl sat silently staring at the carefully packed stacks of one-hundred-dollar bills for a very long time, until Cheryl finally broke the spell the money had cast upon them.

"Tell me, sport," she whispered, "you buying dinner?"

CHAPTER ELEVEN:

NIGHT FALLS IN BEDLAM

THE MOUNTAIN HAD GROWN QUIET OVER THE PAST HALF-HOUR AS dusk began to settle in, crowds grew thin, shadows grew long, and the cyclists and fans began to retire to hotels and bars and restaurants.

Hootie Bosco sat on the floor of the step van, leaning back, feet extended, trying to find the balance point of his butt. He ignored the crowds walking past and staring quizzically inside the van, and held his focus on a point, about two-thirds of the way up the mountain, a slice of orange plastic safety netting that, from this point of view, anyway, wouldn't hold back a kid on a trike, let alone a hurtling cyclist on a 24-pound rolling bullet. He leaned farther back, looking like a low-slung "V" made out of Jell-O, his legs and upper torso shaking, almost imperceptibly, with the strain of balancing.

He was thinking of nothing, which, in turn, helped him think of everything. For some reason, clearing his mind made whatever was in there brighter, fresher, more refined and defined, easier to judge, easier to deal with, easier to find in the mess that was his head.

Most people would see it as nothing more than elaborate screwing around, but he saw it as something more like yoga. Find your focus, find your center, find your … "Shit!"

Caught under the legs, Hootie Bosco found himself tossed upside down and backward, his head slamming against the floor, the side of his skull pinched by the business end of a loose derailleur attempting to gouge a chunk out of his hairline.

Luckily, all it caught was dreadlock.

Hootie rose up and cursed, bending his head to the side as if it would just naturally free up the component from his hair. It didn't, and he pulled and twisted and played with the metal until it broke free, taking a snatch of long hairs with it.

"Are you about done?" came a voice from outside the van.

Hootie sat up and stared at the little woman, less than half of her rising up over the lip of the step van.

"That's not a very nice thing to do," Hootie said, trying, without success, to hold onto the last few moments of his transcendental high. He smiled, without a lick of sincerity. The woman did not return it.

"I have no time for such foolishness."

"What foolishness?"

"Your game with your legs and head in the air."

Hootie examined her carefully, quickly recalling their earlier verbal sparring, and thought of a direction that might twist her tail just a bit before saying, "Well, you don't need to kneel to pray."

"What?"

"I said," Hootie whispered, leaning close to her tight, little face, "that you don't need to kneel to pray."

She raised her cudgel almost as a cross before her in defense against the demon himself. "You blaspheme!"

Hootie smiled to himself. Oh, this one. This one was easy.

"How do I blaspheme? I pray, in an unorthodox position that, rather than showing humility before God, shows supplication. What in the name of heaven, is so wrong with that?"

"It's not right," was all that Marjorie Stump could reply.

"Ah, it's not right. Which means that Buddha is not right. Nor Mohammed. Nor the Torah. Nor the Koran. Nor any of the great prophets or their books or their people. Only you. You are the only one who is right. Only you know the perfect way."

Marjorie rose to the bait and lifted herself to her full height. Even though it wasn't much, her strength of personality made it enough to seem impressive.

"Yes," she said, simply.

"That, my dear," Hootie replied, moving forward and sitting down to cast his legs over the edge of the van, "is the cardinal sin of pride."

"Wha...."

"And beware most of all the sin of pride," he intoned, "for it enters within the soul as the serpent within the garden, unseen, unheard, until overcome is the heart of the servant of the Lord."

Marjorie Stump stared at him, her mouth open in silent, unheard argument.

Hootie stared at her for a moment, his face a mask of intent and silent redemption, before shouting "Poof!" and slapping his hands together, causing Marjorie Stump to jump back a good three feet from the edge of the van.

"Oh," she shouted, angrily, "oh! That was ... oh ... that was horrible!" She raised the heavy blackthorn cane again and advanced on Hootie Bosco.

Hootie put up a finger.

"Don't you dare, lady," he said, quietly, "don't you dare. You interrupted my meditation. It would be no different if I set off fireworks in the middle of Mass. Don't you dare threaten me because I got back at you."

"You are ... you are...."

"I am Hootie Bosco. And you are?" He put down his hand and sat back, leaning against the air as if held by an invisible recliner chair.

She took a deep breath, and, with great effort of will, lowered the stick.

"I ... am ... Marjorie Stump."

"I gather. One of the local constabulary told me all about you and your lap dog." He nodded in the direction of Kelvin, standing off in the gathering dusk.

"Why would they do that?"

"Because I asked them," Hootie said, matter-of-factly. "I like to know, Miz Stump, who is snipping spokes on my bicycles in order to discover why. Why and who lead to what, when and where, which, I figure, puts me ahead of your little game."

"My game?"

"I figure you're your own form of eco-terrorist, playing little monkey wrenches wherever and whenever you can, harassment, mainly, in the hopes of causing whatever trouble you can in an effort to protect the mountain and valley you've come to see as your own from the dull and mindless march of progress."

He sat forward, easily, and watched her eyes widen as she prepared a response.

"Logging isn't big around here, so you wouldn't spike trees. But you would wrench consumers, wouldn't you? Loosen bindings? Sugar in the gas tank? Or is it just the corporation? I'll bet you like to torch mountaintop ski buildings, don't you? Do you go that far?" He smiled. "A signal fire in the middle of the night that can be seen nationwide as a warning to corporate developers and the ski community: Vail is under attack. Vail is off-limits. Vail is mine."

Marjorie Stump stared, silently, for a moment, before smiling in return and whispering, "All things are possible to GOD." She admitted nothing, but her demeanor suggested proof of ownership.

"Yes. Yes. Very good," she nodded, in the way of a teacher. "Yes, that's it, I suppose. Yes. But, you are wrong in one aspect, sir. This is not progress and this is not a game."

"Don't fool yourself, sister," Hootie said, snatching a shop rag to wipe his hands before sliding to the ground and leaning over her for emphasis, "it's all a game."

"I...."

"What can I do you for? You and your little pal?" he said, suddenly, cocking his head in the direction of Kelvin, changing the subject dramatically and once more throwing her off balance.

"I am...."

"Yeessss," Hootie teased, "Iiii aaaammmm...."

Marjorie Stump snorted in defiance, and her eyes grew wide as she forced herself back on track.

"I am looking for somebody."

"And that somebody would be?"

"Somebody named Ross. Do you know him?"

"Do I know who?" he asked with a smile.

"Do you know Ross?"

"First name or last name?"

"Last name I think. Why?"

"Because I know a lot of Rosses—first name," Hootie mused, "went to school with some, did some Army time with another few, even knew a rider or two named Ross—first name."

"Here," Marjorie pushed, leaning forward toward his face, "do you know any here?"

"Here?" Hootie said, raising his eyebrows and gently pushing her out of his safe bubble of space. "No. I don't know any here. No Ross—first name."

Marjorie settled back, disappointed and tired of the games this aging hippie was playing with her mind.

"Let's move on, Kelvin," she said sharply, looking at Hootie with disgust as she turned.

Hootie sat forward and said one word that stopped Marjorie in her tracks. "Why?"

She didn't answer, but, then again, she didn't move either.

"Why?" Hootie continued, "Why Ross? Why now? Why him?"

She turned quickly, so quickly that Hootie was taken by surprise at the suddenness of the move.

"So you do know him."

"No. Didn't say that. I merely asked a question and...."

"You do. You do know him."

"Why?"

"I have a question for him," was all that Marjorie Stump would offer.

The two stood staring at each other for a long moment, before she turned and walked away. Now, she was playing with him.

"That's it?" Hootie called after her. "One lousy question and you fall apart—one lousy chorus of 'I don't care'?"

"Yes, in a way. I haven't got time for games, mister...."

"Bosco."

"Bosco. I ... like the drink, Bosco?"

"Like the drink, Bosco."

"I haven't got time for games, mister ... uh, Bosco. I'm looking for Ross, last name, because I have some information that might be of use to him about a friend of his—a friend of his that has disappeared into the ether."

"Why do you think Will would care?"

She smiled.

"Well, I'm sure Will—Ross—will be happy to know where his friends are, especially one friend that meant so much to him by the message he passed on."

Hootie cursed himself silently without taking the look of distinct unconcern off his face. "I don't doubt that. Ross seems concerned about his friends."

"Aren't we all?"

"Yes," Hootie replied, "aren't we all?" He reached out his hand to her. "Give me the message, I'll make sure he gets it."

"No, I don't think so," Marjorie sighed. "This was one from a friend who prefers to remain nameless. One I prefer to give him myself."

"Oh, okay." Hootie nodded and turned back into the van. Her fish getting away, Marjorie Stump leaned forward and recast her line.

"On the other hand, perhaps you can help me help find him … and … in a way, you help him."

Hootie reappeared from the gloom and looked at Marjorie Stump carefully. He then glanced over toward Kelvin Stump, then back to Marjorie. Marjorie to the mountain. He stared at the green hillside for a long time before he finally said, "No, I think you're right. You're right. A private message from a friend should be delivered clean. Telling me would put too many fingerprints on it. So, go ahead. Let him know."

"So, where do I find him?"

Hootie Bosco thought for a moment, then shook his head. "Don't know. Not my day to watch him."

Her expression didn't change. Marjorie Stump stared at Hootie, but no muscle betrayed her anger. Finally, she nodded and turned.

"Very well, Mr. Bosco, if, in fact, that is your name. I'm thinking that the police would have a very interesting time examining this truck later on for contraband. Anonymous calls can cause a lot of trouble."

Hootie nodded.

"Don't I know it. Don't I know it."

He nodded, his head shaking down, until all Marjorie and Kelvin could see were dreadlocks shaking back and forth, slowly, quietly. When he raised his head, Hootie Bosco was laughing.

"Do your worst, Madame de Farge. For I already know anonymous. And the Vail constabulary will know as soon as they drop by. So do it. Call. Write. Stop by in person. But don't threaten me, lady. I've been threatened by the best and have seen hell from the ninth ring up. Don't threaten me."

"Or me," Marjorie said, her eyes locked on Hootie's face, her anger reaching a point of no return. She could feel the money, the possibilities of the money, the chances to serve her Mother slipping away. She glanced around her quickly, then, seeing few about, nodded to her son.

"Kelvin...."

Without a word, the human totem pole lumbered forward and grabbed Hootie Bosco by the wrist, squeezing the bones to the point that Hootie dropped a bit to his side and flinched.

"Mr. Bosco, it's a simple question. Where can I find Ross? Will Ross?"

"I tell you ... I tell you...."

Suddenly, a silver pole shot out of Hootie Bosco's left hand and into Kelvin Stump's body, just above the stomach. The weight and force of the blow, along with the complete surprise of it, knocked the wind out of Stump and dropped him back a step. The silver pole blurred up toward his face and, with what felt like a flick of light, Kelvin Stump felt his nose turn to mush.

"Ow, God! Jesus God Christ shit goddamn!" He dropped Hootie's wrist as both his hands flew up to his shattered nose.

Without thought, Marjorie Stump said, "Don't curse." Given the situation, with Kelvin trying to push the snot and blood back into his face, Hootie smiled, sadly. This woman, who showed more concern for a blade of grass than for the pain of her son, was a true piece of work.

Hootie turned to Marjorie and held up the 32-inch box-end wrench he had picked up at a Santa Fe flea market for two dollars and one of Bobby J's old amateur jerseys.

"You know, people made fun of this," he said, admiring the dull silver finish of the outrageously large tool, "said I'd never need the thing in a million years. But I said, shucks, you'll never know when you come across a really big nut."

He turned and smiled.

"Know what I mean, Marjorie?"

"My nothe. My goddamned nothe!" Kelvin cried, the blood seeping through his fingertips and palms and spreading across his chin. He pulled his hands away, and, suddenly enraged by the sight of his own blood, took a full step toward Hootie.

"Kelvin!" Marjorie shouted. Kelvin stopped, within a short step and arm's reach of Hootie Bosco and the silver wrench.

Hootie merely smiled, never moving, never flinching, never raising the wrench off his legs where it now rested comfortably.

"Look, pal," Hootie whispered, "I'm not much for listening to my mommy anymore. Drives her crazy, but that's life. On the other hand, in this situation," he nodded toward Marjorie Stump, "I'd listen to her. Otherwise, you're going to be walking home with a useless wing and a mouthful of bloody Chiclets."

Kelvin merely hyperventilated, squeezing his fingers together as he did so.

"I know. You want to kill me. But believe me, pal, you try and you will ache for weeks." Hootie smiled without warmth.

Kelvin Stump reached for his nose, wiped more of the blood away, turned and stalked past his mother. Marjorie Stump watched him go and then looked back at Hootie Bosco.

"You shouldn't have done that. Kelvin has a long memory."

"Yeah, well," Hootie said, leaning over and sliding the wrench back into a black vinyl sleeve against the wall of the truck, "so do elephants, but I've never worried about them, either. Tell him to stay the hell away from me and this van and my people."

"Your people? Like Will Ross?"

"Jesus, you don't give up, do you lady?" Hootie shook his head and turned back into the van.

"Is he in town, that's all I ask," the angry little woman called after him.

"Is he in town, I don't know," Hootie said, jumping down and lifting a last workstand into the back of the van, "but—if he was—I wouldn't tell your sorry fat ass."

"I think that's rude."

"You think right." Hootie pulled the canvas strap that lowered the back gate of the van. It hit the bottom of the step with a hollow "boom" that signaled to those in the know the end of another day on the mountain. Hootie Bosco was the first to open and the last to close. Everyone else was already high or naked or a combination of the two.

He snapped the heavy-gauge lock in place, pocketed the keys, and turned to leave.

"By the way, ma'am," he said, quietly, "don't fuck with my truck. If I find even the paint scratched tomorrow morning, I'll come looking for you with local law enforcement in hand."

"Don't curse at me."

"Don't fuck with me, simple as that. You or bonehead Charlie."

"Kelvin. He has a name, Kelvin," she said with as much dignity as she could muster.

"Really? We had one of his refrigerators when I was a kid. 'Night now." He turned with a final glance at the figure holding his nose in the growing darkness of the distance and turned toward town. Within a few steps he was on the brick walk leading down Wall Street through construction to Gore Creek to Bridge and, finally, to his hotel. He walked without looking back, though he knew, by the feeling that creeped over his shoulders, that the two were either watching him or following. Maybe he'd walk into the parking structure for a minute before stepping into his hotel. While it shouldn't be difficult to find him, there was no need, Hootie figured, in making it too easy for Mama Stump and her angry, smokestack son.

He picked up his pace and turned this way and that through the Bridge Street construction, darted into the parking structure and picked up his pace, changing floors twice, walking the length of the quickly emptying transportation center and wondered what he would tell Will and Cheryl when he got back to the hotel.

No matter how you sliced it, these two would be difficult to explain.

※

KELVIN STUMP PLAYED WITH HIS NOSE FOR A FEW MOMENTS, THE BLEEDING now stopped, the pain subsiding into a dull ache. He tweaked it. It wasn't broken, though the snot and blood had congested him to the point that he sounded like a forties pug after three rounds with the champ.

"Shou I fowwoe him?" Kelvin asked, watching Hootie Bosco disappear through a construction zone and into Vail Village.

"No, let him go."

"He know where da money is."

Marjorie Stump nodded and smiled at her son. "So do we, Kelvin, so do we?"

"Like helw," he snapped, his nose still smarting from the wrench, the pain suddenly forgotten in a new blow to the side of his knee by his mother's cudgel. He fell to the ground holding one knee, one nose and making painful little snorting sounds.

She looked at him without compassion.

"Don't curse."

She stepped over him, which was more like a hop because of his size, and walked to the edge of the sidewalk leading to Wall Street or Bridge Street or any other way into town.

"We may not know where this Ross fellow is, but we do know where this Bosco fellow stays."

Kelvin mewed softly in the background, which Marjorie took to mean "How?" and answered accordingly, snapping her fingers madly as if to recover some long, lost memory.

"A program. I saw a program for this event. And I was surprised because, and I remember this, because each team had its hotel listed. I was surprised because of their greed and need for publicity. And that … greed and desire for publicity and a free room means that they will announce for us where Mr. Bosco is staying. And, since he does know our Mr. Ross, there is an excellent chance that he is staying at the same hotel. Or, somewhere near by. Perhaps he's a teammate. Perhaps a friend. Perhaps a fornicator living with someone in a state of sin.

"Whatever. There is time and there is no need to run and follow him. Let's take care of your nose, shall we, Kelvin?"

She reached out her arm to her son, who stared at her with a hard, cold light that actually frightened Marjorie Stump. She hesitated, a state generally unknown to her, and drew back her arm. Kelvin rolled to the side and balanced himself, pushing himself back onto his knees, favoring the right, then onto his haunches, then, finally, up to his full height. His face was a mass of dark, dried blood, his hands as well, his fingertips covered with grass and dirt that had stuck to the blood from his nose.

Marjorie stepped up to him defiantly, in no way ready to allow him to challenge her authority. But this time, in his eyes, she saw nothing but the dull and slavish Kelvin that she had always known. The flash of hatred she had seen, so clearly, had gone, if, in fact, it had ever existed at all.

The last of the sun took the last comfort of the September day with it. A chill forced Kelvin to shudder and Marjorie to turn up the collar of her windbreaker.

She reached out her hand to her son.

"Let's go clean up your face, dear. We have time to find the money."

Kelvin nodded and began to walk behind her, one or two steps, as they skirted town in a journey home.

Nothing passed between them. And yet, Kelvin kicked himself silently for allowing so many people to make such a fool of him in one, short, September afternoon.

This was his money. His future. It would carry his name.

Never again, he thought to himself. Never again would she take anything from him, his money, his future, his dignity.

Never again.

He had hidden it all so well for so long. Perhaps now was the time to reveal it and destroy her. Bring her and GOD and her dreams of environmental conquest to their knees.

His face and knee continued to throb, one beat of pain just slightly behind the other.

Never again.

The pair walked quietly down Vail Road, nothing said between them, the new darkness of the evening padding their steps and cloaking them from the eyes of those rushing without pause, without conviction, without goal toward an overpriced evening of empty joy.

✿

OLVERIO CANGLIOSI RAN HIS THUMBNAIL OVER THE GAPS IN HIS TEETH, SETTING up a click-click-click within his head. Deep in thought, he didn't realize that the same click-click-click that brought him a measure of transcendental peace, was driving Stanley Szyclinski absolutely stark raving mad.

"Look, friend," Stanley cut through Ollie's random thought, "would you please, for the love of God, stop it?"

"Stop what?"

"That thing with your teeth."

"What thing with my teeth?"

"That thing with your teeth that's making me nuts!?"

"Fine," Ollie shrugged, "I'll stop doing whatever it is I'm doing, even though what I'm doing is really nothing."

"It may be nothing, but it's enough."

The two settled back into the chairs in the lobby of their small hotel in Lionshead and stared out the windows. While people continued to surge around them, on their way to rooms or restaurants, the two continued to stare and chat, quietly, in a verbal shorthand that sounded to the passerby like nothing more than endless touristy chit-chat of older businessmen waiting for their wives to appear for an early dinner reservation.

"So, what do you think?"

"He dumped it. Cut and run."

"No grab?"

"Who?"

"The big guy running after him?"

"Maybe. But that's a long shot."

"So where's the go bag?"

"The half-acre in Leo's duffel? Good question."

"Hmm." Stanley stretched out his legs and arms. "What about the rest?"

"Stuffed away."

"Where?"

"Ha," Ollie cackled, making a nine-year-old girl across the lobby jump and then smile at him out of embarrassment. He smiled back and spoke without turning to Stan. "Could be anywhere."

"With the big man?"

"We were there too soon."

"Not soon enough, for old Leonard, anyway."

"Hmm, maybe not. But soon enough. The box didn't get wrestled away."

"Don't think so."

"Hmm."

"Hmm."

"So," Stanley said, after a long pause in which he almost fell asleep, "what's the next step?"

"Well, the nasty part of the job is already done…. Hello, how are you?" Ollie smiled and waved at the dark-haired girl as her father took her hand and walked her toward the front door. "Have a nice evening…. So Mister Genna has to be happy about that, but, as for the money, I suppose we keep looking for somebody with very expensive tastes who looks like he shouldn't have them."

"Who?"

"God in heaven," Ollie sighed, "I don't know." He paused for a moment and stared at the gas fire hissing in the fireplace. "Thing is, Leonard seemed to know that guy on the bike today."

"Which guy on the bike?" Stanley asked.

"The guy on the bike that got in your way."

"Oooh, yes. That one. The one I stepped on."

"Yeah, that one. Cherylann's friend."

"Indeed. It might be time to call on our niece."

"Even if she doesn't want to see us," Ollie said with a touch of sorrow in his voice.

"Even if she doesn't want to see us," Stanley whispered sadly.

The two rose from the easy chairs that Stanley had found to be perhaps the most comfortable he had ever sat in, nodded to a young woman standing in a daze near the door, and stepped out into the street.

"So where to?" Stanley asked.

"Family reunion," Olverio said, simply.

WILL FINISHED HIS SECOND GLASS OF CHAMPAGNE AND SHUDDERED.

"A bit tart?" Cheryl asked absentmindedly.

"Yeah, just a bit," he answered. "I thought the fruit was supposed to cut it."

"You know, you could afford the really good stuff."

"I'm not sure it's all that different."

"I assure you, it is."

"How do you know so much about champagne?"

"I lived in France, remember?"

"So did I," he huffed with dented pride.

"Yes," she said with a laugh, "but I paid attention."

He watched her smile, then turn and stare off into the distance, through the window of the restaurant, and across a courtyard and toward yet another part of the village that lay on the other side of the creek. The evening was drawing to an early close for most. The riders were already returning to rooms in order to rest for the first day of racing.

"So, what's bothering you? The race, the money, my ruining a perfectly good bike?" he asked, doing a little "hot-cha" and spreading his hands in a bad imitation of Jolson.

"Yeah, I suppose," she muttered, distantly. "I need to crash. I need to rest for tomorrow. All that cash sitting in our room doesn't make me any more comfortable. But it's not any of those, really."

"Yeah, so … what?"

"Did you ever get the feeling….?"

"Yeah?"

"That somebody's looking for you?"

"Well, frankly, no," he answered, smiling.

"Well, I do, Will. Tonight. That, plus, none of the stuff I've got going on for the rest of the weekend, or the people I keep running into, are going to make my life any easier."

She lapsed into a sullen silence, pushing the dinner around on her plate without another word.

Will sat silently, searching for just the right thing to say to take the load off her shoulders, make her smile, make the world a better place for her.

"Well, figure it this way," he said, finally, "all you have to do is make it to Monday morning in one piece and you're home free."

She slowly raised her eyes and looked at him with a mixture of fear and dread and absolute loathing for what he had just said.

"That, my dear," she said in a harsh and angry tone, "is exactly what is scaring the living shit out of me."

✳

FEW IN VAIL SLEPT WELL THAT NIGHT.

Hootie Bosco wrestled with dreams of bikes and step vans and mountains of equipment reduced to pieces by short, angry women and their faceless drones. Marshall Reed dreamed of the bike stolen from him by an interloper, while Jeremy Jettmann and Frannie Draa dreamed of each other, millimeters away, locked in each other's arms.

Will drifted off sleeping above a mountain of money and next to a woman radiating a level of performance anxiety that even what he felt to be Olympic-quality sex could not overcome, the world dropping itself upon her shoulders. Stan and Ollie tossed and turned in their separate rooms. Ollie remained disturbed by the hate that he had seen in his niece's face that afternoon, the visage rising up to meet him whenever he closed his eyes, until he finally sat on the end of his bed and watched ancient reruns of "Have Gun Will Travel," drifting off with an infomercial for plastic breast enhancers as his only companion. Stanley, on the other hand, found himself face to face, in a life-and-death struggle, with Buster again. Buster No Knuckles holding a gun to his head and asking for the money, the money, where's the money, Stanley?

Kelvin Stump honked through the inflated horn in the center of his face and dreamed of homes, thousands and thousands of homes, ticky-tacky boxes with perfectly manicured lawns, the dream marred only by the vision of the little man in the blue suit standing off to one side with his hand out, asking quietly for his payment.

Meanwhile, Marjorie, snoring gently in the room above, dreamed of nothing, nothing in the Vail Valley any longer, the sweep of land nothing more than a green turn of the highway, her job finally done, her promise to the Mother of us all finally complete.

And yet, Cheryl, Cheryl Crane, Cherylann Cangliosi, slept worst of all, lost in the three-quarter sleep that she so completely and horribly dreaded, seeing the faces of those she loved and hated wander through her room, her life, the weekend ahead, and her without the ability to wake up and deal with them in any way, shape or form.

All she wanted to do was ride, but all she could do was dread the riding ahead. She had missed a day of practice on both the downhill and cross-country courses by arriving a day late, she had come face-to-face with her past, and caught a glimpse of her uncertain future.

All around her the lights were dim, the world in shades of grey.

The night seemed to last forever.

SATURDAY

CHAPTER TWELVE:

RIDIN'

RACE DAY, THE FIRST DAY OF A WEEKEND SERIES, AS ALWAYS, INVARIABLY, dawned, and dawned crazy. People ignored wake-up calls; officials ran late; equipment that was sitting beside a bed or locked in a step van where someone knew exactly where it would be, someplace safe, developed legs during the night and walked away, finding a cubby hole someplace stupid, where it was not found until just before the first heat, or even until checkout on Monday morning.

Madness reigned, even if you had nothing to do.

"I've got nothing to do," he said from the edge of the bed, his feet brushing the ochre, shag carpet.

"Sit on your money, consider yourself lucky."

Will frowned and rose, saying, "It's not my money" under his breath as he padded his way to the bathroom for his morning toilette. Cheryl stood next to the sink and was already finished, wearing a Haven parachute-cloth training suit.

"Wow, you must have been up early."

"I'm not sure if I stayed up late or got up early."

"Bad night?" he asked, genuinely concerned.

"Not good, I can tell you that," she said with a sigh, brushing an errant strand of hair back onto the top of her head.

"Busy day, today."

"Don't I know it. The downhill is jammed early with every amateur category known to man—I won't be able to get near it before my run. So, I'll work out on the cross-country course a bit, getting a feel for it before the high-end races tomorrow."

"That's a lot. You don't practice day of race, do you?"

"Not usually, but I missed Thursday and only got a couple of runs yesterday. Today we get serious or we go home early. Besides, I can use the workout. Gotta lotta angst." She smiled sadly. "Gotta run."

She leaned over and kissed him perfunctorily on the cheek.

"Big day. I'm outta here."

"Well, wait, give me ten and I'll go with you," he said, suddenly rushing to catch up with her.

"No, no, that's okay. I'm busy the rest of the day, and you've got stuff you probably want to do, so I'll run and catch some chow and get riding. Wanna catch up."

"I love you," he called after her as she stepped into the hall. She stopped, leaned back in and said, "I love you, too. Thanks." Then she closed the door behind her.

Will felt a pang of loss, the sense that he truly was on his own today and he wasn't thrilled with the company. He caught his reflection in the bathroom mirror and stared at the face looking back at him. Who are you today, he wondered. Who have you become?

The questions were asked silently. The reflection offered no answers.

Will shook his head. The Will in the parallel universe did the same.

They both took a deep breath and stripped themselves down, turning on the shower and stepping in without checking the heat.

One scream and some quick adjustments later, and Will had forgotten about the reflection and was busily soaping himself and wondering about the note Hootie Bosco had left shoved under the door last night:

Gotta talk. Lady named Stump looking for you. Watch your back.

That was sure to make a natural paranoid sleep well. What the hell did any of that mean? What was a Stump, and why should he watch his back? Especially here, especially now?

There was only one reason he could think of.

He pondered that thought for a moment, finished his shower, shaved without thinking of, or bothering with, the man in the mirror, covered the nicks with toilet paper sticking plasters, wrapped himself in a towel and stepped out into the room. First things first, he thought: gear up, hide the money, put the "Do Not Disturb" sign on the door, make the bed, and get outside.

Then, it was time to shut up and ride his damn bike.

All the answers were there.

❈

CHERYL, ON THE OTHER HAND, WASN'T SO SURE WHERE THE ANSWERS LAY.

She strode down Bridge Street, early enough that whatever crowds were on hand were thin. She brushed the last few crumbs of bagel off the shelf her breasts had made in the electric blue, gold and white Haven-TW jersey, and took another sip of latté as she walked. The heat of the coffee steamed in the crisp air of the morning, and she could sense the morning embrace of the fog-laden pine forest that surrounded the village. The feel, the smell, the atmosphere of the forest in the middle of town. No wonder people loved the mountains.

She stopped for a moment and pushed the bushel of stress that was her life for the next few days aside: the team, the race, the boyfriend, the uncles, the money, the weekend itself.

Cheryl Crane closed her eyes gently and took a deep breath. The crisp air, cleaner than any she had ever breathed, despite an interstate highway less than half-a-mile away, coursed through her and scrubbed clean her mind, her mood, and even her soul.

Three breaths and the boom of a truck door in the distance, and she was reborn, even if only for a moment.

Colorado. She smiled and opened her eyes.

How could anyone ever possibly leave here?

Hootie was at the truck.

The day had begun.

It was time to ride.

❈

AS THE SOUND OF THE "BOOM" RACED ACROSS THE FLOOR OF THE VALLEY, Olverio Cangliosi cracked open one eye and stared at the ceiling. Only moments before he had been drifting through a world that was warm and secure and of his own making. Now, in the literal blink of an eye, he was back in Vail, in a world that was, at the moment, anyway, completely out of control.

He opened both eyes, wiggled himself upward until he was leaning up against the headboard, and stared across the room.

He was cranky enough that he wanted to lash out, break the rules, piss somebody off just so he could go for them. Smoke, for instance, in his non-smoking room, in his non-smoking hotel.

Rules didn't necessarily matter to a man like him, but he also realized that to break them, at a moment like this, would only draw unnecessary attention to himself and screw up the job even more than it already was.

His job.

Ollie closed his eyes, tucked his chin down onto his chest, and frantically scratched his forehead, trying to make an idea, any idea, leap forward to a spot in his skull where he could get hold of it and make it useful.

It didn't work.

The money was gone. Romanowski was dead. And he and Stanley were at a loss.

They had one more day, perhaps two, to make it work somehow, before they had to return to Detroit and make the call. At least they could say the contract was complete.

That was something.

The problem was, that, in his original spittle-laden phone call, Angelo had seemed just as interested, if not more so, in having the money back as in having Leonard Romanowski stuffed and mounted as an object lesson.

Ollie smiled. Without that seed money, perhaps Angelo was reduced to once again strong-arming little old ladies for nickels, dimes, and the occasional quarter to continue making the payments on that Jersey dump of his, complete with above-ground pool for the kiddies.

He tore a piece of paper off the pad beside the bed, rolled it into a tube and sucked on it, hoping that might start some thought moving. It didn't, but it did give him something to do with his hands.

He stared at a point of nothing across the room and pondered his next move. There wasn't one, but he pondered it anyway.

❧

THREE DOORS DOWN, STANLEY SZYCLINSKI SHAVED QUICKLY, SMILING AT THE
face that smiled back at him from the mirror, both of them whistling a jaunty,
formless tune, both of them unruffled, unlike their partner, by the turn of events
over the past 24 hours. There was always time, he knew, to put the ball back in play,
and even if it didn't go, there was no reason to ruin a perfectly good mood over it.

Sometimes, these things just didn't work out. Sometimes, these things just
didn't play.

Then again, he thought, working the underside of his chin, sometimes the
strangest things played out in the strangest ways with the strangest timing.

You just didn't know.

Until you knew.

✦

FOR MARJORIE STUMP, THE MORNING ROSE AS A CHALLENGE, TO HER BODY, HER
calling, and her future.

It was getting harder to get out of bed each morning. She still awoke, clear-
headed and vital, each day, but there was a stiffness bordering on agony with
each lift, each twist, each move toward the edge of the bed. There was really no
denying it. Her body was giving up the battle. She was on the losing side.

She hated the thought, for there was so much more to do, so much more
to accomplish, so much more to save and protect and shut off from the rest
of the world.

She shuffled to the kitchen of her small, set-apart home and walked out
onto the back porch. She stared across the valley toward the mountain. Already
there was activity, bicyclists, like ants, riding across the face of the mountain,
warming up for the day's events, causing her more trouble and grief.

There was no way to stop them, she thought, pulling herself up with the help
of her cane and feeling the pain slowly seep from her bones. There was no
way to stop them—directly.

She could monkey wrench, she could harass, but nothing would change,
not this weekend, not ever, because of money. With money you could stage
races in Vail. You could make things happen your way. With money, you had

a measure of power.

With money.

And with money, you could stop them.

She nodded and smiled.

With money.

And somewhere, out there, she knew, there could just be a great deal of it with an absentee owner. A great deal of money that she could put to good use. Money that could make her well, by making the world around her well again.

She'd have the money.

She'd have the power.

They'd have to listen to her.

She nodded with a force that surprised even her and thumped the shillelagh heavily on the deck. Twice. Thrice. The impacts rolled through the little house, rattling everything they came upon like a small earthquake or a cheap blender.

THE SHUDDERS OF THE CANE CRASHED OVER KELVIN STUMP IN THREE SMALL waves. His eyes opened and he faced another day.

Unhappily.

The bag of money that should have been his was now under his mother's bed. The $50,000 in cash he had pulled out and squirreled away wouldn't pay for cardboard coasters given where he wanted to go and what he needed to do.

There were demands on a person like him. Loans and partners and a whole other life. He had to make an appearance, be a driving force, but today was Saturday. The office was closed. The banks were closed. There was nothing he could do until Monday.

Monday. By Monday would he still be stuck here, or free to live his new life? It was a life being frustrated by the one he wanted to leave behind.

Quickly, the anger that built up inside him, behind the frustrations, reached a point where he felt a need to lash out, viciously, at whoever and whatever got in his way.

He took a breath. His nose honked, and the dull throbbing pain reasserted itself.

Kelvin Stump slowly released his grip on the sheet and watched the color return to his knuckles.

He convinced himself to relax, to unwind, to wait for the moment, rather than try to force his own hand. The time would come, he thought, the opportunity would present itself, and he would win, if, in fact, he was ready to act.

The time was coming.

The time was now.

CHAPTER THIRTEEN:

THE LION KING

I
T FELT STRANGE TO BE HAULING A LOOSELY PACKED DUFFEL BAG OF HIS OWN gear through the center of Vail. Will was used to the professional squads of Europe, where all he usually had to haul was his own butt toward the starting line. Flunkies and managers, often one and the same, were responsible for getting the parts he needed where he needed them.

But that was road racing. Big teams, big money, big sponsors.

This was mountain biking. And while there was money and there were sponsors and even a few flunkies hanging about, it was much more a self-serve kind of business. Besides, he thought, what right did he have to wish and hope for a valet?

He wasn't on a team.

He wasn't in the game.

He was a hanger on, a boyfriend, no less, following camp like one of Fighting Joe Hooker's patriotic ladies.

He was, in fact, a flunky.

Will sighed and smiled. Welcome to the real world, my friend.

He glanced at his watch as he turned the corner of the step van: 6:59 a.m. Amateur riders, young ones, in their early twenties, to Will's fading eye, were already gathering around the trucks and the base of the Vista Bahn, pawing the ground, laughing too loud, brightening the day with their enthusiasm and a rainbow of corporate and team jerseys bought at a severe markup from mail-order catalogues.

Will laughed in spite of himself. There were at least two Haven road team jerseys in the mix, the jersey he had been wearing less than two months before in the middle of the Tour de France.

"Bring back memories?"

"Huh?" Will shook himself free of the mob scene before him and turned to look at Hootie Bosco, safe inside his step van castle inside the pit area.

Hootie pointed with his thumb at the assembled masses.

"Beginner men. They're first off today. What, I'd bet," he looked at a schedule taped crookedly to an inner wall of the van, "nineteen to twenty-four and then twenty-five to twenty-nine. I think they're all off at eight."

"Memories?"

"Your days as an amateur? Getting there an hour early and pacing? Sizing up the competition? Doing a psyche job on the new kid who doesn't know what he's doing?"

"I don't...."

"Oh, wait," Hootie cackled, nodding, "you didn't do that, right? You never raced as a lowly beginner, did you? You were always on a team."

"Hey, I did," Will answered defensively.

"Well, not like this. You missed something, pal. Believe me. There is nothing quite as isolated and alone as hanging out at a starting line of your first downhill with your one bike, your one jersey, and your one spare tube, stuck in a line of people just like you who are either scared out of their wits or so full of themselves that their egos could apply for statehood, waiting for the timer's wave so they can fly out of the gate at an obnoxious pace, only to bunch up later behind two slow ones and one fast one about the middle of the course and roll down the rest of the mountain like a pack of cartoon dogs."

Hootie smiled a smile that remembered that past.

"There's nothing like it for excitement or adrenaline or sheer, raw fright, my friend. I'm sorry you missed it."

"I'm not sure I did," Will answered, defensively.

"Oh, you got a fright before the gun, that's for sure," Hootie nodded, "but, like I said, you were always on a team. You always had Kenally and your teammates to hang with and joke with and pick at other people with and make sure you had everything ready to go. Not like these poor suckers. They took the end of the week off work just to be up here and hang their ass over the edge with nothing to show for it Monday but road rash, a knocked knee and maybe a case of bottled water as a prize.

"They got nobody to talk to, nobody to hang with, nobody to make sure of much of anything. Man, you talk about guts. They got 'em—in spades."

Will nodded, then turned to Hootie. "You down on teams?"

"Hell, no," Hootie answered. "Teams have paid my way in life. I love teams. I'd be stacking tires in a Firestone warehouse if it wasn't for teams. But these guys," Hootie jerked his head, the dreadlocks twisting with the sudden movement, "these guys are single combat warriors. They're out there alone with no support and little, if any, skill. That's guts. That's nuts."

"And they're the ones who keep the sport alive," Will added.

"No shit," was the best reply that Hootie could come up with.

Will turned his back on the growing crowd of beginners now stretching and warming up for the ride to a start house that was still nearly half-an-hour away. He raked through the random thoughts that filled his brain and finally found what he had wanted to ask when he first stepped up to the van.

"Where's Cheryl?"

"She's out on the cross-country course. Judges weren't thrilled about it, but the organizers knew she had come in late and let her make a run this morning. She said she needed to ride, to get acquainted with it. Made quite an argument...."

"She's good at that."

"And they let her go."

"Think I can get on?"

Hootie barked a laugh.

"No way in God's green earth, pal. She's a registered pro. You're a boyfriend. No offense."

"None taken," he lied.

"What can I do for you, sport?"

"I need my bike."

"Your bike? Your bike?"

"Hey—you said it—I broke it, I bought it."

Hootie Bosco frowned, caught in his own words of the day before.

"Look, I've already caught hell from Marshall Reed about that this morning. He's convinced that the Colnago was his bike. Hell, I ought to just let you two kill each other over the damned thing and send it off to some bicycle rescue group and be done with...."

"Look, Hootie, I'm sorry, I—I just want to ride. Have you got something?"

Bosco sighed and nodded, "Yeah, I got a yellow Colnago back here that ain't doin' anything." He turned and stepped back into the nether reaches of the van, banged around for a moment and stepped forward with the beauty.

"Set up for your new shoes and everything."

"You're amazing," Will said with a grin. "How'd you know?"

"You bet your ass I am. She told me."

Will took the bike and stepped carefully over the seat. It fit him beautifully, to the point where, even in the midst of all the activity and the race preps, the literally hundreds of riders and bikes now milling about, people stopped and stared at the sight of this man with this bike at this point in time.

Hootie pointed behind him, over his shoulder, away from the mountain.

"You're not going to want to be anywhere near any of this. I'd suggest some of the stuff on the other side of the highway. Off," he squinted into the morning sun, "that way. There's a nice trail or two leading up to the top of Old Vail Pass."

"Old Vail Pass."

"Old Vail Pass. It's like two-lane pioneer shit that dead-ends at the top of the mountain. Very little traffic. Nobody drives up there anymore. Just ride around. Find a trail. Explore. That's what this is all about."

"But do it...."

"Away from here. You get caught up in this shit and it's going to make your adventure on that volcano in France look like Toot's Birthday Party."

Will laughed in spite of himself. He had no idea what Hootie Bosco was talking about. He nodded and pushed off toward Hanson Ranch Road, away from the course and the activity of the day.

"Just head for the frontage road next to the highway and turn right. You'll get there eventually," Hootie called after him.

Will waved an absentminded hand and brought it back quickly to the handlebar. The front wheel was wobbling, not out of any mechanical problem but out of the very simply fact that Will still wasn't used to the bike. Maybe a ride, a long ride with some easy trails, would settle them both out.

One could only hope.

Hootie Bosco watched as Will Ross rode off into the distance, finally lost in the crowd. It was only then that a thought leapt into his head like a horny salmon desperate to breed upstream.

"Damn," he thought, snapping his fingers, "that woman. I wanted to talk to him about that woman."

He stared for a second, then shrugged and went back to the business at hand. He had taught himself not to be concerned with much of anything in life that wasn't under his direct control at any one moment in time.

This morning was busy for everybody else, but not for him. He had prepared, and his people didn't go off until this afternoon.

This morning was Amateur Night at the Bar None Ranch.

And while he enjoyed watching it, in the end, he wanted absolutely nothing to do with it.

❖

CHERYL HAD EXPECTED SOMETHING DIFFERENT, SOMETHING TOUGHER AND less fun on the first of the three cross-country loops out of Vail. She had heard stories of the course having a tortuous climb pretty much right off the bat, but this, winding across a few paved roads, then onto hard-packed single track next to the creek, passing close to a shopping area, didn't seem bad at all. This was the course, there was no doubt about that, everything was marked with enough flags to equip a small army, but, frankly, it didn't seem like a world championship course. Over a small bridge and through what appeared, anyway, to be set up as a feed zone, and, suddenly, it did seem a little more difficult, not like the advertisements, necessarily, all the pre-race gas she had heard, but certainly enough to put the strain on her legs and lungs.

She shifted gears and dug into it. The single-track section that drew her up the ski slope looked new, but was engineered at an odd angle that cut the rate of climb significantly. It was tough, no doubt, but this was no gut buster. At least not yet.

The track cut into a grove of aspens, shining green and gold in the morning sun, and she instinctively cut her speed, her mind focused on watching, seeing, memorizing the course before her, rather than thinking about the week behind or the beauty of her surroundings. It started out so fresh and new, then yesterday and … a root system snaked across the road at odd angles and forced her to cut up high on the bank of the trail to roll past. Keep your mind on your game, she thought, keep it here. Ignore the world around you. Forget looking, forget thinking, just ride … shit.

The turn had come up quickly, almost blind, surprising her and leaving Cheryl blinking her eyes hard with her heart banging in her chest like a twenty-one-gun artillery salute at Eisenhower's funeral.

She popped out onto a wide, almost double-track climb and shifted gears, cursing herself and taking her penance in the burn of her legs and lungs. If she didn't pay attention, she knew, this was just a workout. Nothing more. If she didn't remember the course today, it would be just as blank to her tomorrow as if she had just stepped off the bus from Detroit.

She popped over the top and began to ride the rolls across the Lionshead ski slope. She was already heading down and back toward the village. This, she thought, was nothing. A little more than three miles and hardly any altitude gain or difficult climbing.

Either she was really good or this was really easy. Even the amateurs were going to have fun with this, she thought.

She picked up her pace and buttoned down her mind, keeping her eyes and focus at three different points ahead of her. Far, middle, close aboard, anticipating any and all changes in terrain or pitch.

This was cinchy, she thought, and settled back with the ease of someone about to get a rude lesson in course design.

It came sooner than she expected.

❧

WILL HAD SPED ALONG THE FRONTAGE ROAD BESIDE I-70, MARVELING AT THE clean bite of the air and the showy magnificence of the homes built into and up along the base of the mountain. There was money to be had here, and he idly pondered how he could get his hands on some of it.

Then again, he had been the one sleeping on top of a bicycle box of cash the night before, so his level of envy was nowhere near as high as it possibly could have been. Then again, holding money for someone was nothing like having it in the bank, at your disposal.

Sure was nice to look at, though.

Then came the doubt.

What was it there for? Why had he dumped it with him? Where was Leonard now and was he okay and what was the deal with Cheryl's uncles, the comedy twins? And would they now come looking for him, Cheryl or no Cheryl?

"Damn!" he shouted to the mountain air and slapped his right hand on the grip. Hootie. That note. He wanted to ask about that note. For the life of him, at this moment, he couldn't remember any of it other than a woman and wanting to see him.

Well, it could wait. Given who he was, where he was, and what he was doing, it couldn't really be all that important.

Will shook his head and shifted gears. Keep on the road. Keep on the bike. He picked up the pace, cut under the highway and took a small paved road off the main, heading upwards toward who knew where.

He pedaled for his life.

❧

CHERYL CRANE HELD ON FOR HERS.

The first of three loops on the cross-country course cut back into town, where it picked up the start of the second loop. To get into Vail, you had to go down. And to go down in a ski town, you had to go down stairs, these, called Bahama Mama Falls. Cute, she thought, angrily, as she shifted her weight to keep her balance and tried to control her speed.

"Goddamn it, goddamn it," was all that was spitting out between her teeth as she fought her way down the steps, hit the corner in pedestrian traffic— which, like a school of fish, parted, turned, and broke for her approach. She made a hard right turn, and began the second loop of the cross-country course, the Village Loop. The dirt road climb took her through what appeared to be yet another feed zone. Now, it seemed the climbing got serious. The entire first loop, in fact, acted more like a warm-up, adding distance and building confidence before the serious grind began. And it was a grind, long and steady on the climb, leading into and out of trees on fairly easy dirt, few surprises, but, suddenly, a lot of work, passing a pond on her left which gave the track a soft and soggy feel that she knew would be sheer mud by the time she got back to it 26 hours from now. The climb continued, her speed fell. Crossing another slope, leading into a hard right turn back across the face, she took a quick drink of water and felt it fight the burn back down her throat. The sweat and the effort were starting to take their toll. The burn in her lungs, as she gasped for what little oxygen lived at this altitude, wouldn't recede. The sweat of effort and fear began to pour off her now, forcing her to run a thumb under the forehead edge of her helmet to keep the sudden downpour out of her eyes.

She made a left and caught a section of dirt road that eased her breathing a bit, maybe half a kilometer, then turned hard again into hell's half-acre, a brutal piece of technical single track called Garnsey's Grind.

And she was still climbing. Climbing and burning and focusing no longer far ahead, but at the base of her front tire, just trying to see the next obstacle, just trying to force the next turn of the crank.

Just one more. Just one more. Just one more.

Without realizing it, her world was a million miles away.

She was alone on the mountain, fighting for her balance, desperately struggling for another five feet, three, one foot.

Just one more. Just one more.

❖

IT FELT LIKE WILL WAS GOING STRAIGHT UP NOW.

He was in the smallest rings he could find on the bike, the gears that he had, at one time, laughingly called Geek Gears, but he wished he could go still farther down. He was spinning like a madman, watching his balance, his pace, and the trail ahead. He had wandered off the abandoned two laner and was now exploring, passing through a world of rustling aspen, all on the verge of changing colors, past clumps of mutated scrub pine and a few lodgepole pines. He had no idea where he was, but that was, as Hootie might say, the point of it all.

He only knew that he was up from where he had begun, still going up like a turtle out of purgatory, and wishing he had decided to have more breakfast that morning.

He was already running on empty and, yet, he was still running. The effort and the pace, the basic rhythm of it all, began, slowly, to bring his focus to a point within himself, where he saw the trail and felt the gear, but dropped away from the ride, the effort, and the mountain. The sounds of the day dissolved into an internal monologue, where the only thing heard was the boom of his own breathing, the only thought felt, the click of the internal metronome, the click click click of the next sweep, the next turn of the crank.

Tuck it down. Bring it around. Tuck it down. Bring it around.

His day, his night, his week were all behind him. Spiritual, moral, and ethical thoughts were somewhere lower on the mountain, along with career plans, his mother asking what he would do with his life, how he would live, what he would do. They were all miles away, stuffed in a duffel bag in the back of a step van with his tennis shoes. Money, lots and lots of American green cash money, was miles away, the questions that needed to be asked about it sitting with it, waiting for the return of Leonard Romanowski, thoughts of whom were even farther away at this particular moment in time.

Will had found the pace. Will had found the rhythm. Will had found the bike.

Will had found peace.

After months of struggle and injury and rehabilitation, he had found the spot again, that elusive place in the world of his own making, where the moment, the machine, and the man were all one and the same.

Which made the flat tire come as a complete surprise.

❖

CHERYL PASSED ANOTHER POND ON HER LEFT AS SHE CRESTED THE COURSE and dropped back down the mountainside. She popped out of the woods and picked up the dirt service road on the mountain, fully intending to pick up speed. She didn't. She merely tried to catch her breath and replace the fluids that she was losing with the flood of sweat that was coming out of every pore of her body. She gasped for breath between gulps of water, finishing off the bottle before she turned back into the woods. This was bad, she thought. She'd have to really hydrate herself or she'd never make it to the third loop of the first lap.

She laughed at her own ego.

Oh, yeah. That first loop. What a cinch. So cinchy. Shit, damn, it caught me napping.

She took another gulp of air and picked up speed and turned off the road again into the heavily wooded single track. She left the thoughts of the loop, her ride, her exhaustion, and her dehydration behind her on the service road, focusing on the single track, the obstacles, the tight turns back and forth. Her mind desperately catalogued each and every turn, each and every root and rock and tree limb determined to mangle a tire or rim or fork and throw her out and over the barricades and safety netting and woolly bags into the deep woods where her body would never be found.

She popped up and over the service road, eight full feet of smooth sailing, and dropped back into the woods, her focus lifting for a second, maybe two, then locking down again inside the forest that began to fly past her with a thwup, thwup, thwup as the speed built up, a combination of her gearing and the downward slope. She slowed instinctively as she crossed the service road again, dropped back into the woods and continued heading down the slope at an oblique angle.

Signage and memories of the race bible crowded into her consciousness and screamed for her to graunch on the binders and bring herself to a stop. She didn't, but rolled forward slowly, left onto a service road and then up to a ridge, where something more material shouted at her to fully stop. The track led over a cliff on a five-foot drop and into a steep gully.

She shook her head and tried to stop both her hyperventilation and the banging in her chest. If she had ridden forward as she had been, she would have been out of the race. Maybe for good.

She stepped off the bike, slung it over her shoulder, and slid down the rock face toward the gully track. It wasn't professional, it wasn't stylish, it wasn't happenin', but it got her down the hill in one piece and back on the bike. The course shot down the gully into a section of plastic barricade netting, which she knew she'd see from the other side in just a minute. She flew along the barricades to pick up speed again, then made a hard left back into the technical single track, which, after what she had just been through, didn't seem all that technical or difficult to her.

That, she told herself, was why you ride a course. You get to know it. You get to feel it. You program out the fear and the sense of the unknown. The race bible didn't give you that. You had to see it yourself.

She cut under the Vista Bahn chair lift, came through the chute and took another hard left back onto the streets of town, onto the final loop, the Golden Peak. She emerged from town and looked back quickly toward the pit area and the Haven-TW truck.

Hootie Bosco stood in the back, smiling and waving a red shop cloth like a New Bedford wife waving a doily at her departing husband's ship.

Cheryl laughed despite her exhaustion, turned to the right, and headed back up the mountain.

※

WILL LEANED BACK ALONG THE RIDGE THAT FORMED THE UPPER PORTION OF the trail and reveled in the beauty of the day and the place. A breeze, gentle, and ever so close to autumn brisk, rustled the leaves of the aspen trees around him and almost lulled him to sleep.

There was a calm and beautiful peace here, a peace that allowed a soul to let go of its demons and pressures and small, human thoughts. He looked up at a sky that was almost too blue, too beautiful to be real. The color shocked him and made him squint, forcing him to drop the sunglasses back to the bridge of his nose. The sound ranged between gentle and non-existent, from the occasional sound of leaves singing in a breeze to the sound of silence, that hum inside your ear that told you there was no sound to be heard.

He had broken free.

This, he thought, was the place to be. He took another deep breath and let it out slowly. This was the place to live.

He sat up quickly before he could drift off and blinked his eyes quickly.

No naps. No naps now. Got a flat to fix.

He stripped off the Haven-TW fanny pack that Hootie Bosco had tossed to him before he rolled away from the van, unzipped it, and poked around inside. There was a PowerBar in a flavor he couldn't stomach, a spare, a set of plastic tire irons, and a CO_2 compressed air gun.

He had never seen one of these things, as he had always used pumps. Either that, or he had tossed his wheel to a mechanic who would slap another on and then mysteriously repair the flat out of his sight.

Ah, royalty.

Ah, flunky-dom.

He wiggled an iron between the rim and the tire and stripped it off. Out of practice, perhaps, but it was just like riding a bicycle. Your fingers never quite forgot how to do it.

After he pulled the tube out, returning to a habit years in the making, Will took a moment to check the tire for damage. He poked his finger on a spike of wood, a cross between a wooden nail and what God would make a thorn into if he were in a really bad mood on the third day of creation. Will turned, and pulled it out from the other side.

For as bad as it felt and as much damage as it did, it didn't seem all that frightening once out of the tire and into the sunlight, but the damage was done and the tube was a goner. Will tossed the tube into the fanny pack, pulling out the spare at the same time. He fit it in and, using a tire iron, rolled the tire itself back into place along the rim, taking care not to pinch the tube between the two.

He then fit the compressed air gun to the presta valve and pushed the handle, watching, with surprise, as the tire filled immediately and the valve itself grew icy to the touch.

He popped it off with a smile and couldn't help but say "Hot damn" with a great deal of pleasure.

Toys, he thought, I love the toys that come with this sport.

He fit the finished wheel back into the rear mounts of the bike and wiggled the chain back onto the gears. He checked the alignment of the wheel and tightened down the quick release, then reset the brakes. Leaning the bike along the ridge, he gathered up the tools and spare and expended gas gun and put them back into the fanny pack.

As he stood and stretched and fastened the fanny pack around his waist, he heard a noise up the hill.

He turned his face to the sun and stared passively at the big cat that stood not more than five feet above him.

Damn, he thought, that's great.

I've never seen a mountain lion before.

❀

THE THIRD LOOP WAS PROVING TO BE A MUCH MORE GRADUAL CLIMB THAN the second. Cheryl stayed in the middle ring for the gentle, opening track, then went granny past the death-defying gully drop, then went back to the middle as the track stepped up onto the service road again for the climb to the top of the course. It was a climb, that's for sure, but as she thought her way through this, she realized that this was the place to attack, if, in fact, she still could, before they hit the downhill single- and double-tracks leading to the finish line in the middle of Vail.

She rolled over the top and cut back down across the mountain on a fast section of double-track trail, then cut into the woods again and caught herself as the trail narrowed to single track and Mother Nature made herself known on the front end again. Not bad, and, frankly, she felt later, that it set her up for the tight and difficult switchbacks that cut down the mountainside through the trees. She fought the bike a bit, letting her speed get a bit too high before tightly reining it in on the turns. The trail itself went from rocks to washboard to pea gravel to roots, her front shocks doing a shimmy while she pushed and pulled the fork through a rough approximation of a solid line down the mountain.

She popped out of the chicanes, turned back into the woods, and exploded out the other side onto a stretch of solid trail leading to paved roads and the finish. Cheryl realized, suddenly, that she had completely lost herself in the course for the last drop through the trees.

It was a good feeling, a feeling that said she belonged where she was, with what she was doing.

She followed the course until the crowds grew too thick, then cut up across the base of the mountain alongside the pit area. As she came to a stop next to the Haven-TW step van, she smiled at Hootie Bosco with a large and satisfied grin and said one word:

"Water."

✦

"YAAAAAAAAAH! YAAAAAAAAAH! YAH! YAH!"

Will waved his hands frantically in the air at the lion, screaming at the top of his lungs for any number of reasons: He was frightened out of his mind, which made screaming his only form of communication; he was trying desperately to frighten the mountain cat out of his mind, which didn't appear to be working; and, quite frankly, he didn't have the slightest idea what to do otherwise.

The cat stared at him, then, started turning his head a bit as Will stepped forward toward the bike.

"Make yourself big!" he screamed, trying to remember something he had heard in bear country years before, "Make yourself big!"

Thoughts became words and words became screams.

"Yyyyyyaaaaaggggghhh!"

Will slid a foot next to the bike frame and watched the cat's eyes widen with the movement. Will continued to scream and wave his arms maniacally. His only thought, his thought that was his only hope, was to get the bike between him and the lion. To appear so damned huge and mechanical that it would frighten Mike Tyson away.

He slowly crouched, screaming and waving one arm all the time, the cat relaxing a bit, looking at him now with a bemused disinterest. Will took the bike by the headset, just above the front fork, with his left hand and began to lift it as quietly as possible, keeping all the attention on his right hand waving frantically.

The cat watched quietly until Will swept his hand under the seat and lifted the bike, almost as if to throw it.

In reaction to Will's move, the mountain lion snarled and jerked forward as if to lunge, which made Will scream in a piercing tone that hurt his throat and instinctively made him take a step back on the narrow trail. He caught a foot on a root and nearly twisted his ankle. He tried to re-balance himself, but with the bike over his head, throwing him backward, Will fell back. He took a step into nothingness and crashed backward end-over-end through the trees and bushes, rocks and stumps that lined the side of the mountain.

First, he hit dirt, then he hit the bike, then he hit rocks, then dirt, then the bike, then what felt like a tree, then the bike, then dirt, then a rock, then the bike, then nothing, then the dirt, hard, and then finally, the bike hit him.

Then it all stopped.

Will lay quietly on the floor of the White River National Forest, a grove of aspen rustling gently in the air above him. He watched it all for a moment, smiling at the quiet beauty of nature, then closed his eyes for a little nap, despite the fact that the fanny pack was digging into his back and the front wheel of the bike, twisted beyond all recognition, lay draped across his bloodied leg.

The leg brace that had been such a part of his life for the past eight weeks was nowhere to be seen.

He drifted away on the breeze of an autumn day in the mountains, the pain that he'd be feeling soon deciding to give him a few moments of unconsciousness before making itself known to him.

Nearly one-hundred feet above him, the big cat had watched the fall, the red, black, and gold Haven road jersey flashing in black and white in his eyes.

With a singular snort of disinterest, the lion turned and sauntered back deep into the forest, the pads of its paws making a silent whoosh with each step on the carpet of the forest floor.

CHAPTER FOURTEEN:

MARJORIE MORNINGSTAR

THE GLORY OF AN EARLY SEPTEMBER, LATE MORNING IN THE mountains surrounding Vail is the crispness of the wind as it gently rocks the aspen leaves to and fro, the white noise that movement creates above your head, a sound that adds a gentle peace to the silence, and the vision of an occasional leaf breaking free and dropping gently, roundabout, to the ground where it falls onto the bed of the forest, or, onto the cyclist who is lying there senseless.

"Oh, my sweet Lord."

Marjorie Stump's first thought was that she had come across the body of a murder victim and her first inclination was to leap away in the other direction, gaining a head start that she would build on through determined and forceful powerwalking back toward Vail. She turned, stopped, caught both her body and her fear, and listened for a very long moment that lasted between an eternity and the week she had once spent in Los Angeles.

The forest was filled with its own sounds: the trees, the wind, the rich, full silence of nature. Whatever this was, it was alone and it appeared to be an accident. She carefully moved toward the crumbled mound of body and bike, her shillelagh at the ready. The closer she moved, the more relaxed she became. The body was moving, if only slightly, the bike was mangled, indicating a fall rather than a confrontation, and the rider was moaning, gently.

She stepped forward swiftly, suddenly determined to take action, and knelt beside Will, taking his head in her right hand, and with little gentleness or ceremony, cranked it over toward her.

"Are you all right?"

Through an electric mist that filled his eyes, past the image of hundreds of stiffly marching German soldiers passing the focal point of his brain, the vision shaken loose from some ancient documentary he had seen as a child, Will saw her gnarled face and in the midst of his mind, screamed.

"Are you all right?" she questioned, forcefully, her hand shaking his head, like a shopper checking a melon.

The movement made him want to puke.

"What-is-your-name?" she barked, the words striking Will like a foreigner being taught English by an American tourist.

"Ah'm, Ah'm, Ah'm," he offered, swallowed, then added, "I'm...."

"Yes? Who?" She stopped shaking his head for a moment, then, out of frustration, gave it another mighty jangle. "Who-are-you?"

The sudden movement pushed him back toward unconsciousness, where he found the door already shut and locked. There was nowhere else to go but back to the world of the gnome shaking his head like Carol Burnett with the "Sorry" bell.

"What-is-your-name."

Will smiled drunkenly and said, "Murrrrph. Murrrph."

Marjorie Stump nodded, satisfied, and sat Will up. He felt a few vertebrae in his back snap like starter shots at a high school track meet, then felt like he was coming over the top of that white wooden roller coaster he had seen next to the highway in Denver. He leaned back against her hand, hoping that it would lower him back to the ground so he could sleep this one off, but there was no lessening of resistance. He was up and, by God, she was going to keep him up.

"Well, Murph—how did you get yourself in this predicament?" She looked up the hillside, following an imagined trail back up toward the ridge line, noticing some slide marks and a few small broken branches along the way, as well as a strip of dark-blue mesh wrapped around what appeared to be a silver metal bar. "Did you fall out of sheer clumsiness, or, did Mother Nature somehow let you know how very unwelcome your machine is in the deep of the forest?"

Will turned, his head floating on a bed of BBs.

"Cat," he mumbled. "Cat."

"Cat?"

"Cat," he nodded, dimly, "big fucking cat."

"Don't curse. And don't talk nonsense. There are no big cats around here anymore. There should be, that's for certain, but there aren't thanks to all that," she waved a hand in the vague direction of Vail proper, "and there likely never will be again."

"Cat," he nodded again, defiantly, the child determined to make his mother believe him. "Cat. Big damned cat."

"Certainly, Murph. Certainly. Shhh. You bet. Cat. Can you walk, Murph? Can you walk?"

Will didn't answer, just sat staring straight ahead, his brain still on full tilt, his eyes dancing around in their sockets like lottery balls in the blower.

"Sure you can, Murph. Sure, you can walk." She stepped behind him, braced herself along his back, caught her forearms under his armpits and lifted with her legs. For as small as she was, and with as little help as he gave, the lift was remarkably easy. Will felt himself rise as if in an elevator, hitting the top of the roller coaster again and nearly falling over the top. The bike, still leaning up against his leg, rose with him. Instinctively, he grabbed the top tube and balanced against it, nearly falling over in a dead faint in the other direction.

He flexed his eyes and took a deep breath, feeling the wind roll through a ragged and somewhat mangled interior. God, what have I done now, he wondered. He straightened up, took a step backward for balance, rocked back and forth for a moment, then turned to his benefactor.

"Thanks…."

"Don't mention it, Murph. You've interrupted my morning nature walk, a fact of daily living for nearly thirty years, through your own clumsiness, but I won't hold that against you. I've got enough Christian charity still within me to render aid to an accident victim, even if it is their own fault. I'll give of myself today so that you will be safe. That is the mark of a good Samaritan."

She waved her cudgel in his face for emphasis. "I'll get you back to town, despite the fact that I'm giving of myself."

"I understand," Will said, cutting her off with a raised palm, deflecting the stick and wheezing between each word, "I understand. I've … woof … ruined your day. Wooooof. Sorry."

"Can you walk?"

"I dunno," Will muttered, leaning against the bike, somehow, stupidly, unable to feel his feet, unable to find the balance point that would allow him to stand alone, proud and unafrai … he began to feel himself drift and fall backward. A hand, slapped, hard, onto the middle of his back, brought him back to reality.

"Don't go anywhere without me, Murph. Stay right here, for I have plenty to do today and I don't want you or anyone else holding me up."

Will nodded, brain function at about 55 percent.

"Let's go then. You ready?" She looked at him defiantly, almost daring him to gather the courage to pass out in front of her.

Will had no idea if he was ready or not, but seeing as how he was now on the ragged edge of a balance point and the movie in his head had changed from a World War II documentary to random images of "The 5,000 Fingers of Dr. T," he nodded dumbly and mumbled, "Ready."

She smiled in triumph, her good deed done for the day, and turned, starting off back in the direction she came, deep through the woods, toward the road and the bus stop that would take them both back into town.

Will watched her go for a moment, then, using the bike as a rolling cane, a high-end rolling Italian walker, he pushed along behind her, slowly, at first, then with more confidence, following the trail she broke through the forest. Even with his limited brain function, he followed amazed, amazed at how someone so indelicate, moving so forcefully, could leave no trace of her passing through the forest.

Will, on the other hand, stomped along behind her, the drunken uncle and his Colnago weedwhacker ruining the wedding cake and tearing the train on the bridal gown to shreds.

"Gently, Murph," she called from up ahead, "step gently in Her house."

Will nodded and walked as carefully as he could, until one thought crowded into a brain filled with random thoughts spilled from every drawer of memory in the library.

"Murph? Who's Murph?"

✿

THE COMBINATION OF THE COOL OF THE DAY AND THE WARMTH OF THE SUN was intoxicating. Cheryl stretched herself back, deeper into the folding chair, and pulled the zipper of the Haven-TW jersey down a bit farther across her chest. A sudden breeze raised goosebumps across the rise of her breasts, which the warmth of the sun immediately countered.

Hootie Bosco stood in the middle of the step van door, jealously guarding the woman who sat relaxing before his truck. He waved his hand in mock anger at two teenaged boys slowing their walk toward the downhill course as they passed the vision, vaguely undressed, in the folding chair.

"Move along, come on, move along you two. Nothing to see here, show's over."

The two, embarrassed, moved along. Hootie turned back to Cheryl.

"Just what in the world do you think you're doing, young lady? Exposing yourself to the world?"

Cheryl sat up and blinked, glanced down and, realizing that she was, indeed, exposing more than she expected, zipped the jersey part of the way back up. With a small measure of embarrassment, she turned to Hootie and said, "You could have said something."

"I did. I just said it to the two teenaged boys who were stepping on their tongues."

"You should have said it to me."

"I thought it was a new image you were trying to develop."

"Trying for the Paola Pezzo look?"

Hootie shrugged, with a smile, and didn't answer. He liked the Paola Pezzo look. His smile growing, Hootie turned to work intently on a spare hub.

"What, uh, what's your schedule for the rest of the day?" he asked, blankly, changing the subject.

Cheryl laughed and shook her head. "I don't know, frankly. The women's downhill starts about two, but I also wanted to check on the others. Don't know how I'll schedule everything. Want another ride on the cross-country, too."

"Don't burn yourself out, there, champ. Just go watch for a while, why don'tcha? Frannie's training for the dual slalom today. You can wander over there and watch her, get another feel for the mountain."

"Yeah. Problem is, I'll probably have to put up with Jettman and Reed."

"I wouldn't worry about Jettman. He only had eyes for Frannie today. I think Reed is losing his power over him."

"Really," she said with a smile.

"Yeah. Sex does that."

"Sex?"

"Yeah. Sex. An intimate relationship between two people. You remember the concept?"

She was struck by a momentary embarrassment, surprised by his comment and the veiled insight it held.

"Yeah," she said, "I remember the concept."

Hootie watched her for a moment, the discomfort growing in her eyes, then smiled and tried to relieve the tension.

"Will went riding."

Casting a thumb behind him, toward the village, he said, "that way."

She nodded, looked back toward the village, then turned up toward the mountain. What the village held and what the mountain offered, were two entirely different things to her.

She pulled off her riding shoes, tossed them in a box at the base of the truck, snagged her ancient, torn and mottled Keds out of her backpack and slipped them on. She pulled a light, blue and gold nylon windbreaker from the pack and tied it around her waist.

"I'm going to watch some racing."

"Okay. Amateur downhill?"

"Yeah. Maybe acclimate a bit more."

"Sure. Can't help it when you're in it."

"Get up on the mountain."

"Fine."

"Get ready for my run later, later after they clear the course."

"No probs."

"Downhill."

"That's after lunch. Need some money?"

"You sound like my mother."

"I am. Need some money for lunch?"

"Yeah, as a matter of fact."

Hootie pulled a twenty from his wallet and tossed it to her. "There you go. Pay me back when your rich uncles die."

"What?"

"Pay me back when your rich uncles die and leave you their fortune. In small bills. Unmarked. Cash."

"Why would you say that?" she snapped, quickly.

"Whoa," he raised both hands in mock surrender, "no reason, chief, no reason at all. Jest funnin' wit' chew."

She nodded quickly, suddenly embarrassed by her tone. "Yeah, sorry," she said, tapping the first finger of her right hand against her lips, nervously, as if deep in thoughts that simply weren't there. "I'm, uh, I'm going to watch a few runs. I'll see you this afternoon."

"You said that," Hootie said, carefully, not wanting to set anything else off.

"Yeah, okay," she answered, already walking away toward a break in the course that looked like a prime downhill spectator spot.

"Thanks, uh, for the twenty. I'll see you later, Hootie."

Hootie Bosco nodded and waved, with a smile as insincere as the Joker. "See ya," he whistled through his teeth, and turned back into the darkness of his vehicular cave.

"Man, oh, man," he said to his personal Diamondback frame in the corner, "that is one great woman who is wound way, way, way too tight."

The frame didn't answer, but Hootie didn't mind.

It was a rhetorical statement.

❖

CHERYL WALKED QUIETLY, DEEP IN THOUGHT, TOWARD THE COURSE ON VAIL Mountain. She fell in with a small crowd of people, talking, laughing, wheezing up the mountainside toward the prime vantage points. She looked up and realized that there weren't many spectators this morning. But, then again, it was early and these were the amateurs. She hoped that it would change for the pro runs later this afternoon and Sunday, in a big way, or the Ishmael Coffee Company would bail out of this race faster than a Grande Latte passing through a small bladder.

She smiled at the image and felt her mood rise with those around her.

About four feet behind her, Kelvin Stump smiled as well.

This woman knew a Will. And she was nervous about money.

He had heard it with his own ears. From her own mouth.

This was one to follow.

❋

"DO YOU REALIZE, YOUNG MAN, THAT EVERY TIME YOU RIDE THROUGH A FOREST, an old growth forest, that the tires of your bicycle," she tapped the mangled front tire for emphasis, "destroy a little bit of the top soil, break it down, making it a prime candidate for an unnatural erosion?"

Will pushed and pulled the bike for support, keeping it beside him to keep himself standing at least close to upright. His mind sang like a pinball machine, with lights and bells going off at odd angles and high pitch. He was following her only because she said to, there was no other way he could have done it. Everything in his body told him to stop and sit down on the forest carpet, but he kept walking at her insistence. Every third step he felt a wave of nausea wash over him, reaching a point, where, once, he bent over the bike, retched up a loud and nasty smelling belch, then spit in the grass.

"There, that actually helps the food chain in the forest, it increases the bacteria levels in the composting process on the forest floor. Fascinating, isn't it?"

Will retched again, after swallowing a fly along the way that forced him to spit a ball of yellow goo at his own feet.

"Good, very good," she murmured softly. "You're helping the forest more than you might think. That's why when I need to expel just about anything from my body, I do it outside. In the forest. In the grass. In the world. It's natural and it adds to nature."

Will stared for a moment, the flashbulbs in his mind waiting quietly for the next celebrity at the movie premiere. He looked at the woman blankly while his mind, without any effort on his part, conjured up the image of this women parking herself in the tall grass to leave Mother Nature a calling card.

He shook his head violently to erase the image, thus allowing the next thunderstorm to roll through the space just behind his eyes. The front of the bike dropped back to the ground and rolled along like a drunken sailor driving a rickshaw, carving a sidewinder snake line through the leaves and pine needles on the ground.

"I said, keep that up, keep that picked up. You're breaking down the topsoil, Murph. Stop it. Now tell me, Murph, where are you from?"

Will should have been correcting her, but didn't have the brain power to do it at that particular point in time. He struggled along behind her, lifting the front wheel again, and mumbled, "Michigan."

"What part?"

"West Michigan. Near, uh, Kalamazoo. I think."

"Ah, west Michigan. Let's see, what do I know about that—lots of farming, right?"

Will nodded, blankly. He would have nodded if she had said, "Lot of weenie ranches, right?"

"Lots of farming, corporate farming, with lots of pesticides and chemical fertilizers and genetically engineered fruits and vegetables. Dairy, too, right?"

"Uhmp."

"Growth hormones. You didn't drink the milk while you were growing up, did you?"

"Yeah, I suppose," he said, suddenly alert with the implied threat in her voice.

"Yes, well then. You're a prime candidate for all sorts of things now … you know that don't you?"

"What?"

"Milk. Milk is bad. Unless it's organic. Same for fruits and vegetables. Eggs. Oh, God, eggs are terrible. Grains and what they've been sprayed with. The fillers in bread! You wouldn't believe how some people make bread, the vitamins leached out, the fiber built up with sawdust. A trip to the modern supermarket is no better than playing Russian roulette with food. Did you ever think of that?" She shook her head. "You never thought of that."

Will shook his head, slowly, in response. It was like a mirror image.

"You never thought of that, did you, Murph?"

Her steady gaze made him realize, deep down, that she was expecting an answer.

"No. I never thought of that."

"What do you expect to do about it?"

Oh, God, he thought, she wants me to talk again. He stared into her small grey eyes, pinpricks, really, in a round and wrinkled face, and said, never quite believing it, "I'll never eat again."

Marjorie Stump stared for a second, her face hard and unforgiving, then burst out laughing, slapping Will hard on the shoulder and sending a shot of pain rocketing around his body like a six-bumper billiard shot.

Will's mouth worked frantically and nothing came out.

"Murph, you are a hoot, an honest-to-God hoot," Marjorie said, laughing, shaking her head the entire time. "A card. A living, breathing card.

"I like you."

She kept nodding as she turned and began to trudge through the forest again, with Will slowly following in her path, nodding out of pain and confusion more than agreement.

The shuttered light of the forest played off each leaf and branch and twig and trunk, raising havoc with his mind and balance and stomach.

And yet, he followed her blindly toward who knew where.

"WE'RE S-O-L, YOU KNOW THAT, DON'T YOU?"

"Don't curse."

"I didn't curse. I said, simply, we're s-o-l, which is a benign equivalent and aptly describes our current predicament."

Olverio stared at Stanley for a moment, then nodded his head in resignation. He conceded the point. It was a predicament, and, at the moment, they were, indeed, shit-outta-luck.

They walked up Willow Bridge toward the race course, the crowd growing in dribs and drabs around them. They took care in when they spoke, and how, but didn't make any effort to conceal themselves. In doing so, they simply became two weird-looking older guys in a crowd of bicycle racers.

"And our predicament is…?" Ollie asked.

"No dollars, and multiple lumps starting to turn up. Officers start finding those and life could get real interesting real fast around here," Stanley answered, outlining a predicament that was all too clear to both.

"You're absolutely right," Ollie said with a sigh.

"Coffee? You gentlemen like coffee? You look like you could use some Ishmael French Roast this morning."

The cheery coffee pitch girl held out a Dixie Cup of Joe toward the two men. Ollie shook it away, two cups being his limit with no bathrooms in sight, while Stanley took it with a smile and thanked the girl.

"Glad we came to a coffee race, ma'am, nothing better than the greatest coffee in the world as a sponsor."

The girl smiled wide at the tall, skinny man and returned his enthusiasm.

"Thank you, sir. Ishmael prides itself on a great product and sponsoring great events."

"You've hit both, I think," Stanley said, taking a sip and turning back up the street.

"Thank you, sir," the girl replied, her huge grin disappearing at the sight of Stanley's back, her mind turning to the thought that she never would be able to keep this up all day and, God, the smell of ancient coffee was making her sick.

She turned and regained her smile, thrusting herself upon another approaching and unwitting group of potential java junkies. Ten steps in the other direction, Stanley casually tossed the coffee into the grass.

"Why'd you do that?" Ollie asked.

"Tasted like shit."

"And you've tasted that."

"More times than you'd ever want to know."

"What was wrong with it?"

"Ack," Stanley spit, "wrong beans. Modern coffee comes from the wrong beans."

"It's popular."

"So is jabbing yourself with a dirty tattoo needle, but that doesn't mean that I want to do it."

"I suppose."

At Gore Creek Drive, a race marshal opened up the barricade and let the two pass with a small crowd of other race fans. Carried along by them, Stan and Ollie found themselves at the base of the mountain, walking up, with effort, toward the chicanes of the race course above.

As they approached the downward leg of the Lionshead Loop, a group of three young women, practicing, shot by on the track. Ollie watched them sail past, suddenly chased by a race marshal who wanted them off the course. The three waved nonchalantly and disappeared in the distance toward Bahama Mama Falls.

"Aren't there steps down there?" Stanley asked, pointing in the general direction of town. "I could have sworn there were steps down there."

Ollie watched without answering, but merely stared at the young women riding off in the distance, the race marshal running behind. He cleared his mind of everything, hoping that the thought that was in there, the flash of insight he needed, could find its way to center stage.

"Stanley," he said, his partner turning while still shaking his head that people would be silly enough to ride perfectly good bicycles down perfectly good stairs, "think back. Think back to yesterday morning in the restaurant, when Mr. R decided to make a break for it."

"Yeah, so?"

"Remember how we were shocked to see Cheryl?"

"Yeah, sure. Didn't expect to see her there at all."

"I know. But—do you remember his reaction?"

"To Cheryl?"

"No, to that guy she was with."

"The dork with the bicycle? The one I stepped on?"

"Yeah, him. Romanowski seemed awfully surprised to see him there. Didn't you think? Even excited. Acted like he knew him. Knew him pretty well."

"The guy with all the stuff on his legs?"

"Yeah. Him. That's him. Now, if you were Romanowski...."

"... and you had to stash a present...."

"... who would you...."

"... do it with?"

"I think we need to find Mister...."

"Dork."

"Yes, and have a little talk."

Stanley nodded and turned, looking up the mountain at the scattered pockets of people and riders that covered the hill.

"Do you know where to start?"

Ollie shook his head.

"Cheryl, maybe. Or the hotel. Perhaps."

"Where do racers meet on race day?"

"I dunno. I never followed this stuff. Never could figure out what Raymond and Cheryl saw in it."

Stanley nodded.

"Although," he said, holding one finger in the air for emphasis, "the six-day races were hot back in the early thirties."

"You were only a kid."

"I bet on 'em."

"You didn't bet. You were a baby."

"I matured early."

Ollie looked around, kicked the dirt, then turned to a teenager in a "NO FEAR!" sweatshirt.

"Excuse me, son."

"Yeah, dude?" He smiled at the incongruity.

Ollie nodded with patience and smiled back, showing his teeth. The teenager lost his smile.

"Do you know where I could find Cheryl Crane? One of the riders? Where her team might hang out?"

"Crane. Crane. Crane," the young man repeated, all the while flipping through the race program, "Crane is ... with ... Haven. Haven and Two Wheels. I'd just go over to the pit area, over—there—behind that cyclone fencing near the chair lift, and see if she's hanging out there."

"Thanks, son. And don't call me dude."

"Sorry, dude," the kid said, then added, "force of habit," before he turned quickly back up the hill.

Ollie watched him go, shaking his head at the lack of manners and empty one-liners that swirled around the modern youth of America.

"I hate smart alecks," Stan said, "but—he was right—you are a dude."

Ollie shrugged. "Hmm. Haven."

"Two Wheels."

The two turned and walked toward the break in the race course fencing that would allow them to cross over to the mountain base that had become little more than a truck-and-RV parking lot, a collection of people and vans dedicated to the proposition that staying in the race was the highest calling in life. And, as they reached the pit wall, they stepped forward to look for the truck, the niece, the man, and, finally, the money that was making this a far longer weekend than they had ever anticipated.

WILL LOOKED DOWN THE ROAD IN FRUSTRATED ANTICIPATION, THE BUS nowhere to be seen.

His head rang with the incessant chatter of Marjorie Stump. The topics ranging from the ecology of the forest floor to the migratory habits of the downy headed woodpecker (which didn't seem to migrate at all), from corporate greed on Vail Mountain to the environmental activities of GOD.

"Who?"

"GOD. That's my very own organization, don't you know," she said with pointed pride. "Guardians Of the Domain."

"What Domain?"

"Look around you, Murph," she said with pleasure. "Look around you. What is green, is due to GOD. What is GOD is due to me."

He wasn't following. His eyes couldn't focus on her face, and his ears couldn't focus on her words.

"You did this?"

"Indeed I did. When the corporation tried to expand, I was there to defeat it by any means necessary."

"How?" he asked, the word sounding like it had been spoken by a troll in a fifty-five-gallon drum and causing him to turn to look for the speaker.

She reached up and turned his head back to face her, the small dots of her eyes blazing into the front of his skull.

"By any means necessary, Murph."

"Yeah," he said, dully, "like…."

"My God. Men. You, Murph," she said, shaking her head, sadly, "are as thick as my husband and my son. And I never thought anyone could be quite that thick."

"Sorry," he mumbled.

"By any means necessary means, and I will tell you, everything from leaflets to speaking out at public forums, to gathering money to buy private land before the corporate raiders can get hold of it, to lobbying the legislature, to threatening construction firms…."

Did she say threatening? he wondered.

" … up to and including, and, yes, I will tell you this, Murph, monkey wrenching. Spikes in trees, gravel on slopes, an errant match next to an old mountaintop restaurant, vandalism, eco-terrorism, it doesn't matter. As long as I get it done."

"Get what done?"

"Protect my Mother. Your Mother. Restrict the rape of the countryside. Protect the habitat. Do you know how much habitat the lynx is losing to the recreational needs of the naked ape?"

"Naked…."

"Man. My goal, above all, is to restrict the spread of the animal known as man."

"But…."

"No, Murph, there is no argument. The animal known as man uses far more than he contributes to the world. He is like a parasite. A roach. He does not renew, restore or recycle. He uses and discards."

Her voice and anger had drifted away, and she spoke as if in a trance of her own design. She had found an alpha state in which Will had no part.

He turned and looked desperately for the bus in the distance.

"He procreates beyond his needs or means, greedily destroying his Mother for his own instantaneous gratification. I want to ski today and so I shall drive my fossil-fuel vehicle, alone, but with hundreds of others, alone, in their own fossil-fuel vehicles, toward a pristine mountainside gutted and cut to fit the financial needs of investors who only know the glory of money, and not the glory of sharing a mountain morning."

"Yeah, but isn't it sharing to use the land for farms and fun and maybe a house or two?"

The shillelagh whistled in the air, brushing his bare, if bloodied knee, threatening him just enough to wake him out of his concussive slumber and put the fear of God in him.

"Jesus H. Christ, lady!" he yelped, leaping backward and putting the bike between his leg and her stick.

"Don't curse," she said with a scowl. "Don't take the name of my Lord in vain."

"I'm sorry, but don't swing that stick at me, either."

"Well, then, I'm sorry, Murph. But you have to admit that your argument was silly and stupid."

"What argument?"

"That the animal known as man had a right...."

"Oh, great," he shouted, turning and pointing with almost childish abandon, "the bus! Oh, it's the bus!" He lowered his voice, "The goddamned it's-about-time bus."

The noisy shuttle arose in Will's eyes like a mirage, shimmering in the heat that didn't exist in the distance that did. The woman, Marjorie, he struggled to remember, Marjorie Stump, had driven him like a much-disliked pack mule to the road, considered leaving him there, which, in its own way, wouldn't have broken Will's heart, then felt, once more out of her oblique sense of charity, to stay with him, put him on the bus and get him at least back to town, to his hotel if not to his friends, and then proceeded to pass the time by lecturing at least one of his ears off about various religious and environmental issues.

As the bus pulled closer, Marjorie raised her cudgel in her right hand and shook it furiously. The driver, Will noticed, obviously used to her theatrics, smiled, rolled his eyes, and pulled to the side. The bus rolled to a stop in front of them with a squeal of brakes and the hiss of the door.

"Yes, ma'am, what can we do for you?"

"You can give us a ride back to town," Marjorie answered sharply, striding directly on the bus and flashing a travel pass before sliding into a seat directly behind the driver.

Will noticed that the driver sighed deeply, almost in resignation, as he watched her in the mirror over his head. Will smiled, he already knew the feeling with this woman, and began to wrestle the bike up the steps of the bus.

"You can't bring that on here," the driver pointed out in clipped, officious tones.

"You've got to wait for a bus with a bike rack on it. Mine got smashed in a fender bender."

Will stood stupidly, half on, half off the bus, staring at the man through dull, shaken eyes, the pupils still dancing around like black spots in a clear plastic shell. Without an argument, he nodded and began to roll the bike backward off the bus.

"Stop it! Stop it, Murph!" a voice commanded in a rising, angry tone. "You get on this bus right now. Henry, this man is injured. We've got to get him to town, and he is not about to leave an expensive machine out here in the woods. You wouldn't. You know it. Now, shut up, let him on and drive."

"Can't do it, Miss Stum...."

Bang!

The head of the shillelagh landed with a "crack!" on the floor of the bus next to the driver's seat. The driver jumped a good six inches, while the noise made Will rear back, almost to the point of losing his balance and falling out of the bus.

"Henry, you will take him, and you will take the bike, and since he is injured, you will drive straight to town, ignoring your other stops along the way."

"I can't...."

Bang!

"Don't do that," he sighed and turned to Will. "Get it on, let's go."

Will nodded a silent "sorry" to the driver and wrestled the bike onto the top step, then slid into the first seat, the flush of effort making him see a variety of colors and geometric patterns behind his eyes.

Marjorie Stump tapped her cane twice, impatiently, and said, sharply, "Let's go."

The driver nodded, closed the door, and the bus rolled off, with effort, toward Vail. As it made the turn under the highway and into the upper crust of East Vail, Henry, the driver, flipped a glance over to Will.

"So, what happened? Endo?"

"I'm sorry?" Will shook his head and felt his brain slosh around a bit.

"Endo? End over end? Fall?" The driver stared at him for just long enough that Will wished he'd go back to watching the road. Then, he understood.

"Yeah. Endo. Fell down a hill."

"Says a big cat scared him," Marjorie added, making no effort to mask the sarcasm in her voice.

"A cat, like a house cat?" the driver said incredulously to the small, pinched face in the mirror above his head.

"It was a mountain lion," Will whispered, his voice carrying no further than the center of the aisle.

"He says it was a big cat. A lion."

"A mountain lion?" Henry seemed stunned by the thought for a moment, staring at the reflection of Marjorie Stump and completely ignoring the road ahead. Even if he had intended to ignore her earlier demand and stop at the bus stops along the way, as the bus careened toward Vail Village, he blew through two without a second glance at the road.

"There haven't been mountain lions around here for years, have there? A bear or two, but you've got to go deep to catch a lion."

"That's what I tried to tell him."

"I didn't try to catch him. He tried to catch me."

"You sure, kid?"

Will stared at the man who certainly wasn't any older than he was and nodded, "Yeah, I'm sure."

"You ought to report this," the driver said anxiously.

"I will."

"Oh, nonsense, Murph. You report that, and they'll look at you like you've seen little green men or a platoon of German soldiers trooping across the pass. It wasn't a lion. I would know. I walk those hills every day...."

"She does. She really does," the driver offered.

"And there has been no trace of a cat. No trace of a cat at all. No scat. No trail. No cat."

The driver turned and stared at Will, making him nervous to the point of clamminess and finally leading him to point back down the road.

"Well, Murph?"

The driver turned back to watch the road, while Marjorie continued to stare at him. Will shrugged. He didn't have it in him to argue the point.

He stared across the bus and saw the bandshell of the Ford Amphitheater pass the window.

"Should I take him straight to the hospital?"

"Well, what's your pleasure, Murph?" Marjorie asked.

Will knew that he probably should have gone, but shook his head, just wanting to get himself and the bike back to a place where they could both rest for a while.

"No. No. Drop me in town."

The driver looked up in the mirror again, into the face of Marjorie Stump. Their eyes locked for a moment, and the driver finally nodded.

Will watched the two stare at each other in silent conversation until Marjorie Stump shrugged and he wondered to himself how the driver had managed it. Two miles of driving with one mile of watching the road.

"Where are you staying, Murph?"

"The Bavarian something ... I ... think." He blinked his eyes, hard. He couldn't connect his thoughts.

They passed the huge parking structure in the Village, and Will began to recognize landmarks, the hotel, Bridge Street, and the rest. He pointed out the window.

"This is it, this is good."

The driver stepped harder than he had to on the brakes and made the turn at the end of the transportation center into the Village. As he completed the

'S' turn, he was pointed toward Lionshead, and Will had used the inertia to pull himself up and out of his seat.

Marjorie looked at him with a vague sort of motherly smile.

"Well, Murph, don't go eyeballing any mountain lions, you hear?" she said with a cackle.

"Yeah," Henry the driver added, nervously, "mountain lions."

Will nodded and rolled the bike down the steps and into the street. He leaned it up against the side of the bus and stepped back onto the first step.

"Ms. Stump, Mrs. Stump, I'm sorry, I … anyway, thank you. I do appreciate your help. That was very kind of you."

"No problem, Murph. Happy to help. Go get yourself patched up now."

"I will. And thanks." He began to step down, caught himself and rose back into the bus. "By the way, Mrs. Stump, Ms., Mrs. Stump. I'm not sure where this started, but my name's not Murph. It's Will. Will Ross. Thank you."

"Indeed, Mr. Ross," she answered, her eyes narrowing at the sound of the bell that was ringing madly in the back of her head, "don't mention it."

"Thanks again. I owe you." Will smiled crookedly and stepped off the bus, losing his balance and nearly swooning, before taking the bike, as the door of the bus closed, and leaning on it for support.

"Shit," he thought to himself, "Hootie's gonna shit."

He picked the front wheel of the bike off the ground as best he could and began limping his way through the thin crowds toward Bridge Street and the van and the mechanic and the water and the chair he knew were there.

As he made the turn, if he had looked back, he would have seen the silhouette of Marjorie Stump's head suddenly shoot up from half staff, while her body leapt from her seat and rushed toward the back window, her hands and forehead slapping against the glass as the bus in which she was riding never paused, through the Village toward Lionshead and farther away with each second from the man she had known as Murph.

The man she now knew was Will Ross.

The man she and Kelvin were trying to find. The man already swallowed up by the people and buildings that made up Vail this day.

REVELATION

A T FIRST, IT WAS AS IF MARSHALL REED HAD FORGOTTEN ABOUT THE bike, forgotten about his anger, forgotten about his war of words with Cheryl Crane. He was joking with Hootie, laughing at the amateurs, complaining about his hotel, the food, the pay with the team, the course, in short, acting like every other rider at every other race the world has ever known.

Hootie shook his head at the flash of recognition.

Reed leaned over the back of the step van and peered into the murk.

"You got a bike in there for me?"

"I got a bike for you right here," Hootie answered, spinning the front wheel on the Diamondback that Reed had brought in caked with mud from the dual-slalom course.

"Man, I gotta tell you, I have no idea how you got this thing muddy when there's been no rain here for three weeks."

"Hey, when there's no mud, I find it. That's my job," Reed replied, laughing. He turned and sat on the edge of the van. "I suppose you're trying to save my feelings, aren't you? The boyfriend has the bike, doesn't he?"

Hootie paused for a second, not wanting to be pulled into this battle between Reed and Cheryl.

"No, no, that's okay, Hoot," Reed nodded, "I understand. You get a boss with a boyfriend and, by God, you've got to give up for the boyfriend." His nodding became a shaking. "I don't believe in that sort of thing. Really don't. It ain't going to happen when I'm running a team. That's for sure." The shake became a nod again.

Hootie stopped for a second and stared, as if he were watching Charles

Foster Kane write his Declaration of Principles that he would soon enough abandon. So will you, kid, he thought to himself, so will you.

Hootie went back to cleaning the hub while Marshall Reed stared at the mountain that was proving easy enough for him to conquer, when first a mangled rim, then a dirty bike, then a mangled rider appeared around the corner of the van.

"Home again. Man." Will dropped the bike against the side of the step van, the frame and various parts making a loose, jangling sound when they bounced. He turned, stumbled to the lawn chair, and stretched out in it, sinking deep into the fabric and very nearly hearing his muscles thank him profusely for finally sitting back down.

"What the...."

"Hell." Marshall Reed finished Hootie's sentence.

"What happened to you?" said Hootie as he stepped down out of the truck.

"What happened to my bike?"

Hootie rushed to Will's side, picking up a water bottle as he ran, while Marshall Reed moved just as quickly in the other direction, snatching up a red shop rag to wipe, lovingly, the frame of the Colnago, his Colnago, leaning haphazardly at the back corner of the van.

"What happened, Will?" Hootie said, sliding up next to the lawn chair on his knees, "Are you okay?" He offered water and Will gladly took it, each gulp burning on its way down, picking up the dirt, twigs and bits of leaves his throat had picked up on the way down the mountainside. That woman, he thought, that nasty little forest lady with the God complex. She had never offered him any water. Up and go, up and go, he thought, like she was running a damned army and I was throwing off her schedule of getting the replacements to the front.

"Thanks, man. I needed that."

Marshall Reed appeared at his side and slapped Will's shoulder with the tips of his fingers. The shock and pain, along what had to be a heavy bruise line, made Will rise up in a chair that wasn't meant for rising up gracefully.

"What the hell ... what the hell...." Reed's anger was making it difficult for him to talk. He squeaked, "What the hell happened here?"

Will turned his head up and stared at Reed, whose face, mottled with anger and intensity, stared back and forth between Will and the bike, the mangled machine he himself had intended to ride this weekend.

"I broke it," was all that Will could say.

"You broke it? You're damned well right you broke it, asshole!" Reed screamed, his anger tacking toward hysteria.

"Ease up, man, ease up," Hootie said, his soothing tones making Will smile. The two looked up at Marshall Reed.

"Fuck ease up, pal," Reed answered. He turned, walked toward the bike, then past it, marching down the length of the van, before turning and walking back at a quick-time march.

"What the hell did you think you were doing, anyway? Using your girl-friend to get a bike that you can't handle and shouldn't be riding in the first place? That's a bike from a sponsor, pal, a team sponsor. It's not for you to be riding around town, bending into a pretzel every time you swing your fucking legs over it. That's a bike that I … we're supposed to be riding. Us. And me in particular. I'm supposed to be riding that bike and finding out what it can do."

He glanced back at the mangled front rim.

"Not what it can't do." He finger-slapped Will on the shoulder again, making another wave of pain run down through Will's bloodied elbow and set off a throb in his finger tips, then race back up toward the top of his head, then down through the dings in his side, through both legs at the same time, then back up to his head and, finally, winding up as a sting in his shoulder. He had jerked, he had grimaced, and the entire trip took less than a few seconds.

The pause, uncomfortably long as it seemed, was, in reality, only a few seconds of Marshall Reed staring and panting, Will, looking back with pure exhaustion, and Hootie Bosco, staring at both, his eyes snapping back and forth as if they wanted to split into two separate video cameras pointed at two separate things.

Will didn't want to do it, but knew he had to, so, slowly, and taking as much care as he could, he braced his hands against the arm rests of the deep lawn chair, pushed, leaned forward, felt himself begin to pass out, and, finally, with the help of Hootie, rose up to his full height to meet the gaze of Marshall Reed face to face.

He paused for a moment as the last wave of nausea washed over him, then said, "Look, pal, I've got no problem with you. And, frankly, if I were in your position, I probably wouldn't be happy either. There's a new bike in the house and I don't get to ride it? I wouldn't like that, either."

"Damn right."

"Damn right," Will agreed, nodding his head in three directions at once, "so, I understand. But, I gotta tell you, for some reason, I got the bike today. Out of all the bikes you've got here, this is the one, the one, that can truly be called a spare. It's not assigned. It's only here on spec. Because of sponsors, nobody can ride it, except Cheryl. And for some reason, I keep getting into trouble with it. I'm sorry, Marshall. I'm truly sorry. It's nothing against you, but that's just the way it is."

A crowd slowly began to gather around the edges of the Haven-TW area, no one coming close enough to get involved, no one standing so far away that they would miss anything.

Marshall Reed looked beyond Will for a moment at the people, expectant, standing on the periphery, then glanced at Hootie, before finally turning back to Will.

At first, Will thought, given the way Reed was looking around, that maybe, just maybe, he had finally reached inside that gourd Marshall Reed called a head, but, then, as Reed began slowly moving his head up and down, sizing Will up, taking his measure, Will realized that this was going to get uglier before it got better.

Reed's right arm shot out, the palm flat, catching Will just below the ridge of his left shoulder. The force and the pain turned him a full quarter away from Reed. He rolled back as Hootie blocked another blow. There was a collective intake of breath from the crowd.

"Enough, Marshall. Look at him, man. What the hell are you thinking? He's all busted up. If you're going to try to kick his ass, at least wait until he's able to fight back."

"Fuck you, Hootie. And fuck you, boyfriend. This may be my one opportunity to fuck you up—so, I'm gonna take it." He shoved Hootie, who reeled backward and tripped over a duffel bag. The right arm shot out again and caught Will, full force, just above the left breast. He turned left, fell backward, and stumbled, rolling around Marshall Reed and back toward the truck. The last blow had sent a bolt of pain shooting through his chest and down his arms, knocking the wind out of him and making his finger tips numb. Another shot, palm flat again, same spot, and Will realized that he couldn't move his left arm up to block the attack, cover himself, or even raise his hand to give Reed the finger in one final gesture of defiance. Will retreated again until he fell backward against the lip of the step van, his head banging into Reed's bike, hanging from the workstand, the back of his right hand slapping into a wooden tool tray and sending yet another shot of pain rocketing around his body like an atomic pinball. He tried to push himself up to regain his balance, but one hand seemed lost in a pile of loose tools. He couldn't find any grip, any ground, any bottom to the pile of tools.

Someone in the crowd screamed, "Yeah!"

Hootie Bosco jumped up and ran to the pair, grabbing Reed on the left, blocking another palm strike, this time to Will's head, and turning the man full around.

"Knock it off, damn it, knock it off!" Hootie yelled.

"Aw, too late, Hootie, I'm having too much—fun," and, with that, he pushed Hootie backward again, turned to Will and smiled, "ready to open a fresh can of ass whupping?"

The smile left his face in a heartbeat, as Will smiled back at him and whispered, "You bet, pal." Reed felt the instinctive need to drop back, but was already committed to at least one strike with his left fist. As the arm swung around, Will dropped sideways and low, under and away from the blow, and, using the momentum of his collapse, drove the heavy-gauge two-inch box wrench as hard as he could into Marshall Reed's gut, just below the ribs.

The crowd let out a collective gasp as Marshall Reed's face turned bright red and his mouth exploded with a huge "Ppppppwwwwwwwah!"

Will felt the shock of the blow travel up his right arm and to his shoulder, the pain forcing him to drop the 5-pound slice of steel as he fell to the ground. Marshall Reed, on the other hand, folded up like a cheap suitcase on a one-way trip to Philadelphia.

Hootie stood, panting, above them both, Will on his hands and knees,

Reed in a fetal position, as they wheezed and tried to get up.

Hootie stepped over Reed and reached for Will, talking down to Reed as he passed him.

"Never back a wounded bear into a corner, man. Especially a corner where he can get hold of an oversized box wrench. Come on, now."

He caught Will under the right arm and helped him to his feet, walked him a few steps back to the lawn chair and dropped him, clumsily and with little gentleness, back into the deep sag of the fabric. Both it and Will groaned.

"Thanks, Hootie," Will mumbled through teeth clenched with pain, "I appreciate it."

"No, no, man, I should thank you," Hootie replied, "that was a hell of a show. Haven't seen anything like that since the fourth-grade playground."

Will laughed, which sounded more like a single, heavy breath than a laugh, and swallowed hard. Whatever recovery he had made since the fall down the mountainside was gone now, swept away in a flash of anger, ego, and bully-boy attitude.

His head flopped over to one side, and he watched the crowd slowly disperse. Hootie helped them along.

"Enough, you guys, it's done. Show's over. Nothing more to see now except Marshall Reed's breakfast. That's it. Let's go." He waved his hands and his shop apron at them like an old woman trying to drive flies out of her kitchen. "Don't miss the 4 p.m. show. Fun for the kiddies."

Will waved his hand, never moving his arm off the armrest of the chair, in a gesture of dismissal. As they left, one guy in an ancient Twisted Sister T-shirt walked past him, slapped him on the shoulder, making him jump in the seat, and said, "Nice goin' dude, that was great."

Will smiled politely and nodded, knowing full well that the same guy would have said the same thing to Marshall Reed if Reed had kicked the living shit out of Will.

Hootie walked over to Reed, grabbed him by the collar of his jersey and, with more strength than you would have imagined for his thin frame, lifted him, cleanly, to his knees, then his feet, turned him, and sat him back on the edge of the step van.

Reed still looked like he was breathing at only 50 percent, his breath coming in gasps and whistles and rattles, but Hootie brushed that off, taking Marshall Reed's chin in his hand and turning it up so their eyes could meet. Reed's eyes bounced around a bit, then found their focus.

Hootie watched Reed's eyes finish their hat dance, then said, "You'll be fine."

He dropped the chin with little ceremony or care and turned away as Marshall Reed rose up behind him and pointed an accusing finger at Will.

"That ... asshole ... attacked me with a ... wrench!"

Hootie turned back, looked at Will—already sleeping, or passed out, in the chair—and then back at Marshall Reed.

He nodded. "Yep. He did."

Reed looked at Hootie with a surprise bordering on shock, the team mechanic standing with this interloper rather than with him, a team member, the number two, who, if life was at all fair, could easily hold the future of Hootie Bosco in his hands, and shook his head.

"Hootie, you don't get it. He attacked me."

Hootie nodded, "Yeah, I get it. He attacked you."

"That's assault...."

"...in self-defense."

"Bullshit self-defense. If you know what's good for you, Bosco, when I bring a cop over here, you're going to say that he attacked me with a deadly weapon, then this asshole will spend the rest of the weekend in jail."

Marshall Reed took another step toward Will, who seemed lost to the world.

Hootie dropped his head and shook it in disbelief, the dreadlocks shimmying like palm fronds in a high wind. As Reed passed, Hootie put out his arm and caught Reed just above the elbow. Reed stopped, first because of the surprise of the move, but then, because of the strength that trapped him there. Flex his muscle as he might, there was no way Marshall Reed could break the hold of the mechanic.

Hootie turned his face up to Reed and said, quietly, but with more force than Marshall had ever heard from him, "Go ahead, Mr. Reed, go get a cop. You get a cop, and I will lay it all out for him. How this guy rode a bike you thought was yours, but wasn't, how you attacked him, even though he suffered a bad fall, how you bullied and backed him up, pushing, slapping and taking a swing, and how, when cornered, with you punching at him, just before he collapsed, he dropped you with a wrench to the gut. Got lots of witnesses."

"That wrench was a weapon...."

"Yep. But after the initial blow, he put it back, stepped over you and sat down. He didn't follow up by bashing in your head, which is what most people, myself included, would have done. He simply wanted you to stop and, I think, got you to stop. No court in the world would convict him. Might convict you, though, felony menacing might work. Can't convict for just being an asshole, but folks might try. So, go ahead."

Reed looked at Will, back to Hootie, walked over to the workstand, pulled his bike from the clamp, bounced it once on the ground, retrieved his helmet and gloves from the table bordering Haven-TW's little slice of heaven, and walked off toward the downhill course without another word. Hootie watched him go, took a quick glance at Will, still breathing, then reached into his pocket and checked his change.

He needed a beer.

As he walked away, leaving a sleeping Will to guard the shop, two men stepped out of whatever mid-afternoon shadows existed in Vail and walked into the Haven area, stopping on either side of Will Ross's chair.

The taller of the two reached down to shake him gently, while the other fingered the butt of a .22 caliber Walther, with silencer, in the pocket of his jacket.

※

THE AMATEURS WERE FINALLY WRAPPING UP NOW, AND THE DOWNHILL COURSE would be open soon for the pro races. Cheryl glanced at her watch, it was nearly 1 p.m. They were late. The semi-pro men were just finishing their competition, taking their last lunge at the course.

Most of the day, Cheryl Crane had placed herself within various groups, with or without invitation: a crowd of teenagers from Denver; a tour group from Japan; two families of four with undisciplined sons, which drove her quickly away; and, finally, a Denver TV crew, the reporter, from which, putting her to work hauling the tripod.

She didn't mind. Somehow, somewhere in her head, a bell kept ringing, not allowing her to enjoy the day or the downhill, from the rough-edged smoothness of the semi-pros to the cartoon jangle of the beginners. She felt something. Something like she was being watched. And followed.

She turned many times during the day, scanning the crowd behind her, and occasionally caught a glimpse of a tall, blond man with a purple nose, close by or in the distance, watching the racers with intensity, yet, also, with a strange kind of detachment. She'd move to a different position on the course, the chicane, the drop-off, the straightaway, and he'd be there, most times, anyway, somewhere close, watching the race, following just about the same path she was taking through the day.

And she knew him.

She didn't know from where, but she knew him. She had seen him before.

She tried to shake it off, ignore the bell, not yet grown into a full-grown threat, and settle into watching the downhill, but she simply couldn't do it. Her mind was filled with shouts and screams of things to do and races to ride, this, this annoyance really didn't help. It simply kept her from compartmentalizing the rest of her life. It kept intruding on her focus, pulling her away from everything to the point that she didn't even protest the thousands of pictures the Japanese tourists took of her, with and without them, in her skintight uniform.

The last few riders shot past, the course grew quiet, and the crowds, thin as they were for a Saturday, began wandering down the mountain and toward town for the lunch rush. Cheryl joined a clot of riders from earlier events, hoping to lose her jersey among the rainbow of others, and succeeded in moving close beside the tall blond man she suspected of following her. He was looking up the mountain, squinting into the early-September glare. She could see his eyes snapping to and fro across the face of Vail Mountain, sectioning off each area as if looking for something or someone.

As the crowd of riders drew close, she slid to his side, reached out, and touched his elbow. His head turned as if yanked by an invisible string, and he stared wide-eyed at the crowd passing him. Her face was there.

"I'm going this way."

Her face was gone, settled back into the knot of people, all in cycling jerseys, making their way toward Vail Village.

Kelvin Stump mentally kicked himself, not for being caught, so much, but for being so easily caught and surprised. He turned and followed the riders, at a distance, toward town.

At the base of the mountain, she turned suddenly toward the pit area. Kelvin followed, about 25 feet behind her. She turned and waved and continued on her way. He turned right, cut under the Vista Bahn, crossed the course, and took the long way around.

Cheryl turned again to see him turn away and wondered if he had given it up or was simply trying to throw her off. She watched him for a second and shrugged. She'd be with people again in a moment, her people, and he could stand at his safe distance and watch her as much as he wanted.

She had spent her life fighting off the demons, so she wasn't about to be spooked by this one right now. She stepped across the road and into the pit area, walking crossways between the mechanics and work stations and riders and bikes, thinning out as the first professional downhill runs approached, toward Hootie's world of the step van.

She smiled and nodded as one rider she didn't recognize waved at her, turned back, and realized quickly that something was wrong.

The step van was open. The bikes were out. The tools were all neatly arranged. And nobody was home.

Now, she was spooked.

❊

THE TWO MEN HALF-CARRIED, HALF-DRAGGED WILL TOWARD THE HOTEL AT the end of Bridge Street. Random thoughts kept flashing through his mind with flashes and bells and little cartoon noises. He couldn't seem to bring himself back to full reality, the batterings of the day piling themselves on, one after another, until all he wanted to do was pass out in a corner for the rest of the weekend.

He mentally wandered through the attic of his brain, trying to remember what he knew and didn't know about these two that supported him through the streets of Vail. Don't say what? Don't say what to these guys? Don't. Who? Something would set them off. And if it did, would they hurt me? They didn't hurt Cheryl. Could have. But she got away. What the hell? Family?

Some family.

He turned and smiled at the tall one, who was pinching him just under his left arm. The tall one smiled back, a big, dim, goofy smile. Will noticed that the front of his hair was stretched up into a peak, as if he had scratched it that way.

He turned to the smaller one, who had a better grip on his right arm. There was a hard, uncompromising look in his eye that frightened Will. This guy, Will knew, didn't play around.

"You can let go of me, now. I think I can walk."

"Maybe so, friend, but maybe you can walk faster than we think or want and in a new direction we don't like."

"You don't understand," Will answered. "I'm not going anywhere."

"I believe you," the short man nodded, "we believe you. But there's no reason to take any chances at this late date, now, is there?"

Will nodded, dumbly, for some reason that he couldn't fathom, agreeing with the wisdom of the argument. And so, he was carried along.

"You know, I really appreciate your help, here. I am having a hard time walking this afternoon, but could I ask you a question?"

"Ask away," Stanley said.

"Are you just taking me someplace to kill me?"

The two men on either side of Will looked at each other and didn't answer. Will felt a cold hand move up his spine and a shot of adrenaline give strength back to his knees. He rose up a bit, still putting his weight into their hands, but more awake and aware now and ready to make a move.

But what move? A Jerry Lewis marionette kind of thing thirty feet into a stone wall? Then again, caught in a pair of vise grips, he wasn't moving much of anywhere.

But he was certainly awake. The adrenaline jolt that came with no answer to the question that he didn't want to ask had brought him back from the brink of unconsciousness, real fast.

There was something to be said for that.

The trio continued on in silence, until Will finally landed on a new point, a point in his favor.

"You know, Cheryl told me that you're family. And if you're her family, you're pretty damned close to being my family. Family. That matters, doesn't it?"

"What do you mean, family?" Ollie muttered, darkly.

"I mean, me, Cheryl, you, me. Rose."

"You know Rose?" Stanley asked, brightening.

"Rose, oh, yeah, I know Rose. Rose loves me. I come within twenty-five miles of her house and she starts cooking. She's crazy about me."

"Yeah. Rose is my sister."

"Really? I love Rose. Her stuffed peppers are killers."

The word was out of his mouth before he could stop it. It hung uncomfortably in the air, then disappeared in a gust of wind. Will felt his heart sink.

"Really?" Stanley smiled, "I wouldn't take you for a stuffed pepper kind of guy. Those are my favorites."

Will smiled weakly and whispered, "Love 'em. Just love 'em."

"Stanley," Ollie said, "this is not the time nor the place."

"But, Ollie, he knows Rose."

"And Rose loves me," Will added. "So does Cheryl. And Raymond— remember Raymond? He was my best friend."

"What?" The statement stopped Ollie in his tracks. He turned Will toward him and stared, hard, into his face. Will could feel his chest tighten from the look alone.

"You knew Raymond?"

"Yeah, I knew Raymond," Will said, in all seriousness, "I knew Raymond. I rode with Raymond. He was my best friend in the entire world." Without realizing it, tears began to fill Will's eyes. "I rode with him on the day he was killed. I was just behind him. The truck hit him and I hit the truck. I think. I dunno. I can't remember it so much anymore. I just remember sounds and flashes and screams." Now, his chest tightened for a different reason and Will put his hand to his face for a second, before brushing away the memory and staring back at Olverio Cangliosi.

"Yep. Knew him. I dunno what you fellows want, but let's get this done, okay? I suddenly feel like shit inside and out and just want to lie down."

"You," Ollie whispered. "You were the other guy."

Will nodded sharply and began to walk down the street alone, the two men who had been holding him only moments before standing quietly behind him, lost in their own memories of their nephew.

Will stopped and turned back to them.

"You coming?"

Stan and Ollie nodded and walked up beside Will. Ollie didn't take his arm, Stanley did, but it was more in support, now, rather than restraint. The three continued to walk, slowly, toward the highway.

"So, what do you need from me?" Will asked.

Stanley's eyes wiggled in their sockets, unsure of how to answer such a direct question. Ollie didn't hesitate.

"We want a box or a case, some kind of long, thin, heavy container that a friend of ours might have left with you."

Will nodded.

"Leonard."

"Exactly. Your friend...."

"My agent. He wasn't exactly my friend."

"... your agent did some work on the side in New York, running money for a numbers racket run by a gentleman known as Bloody Angelo."

"Not a nice man," Stanley offered.

"Usually not with nicknames like that," Will agreed, his nervousness beginning to return as the adrenaline faded from his system, taking his courage with it.

"Well," Ollie continued, "one day, after a particularly heavy week of betting, your friend, agent, acquaintance, was entrusted with the whole shooting match and decided to run."

"You can't have that and run a business," Stanley added.

Will nodded in agreement. "Screws up the books. Pisses off the IRS I'd imagine."

Stanley laughed.

"The IRS. Yeah, the IRS do get pissed."

Will immediately recognized the stupidity of the remark.

"So we were hired to find him," Ollie concluded.

"And kill him," Will said, remembering the case under his bed while trying to keep his impression of a Vienna choir boy out of his voice.

"If necessary. But we don't like to work that way."

"But you've done it?" Will asked.

Olverio Cangliosi stopped and stared at Will for a moment and nodded, finally saying, "Yeah, we've done it."

"Not as often as we've been given credit for it," Stanley said.

"No, that's true," Ollie answered, "that's certainly true."

Will smiled, a big, fake smile that tried to hide the fact that his guts were turning to mango mush. They turned together and walked on in silence.

They reached the corner of East Meadow Drive and paused for a second and looked down the street, and, then, toward Will.

Without a question, he provided an answer, nodding at the tall white building next to them and saying, "This one. 401. Corner room."

"Thank you," Ollie said.

"Yes, indeed, thank you," Stanley added.

"No, no, gentlemen, I must thank you," Will joked, hoping to lighten the mood and settle his guts, now leaping and heaving as if they were going to leap from his body and race down the road on their own.

"Hey, dude, bad day at Black Rock?"

The twenty-something dropped out of the crowd and crossed directly in front of the trio, drawn to them by Will's appearance and the need for the single crash story he hadn't seen or heard all day long.

Will felt the pressure tighten on his arms, lifting him up straighter between his two bookends. He smiled and nodded.

"Yeah. Bad endo, but not on the course, dude. I came over the ridge and hit some gnarly single track on the way to Vail Pass and did head stands all the way down the side of the mountain. Luckily, a rock got in my way and stopped me."

"Lucky, dude," the guy moaned.

Will nodded.

"Yeah, now my uncles are haulin' my bones back to my room. Thank god I've got family here, huh, dude?"

"Oh, yeah, maybe, I guess," the guy answered. "My mom's here somewhere and you can have her, too."

"Thanks, send her over."

"Ha, sure, dude," the guy said, laughing, nodding and walking way. "Sure, dude. Stitch clean. Stitch clean, buddy."

"Thanks, dude."

Olverio watched the young man walk away into the construction at the end of Bridge Street and turned to Will.

"What was that?"

"Actually, I'm not sure," Will replied, "I think he was just looking for a story for tonight, and I just looked broken up enough to be it."

"Weird damned sport," Stanley muttered.

"Oh, I agree with you, sir, I do agree with you."

The three turned and made for the front door of the hotel, entered, crossed the lobby and stepped into the stairwell.

"Can't we take the elevator?" Will asked.

"Don't like elevators," Stanley replied.

"Only if you've got to, son, only if you've got to. They're death traps," Ollie answered.

Will stumbled up the steps while pondering Ollie's fear, the only image coming to mind that of Clemenza with the shotgun during the murderous aria at the end of one of "The Godfather" movies. At the moment, he wasn't sure which, as they were all running together in a cacophony of music and murder, and Diane Keaton sounding pained.

They walked silently now, the only sound being the effort of their breathing, all three at altitude for the first time, one just plain damned tired.

They passed two and were halfway up to number three when Will turned to Ollie, one step behind.

His mind told him to just keep walking, to keep moving, and to give them the damned money and be done with it all. But, there was a question he had to ask and there was a point he had to make, not for him, but for the woman he loved.

And he was too much of a coward to ask it or make it.

"Keep moving," Ollie said with a wheeze, waving his hand blindly up the stairs.

"Not yet," Will said, all the time summoning his courage from every point in his body, "not yet. We're alone here and before we go up and you get what you want and take off, I have to ask you a question."

"And that would be?" Ollie stared at him, coldly, his patience ebbing away after a truly bad weekend.

Will looked at Ollie, turned to Stanley—who had stepped up to the next landing, looked, come back and nodded—then turned back to Ollie.

"Why'd you do it?"

"Why'd I do what?"

Will took a deep breath. No matter how hard he tried to focus, to ask the question he needed to ask, his mind refused to go directly to the point and skirted the issue.

"Cheryl's been—running—for years. Europe. Here. New name. Whole mess. Running. From you guys."

"Us?" Stanley said, clearly shocked. "Why would she run…."

"… from us?" Ollie finished.

"She's run from you guys because she was sure you were going to whack her."

"What!?!" Stanley popped. "Where the hell did she ever get an idea like that?"

Ollie simply shook his head. "Explains a lot. Her general pissiness. Running away. Doesn't explain why though."

"Oh, come on, guys," Will said, their confusion at his revelation building his courage in a roundabout way, "why shouldn't she feel this way. She saw you."

"She saw us what?"

"She saw you whack her father!"

The words were out before Will could stop them in a tone he couldn't control. Before they had even bounced off the far wall, Ollie was on him, slamming Will back against the wallpaper and driving the wind, for the third time that day, out of his chest. Ollie clutched Will's throat and began to squeeze. Will gagged and clawed for air, turning his eyes to Ollie's face and seeing nothing but a mask of hatred there, the eyes full dead in their sockets.

In that moment, Will knew he was going to die.

He wet himself.

Stanley stared at them both for a split second, his reaction to Will's accusation ringing in his ears and freezing his heart. He shook himself free and jumped between the two, breaking Ollie's hold of Will's neck and pushing his partner away.

Will fell to the floor and roared with the effort of breathing again.

"Let me at that little fucker," Ollie snarled, reaching past Stanley and back toward Will, "just give me another few seconds with him."

"Ollie. Ollie! Stop it. Stop. Stop." Stanley held him until he could feel the muscles in his arms relax, and the breathing return to normal. "Stop. Stop. Are you calm? Calm, pal?"

Ollie nodded.

"Okay, then, okay," Stanley held both hands up in a gesture of peace and stayed between the two, backing away from Ollie and over to Will on the other side of the landing. He took a glance back, adjusted his step a bit, and brought his heel down, hard, on Will's right hand.

"Jesus!" Will barked.

Stanley turned, lifted Will in one move, and said, angrily to his face, "Jesus, indeed, boy. You had better explain yourself real quick or you'll be explaining it to the man himself."

Will's mind raced to find a word, a phrase, an avenue that might save his life, but all that would come out was a torrent of words, loosely connected, that spilled out over his lips and onto the floor, making no sense to him at all.

"She, she, saw you, she said, Cheryl said she saw you, the day, the day, her father died, she saw you...."

"She saw us what?"

"She saw ... you ... you two, with her father. Her father. She saw you ... with her ... his ... his body. His body. You were standing with his ... body. She ran. You ran after her and she was sure ... sure you were going ... to ... so she ran ... she ran away, okay?" He was crying now. "Europe and stayed there. I met her. Saw her there. We ... you know ... then, you ... she saw you here. Here. Told me. She told me. You killed her.... Aw, shit."

Will became a dead weight, falling out of Stanley's hands and sliding away to the floor of the stairwell, where his eyes focused on a nonexistent pattern in the industrial carpet while his soul waited to see his grandfather again.

Stan and Ollie stood in shocked silence in the stairwell, the only sound being Will's quiet weeping at their feet. Neither said a word for a long moment, until Stanley turned to his partner and said, quietly, "Well, I'll be fucked."

Ollie nodded, the cursing, his and Stanley's, making no impression on his mind.

"So will I."

They turned back to Will, stepped over and gently gathered him up. Will wasn't with them at all. He wept quietly and his body had the consistency of a sack of rice left out in the rain. His face, his shirt, and his pants were wet.

Will Ross was, quite frankly, a mess.

But, for some reason that he couldn't fathom, the men on either side of him didn't seem to mind. They carried him, carefully, up the steps, toward the landing for the rooms on the fourth floor. Stanley opened the door to the hallway and looked in, both ways, and waited until the short, round woman finished moving the black bicycle case into the elevator and the door closed behind her.

"401?"

"That's what the man said."

They carried and dragged Will down to the end of the hall, then fished in his soggy side pocket until they came up with the key card.

Ollie swiped the card, turned the knob and stepped into a small sleeping room, with a tiny bathroom to one side and a view of the creek and the village and the mountain ahead. Holding the door for Stanley, who had slung Will's arm over his shoulder, Ollie watched as his friend and partner carried the broken bicycle rider into the room.

"Where is the case, Will?" Ollie asked, gently.

"Under the bed," Will answered distantly. "Under the bed, but...."

Ollie crouched down, flipped up the comforter and looked under the bed. The space was empty except for one "DO NOT REMOVE THIS LABEL UNDER PENALTY OF LAW" slip torn from a pillow, and assorted dust bunnies. He turned back to Stanley and Will, shook his head and asked, "Any other ideas?"

Will's eyes widened as the calcium found its way in a headlong rush back into his bones. He leapt away from Stanley as if electrified, stood ramrod straight in the middle of the hotel room and shouted at the top of his lungs.

"What!?!"

CHAPTER SIXTEEN:

MONKEY WRENCHING

ILL FELL TO HIS KNEES AND FELT A PAINFUL SHUDDER RUN UP and through his legs and thighs, pelvis and chest, to set up a pounding between his ears. It bypassed his gut, already filled with a lump the size of Wichita Falls, Texas. He fought with an edge of the comforter, in his desperation, now a living breathing thing, yanked it up and looked under the bed, the emptiness there causing him to gasp and inhale a large dust bunny.

He gagged, for that, and a number of other reasons.

Will turned back and sat, downhearted, feeling violated, on the floor at the end of the bed.

"Is that where the case was, Will?" Stanley asked.

All Will could do was nod.

"Are you sure?" Ollie said.

Will nodded again, not quite sure what to say or how to say it.

"You don't forget where you put a box with all the money in the world."

"No, I guess you don't," Ollie said.

Stanley crinkled his forehead, the effort of thought making his face hurt. "A black box, you say? A black bicycle box?"

"How big is that box, Will?"

Will stirred himself, stared at the two men, both looking as frustrated and disheveled as he knew he must, and said, hollowly "It's a box, maybe three by five. Eight inches wide. Black, heavy gauge plastic with silvered edging and locks."

"Has it got little wheels. Lengthwise?" Stanley made a gesture with his hands.

"Casters? Yeah, yeah, it's got casters."

Stanley nodded for a moment, then turned to Ollie. "I think I know where it is," he said, brightly.

"Really?" Ollie replied, in a light and happy tone, "Well, then I think we should leave our friend here to clean himself up, and go in search of our quarry."

"Indeed."

"In-deed."

"Huh?" Will mumbled, dumbly, the electric energy of finding his room stripped of the treasure chest starting to leave his spine.

Stan and Ollie smiled at each other and turned for the door, Ollie opening it and stepping through into the hall. Just as Stanley stepped through, he turned back to Will.

"You wouldn't happen to know an old woman, short, squat, looking kind of like a walking trash barrel, would you?"

"What?"

"Little dame. Grey hair, determined look about her?"

Will started to shake his head, no, which caused Stanley to frown, but then, a spark of memory made him sit up a bit at the end of the bed and say, "Wait a minute. This morning. The woman on the bus. The walker. The lady who was so into nature. Kept riffing on nature. Wacko. Yeah, yeah. There was a woman who was real interested in me. Who I was. Where I was staying."

Ollie leaned back through the door. "Did you tell her?"

Will wiggled his fingers in the air and clutched his head, desperately searching his conversations of only an hour before, hoping that he wouldn't remember what he knew he would.

"Yeah, I think I did. She kept calling me Murph for some reason, even though I think I already met her someplace, then she asked where I was staying and I told her. She had helped me, man, I had a bad fall. She helped me. So, I told her. Then, when I was getting off the bus, I told her that my name wasn't Murph, it was Will and she got real agitated. The bus left and she was pressed against the back window like a Garfield sticky doll."

"Did you ever get a name?"

"Yeah. I did. I did," Will mused, digging through the pain, the muddle and the sheer exhaustion of the day so far, "Stump. Marjorie Stump."

"Marjorie Stump," he said, committing it to memory. "You're sure?"

"Yeah," he said, his head bouncing faster as the excitement of knowing that he could actually still remember something became a physical pleasure. "Yeah. I remember it because it fit her so well. The image and the name are perfect. She's like her own memory game."

Stanley turned to Ollie.

"Marjorie Stump."

"Got it."

"Let's went."

Stanley slid past Ollie and stepped into the hallway, moving quickly toward the stairs. Ollie turned back toward Will and said, quietly, "Sorry about earlier, my friend. Hope you can understand. Get cleaned up and we'll talk later. Tell Cheryl we need to talk, too. Okay?"

He smiled a smile that chilled Will to his very core and pulled the door closed behind him. Will stared at the pale yellow fire door and the hotel information card screwed into a cheap frame at a weird angle on the back and felt himself collapsing internally.

"Can't wait," he said, sarcastically, to the door and the room and the green TV screen.

This had been some morning, filled with one lion, Marjorie Stump, Marshall Reed, and two guys named Stan and Ollie. Of them all, only the lion hadn't really threatened him. His fall was his own damned fault.

He was still on his knees on the floor, but, finally alone, he reached up and braced himself on the end of the bed and pushed himself upward into a standing position. He faded back for a second, compensated, and shakily gained his balance. Everything he had, hurt. He needed a shower. No, he needed a bath. A stop-the-drain, soak-until-you're-parboiled bath where he could think. He stumbled into the bathroom, closed the drain and stuffed a washcloth into the overflow.

Turning on the water, he felt the heat rise up and caress his face. He fought to stay awake at least until he could step in and soak. He had to think. He needed time to figure this all out.

He needed time to decide what to do.

He stood solitary and alone in front of the mirror covering the wall of the bathroom. He stared at the man in the glass, broken, bent, and, if such a thing were possible, even more tired than he. He waved his hand in tired frustration at the image.

"I don't have time for you," he muttered.

Will painfully stripped away the Haven jersey; leaves, grass, and a twig the size of a No. 2 pencil dropped noisily to the floor. He ignored them. He kicked off his shoes and stripped away the soggy cycling shorts and tights, pulling one of his two socks away at the same time.

He ignored the other one and stepped into the tub, shutting off the water as he went, just as it passed the top of the overflow. He slowly lowered himself into the heat of the tub, taking care not to burn his manhood as he did. His butt finally reaching the bottom, he slid out, full length, took a towel from the pile next to the tub and rolled it into a pillow.

He settled in, noticed the sock, and picked it off with the toes of his other foot, setting it free, letting it float on the top of the steaming ocean next to the island that was his left kneecap.

Rather than think, he felt himself drifting away, the last errant thoughts rising with the steam, like four million lighter-than-air bucks.

Marjorie Stump somehow knew about the four million bucks.

And that each and every one of them was in a bicycle case in his room.

And she knew where that room was. And how to get into it. And how to get away with the case.

The case, but not the key. That wouldn't stop her, but it sure as hell would slow her up.

The pain of the morning, the effort, the mind-numbing stupidity of it all drifted away in the vapors that steamed the mirror and in the quiet that surrounded him so completely that it took on a sound of its own.

He floated through it all, his mind losing all shape and focus and function.

One last thought wandered through and waved at him from behind the back of his eyeballs.

It made him smile with satisfaction.

It was the only thing that had gone right today.

"I know something you don't know," he whispered in a weak, sing-song voice, to everyone, to no one in particular.

❀

"TRUSTING SOUL, AREN'T YOU?"

Hootie Bosco looked up from the tray he so carefully balanced as he walked along the uneven ground and visibly started at the sight of Cheryl Crane sitting in the lawn chair in front of the loaded workstation in front of the open step van.

"Whoa! Well, hey, there, you've changed."

"How have I changed?" Cheryl asked, trying to keep her disappointment, bordering on anger, in check.

"Well, when I left, you were your boyfriend. Now that I return, you is you."

"What are you talking about?"

"Like I said, when I left here, it was your boyfriend sitting in that chair. He was on the verge of snoozin', but I felt it was safe to leave for a few minutes to snag a snack. By the way, I brought him a beer, but since he's become you, I guess ownership on that changes, too."

"No, thanks," Cheryl waved him off, "I'm racing today."

Hootie shrugged. "Oh, well. More for me."

Hootie Bosco turned and slid the tray onto the floor of the step van, one of the beers sloshing a bit and sending a wall of froth down the waxed paper cup. He said "shit" under his breath. So much work, so much effort, gone to pot at the last possible second. He ran his palm along the edge of the cup, picking up the majority of the foam before it ran into the tray, and licked it off.

It was cold. It was good. It tasted ever so slightly of dirt and heavy grease, which, to him, was not a particularly bad combination.

Cheryl rose up out of the deep, rump sprung lawn chair.

"So, when you left, Will was here?"

"Yep."

"Watching things?"

"Through half-closed eyes, but yeah. I thought I'd be back quick enough before we lost him completely to Morpheus, but the line was longer than I figured. Besides, it would take somebody with balls the size of church bells to wander in and lift with him even just sitting there."

"Unless he was snoring."

"Well, yes, that would be bad."

"Well, he wandered off. Left the truck wide open, the equipment out. You said he was sleeping."

"Not quite," Hootie answered, feeling himself caught in the lucky outcome of what could have been a bad situation. "But, just by looking around from here I can tell you that nothing's gone."

"You're lucky," Cheryl said, in a quiet tone of authority. "We could have lost a lot."

Hootie nodded, even his dreadlocks hanging, acting somewhat ashamed of their actions.

Cheryl looked up the mountainside and frowned. She was an hour away from her shot at the downhill course, which they were already beginning to open up. In the changing light of mid-afternoon, the Village was filling with racers and fans, grabbing last-minute victuals and supplies before heading up the mountain for the prime viewing locations. The race marshals, she could see, were resetting the race barricades before the course became plugged with humanity.

It was time to fly. From this time on, there'd be no calm in her heart, or time in her life, until Monday morning.

She sighed. The gods of mountain biking were against her. She had come in a day late and wound up more than a few dollars short. The weekend had already overwhelmed her, and her main reason for being here had yet to begin.

Cheryl rubbed her forehead and glanced up to one side, seeing some movement near the edge of a building. She stared at it for a moment, then backed up next to the step van, dropping her sunglasses onto the bridge of her nose as she did.

"Hootie," she said, quietly, "do you have a pair of sunglasses?"

"Yeah."

"Put 'em on, would you?"

Hootie Bosco looked at her for a moment, shrugged, plucked his sunglasses from his shirt pocket, flipped them open and slid them on.

"Just chat with me, would you?"

"Ooo-kay," he said slowly, with just a hint of concern.

"Don't turn your head, but while we're chatting, keep your eyes on the corner of that lift hut over there."

"Which one, there are like a thousand."

"That one up close left, the brown job with the rough edging."

"You're still not cutting it down, but I think I know which one you're saying," he said, cranking his head a bit to the right, pointing at a tool on the ground, but keeping his eyes, behind the sunglasses, peering off to the left, toward the corner of the hut.

In a light and jovial tone he said, as he reached down to pick up the tool, "So, uh, what am I looking for here?"

"I dunno, maybe nothing. I'm just getting the creepiest feeling that some guy is still following me around today."

"Still? Really?" he turned back to her, now shuttling his eyes spy on the corner. As if on cue, a tall, blond figure leaned out from behind the edge, the head at least a head higher than Hootie expected a head to be. The head retreated as Hootie turned his face full toward the corner, staring straight at the spot.

"Well, that's unobtrusive. You'd make a great spy," she said, sarcastically.

"Sorry. Sorry," he apologized. "You just don't expect a head to bop out that much higher than a normal person's."

"He's creepin' me out, Hootie."

A bell suddenly rang in the back of Hootie Bosco's head. He wasn't quite sure what it meant, or what it was, for that matter, perhaps an acid flashback from a bad piece of windowpane thirty years before, but the bell was there and he rose to answer it.

Without another word to Cheryl, he crossed the pit area, picking his way through the crowd of vans and trailers and even an RV or two, toward the corner of the hut.

Cheryl hissed at him in the background in a vain attempt to get his attention, to draw him back, to not give away the notion that they knew this guy was there. Abruptly, she stopped, first because she suddenly realized that it didn't matter if the guy knew, that it might scare him off, and second because it was painfully obvious that Hootie was operating on pure instinct now, drawn to the corner by a mysterious magnetic force than answered to nothing or no one on the planet.

He crossed in close to the lift shelter and walked quickly and quietly along a pile of hoses and board lumber that fronted it, turned the corner and came face to face with Kelvin Stump, who was just then leaning forward for another quick look.

In shock, Kelvin fell back and tripped over a small boulder, crashing to the ground over the edge of a hose, tangling his feet as a small water sprinkler dug into his back and forced him to spit out a curse.

"Don't do that," Hootie said, quietly, eyeing Kelvin suspiciously with a hard look, "don't try to sneak up on us, don't try to spy ... I know you."

Kelvin Stump lay silently on the curled hose, quickly judging his options. He could run, he could punch this guy, or he could just lie here, tangled up, and try to deal with it all as gracefully as he could.

"I'm a race fan," he said, finally, smiling at Hootie Bosco, "I'm a big fan of hers and I'm, uh, too embarrassed to come up and ask for her autograph."

Hootie nodded.

"Bullshit."

"What? No, I...."

"Cut the crap, pal, I haven't got time and now I've got you pegged. I remember the nose. You're that big-drink-of-water son-of-a-bitch that was snipping spokes the other night—which makes you no goddamned fan—and yesterday you came in tow with that mouthy old dame looking for Will."

Kelvin Stump stared at the rock near his feet for a split second, trying to find an answer there, but found none. He finally smiled and opened his hands to Hootie, pulled his feet out of the hose and pushed himself up to full height. He had at least nine inches on the mechanic.

"Yeah, you caught me dead to rights."

"You had better fuckin' explain yourself."

Kelvin stared at the ground for a moment, attempting to simply reek of humility, then sighed, looked at Hootie, and nodded sheepishly.

"You're right. My mother—the little nasty one you were talking about—yeah, she wants to find some guy named Will Ross for some reason, don't ask me why. She told me to follow her," he turned and pointed to Cheryl, still sitting on the edge of the step van, staring at the two at the corner, "and so I did. I'm sorry, it was wrong, but, man, you do what my mother asks or…."

He paused.

"Or what?" Hootie offered.

"Or you get things like this…." Kelvin Stump sighed again and smiled. He thought for a second, then pulled up his right pant leg.

Hootie Bosco couldn't help but gasp at the sight. The man's right knee was a mass of bruises, some old, some new, some high, some low, some right on the knee cap itself, which, in turn, was nothing but a mass of knots and lumps, bulging and receding, all forming a large and indistinct mass on the joint itself.

"Son of a bitch."

"Exactly," Kelvin said, quietly.

"What the … what…." Hootie stammered.

"Her cane. Her blackthorn cane."

"Jesus."

Kelvin nodded. "Same thing I say when she uses it."

His face pinched tight now, in embarrassment as much as anything else, Kelvin rolled down the pant leg.

"So—I do what Simon says," Kelvin said, then laughed. "What Mama wants, Mama usually gets. Sorry."

Hootie Bosco merely shook his head, still shocked by the sight of the kneecap. He finally looked up at Kelvin and said, "I understand. I understand. Makes me sorry about whacking you in the face yesterday."

"That's okay. She wanted me to mess you up. You returning the favor shut her up, but good."

"Still, I'm sorry about that."

"Thanks."

"My papa swung pretty hard, too."

"Then you do understand."

"Yeah. Come on over. You might as well meet her. Maybe we can figure out a way to get Will and your mom together and make everybody happy."

"Except Will, I'd figure."

The line, coming out of the blue, so unexpected, made Hootie pop a laugh. He stifled it and turned to Kelvin. "Sorry."

"Hey, don't worry. You gotta take a joke where you find it with her."

Hootie nodded and waved his hand. "Come on along. You can have the extra beer I've got, then we can figure out what we can do."

"Thanks."

As the two began walking toward the Haven-TW step van, Cheryl rose off the back and took two steps toward them, eyeing both suspiciously. She would have continued, meeting them before they entered the Haven area, which she instinctively considered a "safe" place, but stopped as everyone in the pit area, it seemed, streamed past her.

She turned and looked, following the movement of the crowd, and picked up a trials demonstration down the hill at the corner of Hanson and Bridge. The rider was doing bike-handling acrobatics, bouncing on the bike's rear wheel up each step of a picnic table, dropping down, turning on a single point of the rear tire, then doing it again. He had picked the perfect time and the perfect place for it, drawing just about everyone in the Village to the show.

Cheryl watched for a moment, drawn to the movement, grace and balletic quality of it all, then turned back as Hootie and Kelvin passed the lawn chair and stepped up to the back of the truck. Hootie reached over and pulled one of the two beers from the tray and handed it to Kelvin, who took it with a smile and sipped.

"Thanks, man. I needed that."

Cheryl watched with a suspicious amazement.

Hootie turned with the other beer and looked at her, offering the brew. "You sure?"

"Yeah," she said, with a touch of anger in her voice, "I'm sure. What is this, like some college reunion we've got going here?"

"This guy ... this ... what's your name?"

"Kelvin."

"Kelvin's got a problem and his problem is his mother and his mother wants to meet Will in the worst damned way and told Kel to follow you because you and Will are, well, you know, and so Kelvin did."

"What does your mother want with Will?" she said, quietly, her mind suddenly alive and intending to protect a bike box of money that she had only recently convinced herself wasn't hers to protect.

"Honestly, I don't know," Kelvin said with a laugh, shaking his head, "she gets an idea into her head about riders or the environment or just about any damned thing and she just takes off. Nothing. Nobody. No-body gets in her way. Especially me."

Cheryl eyed him for a moment, then turned to Hootie.

"Any idea where he is?"

"Huh? God, I've got no idea. Isn't really my day to watch him, even if he wandered in here all busted up."

"Busted up?" she said, her voice rising.

"Sorry, sorry," Hootie raised his hands in apology. "I screwed up. Shoulda told you. He totaled the rim again on the Colnago. Said a mountain lion knocked him off the path on the way up Vail Pass."

"Mountain lion?" Kelvin offered. "There haven't been mountain lions around here in a long time. All the development."

Hootie shrugged. "That's his story and he's sticking to it."

Cheryl looked at the mechanic dumbfounded. "Is he okay?"

Hootie grinned. "He was okay enough to kick the shit out of Marshall Reed."

"What?" Cheryl suddenly felt out of control again. All these things were affecting her life and those she loved or knew or worked with, and she had no idea what was going on. "What the hell happened?"

The three turned as the cheers from the crowd watching the trials riders broke into their conversation. They were alone now in the pit area. Cheryl turned back to Hootie.

"What the hell happened with Reed?"

Hootie held up his hands. "Okay. Okay. Will comes in about two hours ago, maybe a little more, I dunno and he's a fucking mess. Okay? Twigs, leaves, fucking branches everywhere. He's a mess. So's the bike. Front wheel is gone—for the second time—and the fork is cracked. He cracked a damned fork. Do you know what kind of torque…."

He stopped as Cheryl waved her arms in circles, to get the story moving again.

"Okay. Okay. So, Marshall Reed walks in here and sees the Colnago. You know—his bike—and he freaks. Goes ballistic. Does that Joe Pesci thing from the gangster movie, you know, 'Goodfellas,' or whatever…."

Cheryl continued to spin her hands, forcing the story forward.

"And so, Reed goes after Will. Just jumps his bones. Tries to kick start his head. And pushes Will back here…."

Hootie backed up and slapped his hands on the floor of the van.

"… so Will reaches over and grabs this …" Hootie said, picking up the heavy, twenty-eight-inch-long wrench, "… and he 'drives it' into Reed's gut. It was amazing, just goddamned amazing."

Hootie smiled for the two-person crowd, coming close to taking a bow for his performance.

"You … are … kidding me," Cheryl said, a small smile crossing her face.

"Nope. This is a no-shit zone. It be the truth," Hootie said, turning to Kelvin. "Here, Kelvin," he added, tossing the five-pound wrench to him, "heft that once. See if you'd like it in your gut."

Kelvin caught the wrench clumsily and made a face. "No way, man, no way. Remember, I caught this with my face yesterday."

"Oh, Jesus, that's right," Hootie said with an embarrassed grimace.

He turned to Cheryl and smiled as another cheer rose from the crowd gathered nearly a block-and-a-half away from them. Kelvin glanced at the crowd, and Hootie turned, following Kelvin's glance. He never saw it coming.

The wrench snapped out and caught Hootie Bosco just behind the left ear. He looked up in surprise, his mouth working, like a fish out of water, and began to fall back. In one smooth move, Kelvin lifted Hootie's body, growing limp, and tossed it back onto the floor of the step van, the mechanic instinctively curling into a fetal position as he hit the floor. His attacker reached up and pulled the door strap down.

Cheryl had been staring at the crowd as well and had missed the punch, the push, and the door. She turned to see Kelvin Stump throw the heavy-gauge door latch to the side, locking Hootie's body in the rear of the step van.

"What the...." was all she could get out before her right arm was pinched in a ham-fisted vise, forcing her to rise up on her toes.

"Jesus."

"Don't curse, Cheryl, dear," Kelvin Stump snarled. "That poke you feel in your side is a three-inch blade. It won't go in deep, but it will go in deep enough to thoroughly fuck you up. So keep your mouth shut and come along with me. Anything. Anything at all and I'll slice you up like yesterday's fish and feed you to the birds."

"Hootie."

"Fuck Hootie. Payback time for my face. It's you you should be worried about. You and that fucking boyfriend of yours and the money you've got."

"Oh, shit."

"Exactly."

He pulled her to the side, crossed over to a break in the fencing at the edge of the pit, away from the village, and pulled her down the embankment. She struggled, then feeling the point of the knife dig through her jersey, relaxed as much as she could in the situation and followed along.

Wait for the opportunity, they had always said.

There's always an opportunity.

A single car approached in the distance.

"Smile," Kelvin ordered, digging the point of the knife a bit deeper into her side. "Smile, Cheryl, for all to see."

Cheryl smiled.

CHAPTER SEVENTEEN:

PLAYING CATCH-UP

ITH HIS LONG LEGS, STANLEY TOOK THE STAIRS TWO AND THREE at a time on the race down toward the lobby, while Ollie rolled and wheezed behind him. For a large man, he was still incredibly lithe, with a dancer's sense of movement and instinct; still, his size and age were both conspiring to slow him down, to add more effort to his movements.

The altitude wasn't helping.

Ollie gasped as he hit the final step and pulled himself through the door into the carpeted lobby. The desk clerk blinked in surprise, caught off guard by the two comically mismatched men who bounded through her lobby in mid-afternoon going far faster than anyone was legally allowed under the unwritten laws of mountain time.

They stepped into the street and looked both ways quickly.

"Which way?"

It hadn't been long, certainly not long enough for the woman, Marjorie Stump, to wrestle the case out of their sight without help. A block-and-a-half down, there she was, waiting for a bus.

Three blocks away, there was the bus. That would only make it more difficult.

Walking quickly, just short of a run, they crossed the busy street, an odd combination of both foot and occasional car traffic hit the opposite side and slowed. The bus was going to beat them.

There was no point in trying to race ahead and change that fact.

Marjorie Stump had been casting suspicious looks around while walking, but now the bus held her focus so completely that she didn't see the two come up behind her.

The bus stopped, the doors opened, and, as she began to drag the case forward, two men stepped to either side and said, in nearly perfect unison, "Here, let me help."

"No, that's fine," Marjorie snapped, more out of exhaustion and paranoia than anger.

"Oh," Ollie answered, sounding like a southern Indiana minister on holiday, "I'm sorry. Of course, if you don't want help."

He stood back politely. Stanley followed suit. Marjorie smiled, wanly, and continued to fight with the case.

The bus driver leaned down from his seat. "Come on," he whined, "I've got a schedule to keep here."

Stanley stepped to the door with a quiet and determined indignation.

"You will just have to wait, young man. This lady has a case she needs to move...."

"I can't take a case on this...."

"If this is public transportation," Stanley intoned, his voice deepening and the volume rising slightly as if reaching the high point of a Sunday sermon, "then your job is to provide transportation to the public—to those who have decided to forgo owning personal vehicles. You are obligated, morally, to aid her now with her ..." he turned and looked at the case, fishing for a description, "... package."

The driver sighed. Old people. Jesus.

"Yeah, yeah, yeah. Come on. Let's move along."

Marjorie had ignored the driver, wiggling the case, on its rollers, to the base of the steps. In doing so, she had very nearly exhausted herself. She stood, breathing deeply, leaning on the case, her hands sweating, her anger now turned inward toward the slow and emotionally painful effects of aging.

She took a breath, turned quickly to Ollie and said, merely, "Please?"

"Of course," he said, with a shy smile, and reached for the suitcase handle on the forward end of the black plastic case.

"Brother?"

Without a word, Stanley nodded, and positioned his hands at the handles in the middle and rear of the case.

"On three," Ollie whispered, bracing himself for the effort. On the count, the two lifted and stepped forward, bringing the lip of the case to the top of the first step. It was heavier and more unwieldy than either had imagined. The contents shifted toward the back, forcing Stanley to quickly reposition himself for the next step.

The driver looked down with amazement.

"Christ, lady, what do you have in there, rocks?"

"I'd ask you not to take the name of my Lord in vain, young man," Marjorie snapped. "And for your information, not that it's any of your business, it's … magazines. Classic magazines. Life magazines. From the war. Very nearly a complete set."

Stan and Ollie grinned. She was good. Damned good.

"Uuuuuup!"

The two lifted the case to the second step, catching a caster for a second, then bringing the case, free, to the floor of the bus. They pushed it forward, turned the case, pushed it forward and turned, finally working it on board.

"Where would you like to sit, ma'am?" Ollie asked, gently.

"In the back, please," Marjorie answered, stepping up behind them.

They moved the case down the center aisle, suddenly aided by the inertia as the driver closed the doors and stomped the accelerator in an effort to pick up time. They brought it toward the side and propped the case up as Marjorie slid into a rear seat. Casually, the two sat on either side of her.

"Wooo," Stanley barked. "I hate, just hate, moving things like that, don't you, brother Marcus?"

"Large, long, and unwieldy. Like the church piano," Ollie said with a chuckle. "Remember that? Iona giving directions and you and me wrestling with it? What was that sign we put on it? 'You haul, it's yours.'"

Ollie nodded. "That's it. That's it."

Marjorie Stump sat silently between them, her nervousness at what she had and what she was doing to get it boosting her blood pressure to dangerous levels.

"Are you all right?" Ollie said, soothingly. "You look pale."

"I noticed that too," Stanley added. "You're scarin' me, ma'am."

"Oh, no, no, no," Marjorie replied in a light, sing-song voice. "I am just fine. Not used to moving such a heavy weight."

"Magazines," Ollie nodded in sympathy, "they can be heavy."

"Indeed," Stanley added.

Quickly changing the subject, Marjorie took a deep breath and shifted her glance back and forth between the two.

"And so … what brings you to Vail?"

"Just a vacation," Ollie said, lightly. "A chance to get outside and get in a little…."

"Fishing? You're here to fish, aren't you?" she said sharply, drawing the needle to attack and, thus, drive them away.

"Fishing? Noooo," Ollie soothed, "no, no. We don't fish."

"Don't fish at all," Stanley added.

"The lives of fish are tough enough without human beings getting in their way, ripping them from their homes and gutting them…."

"Gutting them," Stanley added, "for a dinner the kids won't even eat. No, we're not fishermen. Just tourists enjoying a mountain town as carefully as we can."

"Carefully?"

"Public transport, the concept of light hike, silence in the wild, photography rather than firearms." Ollie stopped at that point and looked out the window as casually as he could, knowing that to push on with more information would only unmask the complete and utter nonsense of everything he was saying. They were pulling out of the Lionshead shopping area and onto the frontage road.

They rode in silence to Cascade Village. The bus stopped quickly, then moved on again, this time toward West Vail.

Marjorie Stump visibly relaxed a bit, a part of her mind telling her that she was among friends, right-thinking people who meant her no harm. The money, leaning in its black case against a line of seats, was secure and hers for the moment. But even as a part of her grew more comfortable, another grew more anxious, a primitive sense of danger racing up her spine, trying desperately to make her mind understand.

She was torn. She was conflicted. She was at her stop.

"Here! Here!" she shouted toward the back of the driver's head, a full bus length distant. "My stop is here."

"We're between stops," he shouted back.

"Just stop. Just stop here."

"Yes, driver," Ollie shouted, realizing that he was sounding vaguely English, "pull up. This woman has a case and this is where she has to go."

Rolling his eyes, the driver pulled up, very nearly directly across from a slender dirt road leading to a small house, completely out of context among the big-money, high-end condos that surrounded it.

"Let us help," Ollie offered.

"No, that's fine," Marjorie replied. "I'll be just fine."

"Insisting. We're insisting," Stanley said.

She nodded, as if it were simply better to agree and be done with them than fight them off with her shillelagh.

"Ready?"

"Ready."

The two put their weight behind it and slid the case quickly toward the front of the bus. One quick turn and it was down the stairs and out the door, landing on its side with a crash.

"Thank you, gentlemen," Marjorie said with a smile. "I'll take it from here."

"No, no," Ollie said sweetly. "We'll help. That's what we're here for."

Marjorie sighed with exasperation and nodded. "Fine. Fine." She turned toward the driver and said, sharply, "When you return they'll be waiting right here. Pick them up. Stop and pick them up. Do you hear me?"

In a sing-song voice left over from answering his first-grade teacher, the driver responded, "Yes, ma'am." He curled his mouth into a half-baked, fake smile and closed the doors, stomping the accelerator again and making the bus fairly leap back onto the road.

"Where to, ma'am?" Stanley asked, the stupid grin on his face actually beginning to hurt.

"This way. Across the road. That house."

"Indeed."

The trio stepped across the road and began rolling, pushing, and pulling the case toward the small, white clapboard house. As they did, Ollie turned back toward Marjorie, who stomped silently behind them, obviously unhappy at the current turn of events.

"Miz Stump. Do you have a phone?"

"Yes, I … how did you know my name?"

"I'm sorry?"

"I never introduced myself to you," she said, suspiciously, slowly beginning to step around them toward the house. "I never mentioned my name."

"Now, Marjorie," Stanley added, "of course you did. On the bus. When you told us about the money."

"Money?" The word popped out of her unexpectedly, whatever color having returned to her face fleeing now in the shock of being uncovered. Completely.

"Yes, Marjorie," Ollie said, darkly, "money. Money that is not yours. Money that is ours. Money that you should not have bothered trying to take."

"I didn't. I…." she pointed frantically at the case, "*Life* magazines."

"Don't insult us, Miz Stump. We know what is in the case. We know where it came from. Even the room number. We just want to know how you knew it was there."

In her shock, she answered without thinking. "Kelvin. My s…."

She caught herself and went silent.

"Calvin?" Stanley questioned.

"Kelvin," Ollie corrected, slowly. "Strange name."

"Your son?"

"Her son."

The two nodded to each other and turned back toward Marjorie.

"A phone, Miz Stump. We're in need of a phone."

Marjorie Stump stared at the two men, both suddenly taking on the look of being far more dangerous than she had ever imagined. How had she been so foolish, she raged. She looked, longingly, at the case, leaning now against the front railing of her porch. So close. So very, very close. She clutched her shillelagh close to her. Her one chance.

Wait for it, she thought, wait for it.

She took a deep breath and turned toward her door, opening the screen, fumbling with the lock, pushing the inner door open as well, holding it for the two who stood, so threatening, behind her.

"I have a phone. You are welcome to use it."

"Thank you, ma'am."

"Yes, indeed."

"For a fee," she said.

The two men laughed and pushed past her into the small entry room. Marjorie Stump closed the doors behind her and pointed them toward the kitchen.

The three walked silently while Marjorie mused.

She hadn't been joking about the fee.

CHAPTER EIGHTEEN:

PHONE TAG

WILL'S EYES SNAPPED OPEN. HE WATER WAS COLD. THE LEVEL HAD sunk to the point that the dirty, abandoned sock was sticking to the side of the tub.

He yawned, braced himself, and sat up carefully.

Nothing swam before him, anymore, though he still felt just the slightest bit queasy. Queasy. A mom word. He smiled at the thought of the vocabulary she had given him. Queasy, zany, wacky.

He slowly pulled himself up, feeling stiff rather than sore, and rolled out over the edge of the tub. Now, he was cold. A mountain afternoon could be in the eighties, could be in the thirties. He sat on the bath mat and listened. Could be an air conditioner, too. Somebody had turned on and cranked up the air conditioner.

He shuddered, then pulled himself up onto the sink and looked into the mirror, wondering who would be looking back at him this afternoon. This morning, it had been Will the bum, sullen, forlorn, ready to leap off a cliff for a new ride.

Mission accomplished on that, he thought.

Now, it was a man who had stepped back from three brushes with death in just one day. Defiant, maybe, somewhere deep behind the eyes, but mainly tired. Just looking for a bump and a beer and a broad.

"Wanna make sumptin' of it?" he swaggered, dully, then waved his hand in dismissal at the image.

He picked up a brush and stroked his hair straight back, grimaced to see his teeth, swiped at himself with deodorant and padded into the bedroom.

He shivered.

"Jesus," he swore, it was like a damned icebox. Will turned off the fan and stepped slowly over to the suitcase, on a table in front of the open curtains. There was a flash of shame when he realized that he was naked to the world, as a jaybird, for all to see. It was a sad realization, in a way.

As a rider, in Europe, he had never felt any shame at stripping down, in a crowd, standing as fresh as a newborn in a sea of people. You had to, as there were usually no facilities around, or, at best, nothing bigger than the back of a Fiat Uno in which to change, peeling off riding gear, which, over seven hours in the saddle had become something close to an experiment in biological warfare.

An ugly thought.

He bent slowly and pulled on the underwear, almost in a dreamlike state, his eyes shuttered, his mouth curled into an odd, satisfied grin. Then he realized that the Hanes seemed tighter than usual. Not much. Nothing ugly. Just tighter. A bit more bite in the middle.

Maybe not time to worry, but certainly something to think about.

He reached into the bag again and pulled out the red, black and gold Haven parachute-cloth training suit, the baggy nylon that he hadn't worn since the Chunnel transfer in the Tour. With Bresson, Henri Bresson, what, mid-July, less than two months ago. Not long, but certainly enough time for a lot of people to die.

In a way, he wasn't quite sure why he was putting it on. The company had promised him the world, then screwed him royally. He was no longer a rider, or a trainer, or a manager, or an assistant, all jobs promised, all jobs gone in the crash of a corporate jet.

That's what happened, he mused. Losing Bergalis. That's what happened, he forced himself to believe.

So maybe he wore the colors out of loyalty. Even though the company had shown none to him. Maybe he wore them out of memory. The thoughts still did warm him. Then again, maybe he wore them simply because logo-covered sportswear was about all he had to call his own.

He zipped up the jacket, slipped on socks and shoes and stood up. The nap-time soak had done wonders, even if it had been only about twenty minutes. There was still a line of pain and stiffness along his ribs, but nothing like what had been there before.

Now—four Advil, dinner, and a beer, and he should be right as rain.

Right as rain.

As long as she was … shit. The realization shot through his brain like a bottle rocket. Her run. Her downhill was … he scrambled for his watch on the table top. Now. Her ride was a few minutes ago. And he had missed it.

He leaned forward and braced himself on the Formica top of the low hotel dresser. He looked up and stared into the room mirror, seeing someone completely different again. This man was a bit older, a bit more broken, with an incredibly crappy sense of timing. His eyes were puffy and sad, finally empty of the light that had been there for so long this spring and summer.

He had let her down. After all that she had done for him, after all the times she had been there to cheer and support and give him life, he had let her down. For what? For a bath. For himself. Dragged away, sure, but as soon as they left he could have hustled back in the other direction, back to the mountain.

For her.

Nice going, creep, he thought. But it fit, didn't it? He was a leech, in a way, hanging onto Cheryl, draining her energy, making her look after him, find him bikes, while he took his own sweet time recovering from the bust and chop of Le Tour, searching for his plan, himself, his ego. Everything for him, no time for her.

"What a fucking cliché," he muttered, pushing himself away from the desk and turning to stretch walk himself around the room.

It was time to start living with her, as a partner. It was time to wake up and discover whatever else lay in store for him, and her, and them. It was time to be a man, not an attachment.

There was a quiet commotion just outside the door of the room. Will was on the far turn of his walk from the hall, turned, and walked back quietly to the door, straining to hear the conversation just outside.

There was a sharp, "Sorry!" in a voice he recognized as Cheryl's, then a man's voice saying, "You would forget the key."

He glanced at his watch. Either that was the fastest run in the history of riding, or there was something wrong. And he didn't like the sound of that voice.

He pulled open the door, quickly, forcing Cheryl to jump and Kelvin Stump to fall back a step. Cheryl, recovering first, dove into the room, body slamming Will back and away from the door. The pains that had been quieted for a time rose up again and Will began to wonder, vaguely, if he was the designated punching bag for the Village of Vail today.

Cheryl turned where she landed on the floor, and tried to kick the door shut with her feet, automatically locking Kelvin Stump out, but the big man had recovered quickly from his surprise in the hall, and pushed his way through the doorway and into the hotel room itself.

As Cheryl pushed herself away from Kelvin with disgust, standing up and walking into the room, Kelvin shut the door quietly behind him.

"If you don't have a key, then have a boyfriend with a key, that's what I always say."

"Is that what you always say?" Cheryl snapped. "How sweet, how goddamned sweet."

Will lay on the floor for a moment, then rolled to his side and, with a painful effort, pushed himself up again. He was getting tired of doing this today.

He watched Cheryl touch her side, and pull away two fingers tinged with blood.

"Jesus, Cheryl," Will shouted, stepping up to her side, his own pain forgotten for a moment, "what the hell happened?"

"He happened," she said, nodding back toward the man in the doorway. "He happened and his mama happened and my uncles happened and everything just plain happened." The last words were spit out through clenched and angry teeth. She sat down, hard, on the edge of the bed. Will sat beside her, ignoring Kelvin Stump, never noticing the tiny, belt buckle knife he had in his ham hock of a hand. Will leaned over and stared at the tear in her uniform, the cut in her skin.

"What the.... Well, it's not deep, anyway. But, Christ, it looks more like a slice than a scratch, what the hell did you run into?" He reached to touch it and she brushed Will's hand away.

"Leave it. It's fine."

266

"Not any more. Maybe when you were a kid, but now we got supergerms everywhere." He got up from the bed and walked to the bathroom, passing Kelvin Stump without a second glance. "Don't you read *Newsweek*? Supergerms are growing. You don't get just old plain germs anymore, you get supergerms." He gathered up a tiny bottle of alcohol, a tube of antibacterial ointment and a self-adhesive bandage, his patter never stopping, as much out of relief at seeing her as concern over her injury. He smiled at the thought. His anger, his concerns, his moment of insecurity had flown, as soon as he saw her face. No matter what mood she was in, he was happy that she was spending that mood with him.

The man standing before the closet didn't enter into the equation.

"Excuse me, pal." He stepped into the room and continued his monologue with Cheryl. "You see, people have been over-prescribing and misusing antibiotics for years, and so these supergerms have developed. They mutate. Get huge and big and ugly." He moved up beside her and waited for her to open her shirt. "Don't worry about him," he wobbled his head in the direction of Kelvin, "open up."

Without taking her eyes off Kelvin Stump, Cheryl unzipped the top of her jersey and peeled it down along her sides. A bit of the blood, the first blood from the cut, had already dried, and she grimaced as it tugged at the edge of the wound when it pulled away.

"This is going to hurt a bit," Will said, dabbing the area with alcohol. He could see her muscles tighten and hear a quick intake of breath. He wiped it clean, and put the bottle of alcohol down. "So, you see, according to *Newsweek*, you can't play around with these germs, cuz they're really bad and they'll kill you. Eat your flesh clean away."

"Really? Did you read that?" she said, distantly, never taking her eyes off Kelvin Stump.

"No. I just saw it on the cover. I bought the *Time* with the story about sex."

He smiled at his own joke, peeled the backing from the pad and pressed it onto the cut, sliding his hand back and forth to smooth it out and to touch her skin … suddenly the thought crowded into his head: Who the hell was this guy?

As he turned to ask, the phone rang. Cheryl visibly stiffened, which caused Will to ignore their guest again and throw his attention and concern toward her.

What the hell was going on?

The phone rang for a second time.

Will looked at Cheryl, who didn't move, then toward the tall man leaning against the wall.

"Why don't you get that?" the man said, the small knife blade, almost a toy, it seemed, emerging from the hiding place in his hand. The why's were still unknown to Will, but the sense of threat he could see in Cheryl's eyes made him understand the danger he suddenly felt.

Will's eyes squinted suspiciously, and he reached for the phone next to the TV set. He slowly picked up the receiver and said, "Hell-o?"

"Will?" came the answer.

"Yeah. It is," he said, slowly. "Um, who is this?"

"This is Stanley. Ha. Your, uh, Uncle Stanley."

"Oh, yes. Hello, Uncle Stanley." He said the last two words with just a hint of expression. If Cheryl heard it, she never flinched or turned away from Kelvin Stump.

Will turned back to the phone.

"Careful," Kelvin whispered.

"You bet. So, what can I do for you, Uncle Stanley?"

"Just wondered if you still had the key to that case we had been discussing?"

"Yes, sir, right here."

"Good."

"Right here, in our room."

"Great."

"Right here on me."

"Good, Will, that's good to know."

"Yep, right …" Kelvin wiggled the knife in his direction "… right here."

"You okay, Will?"

"Oh, not particularly. But I've gotta go. We've got company."

"Company? Good company or bad company?"

"The latter, Uncle Stanley. Ha."

"Hmmm. Big guy? Wants the cash?"

"Bingo, sir. Bingo."

"Got it, kid. Put 'em on the phone."

Kelvin mimed hanging up the phone. Will nodded.

"Gotta go, pal. Say hello to Aunt Olivia. We'll see you both in Denver on Monday."

"Will—put him on the phone."

Will paused for a second, took a deep breath, then nodded to himself in the mirror, before turning and thrusting the phone toward Kelvin Stump.

"He wants to talk to you."

"What?"

"He wants to talk to you." Will shrugged, as if to say he didn't know what to say, then shook the phone at the man with the knife.

Kelvin Stump stared dumbfounded at the phone. Will shook it again until Kelvin acted like he finally saw it. He walked over and slowly took it, as if it might bite, lifting it carefully to his ear.

"Hello?" he said, slowly.

"Hello, yourself," Stanley said, all traces of the lightheartedness he had had with Will gone. "I hear I have something you want."

"What?" Kelvin muttered, still dumbstruck by the notion of someone on the telephone knowing he was there.

"Listen, pal," Stanley said, coldly, "I have a whole boatload of money here that some little old lady was trying to cart off. You wouldn't have an idea who she is, would you?"

"Mama," Kelvin whispered before he could stop himself.

"Ex-actly," Stanley replied.

In the background, Kelvin could hear two voices, a man's and a woman's, arguing about going to the bathroom in the high grass.

"Thing is," Stanley continued, "we got it. We got her. You want both. You got some friends of ours. We want them. Simple."

"I'll kill them."

Both Will and Cheryl sat up straight at the casual mention of their death. Kelvin turned toward the wall for more privacy. As soon as Kelvin turned,

Will quietly tapped Cheryl on the leg and motioned with his head. As subtly as possible, the two began to slide toward the door.

"No you won't, son. It's not that easy to kill a human being. I know from personal experience."

"What, the Big War, Grandpa," Kelvin spat bitterly, the tail of his ego twisted just a bit by the man's demeaning tone. It was another demeaning tone in a life full of them, one more voice talking down to him, one more telling him that he didn't know what he was talking about, that he wasn't aware, that he couldn't fend for himself. The anger built inside him, cresting and crashing over his mind, forcing his face to flush, and one arm to snake out and grab Cheryl Crane, sliding past silently, by the neck of the jersey.

The shock and force of his attack caused her to gag, the jersey twisting suddenly in his hand like a crumpled sheet of paper until she couldn't breathe. Will took a longing glance at the door he was so close to, abandoned it without another thought, and moved quickly back to her side, unzipping the jersey and freeing her neck from the noose of Spandex.

As soon as the fabric loosened, Kelvin Stump, without another thought in the world, released his grasp and Cheryl fell back against the bed.

"Listen," he hissed into the phone, his anger building into a wave, "I know what it's like to kill something, asshole. Animals. People. You name it."

"No offense, friend, no offense," Stanley said, quietly, backing off.

"In fact—in fact," Kelvin continued, his anger controlling his emotions completely now, "there are two people who were alive on Wednesday morning who are no longer alive today because of me. Two. So don't fuck with me. I can easily make it four, right here, right now. You got that?"

"That's good to know, son, that's good to know," Stanley nodded into the phone, his measure of the man fully recorded in his mind, "but now we have some business to attend to. We have your money and we have your mama."

"Where?"

"Well, at the moment, where we are isn't important. Where we will be in fifteen minutes, that's important."

Kelvin nodded into the phone.

"All right. Where?"

"Just a minute, let me check." Stanley turned away from the phone and talked to whoever he was with. Kelvin could hear two voices in the background talking back to the man on the phone, one, clearly his mother, the other a man with a deep and serious voice.

"Where were all those people going?" Stanley asked. "When we were on the bus?"

"There's a bike show," a sullen and angry woman's voice answered. That was mama for sure.

There was a pause before the other voice, the man's voice, the deep and serious one, said, "Where is that?"

"The ice arena," Kelvin could hear mama answer, "Dobson Ice Arena."

There was another pause before the voice came back on the phone, "Dobson Ice Arena. Do you know that, son?" There was another pause on the phone, then the voice was back. "Kelvin? Do you know that ice arena, Kelvin?"

"Of course, I know it, I was there when they built it. I worked there," he answered, somewhat shocked at hearing the man use his name. Damn you, mama.

"Fine, son. We'll see you there in twenty minutes. And bring your friends."

"They aren't my friends."

"I realize that son, but bring them anyway. Otherwise, you won't see mama...."

There was a long, silent pause, before Stanley continued, "... and ... you won't see any of the money."

Kelvin nodded and said, quickly, "I understand."

"Twenty minutes, Kel, we'll see you in twenty minutes."

"Bring the money. The case and the duffel bag. And no tricks."

"Of course, Kel. Of course. I'm not the tricky kind. The duffel?"

"The gym bag. Mama's got it. Bring the gym bag, too, or there's no deal. They're dead."

"Understood," was all Stanley said.

The phone clicked in Kelvin Stump's ear and he felt his anger build again, the first wave having crashed on the sands of his mind, the second, third, and fourth all rolled up close behind, the gaps shortening between them until they were one on top of the other, so close that he couldn't think, couldn't find a spot between each wave to breathe, to think, to function. With a roar, he slammed one fist and a now buzzing phone against his temples, twisting himself backward and pressing hard against his head as if his hands were the only things keeping his brain from squirting out the fault lines in his skull.

His whole life, his whole world, everything that he had planned and worked for, so long, so hard, even killed for, everything was turning to shit before him. He turned to Will and Cheryl.

Because of these two. Because of them. Because of their friends. Because of mama. Because of his goddamned mother.

Will and Cheryl sat, petrified, on the bed, the raging man blocking the route toward the door. The only possible escape, now, was through the window behind them, a window that Will knew from trial and error wouldn't open more than six inches. Even as frightened as he was, he knew he couldn't get through a six-inch-wide opening in an aluminum window.

Kelvin turned to them, his face a mottled mask of red and white splotches, the fury that had built up inside his head only now receding. He flashed the short-bladed knife toward them and hissed, "Come with me."

Neither moved.

"Come with me!" he bellowed, reaching over, grabbing Cheryl by the shoulder and lifting her, almost without effort, off the bed and into a standing position beside him.

"All right, all right," Will squeaked, desperately trying to find his voice, his wits, his testosterone reserves. He stood on shaky legs and waited for some indication as to where he should go and what he should do.

An arm wrapped across Cheryl's back and in to her armpit, pulling her close into Kelvin. She could feel the knife pinch up into the muscles between her right breast and her shoulder. She shifted quietly to take some of the pressure off her side, then, felt him shift again to bring the blade in even harder against the bandage Will had applied only moments before. It already seemed like years.

"Watch it with that," she whispered, frightened.

"Don't you worry." Kelvin spit, "I know what I'm doing and I'm not going to hurt you...."

The last word was phrased oddly, she thought, and she finished his statement before he had a chance to continue.

"Yet," she said.

"Yet," he answered honestly.

"Yet?" Will asked, his voice taking on the timbre of Alfalfa singing "The Barber of Seville."

Kelvin stood quietly for a moment, his anger at the shift in his fortunes subsiding. He should have the money now, but mother, dear mother, had once again thoroughly screwed up his plans. His life. Still, there remained a chance. He had these two. He didn't like extra baggage at a business meeting, but if he could convince everyone that he was willing to die for the deal, or, better yet, let others do the dying for him, then he could still win the game, the set, the match, the money.

"I don't have any more time to play with you two, sorry." He glanced down at Cheryl, now tight beside him. "Don't you think of trying anything, sister, or I'll gut you like a tenth-grade biology experiment. And you, boyfriend," he said to Will, who stood sweating beside the closet door. "It'll be quick, it'll be messy, and she'll be dead. Don't say anything. Don't try anything. Don't run."

Will tried to keep calm, but simply couldn't. His mind raced, splitting into two, four, maybe six different compartments, this moment in time only being one of them. Another concerned itself with his bladder. Yet another wished he hadn't turned off the air conditioning, as the room was becoming stifling. And yet another wondered if he should speak up and spill the one last secret he held, or might ever hold, in order to save his skin just one last time.

And at that, one final compartment screamed: "Nnnnnnooooooo!"

And so he remained silent, the secret remaining with him. Will's eyes shifted rapidly between Cheryl's face and that of the man enveloping her as if he were trying to absorb her essence.

He nodded. He understood.

Kelvin took a deep breath and motioned Will toward the door.

"Carefully," was all Kelvin said.

Will nodded and began to walk toward the short entryway leading to the door and the narrow hall and the tiny elevator and whatever lay beyond for them.

He suddenly felt electrified and alive, as if each nerve ending was desperately searching for a final sensation of life. He had felt danger before, but nothing like this, as if every fiber of his being realized that the end was coming soon, and now was the time to really appreciate life.

His life didn't flash before his eyes, but the colors did, the bright yellows deep in the carpet, the mottled brass of the door knob, the bits of dust hanging nearly motionless in an errant sunbeam near the door.

Will opened the door and stepped through. He took a deep breath and turned, looked at the two behind him and said, "You're going to kill us. Aren't you?"

Kelvin Stump stared at Will for a second, turned to Cheryl, then back to Will and nodded, thinking that, in the end, they just might appreciate his honesty.

CHAPTER NINETEEN:

TRAVELIN' MUSIC

THE TRIO STEPPED OUT OF THE FAUX-TYROLEAN LOBBY AND INTO THE street. There was a lot of hustle and bustle about, enough so that Will felt sure somebody, somehow, would see the terror hidden in their faces and actually do something about it.

For a moment, he actually convinced himself that it might happen, might just happen, before he realized that even those who looked directly at him, even those who stared as they walked by, showed no light of recognition in their eyes, not even a spark of acknowledgment. Their eyes were all dead, as if they looked, but could not see the world around them.

Great time to get philosophical.

Will felt his heart drop again.

They were alone in a world filled with people.

As they walked silently down the street, Kelvin Stump driving the parade, Will began to wonder what a passerby would see even if he or she looked at them attentively. Three people, maybe friends, unhappy, by the look of it, at some turn of events, the tall man with his main squeeze tight beside him, walking stiffly, holding her tight as if afraid she might run away. The woman sullen and angry, perhaps concerned. The second man, the odd man out, walking close beside, the friend, the buddy, the pal, eyes moving quickly, side to side, back to the couple, away into the crowd and back again.

They'd see nothing because, quite frankly, there was nothing to see.

They crossed a main intersection and passed a small mall. A two-screen movie theater was showing a film starring Bruce Willis.

"How much farther?" Cheryl hissed.

"Not far," Kelvin said with a false cheer that failed to mask the nervousness he was beginning to feel. "Two long blocks and we're there. Just past the hospital."

"How convenient," Cheryl whispered.

"You're not going to need it," Kelvin answered.

"Oh, don't worry," Cheryl said, modulating her tone into a calm voice of reason that made Will marvel at her composure, "I wasn't thinking of me. I was thinking of you."

"Me?" Kelvin said, genuinely surprised.

"Yeah, you. You are stepping into a situation…."

"Cheryl, don't," Will cautioned.

"No, Will, I like to let people know who and what they're up against. It's only fair. You have any idea who was on the phone with you?"

"No."

"That's too bad. Because, if you had known, you'd already be in a car and racing toward Denver and a flight to Aruba."

"Ooooo, you're scaring me, sweetheart," Kelvin said, then laughed for the benefit of a passerby, turning and lightly kissing the top of her head.

She cringed.

"I'm not scaring you, man, but I should be. And don't you ever touch me like that again," she said, with a hard smile. "I'm giving you one last chance to save your life…."

"You mean to save yours."

"No," she answered, "I mean save yours. Your own sorry ass. The people you're about to meet are killers."

"So am I."

"I'm not talking about breaking the necks of housecats, pal, or plinking squirrels," she whispered, breathlessly, "I'm talking about stare-you-in-the-eye, without blinking, killers. I'm talking about guys who would rather watch the life seep outta you than watch a ball game." She smiled sweetly and nodded at a woman with a stroller walking in the opposite direction. The woman smiled back, her eyes widening a bit at the sight of the thoroughly mismatched couple walking so closely in the opposite direction.

Kelvin swallowed hard. Then he thought of the money and pulled Cheryl in even tighter.

"Give it a rest," was all he could think to say.

"You won't get the money, friend," she whispered, sweetly, a hard smile on her face, "you won't get anywhere near it."

"I've already got some of it," Kelvin answered, his face set, "I'll get the rest, don't you worry. I'll get the rest."

"You won't get within a hundred yards of the rest of the money, love. In a few minutes, you won't even care about the money. You'll be too busy trying to shove your brains back through the little hole they're going to put in your skull."

"Shut up, bitch," Kelvin snapped, pulling the tiny knife in closer, cutting through the bandage and back into her side.

She grimaced and rose up on her toes away from the point of the blade.

Will stepped in and put his hand on Kelvin Stump's arm.

"Look, ease up, pal," he whispered, a frightened smile the final act of pretense he had left in him, "it may sound like she's dissing you, but she's being honest. She's giving you a head's up on these guys. I know what they can do."

Cheryl nodded.

Kelvin stopped and stared at both of them for a moment, then relaxed, recapturing the easy façade of a smile on his face and stepping off once again for Dobson Ice Arena, now less than a block away.

"So tell me, friend," Kelvin asked, "what can they do?"

Will frantically built a story.

"Let me tell you about these guys, bud. When I was a kid, there was a case in Detroit. Two guys. Found in a warehouse. Mob hit. It was in all the papers. They were some kind of stoolie's for the cops. One of the guys was found in pieces. His arms and legs had been chopped off. The cops figured, the way he was tied up in tourniquets, that he had been alive for most of it. Alive for most of it. Awake. He watched them do it to him. The other guy, just watching it from across the room, they think, had a dishrag in his mouth to keep him quiet. And he swallowed it. He swallowed a towel, man. Just out of fear. Out-of-his-mind fear. He choked to death. They found the rag in his stomach.

"They told me today," Will said, solemnly, "they told me today that they did that. They did that job."

Cheryl's eyes widened at Will's admission.

"Bullshit," Kelvin said, quietly.

"No, no bullshit," Will said, his voice flat and emotionless, "I remember that one. One of the guys, who died, his name was Virgil—something—Sollotzo—something. When I tried to run from them today—they told me. When they came for the money in my room. They told me. They did it."

Kelvin poked Cheryl in the side with the knife. She flinched.

"No shit?"

"No shit, man. No shit," Will said quietly, if frantically. "They claim thirty-four hits and no convictions."

"Runs, hits, and no errors," Cheryl added.

"That's bad luck for me," Kelvin mumbled, "and bad luck for you if we don't make the deal."

Will blanched. He had stolen the story from the book "The Godfather." Virgil, too. Kelvin had replied with a line from the movie "The Godfather."

"Hey," Will pushed ahead, turning and stepping backward, raising his voice just a bit, causing a few passersby to turn for a moment, then continue on unconcerned, "all I'm saying is this—these are bad-shit dudes. They are related to her...."

Cheryl's eyes widened, unhappy with that sudden bit of information.

"... and they care about her deeply. You mark her up any more with that frog sticker of yours and they are going to be really pissed. Really pissed."

"Yeah, so...."

"You think for one second," Will leaned in, whispering, "that two hit men, two professional, experienced killers, are going to give a rat's ass about that little knife of yours?"

"I'm not running."

"I know that," Will answered, blithely. He chuckled. "They know that. They're counting on that."

"What?"

"There's a lot of money at stake, give or take a hundred for last night's dinner. They know you'll be there. Like a lamb to the slaughter...." His tone brightened, as much out of fear as happiness at having arrived. "Here we are,

Dobson Ice Arena," he sang out like Debbie Reynolds in "Singin' in the Rain."

He pulled open a door, only to be greeted by the face of a teenaged guard wearing a yellow apron with "EVENT SECURITY" stitched across the front.

"You can't come in—hall closes in ten minutes."

"Aw, sure we can," Will said, brightly. "We still have ten minutes, and we're supposed to meet the guys from Richardson Bike Mart in here. Jim and Rhonda are taking the three of us to dinner."

Will turned to Kelvin and asked, brightly, "It is Jim and Rhonda isn't it?"

Kelvin looked frozen, the conversation of the past few minutes finally reaching the marrow of his bones where, as the confrontation actually approached, it began to eat away at him. He merely grunted.

"Yeah, Jim and Rhonda," Will chirped.

"You can't come in—we start shutting down the doors at 4:30."

"Ah, I see. That's why it's open till five, so you guys can run everybody out at 4:30."

The teenager's voice squeaked a bit. "Look, man, I don't make the rules...."

"I understand," Will answered softly, leaning in conspiratorially, "but look, pal. I've got a chance for a good dinner in Vail, Colorado, paid for by somebody else. And these folks have good taste, so it will be a nice place. Expensive, too. I don't get that very often." He paused. "Come on, I'm just heading to their booth. Let us in, and we'll be out of here in eleven minutes. 5:01.... 02 at the latest. Whattya say? You'll be in the private sector sometime soon. Help a guy out and God blesses you tenfold," he lied, mangling some saying of his mother.

He smiled a hundred-watt grin at the kid and cocked his head as if to say they were both in this world together, let's help a buddy out, and jerked his head toward the first of the booths.

The kid looked at him, glanced at his watch, and nodded, stepping back and letting the three pass.

"5:02."

"No doubt," Will answered quickly, already moving past. "Jim likes his dinner by 5:24 at the latest."

"Thanks," Cheryl said without enthusiasm.

"Don't mention it," said the kid, never noticing the pale, cold sweat beading up on the face of Kelvin Stump.

The three moved quickly into the large, colorful hall, ignoring the teen, striding past the first three or four booths, two selling energy supplements, the third selling titanium rims. The energy supplement booths had lines of people slurping up free samples of some kind of goo out of community pump bottles, while the cranks were being manhandled and fingerprinted by lookyloos, guys drooling over the material without any intention to buy.

Despite the overhead lights, the room was oddly dim. Will rubbed his eyes and tried to get them to focus as he stopped in the midst of the quickly diminishing crowd and turned to Kelvin Stump.

"Okay, Admiral Byrd, we've reached the pole. What do we do now?"

"We wait," was all Kelvin could answer.

Cheryl felt the fear run down Stump's arm and envelope her. Maybe they had gone too far, she thought. A frightened man was a man who made mistakes.

"You know," she whispered, "you've still got time. You could still save your own hide."

"I know," Stump answered with a smile that chilled her to her very core, "but we wait. I've come too far. There's too much at stake."

She nodded and turned her face to the floor, her eyes widening at the situation she now found herself in: held by a greedy psychopath, while set to be rescued by two murdering sociopaths who she just happened to call 'family.'

The vision of her father came to mind. The cold grew more intense and blanketed her soul. She made a pledge to herself. She would survive this. She would live. She would beat them all.

She looked at her watch. Her mind leapt away from her predicament. Her downhill start was more than ninety-six minutes ago. The clock was running.

Kelvin Stump snapped his head this way and that, scanning the crowd for two people he didn't know in the company of one he did, but didn't want to know.

"This is ridiculous," he muttered, reaching across his body with his left hand and digging in his right pocket for his keys. The movement made the knife dig into Cheryl's side and she tried to pull away. He held her tight.

"Hang on there, sweet meat."

"Sweet meat? Excuse me, ahhh, sweet meat?" Cheryl felt her anger rise and her skin crawl. She reached up and, despite the pressure he had kept on her side, slipped her hand through his arm and pushed the blade away. "Knock it off. I'm not going anywhere."

"You're a brave man, calling her that," Will said, trying to keep the tone light. "The last guy who did is still trying to find his nuts in a Belgian sewer."

Stump let her go, surprised by her strength and anxious to get at his keys. He slipped the belt knife into its sheath and dug with his right hand, pulling out a set of perhaps ten keys and fiddling with them. One eye was always on Cheryl, the other looking for a specific key. He found it. He took Cheryl hard, by the left arm, and pulled her back. She sighed and fell in place beside Kelvin.

"I've never believed in me having to find somebody—you know," he said, directly to Will, ignoring Cheryl completely. "I've always believed in them having to find me. So—if you want to see your girlfriend again, you will go find your uncles."

"Her uncles."

"Go find them. And bring them…" he paused and turned, scanning a distant wall with his eyes, "… and bring them there. Right over there. Visitors' locker room." He held up the keys and rattled them. "I've worked everywhere in this town. I know places that aren't even places."

"You must be so proud."

Kelvin stopped for a moment at the insult. "You know, I am. You don't know the half of it, asshole," he whispered, angrily, punching a finger into Will's chest, "you don't know the half of it." He looked back at the door in the corner. "We'll be there. Come find us.

"No tricks."

"No tricks," Will answered.

Kelvin rose up to his full height and turned, tugging Cheryl along with him. "Come along, darling."

He said it in a light and playful tone, but, as he turned, and Cheryl's eyes were pulling away from Will's, Will noticed that Kelvin Stump was sweating heavily through his shirt, the fear of what he faced taking physical form.

Will watched them go, Stump pausing on the other side of the arena, glancing about for security, before quickly unlocking the door and stepping inside.

Will sighed and scratched his head. Jesus, what a day.

＊

STANLEY ROLLED HIS EYES AS HE AND OLLIE WRESTLED THE CASE OFF THE bus again in front of the ice arena. He slung the duffel bag over his shoulder and pushed the case on alone, leaving the two behind him to continue their argument.

Ollie and the woman hadn't stopped chattering since they had come in from outside the house, where she had been relieving herself. Now, after the trip back into the village, it sounded something like a mating dance.

"But you can't say that man has no rights," Ollie argued, "because even with your philosophy in place, man is an animal, and animals have rights to life on this planet."

"But man misuses that right," she countered, "by misusing, overusing, parasitically spreading out over the whole of the earth, destroying habitat, rain forest…."

"But Earth, you have to admit, is remarkably resilient."

"Ah, but for how long? How long before the only thing living here is the cockroach? We have to recycle, renew, reuse. Protect habitat. Stop mindless development."

"I agree with you there; Michigan is seeing too much growth," Ollie said, sadly, shaking his head. "Old-growth forest being cut away, industrial growth, new condos, forest developments. It's amazing. Ugly."

"You may not agree with me completely," Marjorie said, with a smile, "but you see. You see it."

"But you can't stop people. They move. They grow. They…."

"Take?"

He nodded. "They take."

"Perhaps I can't stop them, now. I'm only one person. But, with that," she nodded sadly toward the case, "I could have reached more people. Convinced them. Made some noise in a productive, rather than destructive, way. We'll never know."

"I'm sorry. I'm truly sorry."

Impulsively, Ollie reached out and took her hand, giving it a bit of a squeeze. Marjorie Stump jumped as if electrified. She didn't pull her hand away.

Olverio Cangliosi looked at her earnestly, then moved their clasped hands to emphasize his words. "I wish ... I wish there could be ... some way ... that this could work out ... for all of us."

She nodded. "This is blood money, isn't it?"

He agreed.

"We could turn it green," she said with a shy smile.

Ollie laughed in such a way, never releasing her hand, that Stanley felt the need to step between them at the door of the ice arena.

"It's green enough already, kids. Watch the stick, there, lady. I only let you keep it because you said you needed it to walk. Ollie, can we pay attention to business? Shall we get this done?"

Never taking their eyes off each other, Ollie and Marjorie nodded.

Stanley rolled his eyes and shuffled toward the door, pushing the full weight of the case beside him.

✳

WILL BEGAN TO MUTTER TO HIMSELF AS HE WALKED THE AISLES AND SCANNED the crowds for his "uncles" and the Stump woman. Within twenty-five feet, his eyeballs had been overwhelmed by the fluorescent lights and the booths and the colors. He looked at things without seeing them, passed people without knowing they were there.

He called it the "thousand-yard stare," and could only overcome it by stopping in one place and looking at one thing in particular. He stopped at a booth and picked up an ultralight seatpost, turning it over in his hands and letting his eyes readjust.

A petite woman wearing a straw hat and one of the largest smiles he had ever seen approached the other side of the table.

"You in the market?" she asked.

"What, oh, yeah," Will muttered, an idea forming in his mind, "yeah. Do you have this in steel?"

Her eyes fluttered in surprise for a moment, before she leaned forward conspiratorially. "No, sweetheart—you want it lighter, not heavier."

Will whipped his wrist, flinging the seatpost back and forth. The impact might work for surprise, but he'd still want more weight behind it.

"I'm just freaky about strength. I had one break on me once."

"This won't break."

Will smiled, then, shook his head. "No, I think I need something heavier."

"We've got this. It's not much heavier, only a few grams, but it might work for you."

Will hefted the aluminum. It was heavier, but had a different feel. The titanium, despite its weight, still carried more authority.

"I'll take this one," Will said, digging in the rear pocket of his parachute suit for his money.

"Fifteen bucks. Great show deal."

"Yeah it is," he said with a nod. Glancing up, he noticed the sign: Richardson Bike Mart. He had found them after all.

"Oh, hey, I read about you guys. Say 'hi' to Rhonda and Jim."

She smiled, handing him his change and a receipt. "Well, I'll say hello to Jim for you."

Will smiled and took the post, pocketing his change, along with the business card picked up without a thought, and slid the stem inside the front elastic waistband of his pants. He carefully put the receipt with his money, as he suddenly realized either he'd be nailed for shoplifting or picked up as a Viagra addict.

He began walking the center aisle again, continually shifting the somewhat obvious bulge that presented itself with every other step. The crowd continued to thin as 5 p.m. approached. As Will reached the far end of the arena, he caught sight of Stan and Ollie, Marjorie Stump, the three together looking like a refinery in human form, the black, rolling case between them. They were talking with another of the teenage security guards.

"But we have to deliver this," Ollie was saying patiently. "We're late, we know, but have to get this to one of the booths…."

"Which one?" the teenager said, his voice no longer changing, but sounding, for all the world, like it desperately wanted to crack.

"Richardson Bike Mart," Will said sharply, reaching in his pocket, taking the business card and flashing it, quickly, with authority, in front of the teenager's eyes.

"Let's go, folks, you're late. Colnago won't be happy if the bike isn't set up and on display first thing tomorrow morning." He stepped forward and took the top handle of the case from Stanley. Turning back to the teenager, Will asked, "What time do you want vendors out of here, again?"

The teenager shook his head. "I dunno, six, I guess."

Will sighed.

"Shit. Only an hour for set up. Come on. I'm going to need your help." He tugged the case and began rolling it toward the far wall. He turned back to the group at the door. "Well, come on. We've only got an hour and it's gonna be close, so let's do it," he barked.

The four watched him go, one of the wheels of the case sticking for a moment and leaving a white streak on the shiny gray concrete floor and a squeal in the air. Then, Ollie shrugged and followed behind, pulling Marjorie Stump with him. Stanley followed, smiling at the teen and saying, "Have a nice day."

"You, too," the kid answered, before turning back to his door.

❋

OLVERIO WRAPPED HIS ARM IN THAT OF MARJORIE STUMP, WHO IMMEDIATELY began to pull him toward the path between the booths. Instinctively, they were fighting over who would lead their dance. Stanley shook his head, then picked up his pace to catch Will.

Stepping up beside him, Stanley whispered, "Okay, so, what's the deal?"

"He's in the locker room," Will said, simply, nodding his head toward the door they were approaching. "He's got Cheryl. That's the deal."

"Weapons? Anything?"

"Little frog sticker," Will replied. "One of those belt knives you get out of karate magazines. Maybe a two-and-a-half, three-inch blade."

"Cherylann?"

"She's okay. Pissed off. A bit cut up, but okay."

"And she does get pissed off," Stanley said, simply.

"Okay," Ollie said, stepping up with Marjorie Stump in tow, "we'll take it from here. I suggest you go back to your hotel room and wait. Cheryl will be right along."

Will stared at the man who had so recently been squeezing the life out of him and shook his head.

"No."

"What?"

"No. Whatever your plan is, no. It includes me. I'm not trooping off without Cheryl. I'm not leaving without her."

Olverio stared at the skinny young man with the odd erection, about to continue the argument, when an older security guard walked past.

"Time to leave folks."

"Thanks, officer," Will called. "We drop off this case and we're gone."

He smiled and waved. Without dropping his smile he turned to Ollie and said, simply, "I'm in. Deal with it."

He waited a moment for the guard to turn a corner, then knocked on the locker room door.

❀

KELVIN STUMP HAD BRUSQUELY PUSHED CHERYL THROUGH THE DOOR, TURNED and locked it behind him.

"Find someplace to sit. In the back."

Cheryl sighed and turned. This was getting tiring. She shuffled to the back of the locker room, the windows sealed and doors locked, capturing that peculiar bouquet of sweat and mold and trapped humidity.

She walked into the bathroom, found a stall, and pulled a handful of toilet paper off the roll. Pressing it against her side, she grimaced, as much at the predicament she now found herself in as at the wound in her side. A dark brown door with a latched deadbolt in what appeared to be an outer wall beckoned to her for a moment, but the opportunity passed quickly. Kelvin Stump stepped to the bathroom arch and stood on guard.

Ignoring him, Cheryl unzipped the jersey and raised up her arm, pulling the fabric away to stare at the cuts themselves. There were three, it appeared. Two small slits outside the bandage and the one original under it. He had cut back through the pad and reopened the original slit.

There were also four or five punctures around the edges where the point of the blade had punctured the skin. She pushed the toilet paper against the cuts and pulled the jersey on again, zipping it up.

She sighed.

This was not the way life was supposed to go.

She was supposed to be riding today. She was supposed to be winning. She was supposed to be leading a team.

She was not.

She was standing in an aging, smelly locker room, trying to breathe, while five other people fought over a pile of money that had certainly impressed her, no doubt about it, but meant nothing to her in the long run.

It was money, but it was not hers.

And it brought her into contact with her uncles, which, frankly, put the mark of Cain upon it, as far as she was concerned.

She sighed, got up, and stepped past Kelvin into the locker area itself, situated between the showers and the toilets. She sat down on a wooden bench and waited for deliverance.

From whom, by whom, with whom.

Her heroes. Jesus, what a turn of events.

She suddenly didn't care anymore.

She heard a knock at the door.

❦

AT THE KNOCK, KELVIN STUMP STRODE PAST HER, STEPPED INTO THE ENTRY room, slipped the keyed bolt, then, before the door opened, stepped quickly back into the locker room area and slid up tight beside Cheryl. She tightened herself and pulled away, then drew in close to him as the point of the knife blade pressed against her temple.

They both heard, rather than saw, the door open, heard the noise of the case being slid into the room, a quiet collection of voices, then felt the change in air pressure as the door closed behind them.

"Lock it," Kelvin called out. "Bring me the keys."

One of them in the next room slid the deadbolt home again.

From the sound, Cheryl could tell that the group in the next room was beginning to step toward them. The point of the blade began to dig deeper into her temple.

"Hey, watch it, pal," she hissed.

Kelvin let up a bit, for only a moment, the tension of the situation forcing him to unconsciously dig the knife in again.

Christ, she thought, I'm going to have Band Aids everywhere.

Will and Marjorie Stump stepped into the locker room first, Will turning the corner quickly, relieved, for a moment, to see Cheryl, then immediately concerned to see her with a knife at her temple.

Marjorie Stump, unsure of what she would find, was momentarily shocked to see that same knife at that same temple, but smiled when she realized that Kelvin had, for once in his life, stepped forward and taken command.

Now, she could take it from him and regain control of a situation she had lost control over merely an hour before on a bus out of town.

"Kelvin," she ordered, "this one," she said, unwrapping her arm from that of Ollie, "this one has a gun. A pistol. He has it in his right front jacket pocket. It is a small gun, with, I believe, a silencer."

"Thank you, mama," Kelvin whispered, raising his arm perpendicular with Cheryl's head. "The gun. Now. Or your niece. Your niece, right? She'll go from animal to vegetable in a split second."

The tone of Kelvin's voice took Marjorie by surprise for a moment, but she stepped away from Ollie, Will and Stan, toward the bathroom, before turning back and crossing her arms with a smug and satisfied grin.

"Right front pocket, Kelvin. Watch him."

Ollie's face didn't register emotion, though Will could see his eyes shift, slowly, from Kelvin to Marjorie and back again. Stanley was taking in the full layout of the room, before his eyes came back to rest on his niece and the man threatening her.

Kelvin twitched his arm again. Ollie raised his hands in surrender and with his thumb and first finger of his right hand, drew the Walther TPH out of the pocket by the silencer.

Kelvin blinked.

"Oooh. That is tiny, isn't it?"

Ollie shrugged. "It does the job."

"I bet it does," Kelvin whispered, his voice tight. "So does this," he flashed the knife. "Kick it over here. To me. Careful now."

Ollie paused for a moment, before squatting down and placing the gun, with silencer, carefully on the shiny brown floor. He then slid it over, by hand, to Kelvin's feet before standing up again.

Kelvin unwrapped himself from Cheryl, but intertwined the fingers of his right hand in the collar of her jersey and pressed the knife blade against her throat before bending down and picking up the gun with his left hand, his eyes never leaving the three in front of him.

"Sorry, boys," he said, leaning back. "No chance for heroics today. Lean the case there. Gym bag beside it. I win. Game, set and match."

The tension seemed to visibly go out of Marjorie Stump.

"We do indeed, Kelvin. We do indeed win."

He acted as if he never heard her.

Ollie looked at Marjorie with a trace of sadness. She eyed him for a moment, a look of apology in her face, then shrugged.

C'est la vie.

Kelvin released Cheryl and stood up, waving his fist, holding the gun, in a small, loose arc. "This way, now. Over here."

Slowly, the trio moved, reversing positions with the man with the gun, until they were next to Cheryl at the wooden bench. Marjorie Stump stood her ground at the entrance to the toilets. Kelvin paid her no mind.

Will slid up beside Cheryl and sat as carefully as he could, the titanium seatpost digging into his bellybutton and his penis.

"Are you okay?"

"Yeah, yeah, I'm fine," she answered without a trace of emotion.

"Well, you certainly sound it," Stanley said.

Ollie snorted, "Just like her father."

The comment made her head snap angrily toward him.

Kelvin wiggled the Walther in their general direction. "Let's can the family reunion shall we? Shhhh." He raised a finger to his lips and smiled, leaning back into the entryway near the door to listen. He leaned forward again and said, "It should only be a few minutes and we should be on our way."

"On our way?" Will asked, rising up on the hard wooden seat. "We going somewhere?"

"To hell," Ollie said, his eyes shifting slowly between the gun and Kelvin and Marjorie, guarding the john.

"In a handbasket," Stanley added.

"Huh?"

"Will," Cheryl said, quietly, "he intends to kill us all."

"Oh," was all that Will Ross could find in himself to say.

CHAPTER TWENTY:

LOCKER ROOM BLUES

KELVIN STUMP STARED AT THE QUARTET SITTING MOROSELY ON THE bench and smiled. He had won. The smart-assed rider, the woman and the two "killers," were all arrayed before him, looking like a set of mismatched bookends. All slumped, all dejected. Except the guy on the end, the young guy, who sat up pretty much straight, continually digging at his belly. His mother must have beaten the idea of posture into him.

Just like Kelvin. Literally. Kelvin stepped back into the entryway to listen quietly at the door again.

"Who has the key to the case?" Kelvin asked the four. No one answered. No one moved. No one raised their eyes to meet his.

"Let's see," Kelvin asked himself aloud, "do I beg for it, or do I simply shoot the girl in the kneecap and have done with it unless somebody tells…." He lowered the gun toward Cheryl's leg. Will stood up immediately.

"I've got it. I've got the key right here." He dug in the front pocket of his parachute pants and produced a small, silver luggage key.

"You're sure?" Kelvin asked, wiggling the gun toward Cheryl.

"I'm sure," Will answered.

Kelvin took the key and stepped back, fitting it into all three locks and turning them. Will watched him unlock the case and felt a cold sweat break out across his back.

"Very good. Very good." Kelvin laughed. "I hope you don't mind if I don't open it here and now, as it's always so difficult to repack money once it's out on the floor."

He tossed the key back to Will. "Here, keep it. Souvenir."

Will caught the key out of instinct and slid it into his pocket as he sat down on the bench. The seatpost dug into the top of his penis and made him shift uncomfortably.

"If you need to crap," Kelvin said, noticing his discomfort, "the room's in there. Just don't make a smell, okay?"

Kelvin leaned back again and listened at the door. The floor of the arena was growing quiet. It was almost time. Three hours from now and he'd be rich beyond belief in Denver, Colorado, living a whole new life, as a whole new person and with no one the wiser.

"Kelvin," Marjorie hissed, "Kelvin!"

"Mother," he said quietly and calmly.

"What are we going to do, Kelvin?"

"We?"

"He's going to kill us, Mrs. Stump," Will interrupted. "Do you really want that on your conscience, Mrs. Stump?"

She paused and turned to Will, Murph as she knew him, and let her eyes move slowly down the line of people until she reached Ollie. In a way, he had been her tormentor, her kidnapper, but in another he was also the only man who had ever stood up to her on an equal footing, their conversations and arguments, on everything from defecation in the high grass to recycling, taking on the sense of equals sharing thought, soul, communication.

Strange, that in a single afternoon she may have found a soulmate. He smiled at her, a wan, distant smile, she thought, of romantic opportunity gained and lost in the blink of an eye.

She turned her gaze back to Will.

"No, it doesn't really bother me."

"What?! Four people, dead on the floor, and you're thinking you're not going to be bothered?"

"Shh-shh-shh-shh," Kelvin warned.

Will glanced his way, stood and leaned toward Marjorie.

"Look. I've watched you in the forest. I know what you think about life. How you feel. How you feel toward life and nature and everything in this world. How can you even think to watch four people murdered?"

Every eye in the room shifted toward Marjorie Stump, who pondered her answer.

"Well, Murph," she said, in a voice thick with rationalization, "you see, I've never really liked human beings, despite being one myself. They're dirty, for the most part, mean, thoughtless, reproduce like rabbits, and, worst of all, as far as I'm concerned, they foul their nest."

"And so...."

"And so, they're parasites, Murph. Parasites. Four less—and I'm sorry it has to be you four—will not make that much difference to me."

"But you're one, a parasite, right along with us."

Ollie interrupted, quietly, never taking his eyes off Marjorie Stump. "She is, and she'll admit it, but she leaves no trail, unlike the rest of us. When she dies, there will be little to indicate she was ever here, except what she has saved and what few memories the forest itself has of her."

Without thinking, almost without control, she flashed a sweet, shy smile at Ollie. He knew her, she realized. In only a few hours, he had seen inside her very soul, to the very kernel of her essence. Oh, my Lord, she thought, this is one to save.

Will watched the looks that traveled between the two in absolute amazement. All this needs, he thought, is a violin somewhere in the distance.

"That's all well and good, Mrs. Stump, but four bodies leave a trail. And, unlike you in the deep woods, a trail that comes back to you. And no matter how the law might handle it, no matter who may take the fall for the crime, I'd think that Mother Nature even loves her parasites." Will's tone began to take on a slight patina of panic, the words racing out in a rush, like a blind man shooting wildly in the hopes of hitting a target, any target, in the distance. "Think about that, Mrs. Stump. Who are you to stand above Mother Nature herself and judge her creatures? Hmm? Who are you? And what would your Mother say? Even the worst mother in the world loves best ... those children ... with the most problems."

"Oh, brother," Kelvin moaned.

"He's right, you know, Mrs. Stump," Ollie said, softly. "We're all her creatures. We're all a part of this…." He waved his hands in a great circle before him.

She nodded in agreement, her eyes never leaving his.

"Oh, that's grand," Kelvin said, "coming from a guy who hacked somebody up with an ax and stuffed a towel down his mouth."

Ollie looked at him in shock, then at Stanley, who shrugged, then back at Kelvin. "Where in God's green earth did you get that idea?"

Kelvin leaned back a bit, shocked by the reaction.

"Well, from him."

He pointed the gun loosely at Will, who smiled and shrugged.

"He said you were killers," Kelvin said.

"Killers?" Ollie laughed. "I hardly think so. We can be pushy, I grant you that." He turned, as if trying to convince Marjorie of the fact as much, or more, than Kelvin. "We can be mean, we threaten people to get what we want, but we've never killed anybody in our lives. Certainly not with an ax."

"Certainly not," Stanley agreed with a nod.

Everybody turned to Will, who shifted uneasily from cheek to cheek on the wooden bench.

"I … uh … I got it out of a book." Will shrugged, sheepishly, at Ollie.

Kelvin's face tightened. He didn't like being played for a fool. It brought out the worst in him.

"You," he pointed at Will, "you, I'm going to kill first."

"Well, can I go to the bathroom first? I don't want to pee my pants again today."

There was a shuffle and a scrape and an intake of breath from the woman standing in the arch leading to the toilets. Marjorie Stump had watched and listened and had been thinking. Thinking about the people she was with. Thinking of the money in the box.

She rose up to her full height and turned to her son.

"No. No one is going to die this day."

"I'm sorry?"

"I said, Kelvin, and I wish you'd listen, no one is going to die this day."

"Mother…."

"Kelvin! No one is going to die this day! Don't you understand? Listen to me: You are not going to kill these people."

She walked over near Kelvin and defiantly stood her ground.

"Give me the gun, Kelvin, give me the gun."

"No mother," Kelvin answered, quietly, "there is no way I'm going to give up the money in that case," he pointed behind him at the bicycle case, "or the half mill in there," he pointed at the duffel bag next to it.

"No way in hell, mother."

"Kelvin, you listen to me. There is plenty for all of us, here. I wanted it all as well, just like you, for my plans. But even half," she turned quickly to Ollie, "half?"

He nodded. "Half. For our lives, we can do half."

Will nodded in agreement while Cheryl stared straight ahead. Stanley nodded slowly as well.

"Half would send us well on our way."

"No deal."

"Kelvin. You're making me angry. Half would save a lot of what I intend to save…."

"And it wouldn't do shit for what I want to do."

"What, pinwheels and comic books? Beer at that saloon in Edwards? Hmm? You think," she said, moving in close, "that I don't know about that? Those regular trips to Denver to buy that obscenity you have hidden in your room? The filthy magazines? Oh, Kelvin. You must think I'm so incredibly stupid. Half," she nodded at Ollie, "half will be fine."

Ollie smiled at her, but didn't move, his eyes still on Kelvin. As he watched the play in the young man's jaw, he knew that it wasn't fine with him.

"Mother—I am forty years old. Forty. And I hate to break this to you, but I have plans for that money that aren't about to make you happy. Step back."

She stared at her son in disbelief.

"Step back, I said," his voice taking on a deep and commanding tone, as if he had spent his life playing a character and the curtain had finally rung down.

She raised her hand as if to make a point, and in a flash of movement Kelvin Stump brought the silencer to the middle of her forehead, putting pressure on the trigger. Cheryl shut her eyes, automatically. Will watched with fascination, the scene so unreal he lost track of himself and felt like reaching for popcorn.

Marjorie Stump, for the first time in more than forty years, was at a loss. She had no idea what to say, what to do, how to react. When her son pushed with the gun, like someone pressing a single, metal finger against her head, she stepped back into the archway leading to the toilets, her world in disarray, her sense of self suddenly in tatters.

"Kelvin," she muttered with a shocked and saddened tone.

"Yes, mother," he answered bitterly, forty years of listening and surrendering himself finally fraying the wires to the point of ignition, "Kelvin. No offense, dear, but I want you and that damned stick of yours as far away from me for the rest of my life as I can possibly get it."

"Son...."

"Shh-shh-shh-shh," he whispered. "Not any more. Not now. I don't want to hear it."

"He's not listening, Marjorie, because he's got plans for the money. Don't you, son?"

"Son? Don't call me son. I am not your son. My father was Elmo Stump, and I never got to know the man. I never got to know him because—somebody," he said, his voice rising with a long, buried anger, "somebody—crushed his nuts in a hospital delivery room."

Will grimaced and brought his legs together instinctively.

"That was an accident, son," Marjorie said, her surprise at Kelvin's actions turning to anger at the memory, "the mindless act of a woman in the midst of childbirth. I was exonerated by the magistrate."

"Don't give me that shit," Kelvin spat, "I've seen the articles. I've read the articles. Even the police report. That's the obscenity that's hidden in my room. Not this month's copy of *Juggs*. That's the obscenity. That you got off on a murder charge."

"Don't curse, Kelvin. And don't say that about me," Marjorie said, sadly, a forty-year truth, long buried in her own mind, suddenly coming back to haunt her.

"Fuck you."

"Don't curse, Kelvin," she said again, her mind trying to regain equilibrium, her voice desperately trying to regain the upper hand of the situation.

"Shut up."

All eyes in the room shifted back to the tall man with the gun near the door.

Will had completely forgotten that one of the bullets in the gun had been promised to him.

Kelvin stood silently, his eyes on his mother, the other four forgotten, the gun aimed directly at the center of Marjorie Stump's being.

"Mother," he finally said, very quietly, "I am not leaving this room without this money. I have earned it."

"We don't need...."

Ollie interrupted, quietly, "Marjorie, dear, he wasn't thinking about 'we,' were you," he paused, "son?"

"No, Dad," Kelvin said, sarcastically, "and don't call me that again, asshole." He waved the gun in Ollie's direction, the movement reminding Will what could soon be heading his way.

"But, no, I wasn't thinking about 'we.' I was thinking, for once, about 'me.' Yeah, me. And, frankly, I earned it. I've got this purple-and-green nose on the bill thanks to these assholes...."

He waved the gun at Will and Cheryl. Will stifled the impulse to speak up and blame Hootie Bosco for Kelvin's nasal injury.

"... and years of being treated like shit by you and everybody else in this town, mother. I've earned it. I've earned it. And you know what else, this will spin your wheels, mother. I need the money. All four-and-a-half million dollars of it. I need it. And I'm not leaving without it. Because, mother dear, you see, I've got bills to pay. Mortgages to make. Construction loans to pay off. I'm in hock up to and including my eyebrows."

"You have no bills, Kelvin. I pay for everything."

"Yes, you pay for all the glory that is living in that tar paper shack of yours in the midst of all this glory."

"This is not glory...."

"Shut up, mother. How do you think I felt growing up and watching this place grow? Me, with nothing, working here, working there, mopping up the puke and the slop for all the rich ski snots from Denver. 'Oh, boy, mop up that puke, would you, boy. Oh, boy, Johnny has thrown his food on you. Bring him a new plate, huh, boy?'

"And, so, I saved. I saved every penny I could that you didn't take out of my hand and give to some damned environmental organization. I saved. And then, when I could, I caught a bus to Denver and I invested it with a builder I had met up here. I invested it on the ground floor and we made a mint. My eleven grand brought me thousands. We built in Grand County, we built in Routt. We built in Summit. And, then, when we thought we were ready, we started to build here."

"What are you talking about, Kelvin?" Marjorie blurted out, her panic at the fear of the answer getting the best of her.

"What I'm talking about is Vail Mountain Terrace, mother, an MSC development in the heart of Vail Mountain."

"Oh, my God," she whispered.

"Oh, my God is right. Manfra Skell Construction. I am a part of that, a honcho, to my friends in the business. Right down to my Social Security number and birth certificate. Although—there ain't no Manfra no more. He was beginning to wonder about me. Double life and all. Horrible accident in Denver on Thursday. Shot by an intruder. Horrible, horrible, horrible. I suppose I will have to talk to the police about that, my partner being kacked and all. Speak at the funeral. But, gosh, I was out of town. Have been all week. Return tonight."

Kelvin turned and looked at Ollie and Stan.

"See, guys? You aren't the only tough ones around here."

"You killed your partner?"

"Oh, no. Nope. Intruder. That's my story and I'm sticking to it. Stole some silver, a CD player, few odds and ends. Not me, though. In-tru-der."

Marjorie Stump recovered from her shock sufficiently to whisper, "Kelvin … you?"

"Yes, mother, Kelvin, me. And I need this money to make the next payments on the land and on the construction. I'm running on fumes here. Four-and-a-half million, laundered, would come to about three-and-a-half. That should cover me through construction and early sales, by which time, rich Texans should be leaving much of their disposable income directly with me."

"Manfra Skill," Cheryl muttered.

"Actually, it's Skell. S-k-e-ll. Skell."

"Your paternal grandmother's...."

"Maiden name. Yes, mother, I know. I know a lot about the family that you tried to hide from me."

"You, I can't believe, you...." Marjorie whispered, the shock slowly turning to a realization that what she had accepted for all these years was a lie, the blank face, the stupid expression, the blind obedience. All a lie. And, now, a lie that had to be fought, face-to-face—another builder. Another developer. Another man working to destroy her Mother. Her mountain. Her life.

The realization burned inside her, rebuilding her strength, pushing aside the shock and the sadness, giving her the will to do what had to be done, finally, to her own flesh and blood.

"Kelvin. Kelvin," she muttered, the volume growing as she spoke, "I vow this now. I vow this forever. I will fight you. I will fight you with everything I can think of—the law—monkey wrenching—whatever. I will fight you as I have fought no one else in my life. I will fight you. And you will lose, son. You will lose. You will lose the money and your little company and your freedom. For I will turn you in. I will lead the authorities wherever I have to lead them to bring you down. For you, least of all in this world, will not bring down my dreams for this mountain. You will not ... will not ... will not!"

And with that, her frustration boiling over in her mind, Marjorie Stump raised her shillelagh, the one she had intended to bring down on the heads of her kidnappers, and stepped toward the son who had shown her so little faith, so little loyalty, so little love.

Before she said another word, Kelvin calmly lowered the gun and shot her in the stomach. The bullet hit her high and right, pushing her back and collapsing her on the floor of the bathroom, around the corner of the arch.

The room was filled with the silence of shock, until Will jumped to his feet. "Jesus Christ," he shouted, out of pure adrenaline as much as shock at the act, "that was your mother!"

As he stood, the titanium seatpost slipped free, fell through his parachute pants and rang with two distinct sounds on the concrete floor of the locker room.

Kelvin Stump smiled.

"Ding, dong, the witch is dead."

Will slumped back to the bench.

"You son of a bitch, you son of a bitch," Cheryl growled, turning her face up toward him, her head shaking back and forth. "You son of a bitch."

"Exactly," Kelvin agreed.

"You had better get on with your business, pal," Cheryl continued. "Kill us now, kill us quick, for I swear I will follow you to the ends of the earth and I will destroy you."

"Right, sweetie. The granddaughter? Is that it?"

"Niece," Stanley said, quietly, the words ringing with the faintest patina of fear. He patted Cheryl's wrist to calm her down.

"Niece, thank you," Kelvin said, sarcastically. "The niece of a couple of Detroit muggers will track me down and make my life a living hell. Indeed. You'll have enough hell of your own dear, for at about the Evergreen exit on I-70 I will a make a call to the Vail police. They will find you here with this gun and all those bodies around town and a locked door. There's a keyed deadbolt on it right up there, you see? And having worked here—I kept a key. Imagine that. And as for me—I will have an alibi in Denver. Beautiful one, too. Responsible. Works in TV. Community leader. Smart. Smart enough to know enough to say what I want her to say so that the gravy train never stops. How about that? How about that?"

"How do you know the cops won't believe us?" Cheryl asked, measuring the space between her and the door and the small, but proven, deadly gun he mashed in his fingers.

"Because I'll tell them about the money. And you'd have to explain the money. It's not easy to explain four million dollars in cash. Is it boys? Especially if only a bit of her story," he nodded at Cheryl, "is true. Got records, boys? Got police records? They're gonna love to talk to you."

Stan and Ollie didn't move and didn't respond. Cheryl was shocked at how they looked, so old, so small, so afraid.

"No matter," Kelvin continued. "Maybe you could talk around it for a while, 'I lost my bike case, man,' but it would come out sooner or later. The money would. Because I'd tell them. They'll love you down at the station."

Cheryl looked at Will, then looked at Kelvin, the hatred and anger burning brightly in her eyes.

"How did you know about the money?" she asked directly.

"Your friend, his friend," Kelvin waved the gun loosely in Will's direction, "the man running with this money, he told me. Just before he died."

"Died?" Will asked, his voice taking on a fearful and exhausted waver.

"Oh, Mr. Leonard, he's not with us anymore, bud. Sorry. He's gone on to the great beyond. Dead and stuffed in a trunk. Stabbed him. Then, had to break his neck to stuff him in the trunk."

"But you…."

"Me? Not me. I have no contact with these people. Even my mother. Kelvin Stump did it all. And in a while, Kelvin Stump will no longer exist on the face of the earth. I've got a little insurance policy, you see, back at my mother's house." He looked at his watch. "About forty-five minutes from now, a little incendiary device will go off and, oops, my policy goes into effect. I'll clear out, live quietly on my millions and just plain disappear. It's a lot easier than you might think."

"You stand out in a crowd."

"Oh, you're wrong there. I never have and I never will. I know the art, you see, the art of living small. I'm tall, but I'm small. Folks just don't notice. It's kept me alive all these many years. And I've got alibi's up the wazoo in Denver. Who they gonna believe, two crooks in Vail or a Denver developer and his anchorwoman girlfriend?"

Will nodded in agreement, without realizing it. What Kelvin said was true. Even the biggest man could disappear in a crowd that wasn't looking, that didn't care, that couldn't be bothered. The police would go for the most obvious possibility. And that included him.

Kelvin smiled at the four before him, stepped back, bent at the knees and picked up the duffel bag.

"Five-hundred-thousand dollars, courtesy of my mother," he nodded in the direction of the toilet room arch. "Thank you, mom. And four million dollars courtesy of you fine people. I do appreciate it."

Kelvin Stump smiled and backed toward the door, listening for a moment, before flipping one of the two deadbolts, swinging the door open and stepping back into the darkened arena, dragging the bicycle case behind him.

"My friends, and I do mean, my friends, it has been a pleasure." He racked the remaining cartridges into his palm and wiped the gun carefully with the tail of his shirt.

"And now, I must go," he said with a smile, sliding the gun across the floor to Ollie's feet. "Enjoy yourselves. Think up a good story. Keep in mind, however, that no matter how good your's might be—mine will be better. By the way—I could use some muscle out here … oh, no, I suppose not."

He nodded and turned, then turned back, saying quietly, almost wistfully, "You know, it's too bad you guys weren't better. I'd like to test myself against you. Too bad." He smiled and shut the door behind him. There was a rustle of keys and the sound of two deadbolts turning into place, followed by a squeak as the wheels of the case began to move into the distance.

Ollie stood and turned to Stanley. Cheryl was shocked by the transformation. He was younger, alive and vital again, the cloak of age and infirmity cast off like a cheap Halloween mask.

"Well, this is certainly another fine mess you've gotten us into."

"Me?" Stanley stood quickly, his ego calling for him to go on the offensive. "I didn't have anything to do with this one. You—you were the one playing footsie with the old lady and letting him," he pointed at Will, "put four million bucks under his mattress."

"I've gotta ask," Ollie said, pointing at the ten-inch metal bar on the floor. "What is that?" He turned toward the bathroom, not waiting for the answer.

Will stared down. "Seatpost. Thought I could use it as a weapon."

Stanley laughed.

Cheryl stared with a sullen, blank expression on her face. She didn't find the company or the situation amusing in the least.

"Oh, God," Will said, suddenly realizing what had happened over the past few moments, "Marjorie. What about Marjorie Stump?" he asked.

Ollie stood in the arch leading to the toilets, staring down at the floor, then up, then down, then up again.

"How is she?" Will called after him, but got no response.

"How is she?" he asked again, this time louder. Cheryl and Stanley turned, following his gaze to the figure of Olverio standing silently in the door.

"She's gone," Ollie said, quietly.

"Oh, goddamn it," Stanley said, a genuine touch of sorrow in his voice. "You mean she's dead."

"No, I don't mean that at all," Ollie answered slowly. "I mean she's gone."

"Gone?" The three of them asked at once.

"Yeah. Up and gone."

CHAPTER TWENTY-ONE:

SOOPRISE, SOOPRISE, SOOPRISE

ELVIN STUMP MOVED WITH CONFIDENCE TOWARD HIS CAR, THE LATE
model Saab 9000 he kept hidden in the public parking lot at Lionshead. The silver car with the black leather interior was hotter than
hell in the summertime, but, oh, it looked so very, very good every other time.

Taking the elevator up to the second level, he wheeled the case to the hatch-
back and opened it with the remote, his nose being ever so pleasantly assaulted
by the rich scent of the leather. He slid the case along the back, releasing the
seat as he went, until it hit the two front buckets. He resisted the urge to open
and look, as much as he wanted to—to simply gaze upon the fortune that was
now his, finally, and justifiably so—because of the urgent need to put miles
between the ice arena and himself. He had to put some distance, and quickly,
between himself and the day, between the body of his mother and his gun
hand, between four survivors and his alibi, between the present and the life
that came before.

Time to drive.

He slid behind the wheel and started the car, the purr of the engine reminding him how far he had come and how little he still had to travel. He had won
the battle, won the war.

He cranked up the heat, the burst of cold inside the car making his nose
ache. But, then again he thought, what was a little ache at a moment like this?

He was a rich man.

He put the car into gear and turned to look backward as he pulled out of
the parking spot. As he leaned to the rear, he gazed across the shiny black

plastic of the case. He smiled, shifted gears and sped up to the top level of the parking lot, off the structure, onto the frontage road, and toward the roundabout leading to the highway, Denver, and his future.

A momentary flash hit him, a flash that said, "leave no witnesses," but he quickly dismissed the thought. Everyone and everything in that room was interconnected, as was the death of the sports agent, even the death of his mother.

Leaving two criminals at the scene could only be a help down the road.

⟡

"I DON'T MEAN TO QUESTION YOU, OLLIE," WILL SAID, RUBBING THE WELT THAT ran along his stomach from the seatpost, "but where the hell could she have gone?"

"Maybe she dissolved," Stanley answered, with all seriousness, staring at the spot where Marjorie Stump had been lying, only moments before, a spot now occupied only by a single drop of blood. "I've seen that in movies."

"That's movies," Ollie barked, angry frustration in his voice. He pushed himself up with a grunt off the floor. "This isn't the movies." Whatever heart beat in that magnificent little soul, he thought, was still beating, somewhere, just not here.

He stared at the single drop of blood and raised his eyes. Stanley followed his gaze toward a grey, steel fire door in the rear of the restroom. Just looking at the way it sat in the frame, both men could tell it was unlocked.

"Jesus," Stanley said with no little amount of respect, "that's one tough old broad. How'd she reach that bolt?"

Ollie nodded his head in agreement.

"She certainly is," he muttered.

Cheryl left Will sitting on the bench and joined the two, keeping her distance, her hatred of them quieted—though not reduced—because of the situation they shared at this particular moment in time.

"Where is she?"

Ollie looked at his niece and noticed, immediately, the wall she had put up between them.

"She's gone," Ollie said, simply. "Out that door. Probably to the hospital. I think we should follow her."

"What about your money?" Cheryl asked, sarcastically.

"That can wait," Ollie said.

"What, a few more to kill before your big payoff?"

Olverio turned and stared at his niece, a fingertip of sadness touching his heart. He never talked about his work. He wanted to make an exception here, to release the hatred she felt, but wasn't sure if he ever could, even given a chance.

He stared at her for a moment, the emotion of everything he was and everything he knew, the joy at simply still being alive rushing to his face and turning it bright red, filling his eyes with tears.

Her face curled into suspicion. "What's with you?"

"Nothing. Nothing."

Ollie took a deep breath and looked at Stanley.

"Get a paper towel and wet it—just a bit—and wipe up that blood. Don't throw it away, we'll need it for the doorknob." He turned and looked into the locker room at Will. "You ready to travel?"

Will turned and stood, stretching painfully as he did. "Yeah, I'm good to go."

"Good. When we open the door, I want you to turn off the light with your elbow."

"My elbow?"

"Just do it." He watched as Stanley carefully wiped up the drop of blood with the paper towel, then folded it over itself. Ollie stepped back into the locker room, pulled out a handkerchief and picked up the Walther by the silencer, sliding it into his pocket.

"Ready on the door?"

"Ready on the door," Stanley answered.

"Open it."

The door slid open with hardly a sound, only a soft "thunk," as the weather stripping pulled away from the base. As the door slid open, Will turned off the light with his elbow and stepped quickly through the darkness toward the dim light coming through the opening. Stanley took a quick look outside, then stepped through, followed by Cheryl, Ollie and, finally, Will.

Stanley pulled the door closed and heard the doorknob-lock engage with a snap.

"Hospital is ... there," Ollie said, pointing. "Let's check on Mrs. Stump to make sure she made it in one piece."

"And is thinking nice thoughts about her friends from Detroit," Stanley said with a smile.

"Oh, nice thoughts for nice guys," Cheryl said without thinking.

They both turned on her.

◉

THE SAAB ZIPPED IN AND OUT OF TRAFFIC SMOOTHLY, THE STEERING SO TIGHT that even at 115 miles an hour it was like thought-response driving, in and out and in-between, with a feather touch on the wheel.

Kelvin slowed as the car topped the hill, rounding the turn into Copper Mountain. He knew this zone as a favorite speed trap, but tonight his dual detectors were silent.

He slowed to a snail's pace of 82, zipped past the exit and through the night, then sped up again, hitting 125 on the flats as he concentrated again on his driving and the heady promise of his future.

❀

"WHAT IS YOUR PROBLEM?" OLLIE SAID IT, STANLEY THOUGHT IT, AND WILL stepped away from it toward West Meadow Drive.

"I'll just ... head toward the hospital and check on ... Mrs. Stump ... uhh ... yes," Will said toward the three, none of the three paying the slightest bit of attention to him. He waved his fingers loosely in the air, in the general direction of the hospital, and finally simply turned and shuffled away toward the emergency room.

Cheryl stared at the two men, two men she had loved for years and now hated. She had wanted to tell them just how she felt for so long and never had the chance, because of her mother, because of her fears. Tonight, however, there was no one else around and the fear had been stripped away.

She stood before them, not caring what they felt or how they might react to her anger. She had already survived one killer tonight. Perhaps she could finally survive the two she feared most in the world.

"What is your problem, Cherylann?"

"You. That's my problem. You two. I know you. I've seen you. I know what you can do. I'm ashamed that I am related to you in any way, shape, or form."

"Why?" Stanley asked.

The question was so simple, so direct, it knocked Cheryl back just a bit. She wasn't sure she knew how to respond.

"We have to hear it from you, Cheryl," Ollie said, quietly. "Not from your boyfriend. We need to hear it from you. We need to hear it all."

She looked between them, the torrent of emotions overwhelming her and crushing her heart in her chest. She bent forward a bit as if to throw up, to drive the feelings and fears and hatreds from her, then rose with anger and stared them down. The look on her face was chilling, even to the two men who had seen the mask of death so close before them.

"You," she said again, her voice strong and vibrant. "You. I know you. I know who you are. I know what you two are capable of doing. I saw you."

"Saw us what?" Ollie asked, sharply.

"I saw you ..." She paused, a bubble of fear holding down the words she wanted to, needed to, say, "... with my father."

"How?" Ollie said.

"How? How? I don't know how ... I opened my eyes and 'poof' there you were. You," she pointed a finger accusingly at Stanley, "on one side of him, you," she pointed at Ollie, "bent over him on the other. Him," she looked at the ground, tears streaming uncontrollably from her eyes as she recalled the image, "him on the ground. On the floor. His feet, his feet, in his shoes, the dark brown shoes with the black toes and the fancy work on the toes, his shoes, turned," she bent her hands before her like a pair of wings, "turned out, and not moving," she wandered, suddenly unable to control the emotion or the memory of her father, her father dead on the floor of his office. Dead from, dead from ... she turned and looked at the two, her hatred rising again. She swallowed her tears.

The three looked at each other in silence for a moment.

"When he told us, this afternoon," Ollie said quietly, "I didn't believe him. I wanted to kill him."

"Who?"

"Will. Your friend."

"What—plan to kill everybody in my life? I should hang a sign: Spend an afternoon with me now and see heaven tonight."

The words were out before she could think, before she could stop them, just as Ollie's hand snapped out and slapped Cheryl, hard, across the face, before he could think, before he could stop it.

"Enough. Enough of this foolishness. You can hate us all you want. You can change your name. You can run forever for all I care. But this … this I will not allow to continue, this … anger, this self pity, this poor girl who saw her father die…."

"Well…."

"You didn't, you stupid little bitch."

Cheryl was taken aback by the curse, especially coming from a man who didn't … who never … who always admonished others for using the words.

"You never saw us kill your father…."

"Because we never killed your father…." Stanley interrupted.

"You saw us there," Ollie continued, "but we were late. We were there to stop it, and we didn't make it on time. We heard about the mark. We heard that your father was on the mark because he had swept up a legal mess for Buster No Knuckles…."

"And Buster No Knuckles didn't like anybody," Stanley added, "anybody knowing his business."

"It was a bad choice to do anything, even a favor, for Buster," Ollie continued. "We tried to tell your father not to do it, that it was dangerous…."

"But your dad," Stanley said, "your dad was sure he could handle Buster. He had handled everybody else. He was liked. He was respected…."

"Nobody handled Buster," Ollie said.

Stanley nodded, then looked at his niece. For the first time in her life, Cheryl noticed tears in his eyes. "I'm sorry, sweetie. We tried. We were late. We were just too damned late."

"I dunno," Ollie said, shaking his head slowly, "we got there and saw it and called it in to a friend on the force and saw you. We tried to talk to you later, but your mother said to leave you be, that you were in shock. You'd have to deal with it later, on your own. But I guess you never did. Because you didn't know what you were dealing with to begin with." Ollie lowered his head and murmured, "I'm sorry sweetheart. We should have talked to you. We should have talked to you right away about it."

Cheryl stood in shock, staring at the two men she had hated for so long, and felt the hatred sliding slowly away. Though there was always the possibility that they were lying, their tone and their openness, an openness she had never known before from them, made her believe them. The pain she had carried so long was finally beginning to fade, leaving only a heart heavy with loss—loss of time, loss of family, loss of life.

She took a deep breath and asked the question that hung in the cold September dusk before her.

"What, uh, what happened to Buster, uh, Buster No Knuckles?"

Ollie smiled.

"We happened. We happened to Buster No Knuckles."

"You?"

Stanley nodded quickly, a stupid grin filling his face.

"You bet we did."

"You see, Cherylann," Ollie explained, "we, Stanley and myself, have this horrible reputation in Detroit...."

"I know...."

"Well, no you don't," he corrected. "We've got a reputation for being maniacal killers. Enforcers. Hit men. Everybody in the entire damned city is afraid of us."

"Even people we've never met," Stanley added. "That story Will told ain't that far from what people say about us."

"But, we're businessmen," Ollie continued, "businessmen. And in our business you let your reputation speak for you, and the mark will usually do your work for you."

Stanley nodded. "It's true. Charlie Munk. Remember him?"

"We were ready," Ollie said. "Stepped out into the street to hit him quick and clean. He saw us, panicked, jumped into his car and drove full bore into a street light. Gas tank exploded. We got credit."

"That farmer," Stanley said, "that farmer who killed Raymond? Him, him we wanted to kill. Bad ugly. He saw us, ran, slipped on the edge of the loft and did a high dive onto a manure spreader he was washing out."

"He had turned it on to clean it. He put his face in it. Hideous, horrible—accident."

"And what about," Cheryl said, slowly, "what about Buster?"

"Buster was a mad dog," Ollie said, quietly, "even if he hadn't done anything to your father, Buster was a mad dog."

"And you always put down a mad dog," Stanley opined.

"And so…."

"So, Cherylann," Ollie continued, "Buster No Knuckles was sitting in a bar on Michigan. Near Tiger Stadium. He was alone. The place had a few people in it. Not many. But a few. Witnesses. But it didn't matter. If we were going to go down, that was the one to do it for, wasn't it Stanley?"

"It certainly was," he answered, nodding his head for emphasis.

"We walked in, each put a gun to his head, and blew two chunks of it away."

"Two chunks," Stanley agreed.

"The bar went silent and we turned to them all. Your uncle Stanley said…."

"You didn't see nothin'. That's what I said."

"That's what he said. The Detroit organized crime squad…."

"All three of them," Stanley laughed.

"All three of them were so happy that Buster wasn't going to be littering the streets anymore that they slapped him with the murder of your father, wrote him off as the worst suicide they had ever seen, and buried him under two tons of concrete at taxpayers' expense."

"Really?" Cheryl asked, quietly, a tone of fearful relief in her voice.

"Everything except the concrete. They skimmed the cost of that and were all driving new Fords by the end of the week."

The three of them stood silently for a moment, the breeze of the evening moving the weeds and wildflowers near their feet.

Cheryl turned her face to the breeze and felt it wash over her like a cleansing hand, clearing her mind and her heart, releasing the fear and the hatred, giving her back her sense of freedom, the ability to be who she was, anywhere she wanted to be in the world. In her mind's eye she could see her father, who had inhabited so many dreams, filling so many nights, with an angry, disappointed visage. She had always taken it to mean that he was disappointed that she hadn't avenged his death. But it wasn't that at all. She had merely to confront her fear and find the truth. And once she did, she felt the spirit of her father upon her, enveloping her soul, making her free, bringing her home.

"Cherylann," Stan asked, quietly, "Cherylann ... are you with us, sweetheart?"

"Hmm, oh, yes, yes, Uncle Stanley," she said with a smile. "I'm with you."

Will ran up to them, unconcerned with what he might be interrupting.

"Well, I'm glad you're with them...."

Cheryl turned with a start, the mood broken, her voice on edge, "What the hell is that supposed...."

"What that's supposed to mean," Will said anxiously, jumping his cue, "is that I'm glad you're with them because the woman we're looking for—isn't with them."

He pointed back over his shoulder in the direction of the hospital.

❦

KELVIN STUMP SLOWED AS HE APPROACHED THE EISENHOWER TUNNEL. THERE were always enough cops around here to make life interesting, even though to this point his detectors had remained silent for the entire trip, which was unusual. Normally, a burglar alarm at the outlet mall or a fast food joint in Silverthorne could be relied on to set one off, wake the driver up, make him check his speed for a split second before kicking it in the ass again.

Kelvin dropped down to 80, right along with the flow of traffic. As he entered the tunnel his greed got the better of him. He bent, picked up the gym bag from the floor and wrestled it into the seat next to him. The car swung back and forth between lanes. His body twisted and turned the wheel, sending the car skittering toward the far wall of the tunnel. He cut off a family Ford and endured the frantic horn and curses that followed. He turned himself forward again, flipped the driver behind him the finger, and roared away, hitting 90 as he shot from the end of the tunnel like a bead of puffed rice.

"Fuck that, that was too close," he said to the leather interior. "I'll just play with my money out here in the wide open spaces."

He unzipped the bag and then relaxed, focusing on the road and building his speed back up to 101 on the descent. He was making excellent time.

❦

"ISN'T?" STAN AND OLLIE SANG IN TANDEM.

"She isn't what?" Cheryl asked.

"She just isn't," Will replied, breathlessly. "She's not at the hospital, she's not in the parking lot. She's not on that side or this side of the hospital in a lump. She's gone."

"Gone?"

"Gone."

"People," Ollie whispered, "especially old people with gunshot wounds do not get 'gone' that easily."

"Well, this one did. And remember," Will added, "she might be old, but she's not infirm. She hikes in the mountains every day."

Stanley laughed. "And shits in the high grass."

"Back off, leave her alone," Ollie said, testily.

"Sorry, friend, sorry."

"There are two places she could go," Ollie pondered aloud, "the hospital or home."

"She's not in the hospital," Will said.

"Then, home," Ollie decided with a nod. "Home it is. Come along, Stanley."

"Aren't you forgetting something?"

"What?"

Cheryl stepped in. "What about the money?"

"The money? Oh, the money. The case of money," Ollie murmured, the reminder a sudden and unwelcome addition to his life.

Stanley piped up, "Well, he's got a lead, but you gotta know the guy leaves a trail like a dinosaur with diarrhea. Kelvin Stump. Skell. He won't be difficult to pick up in Denver."

"No, but it will be difficult to find the money. Might be difficult to get to him as well, if he's really as big as he said he was...."

Stanley nodded, taking on the tone of his partner, "They rarely are, but, if he is, then we've lost it."

"Never lost one before."

"We may now."

Will stared at them quietly for a moment, then at Cheryl, who leaned in and took, for the first time in years, her Uncle Ollie's hand.

"Guys...."

"Not now, Will," Cheryl admonished him, gently.

"No, guys...."

"Will," Cheryl snapped, "they've just lost four million dollars—cash money. Leave them alone."

"Well, that's just it," Will mumbled sheepishly.

"What?"

"They haven't lost it."

❦

KELVIN STUMP CHECKED HIS WATCH. HE WAS MAKING BEAUTIFUL TIME. EVEN if they got free now, by some stretch of the imagination, by the time they got in touch with Denver police, he'd be home and stretched out in bed with his beautiful TV anchor alibi.

Forty minutes out, by his clock—with this speed, thirty minutes to freedom and financial security.

The silver car rocketed past Silver Plume without a break in speed to note its passing. The road was straight now, for another mile, until the big turn above Georgetown.

Kelvin reached down and finished unzipping the blue gym bag, pushed the zipper open and caught a glimpse of a green corner. New bills, he thought, lighter in color than the old. Yet, even in the dim light of the car, something about the look of those bills nagged him. He reached into the bag with his right hand and grasped a pile of slick paper, all cut into the size of bills, but, in fact, brochures for a Guardians of the Domain meeting on October 1.

"Mother," he croaked, the air from his lungs choked off in his throat by a realization the size of a medicine ball. "Goddamned mother."

His anger increased with the sudden comprehension that his mother, dear sweet goddamned mother, had pulled a switch, hidden the five-hundred grand somewhere safe, so he couldn't get at it before the goddamned tree huggers.

His speed increased in direct proportion to his anger.

He threw the bag on the floor of the car, his attention directed completely away from the road ahead, from the speedometer that was rising steadily, from the tach that was approaching the red line.

Kelvin Stump began to hyperventilate, the creeping dread that filled his mind making one thought, one horrible, inconceivable thought, paramount in his mind. He turned, one hand still on the wheel, and began frantically clutching at the latches of the bike case, scrabbling at them in a growing frenzy. He popped the first, corrected his line on the highway, then reached farther back for the second, center lock, pawing at the latch until it, too, burst open. He reached inside, grabbed one of the sheets of paper and pulled it madly toward him.

Instead of Benjamin Franklin, the face of a single mountain bike rider, covered with mud, in full color, stared back at Kelvin Stump from one of nearly two hundred copies of *The Vail Daily*. He reached back again and dug desperately through the newsprint, in search of the money, his money, by rights and action, his money and his money alone, oblivious to the fact that, in his fury, he was driving at nearly 140 miles an hour toward a highway guardrail that was in place more as a suggestion than a hindrance to driving off the cliff high above the village of Georgetown, Colorado.

Just before he hit the rail, Kelvin Stump screamed at the top of his voice, "Where the hell is my money!?!"

❀

"I MOVED IT."

"You what?" the three said in unison.

"I moved the money. I didn't like having it in my room so I moved it."

"Moved it where?" Ollie asked quickly, leaning forward to hear what had to be a most amazing answer. "You told us it was in the room."

"It wasn't. I'm sorry. It's not," Will bumbled. "It's ... it's ..."

"Where, Will?" Cheryl prodded.

"It's in five paper sacks in the trunk of our rental car."

❦

THE DISTANT CRASH AND RENDING OF METAL MADE MIKE COGDALL LOOK UP from the darkened streets of Georgetown toward two lights that seemed to fly off the highway and in a direct, if distant, line for him.

"Wow, Bo. You don't see that very often."

"What, hon?" his wife Kim muttered, juggling a handful of pink flamingo lawn ornaments before turning her eyes up to follow his gaze.

"A flying car."

As Cogdall pointed at the apparition, it hit the side of the cliff once, bounced, then hit again, bursting into a ball of flame on the second bounce.

The noise continued for a long time, but the Cogdalls weren't there to hear it. They were already in search of the authorities. Meanwhile, four pink flamingoes, the only inhabitants of the street, now stared blindly at the fire dancing gaily in the distance.

❦

OLLIE LAUGHED FOR A LONG TIME.

Despite what had happened that evening, and the worry about a woman still wandering the village with a gunshot wound, Cheryl couldn't help but smile as well. Stanley dropped his head, grinned, and scratched the top of his head absentmindedly.

Will smiled stupidly with them.

"Oh, God, Will—you deserve a great Christmas present for this one," Ollie said while chuckling. "Oh, Lord, at this very moment, I'd give my life for one thing."

"What's that?" Will asked.

"Just to see the look on that guy's face when he opens that case. You don't get a treat like that very often in life."

"Whatcha put in there?" Stanley asked.

"Newspapers," Will said with a grin. "Lots and lots of newspapers."

❦

IT WAS OBVIOUS FROM THE MOMENT GEORGETOWN RESCUE ARRIVED AT THE accident scene what had happened. Two of the paramedics peered into the seared car at the broken, battered, and burned beyond all recognition body of Kelvin Stump, while a police officer gazed up at the break in the I-70 guardrail high above, wondering just how fast someone would have to go to break the rail and still sail this far out and down from the cliff wall.

Pretty damned fast was all he could think.

He bent over and picked up a copy of *The Vail Daily* that a breeze had pushed against his foot. He looked at the photo of the mountain bike racer on the cover, folded the paper neatly, and stuffed it into his back pocket.

CHAPTER TWENTY-TWO:

OH WHERE, OH WHERE

THE FOUR OF THEM STOOD, SILENTLY, IN THE TALL GRASS BESIDE THE ice arena, each staring in a different direction, each lost in another thought. Ollie finally spoke.

"We'll look for Mrs. Stump. Back at her place. She'll need a doctor...."

"Let's hope she still needs one," Stanley offered.

Olverio shot him a look and then nodded.

"Yes, let's hope."

He turned to Will and Cheryl.

"You two go back to your hotel room. Relax. Get some rest. We'll be in touch tonight."

Cheryl smiled and nodded, turning to go back to the hotel. Will stayed and scuffed at the ground with the toe of his shoe.

"What he said," Will whispered, as if afraid to ask, "what he said about Leonard. Was that...."

"True?" Ollie nodded. "Yeah, Will. I'm sorry. Strange, in a way. Leonard ran with him because he thought he'd be safe. He would have been safer with us. We just wanted the cash."

"No matter what Angelo wanted," Stanley added.

"No matter what," Ollie said. "Some reputation, huh, kid?" He smiled and chucked Will on the arm.

Will agreed. He turned and joined Cheryl. The two of them walked slowly to the street and began the ten-minute walk back to the hotel. A few steps down the road and Will turned back, but the spot where the four had stood just seconds ago was already empty.

"Who were those masked men?" he joked.

Cheryl smiled. "Them? They were 'The Lone Uncles.'" She took his hand and they walked, silently, for a block, the pleasure of touching him, the night, and being free from the tension she had carried for years, giving her a sense of rebirth.

It was going to be a lovely evening. It was going to be....

"Hootie!"

"What?" Will jumped. The sudden shock of her voice had made him jerk away.

"Hootie, Jesus!"

"What? What?"

"Hootie. Hootie, that guy, that, Jesus. Before he dragged me off in search of you, he tagged Hootie, full square on the head with that damned box wrench of his ... oh, shit."

"Where is he, where is he?" Will said, slowly, trying to break through her sudden panic.

"He's back at the van. He's back at the truck." She was gone, her legs carrying her in a shot back toward town, back toward Vail Road, back toward the truck and Hootie and her job. One problem had resolved itself, now it was time to take on the others.

She was a manager. These were her people.

She was on call.

Will galumped along behind her, his shuffling gait a cross between a demented Howdy Doody and Chester from "Gunsmoke." At the turn to Vail Road, he felt a twinge in his calf and pulled up, turned, and walked, as quickly as possible, over the bridge, hoping to make up in distance what he was losing in speed. He could see her turn in the distance out toward the mountain.

She was going the long way around.

She usually did.

But, damn, she did make it look good.

✤

IN THE DARK OF NIGHT, THE TWO TURNED DOWN THE NARROW, UNMARKED dirt road leading to the small and lonely, white, clapboard house. They moved quickly, but without hurry, scanning the ground, the edges of the road, the wild fields of grass along the drive for any sign of her or her passage or her death.

"Shh," Ollie demanded. "Listen."

"Anything?" Stanley asked, quietly, a moment later.

"Nothing, friend," Ollie answered. "Nothing at all. I'm thinking...."

"I know...."

"I'm thinking she didn't come this way," Ollie said.

Stanley merely nodded.

The two moved toward the back of the house. Ollie took out a handkerchief and quietly opened the back door, quickly stepping into the darkness of the kitchen.

"You have your small light on you?" he whispered over his shoulder.

"Uh-huh," Stanley grunted, shutting the door behind them.

A second later, a small line of light ran along the baseboards of the room, methodically searching for any sign of Marjorie Stump's return.

"Check that front parlor. Near the door," Ollie said, almost reverentially, "look for any sign she's been here."

Stanley cupped the light to cut down on the beam and stepped, lightly, into the next room. Ollie watched him go and then stepped into Marjorie's bedroom.

There was enough moonlight and starlight shining through the window to give him a sense of what was here, and the sense it gave him was a sense of her. He could see her, he could feel her presence. The room radiated her, even when she was nowhere near.

Nowhere near. Ollie nodded.

The house, he knew, was empty.

He crouched down and glanced under the bed, for no reason that came to mind. A large, overstuffed grocery store bag was tucked high under the frame, behind the edge of the nightstand.

Without thought, he reached up and pulled it down to him.

Unrolling the curled-down top, Ollie glanced in and smiled.

What appeared to be the vault of a very small bank stared back at him.

"Bingo," he whispered.

He pulled the bag in tight and hugged it, thinking, in a way, that it brought him in touch with her.

And it did. As he sat quietly on the floor of her room, in her house, surrounded by the essence of her, he knew. He knew where she was and what she was doing and why she had to do it.

He felt his face grow warm and his eyes grow heavy. He shut his eyes to push back the feeling and pulled the money tighter to his chest. If you make it, he thought, this is yours. This is yours. I leave it with you.

Just make it, Marjorie. Wherever you are, please, just make it.

He knew it was only a dream. She had gone off to die.

The small beam of light entered the room just ahead of Stanley and found Ollie's legs. It never moved up to his face.

"You okay?"

Ollie nodded, then, realizing that Stanley couldn't see him said, "Yeah, I'm okay."

He turned and pushed himself up, using the edge of the bed for support.

"We've got the rest of the money."

"What do you mean?"

"The duffel bag stuff. The half-mil that smart boy thought he carried off in the duffel bag. No bag. No case. No money a-tall."

"Shit."

"Don't curse. Though I'll bet," Ollie laughed, "he sure as hell will."

"He'll be back," Stanley whispered, darkly.

"He will. And we'll be gone."

The two nodded, then, without words, slipped silently through the kitchen and out the back door, Ollie stopping, for just a moment, to carefully slip the Walther TPH, fully silenced, carrying the prints of one Kelvin Stump, who never wiped the silencer, under the pillow of that same Kelvin Stump, in the home of his mother, Marjorie Stump, who, when found, would be carrying a slug from this same gun.

He thought of her again and smiled. If only it had been another place.

If only it had been another time.

The two men strode toward the shed in the back yard, making one, quick, final check of where Marjorie might possibly be. Opening the shed door, Stanley was pushed back by the stench.

"Bingo," he whispered.

Ollie shone the small flashlight in through the door, dimly illuminating the body of a man, tall, big, face down, his head next to a five gallon jerry can of gasoline.

"What the hell ..." Stanley pondered aloud. "Goddamned bodies everywhere in this town."

"Insurance policy," Ollie answered quietly. "This is Kelvin's insurance." He stepped forward and fished his hand into the man's back pocket and withdrew the wallet he found there. He opened it to reveal the driver's license of one Kelvin Stump.

He flashed the tiny light over to the can. A small model rocket engine, attached to a timer and a wire igniter, sat poised above a small hole in the can.

"Burn him beyond recognition and the police will just assume it's Kelvin Stump. I'll bet this poor sap's prints are all over the inside of that house."

Stanley nodded in agreement as Ollie reached over and pulled the wires from the timer on the gas can.

"How'd he die?"

"Don't know, but I'd figure strangulation."

"What do we do now?'

"Leave it. Another nail in Mr. Stump's coffin once the police find it. The more the mess leans his way, the less we are to get wet."

Ollie rose, switched off the light and backed out of the shed. The two shut the door on the scene and began to walk calmly, without hurry, back toward Vail.

Along the way, Ollie looked at the stars and thought of her.

꽃

CHERYL WAS THERE FIRST, RACING, AS FAST AS SHE COULD, PAST THE LODGE, then across the face of the mountain, losing her bearings for a moment, at night, the streets and intersections becoming a maze of Tyrolean shops and dark figures and darker thoughts.

As she finally reached the back of the Haven-TW step van, she jumped, as Will shouted from the edge of the pit area. She turned back to the van and slapped her palm, flat, on the door.

"Hootie," she shouted, "Hootie. Are you okay?"

Will stumbled up beside her and, in the darkness, fumbled with the latch.

"Got it. Got it," he barked, "step back."

He threw the latch and grabbed the hanging strap, bending at the knees and putting his legs and back behind the lift. With a roar, the back gate of the step van rose and boomed against the metal bumpers at the head of the track.

The noise shook them both, as did the sight of what they found.

Through a thick haze of blue, sweet smoke, emerged the vision of Hootie Bosco, sitting in a lawn chair, a huge doobie hanging from his lips, his hair pulled back in a tight pony tail, two cans of Classic Coke duct-taped to a large, purple lump on his forehead, his legs stretched out, his face smiling, his hands holding "Moby Dick." He was reading by the light of a Coleman lantern, vented by the small hatch at the top of the truck.

Will bent at the waist to catch his breath from his panicked rush across town, gagged a bit at the heaviness of the smoke, turned, spit, and turned back with a laugh.

"We're out of our minds with worry, and he's spending Saturday night in the dorm."

Cheryl stood, silently, in shock.

"Hi, kids," Hootie chirped, "knew you'd come. Eventually."

"Well, the least you could have done, when you heard us at the door, was lay down and play dead," Will noted.

"Oh, no. No dead games. Not since Jerry died," he shook his head, the dreadlock ponytail dancing back and forth like it was swishing flies. "It was a glancing blow, nothing deadly. For such a big guy he was pretty much a wimp, wasn't he? Anyway. It rang my bell. I blanked. Got up, shouted for a while, but everybody was off drinking, so I just opened up the party tray and relaxed. Took you longer than I expected, but I got a lot done," he smiled, holding up the book for emphasis.

"Jesus," Cheryl sighed with relief, "at least you're okay."

"I got a hell of a headache. I'm beginning to understand what Ahab went through, especially now that I've got my own white whale to track down and kick the crap out of."

"Sorry, he's split," Cheryl offered. "But it's no wonder you've got a headache, smoking this shit and burning a gas lamp in a closed truck."

"Naw, got a vent," he said, pointing up, "I suspect it was the blow to the head that is causing the majority of my pain at the moment."

"Well, let's get you to the hospital, party boy," Cheryl said. "Sorry to interrupt your reading."

"Christ, we just came from there," Will whined.

"Well, we're going back," Cheryl said, stepping over and helping Hootie out of the chair. She reached over and turned out the gas lamp.

In the darkness, she spoke directly to the silhouette of Will.

"After all, I've got a team to look out for."

❧

THE SOLITARY FIGURE STRUGGLED THROUGH THE DARKNESS, DRIVEN BY PAIN, by hatred, and by a determination to die on her own terms. She had crossed under the highway in the Village and taken dirt roads up the hill, turned off them early onto horse paths, and then taken her own trails, cut through the brush by years of tramping. Alone. With Kelvin.

With her son.

With her killer.

She stopped for a moment and leaned against a tree, her vision going from reality to a burst of kaleidoscopic colors and back again. Marjorie Stump took a deep breath and stood, shook off the neon mirage and struggled on through the alpine forest.

She made no attempt to travel silently. She made no attempt to leave no mark in the forest. This was not a forest trek as much as a death march. A death march she was determined to complete.

And she had miles to go before she slept. Miles to go.

SUNDAY

CHAPTER TWENTY-THREE:

COMPANY

CHERYL CHUCKLED.

The hospital staff had been surprised into silence by Hootie Bosco's version of an ice pack. They also had the good grace to credit his creativity in keeping the swelling down on his head.

Still, the wrench had left its own, peculiarly shaped goose egg on the front part of the mechanic's skull, which, after X-rays and examination and a good-sized bill, the Vail Valley Medical Center had written off as merely a bump. A large, ugly bump caused by a falling five-pound wrench hitting an eight-pound melon.

"A bump!?! A bump the size of Cleveland!" Hootie had cried, asking for something more powerful than Tylenol with Codeine for the pain. They shook their heads, noting that there was enough chemical residue in his clothing to qualify as a prescription in California.

On the way back to the hotel, stopping at a liquor store, Hootie bought a six-pack of Coors outside the store, popped one open, then tossed one each to Cheryl and Will.

"Medicinal use only," he said with a smile.

"You sure you should be doing that?" Cheryl asked, popping the top on her own and taking a long pull to compensate for what had been a long night. "I think I read somewhere about not mixing Tylenol with alcohol, or something."

"You probably did. But, at this stage of the game, it is probably the nicest thing I've ever done to my brain or my liver, so I'm not going to worry about it. Another, Will?"

Will looked over, embarrassed, having drained the first can in two long gulps. He hadn't realized it as he had been doing it, but the can was now empty, nonetheless. He thought back and recalled that he hadn't had anything to eat or drink since before his ride this afternoon.

Long ago, this afternoon.

He looked at his watch: yesterday afternoon.

He held out his hand. "Yeah, please."

Hootie smiled, and tossed another can his way.

"Just don't open it in my direction."

Will popped the top, belched loudly, and took a long pull.

"Whoa, slow down, there, buckaroo—you're actin' like you need that real bad," Hootie muttered to Will.

Will didn't respond, but simply guzzled the beer for maximum effect.

Cheryl watched, then turned to Hootie.

She considered what she was going to say for a moment, then whispered, "Bad day—he lost a bundle today."

"A money bundle?"

"A money bundle. A good-sized money bundle."

"A Montana-sized money bundle or a fit-in-your-wallet money bundle?" he probed.

Cheryl laughed. She turned and looked back toward the ice arena, where she had last seen her uncles. "Montana sized."

Will belched loudly.

"You'd be depressed, too," Will grumbled. "Worst part of it all," he wheezed, the altitude and alcohol playing havoc with his brain cells, "I lost it to her family."

He pointed a weaving finger toward Cheryl and belched loudly again, this time going for distance.

"Yes, that's why I keep him … " Cheryl said, sadly, " … the sophistication factor."

Hootie merely shook his head.

"Man, worst thing I ever lost to my family was a game of euchre."

The three then walked, with an occasional belch, the rest of the way to the hotel, all three of them letting fly with a spectacular trio while passing the elegant woman returning from a party at the home of former president Ford.

Sheila Burns merely shook her head, kept walking, and pondered the death of etiquette in the world.

Hootie had asked, once, what had happened to Kelvin, but Cheryl just shook her head. While Will wanted to relate their adventures, Cheryl had stopped him, simply telling Hootie that, "someday, you'll know, but for now, let's just say that ignorance will be bliss."

Hootie nodded. "Understood." He raised a single finger. "But—some day, after lots of drinking, I want to know."

"You will, I promise."

The rest of the trip to the rooms was in silence. Hootie nursed a swollen head, while Will and Cheryl lost themselves in memories of the evening, concerns for Ollie and Stan, and, strangely enough, Marjorie Stump; thoughts about Kelvin and where he might be and what would happen to him; and guilt about Leonard Romanowski. Not being able to save him. Save him from Kelvin. Save him from himself.

Questions of what to say, if anything, and who to say it to, if anyone, and when to say it, if ever.

Will sighed and dropped his head back on his shoulders while Cheryl fit the key card into their door. She waved at Hootie, who closed the door to his own room behind him, then she opened the door, Will standing silently in the hall caught on the horns of a moral and ethical dilemma.

Okay, hot shot. Pop quiz. Your nasty little agent is dead in a car trunk, while a nasty little old lady is wandering the night, gut shot. You can't save one, but you can maybe save the other. In either case the police should know, that's your responsibility as a citizen … but … you're not directly involved, not yet, anyway. Not until you talk. What do you do. What do you….

"Whoa! Jesus!" Cheryl shouted from the middle of their room. Will broke himself away from his philosophical debate and rushed in to stand beside her. Stretched out on the bed, messing up the bedspread, were Stan and Ollie, waiting patiently for their return.

"Holy Christ, you scared the shit out of me!" Cheryl wheezed, clutching her chest.

"Don't curse," Ollie said, quietly.

"We really didn't know where else to go tonight."

"What about your room?"

"We've already checked out. We're leaving tonight for Detroit."

"What about the money?" Will wondered aloud.

"We've got the money, Will. That trunk of yours is notoriously easy to break into."

"How'd you know which … never mind," Will said, accepting the idea that these two knew more about him and Cheryl and their rental car than they'd ever let on.

"Did you get it all?" he questioned, a faint trace of hope in his voice.

"Your boyfriend is greedy, Cherylann," Stanley noted with a chuckle.

"He is, indeed," she answered, joining in, casting a glance back toward Will.

"What? What did I say," he whined, defensively. "Geeze. I just wondered…."

"If we had left any for you?" Ollie said, finishing his sentence. "Don't worry. If you stay in the family," he paused, casting a glance toward Cheryl and then back to Will, "you'll never be hard up. We watch out for our own."

"Yeah, I know," Will said, thinking of Fredo at the end of "The Godfather, Part II," "that's what I'm worried about."

"You've seen too many gangster movies. Comedies, all comedies," Stanley said through a huge smile.

"Okay, I've seen too many movies, but tell me this—what should I do? I feel like I should call the cops."

Ollie shook his head. "I wouldn't worry about that. We'll let the police know about our buddy Mr. Stump. They'll know what to do with him."

"And believe me. Trust me…."

"What?"

"Trust me on this one: When all this particular shit hits the fan, you're not going to want to have your name linked to it in any way, shape, or form."

"But my name is. He's my agent."

"That's weeks to go in an investigation," Ollie said, slowly. "Who knows if they'll ever get around to checking client lists. Then, if they do and they come to your door, you just say, 'Huh?'"

"Huh?"

"Yeah, just like that."

"No, no," Will stammered, "I don't understand."

"Look, Will," Stanley said, gently, "everything is in Cherylann's name, right? Car, room, meals…."

"Yeah," Cheryl nodded.

"From all they know, you've never even been to Vail. It's a stretch. They don't like to stretch that far," Ollie said, quietly.

"Besides, a few words dropped in the city and NYPD writes it off as a mob hit. Vail nods and clears the books," Stanley added.

"Well, I still feel bad. I feel guilty."

"That's growing up Catholic. It's a good feeling. Use it to do good around the world. But …" Ollie pointed at his head, "… stay out of this one. You did-n't do nothing. You don't know nothing."

The two turned, as one, and slid off opposite sides of the bed.

"Well, my dear, it is time for us to go."

She surprised them. She surprised herself.

"Do you have to? Can't you stay and watch me ride?"

The two men smiled at each other. Cheryl looked at Ollie, then across to Stanley. Two uncles she had denied so long. She took a breath, her heart filled, followed by her eyes. She stepped forward and tightly hugged the short, round man.

At first, he didn't know how to react. It had been so long, there had been so much anger, confusion. Then, as if it were a natural part of living, he found himself relaxing at her touch, reached around and pulled her close to his chest.

"I'm sorry," she whispered, the voice thick and slurred in her throat. "I'm sorry for what I thought."

"That's all right, dear," he said, a shiver in his own tone, "that's all right. That's all right."

"Yeah," Stanley said, "maybe we needed the time apart so you could go off on your own. Maybe that anger gave you great courage. Great co-jones."

Ollie sighed. "It's co-hone-ays, and don't use that language around my niece."

"Ah, sorry."

Cheryl broke from Olverio and stepped quickly around the bed, her face red and wet. She hugged Stanley tightly.

He sniffled.

"Welcome home, Cheryl Crane. I missed you. I missed you every day you were gone."

In the quiet of the room, with the heater fan and an occasional sniffle as the only sound, a heart was mending and a decision being made.

Stanley pulled back from Cheryl and held her at arm's length.

"You're the picture of your mother," he said, his lips quivering at the thought, "the very picture of your mother."

"Except, Cherylann here's rock hard," Ollie said with a laugh.

"She doesn't cook as well," Will added.

All eyes turned at the insult as if Will had just led a cow into the cathedral. He started.

"I'm sorry. She doesn't. Nobody in the world cooks like Rose."

Stanley relaxed a bit and nodded. "Well, he's right there."

"Hmmm," Ollie said, letting the imagined slight pass. "Maybe. Maybe."

The two men glanced at one another and nodded.

"Time to run," Ollie whispered, reaching out, taking Cheryl's hand and squeezing. "You take care." He glanced at Will. "You keep quiet." He looked back to Cheryl. "You ride well this weekend. Everything has been taken care of. You are not a part of this. It is not your responsibility. It is not your concern. Your job is to ride well. Make us proud. Make your mother proud."

"Make your father and Raymond proud," Stanley said.

"Yes," Ollie agreed. He took a breath and sighed. The memories were still painful for him. "Yes, make your father and Raymond proud."

Alone, to the side, Will lowered his head, the flush of heat from the thought of his best friend, the accident, the loss, the memories of what he was and what he had become, burning his face and bringing tears to his eyes.

Cheryl was already crying. The mention of her father opened up a new burst and she clutched Olverio's hand, pulling it tight to her face.

"He's proud of you, Cherylann. Wherever he is, he's proud of you."

Stanley nodded in agreement. "So are we."

The two slowly pulled away and stepped toward the door of the room.

"See you in Detroit. Thanksgiving?" Stanley asked hopefully.

"Sooner," Cheryl said. "Sooner. End of the week."

"Good. Good."

"That would be nice," Ollie said. "You going to bring him?"

Cheryl turned and looked at Will, now red-faced himself with tears.

"Yeah, I suppose I'll have to. He makes life amusing."

"Yes," Stanley noted, "he does that, doesn't he?"

Will smiled stupidly at all three of them and wiped his eyes.

Stanley opened the door and stepped into the hall. Ollie followed him, Cheryl close behind. At the door itself, he stopped and turned to his niece, remembering what he had almost forgotten.

"By the way, while we were waiting here for you, some guy named Reed, Marshall Reed, called, screaming bloody murder. He said he was officially quitting the team, since you were nowhere to be found and missed your race and something about no one at the truck at night and this being a two-bit amateur operation, and that you could go, excuse me, screw yourself, and that no matter what the contract said, he was taking a new ride with somebody else. Go ahead and sue, because no one in the world could make him ride, excuse me again, for a bitch."

Cheryl sighed. "Message received." She shook her head, almost with relief. "What did you say to him?"

"Me? I hope I didn't ruin it for you, but I told him nobody really gave a fuck what he did."

"Ha!" she snorted, "Ha! I thought you didn't curse!"

"I don't. When I do, you know I mean business. Like I said, I hope I didn't...."

"Don't worry about it," she laughed. "It's just about what I would have said. I should have told him that a long time ago. Same words, same emotion. I'll deal with the little shit tomorrow—full bore."

"Watch your mouth, young lady," he warned, "people judge you by your tongue."

"And," Stanley added from the silence of the hall, "you're a leader. People expect certain things from you."

She smiled, then nodded, then put her head on Olverio's shoulder.

"I love you."

He smiled in return, as much for the action as the words. "That's nice to hear. We've never stopped loving you."

He pulled away, smiled and winked, then pulled the door closed behind him. Cheryl stood looking at the door for a long moment and considered the decision she had made only moments before. It was a good one. It was the right one. It was, in fact, the only one she could possibly make.

She would deal with it tomorrow.

She turned to face Will, who stood, puffy eyed, tears streaming down his face, waving a single hand toward her in a loopy, disjointed way.

"I hate good-byes," he mumbled.

"Who said anything about good-bye?" she said, his tears causing hers to return. She stepped across the room. They took each other in their arms and stood, for a long time, silently supporting each other.

Cheryl pulled him tight, feeling the wall of his chest against hers.

In a room far removed from all that she knew, she was finally home.

In a burst of emotional release, the horror and hatred of years falling away in a rush, Cheryl Cangliosi Crane felt reborn, released, full of a fire to live. She filled her lungs, turned to Will, grabbed him by the lapels and fell to the bed, pulling him with her. She pulled frantically at his clothes and spent the next hour pushing him toward a feeble and exhausted state of consciousness.

Though his eyes grew wide at many moments—and at one moment he vaguely remembered actually shouting "Whoa!"—Will didn't fight her in the least.

THE TWO MEN STEPPED FROM THE HOTEL LOBBY INTO THE STREET, DARK, silent, and cold in the early morning of Sunday. Unconsciously, and in perfect unison, they rolled the collars of their windbreakers up against the chill of the night, the Hawaiian print shirts providing little warmth against the deep darkness of the witching hour.

"Where to now, bud?" Stanley asked, quietly.

"Denver to the banker, he'll ship the money back to Angelo, then the airport, then home."

"First class?"

"First class, always."

"What about them?"

"What about them?"

"You were acting like you were going to leave them a gift."

"We should leave Will our Hawaiian shirts," Ollie said with a smile.

"Let's save those for someone else," Stanley said. "What about...."

"Cherylann? Don't worry about Cherylann. By the time she gets home at Thanksgiving, five-hundred-thousand dollars from a paper sack should be washed and dried and freshly laundered."

"Make a nice trust fund."

"Make a nice wedding present."

"Think so?"

Glancing back up at the hotel, receding in the distance behind him, Olverio Cangliosi couldn't resist a smile.

"I think so. Yes, I do. I think so."

The two turned and continued their walk, silently, to their car, both lost in their singular thoughts. Stanley wondered about breakfast, while Ollie lost himself quickly in thoughts of her.

She was nasty. She was bitter. She was mouthy and opinionated.

But she had a fire he didn't often find in older women.

And it intrigued him.

He thought for a moment about taking the morning to look again for her, but knew, instinctively, what she had done, what she was doing.

He hoped she made it. He hoped she found her peace.

Still, he would always wonder.

Where did you go, my dear?

Where are you now, Marjorie Stump?

SHE HAD WALKED AND STRUGGLED THROUGH THE NIGHT TO GET TO THIS ONE place, never losing sight of where she had to go, this one place she loved more than any other on earth. Nestled at the base of the hill, hidden from the old two-lane tarmac that split the earth, leading up to the top of old Vail Pass, she finally found her peace, here in the clearing, where the aspen and lodgepole pines created her cathedral.

Silence was her music, the breath of nature her hymns. She leaned back against the old aspen, like herself, soon to leave this world, and felt comfort, sliding down the trunk until her feet dug little trenches in the carpet of leaves before her. Finally, she had found her place to rest.

She could now rest forever, in the forest that she loved so well.

She took a deep breath and felt the sweetness reach in and through her, silencing the pain that had gripped her stomach, gripped her heart, since late yesterday.

Ungrateful child, she wailed in her mind. Ungrateful child! After all she had given him, all she had sacrificed, all she had taught. To have him be nothing but a larger version of his father, or worse. A developer. A builder. Defiler of the valley. Oh, oh, oh, she drifted away on the chill of the morning, then drifted back. Oh, the tragedy. Of all things for him to be. The pain of it all. It was as if his father's ghost had reached across the decades and miles to tarnish the soul of her son.

His son. In the end, Kelvin had been his son after all.

She hadn't run far enough from her past. So many miles, so many years, and it had never been far enough.

Her breath rattled in her chest. It had never been far enough.

She had never stopped running.

She blinked her eyes and opened them, wide. Across the forest floor she could see a disturbance in the clearing, as if something had landed there and rustled about before leaving. Murph? Was that where she found Murph? Yes, yes, indeed. Murph. A goofy boy. I think Kelvin shot him, too. Maybe so. She thought he did. In the locker room. Oh, how sad, to die in a locker room. A smelly, toilet-filled washroom for overpaid athletes. She moaned and felt the burn in her gut. The pain, the actual pain of it had drifted away earlier in the night. But now, with the sun rising, it was returning, not so much as a pain, but as a burning memory.

She shifted her position on the tree and took another deep breath. She knew, instinctively, that there were very few left within her.

Ungrateful.

Another breath.

Did the others make it away, she wondered. Did he? She had abandoned them all to their fate, which, in a way, made her feel guilty. But then, then again, she had abandoned them so she could die on her own terms. Not in a hospital. Not drugged and alone, a TV set and Bob Barker her only companions. No. She had to leave the girl and that tall, skinny man and, what did he call himself, Ollie, no, Oliver. No. She struggled with her memory. Olverio.

A fine, rich name, for a fine, strong ... she struggled to breathe ... man.

I'm sorry, dear, would have liked to stay. Would have liked to talk more. Sorry to leave you to die at Kelvin's hands, in that place. Sorry.

Marjorie Stump felt warmth on her face.

She smiled to herself as the rising sun began to light up the world around her, the aspens changing early, right before her eyes, the green turning to gold, each leaf lit up from within, until the cathedral was awash with golden streams of light.

And through it, the beasts of her Mother walked, silently, for her. They drifted in and out. The wolf. The bear. The moose. The elk. And the lion. The proud lion, who walked differently from the rest, the only creature before her who took an interest in the wounded old woman stretched out beside the tree.

She smiled and reached out her hand to the dream of the beast, a gift from the Mother she had served so long and so well.

The beast gazed at her with bright and tawny eyes, like the leaves, seemingly lit from within.

Marjorie Stump smiled at the beauty of the image before her, the final gift of her Mother, a beautiful place in which to die.

For she had been a lion in protecting the wild, in battling the greed of the developers, of facing down the builders and their crews, of blocking the village council and its plans, so shortsighted, so shortsighted. She herself had been a lion, attacking, feeding, never frightened off, not when they threatened her land, her home, her very existence.

She had fought them on her own terms. Torching, destroying, sabotaging anything and everything that threatened her valley. Her valley.

The place she had come to live. The place she had come to die.

The warmth of the day, the peace of the place gave her comfort.

She sighed, raising her arms to embrace the dream of nature striding before her. And the lion was upon her.

CHAPTER TWENTY-FOUR:

GRUDGE MATCH

THE MORNING DAWNED COLD. DESPITE BRIGHT GOLDEN STREAKS OF sunlight splitting the sky over the valley, giving it all the look of a great green church, it was still damned cold.

Cold enough that Cheryl Crane could feel the goosebumps on her shoulders fight the Spandex of the jersey for space. The goosebumps were winning.

Will slogged along behind, his stilted gait a result of still compensating for a cast and a brace that were no longer there. As he rolled along behind her, coffee spilled on his hand, his wrist, the ground.

By the time they got to the truck, he'd have two slurps left in the cup.

Her race wasn't up for nearly three hours. Eleven o'clock. The amateurs were on the cross-country course at the moment. As they had just started an hour before, there was still plenty of time to eat or sleep or watch the day begin—but he wasn't driving the schedule this morning.

She was marching with a steady tread in front of him.

He spilled another splash of coffee on his wrist, cursed under his breath, and tried to smooth out his pace, at the same time picking it up in a vain attempt to catch up with her. She was someplace else this morning and had been since the phone call.

❄

"MARSHALL REED? CHERYL CRANE."

"Jesus, it's 7 a.m.!"

"You didn't seem to have a problem calling me at two this morning. Why should I care about you sleeping in?"

"Get lost. We've got nothing to talk about, bitch!" he barked in a thick, sleep-clogged voice.

"Oh, you're wrong there. I have a proposition."

There was silence for a moment on the other end of the line, then a rustling of sheets as Reed realized what was being said and sat up in bed.

"I'm listening."

"9:30. One race. Your choice. Winner takes all," Cheryl said, with quiet determination.

Will sat in the corner chair shaking his head. Grudge matches near race days were a bad idea. Grudge races on a race day were unheard of.

"My choice?" Reed asked, a smile in his voice.

"Your choice. One run. You win, I'm gone. I win—you're gone. Either way, you win."

"What time?"

"Eight a.m. at the truck. Hootie will set you up with whatever you need. Any bike you want. Choose the course. Race at 9:30."

"I've got a race that afternoon."

"Not 'til 1:30. Plenty of time for recovery. Mine's at 11 and I'm making the challenge. What do you say, Marshall? Either way—you're golden."

The phone was quiet for a moment, to the point where Cheryl wondered if they had, in fact, been disconnected.

"Well?"

"You're on. Let me think about where. But then—winner take all?"

"Winner take all."

"See you at the truck. One hour. This is going to be fun, Crane. I can kick your ass and drive you out all at the same time. Should make for a great morning."

"We'll see."

Without another word, she hung up the phone and looked over at Will.

"Bad idea, grudge match on race day," he muttered.

"You've done it."

"Not on race day."

"No time left. Today's it."

"Yeah, but there's no reason in the world to risk your race or your career to beat one asshole."

"But he's my asshole, Will." She sighed. "It's stupid, I know, but there comes a time when you've got to take the bull by the tail and face the situation."

She stood, turned and walked into the bathroom.

Will stared at the wall for a long moment. He understood what she meant, but couldn't get over the visual image it left behind.

❉

HOOTIE BOSCO RUBBED THE HUB WITH THE RED SHOP CLOTH LIKE A PILGRIM to Lourdes rubbing his rosary beads. Much more and the hub would look like a Uri Geller spoon after a ride on the In-sink-erator.

"You don't want to do this, Cheryl Crane. You do not want to do this."

"I realize all the arguments, Hootie. Will has rattled off each and every one of them this morning already. I know what I'm doing."

"Like hell. You have no idea what you're doing, missy. You win and life goes on, just fine. But you lose and that asshole thinks he's the boss. Which means I have to go looking for another job and, frankly, I like this one."

He angrily sucked at the plastic tube that hung near his mouth, the other end jammed in a bottle of Snapple taped to the lump on his head. The image made her smile.

"Don't worry, Hootie. I'm not about to lose."

"Yeah, convince my guts of that, dearie," he said, then turned and angrily spun her bike's front wheel.

Marshall Reed stepped around the corner. He eyed Hootie, then Will, sitting in the sunken lawn chair, then let his eyes drift back, slowly, to Cheryl.

"Well, chief, you ready?"

"Am I ready for what?"

"Are you ready to go on the unemployment line?"

"We'll see. Where are we doing this, Marshall?"

"Ooooh. Cool as ice. I like that in a victim." He chuckled.

"Cut the psych crap. Just where, Marshall?"

"Dual slalom, Miz Crane. Dual slalom."

"I've never ridden slalom," she said, suddenly, immediately cursing herself for letting the words pop out.

"Oh, really? Well, if you've never shot a gun, you should be more careful about giving your opponent the choice of weapons, now, shouldn't you?"

Hootie and Will stared at them silently. Both wanted to shout out, to leap into the confrontation, but this was her show, her challenge, her ride.

They had nothing to do with it.

"Done," was all she said.

"Good. The course is clear. Races were yesterday. Gates are still up." He laughed and nodded at her, then Will, then Hootie. "This should be fun." He stared into the back of the van and eyed the bike he wanted to ride.

"Give me the Colnago."

"You sure?" Hootie asked.

"Yeah, I'm sure. You replaced the rim? Checked out the fork?"

"Yeah. It's ready to ride."

Marshall Reed glanced over at Will. "Then, I'm gonna ride it. Show these Tour dee France folks how bikes are meant to be ridden. Bikes that in about forty-five minutes will be my bikes. To give to my buddies. See you at the top of the hill, gorgeous."

He snapped Cheryl an ugly smile then turned and rolled the bike away toward the lift. Over his shoulder he called, "See you at the top, sweetie, then see you at the bottom."

Will rose up out of the chair, walked to Cheryl's bike, spun the front wheel, angrily spun the crank, then spun the release at the top of the workstand and pulled the bike free.

"What are you doing?" Cheryl asked.

"From this moment on, consider me your Sancho Panza, Don Quixote. Let's go tilt at some windmills."

"Will," she said, sullenly, "I've never ridden a slalom."

"Nothing to it," Hootie said with a determination that she had never heard in his voice before. "Nothing to it," he repeated, reaching for the race bible and flipping to the slalom course map.

"Twelve gates, each one about 40 feet apart. First three are steep and tight, maybe 35 feet of break. Then a speed run on a flat ridge before four, five, and six, forty-foot separation. Then a drop into the gully for seven, eight, and nine. Ten, eleven, and twelve are on the top of the finish run. Catch the last one and fly."

"Any particular rules I should be aware of?"

"Go between 'em. Don't miss. Ride like hell. That's all there is to it."

"Yeah, while going straight down."

"Nothing to that, either. Frannie Draa does it all the time. Jettmann. Reed. And shit, if Reed can do it, anybody can. I've never seen such a klutz on a bike."

"He's got bike-handling skills," Will offered.

"Yeah, apes got bike-handling skills, too. Seen it at the circus. Not that I want 'em ridin' for me, though." Hootie shook his head as punctuation, his hair dancing like an explosion inside a muskrat fur coat.

"Since we are," he said, "breaking with tradition. I'd best step over to the Ishmael tent and let them know we'll be using their slalom course this morning."

"Think they'll throw a fit?"

"Maybe. The race officials will freak. But who gives a shit. Don't worry. I know the promoter. He loves this stuff, especially if he can get it on video."

"Video?" Cheryl said, startled.

"Yeah. Sell it off to ESPN. Show them what a loose and funky Gen-X race they got here." He turned to walk to the officials' tent, over his shoulder he tossed, "Lovely demographics for TV. It'll sell a billion tubes of Clearasil."

They watched as Hootie and his hair negotiated the uneven ground between the trucks and tents, tables and RVs, leading to the Ishmael tent. After a long, cool moment of silence, Cheryl turned to Will.

"This was a better idea earlier this morning."

"Always is," he replied, "but Hootie's right. Reed's a clown. You can beat him."

"I don't know the course, I've never ridden slalom, I'm gonna get my ass kicked."

"Maybe so. I can't give you a magic pill or a speech or words of wisdom. All I can say is shut up and ride your bike. That's what it comes down to, Cheryl.

"Shut up and ride your bike."

⚜

SHE PAUSED AT THE LIFT, STARING UP THE MOUNTAINSIDE. SHE LOOKED OVER at the signage marking the end of the run, then back up again. She took a very deep breath that calmed absolutely nothing.

Hootie Bosco quietly stepped up beside her.

"Look, Cheryl, I've been in this game a long time. And the one thing I know about blind runs is this: You start at the top, you end at the bottom. To get from one place to the other, you throw your heart down the mountainside and just chase after it."

"That's beautiful, Hootie," she said.

"Thanks. I got it out of an Annette movie when I was a kid."

She stared at him for a long second, then burst out laughing.

The chair swung into position, Will handed her bike to the attendant who smoothly mounted it to the rack. Cheryl Crane stepped in, sat down, and was lifted toward the starting line.

Will watched the chair disappear up the mountainside. He never took his eyes off her. She never looked back.

He didn't expect her to.

✤

"YOU WANT A START ON THIS?"

Cheryl shook herself free of the vision of the White River National Forest that spread out, horizon to horizon, before her. She had meditated herself from animal to vegetable and wasn't quite sure, for a moment, where she was or what she was about to do.

"Huh, yeah, I suppose."

Marshall Reed rolled up into the starting block beside her. He stared at the young man with the red and blue bandanna hat.

"Where the hell did you come from?"

"Cross-country course. I bet right about now the senior expert women are screaming bloody murder because you two have pulled away all the fans."

"What are you talking about?"

"You cross that rise down there, pal, and you'll find out what I'm talking about. About the eighth gate in, other side of the gully, everybody and their dog is waiting for you. Grudge match. Winner take all. Shit, you gotta love that."

"How'd you … Hootie. Hootie Bosco."

Cheryl nodded, smiling.

"I dunno. I just heard. Thought you might need a start. Besides...."

"Shut the fuck up," Reed barked, far more nervous, suddenly, than he had been at the bottom of the mountain. "Just start us and get the hell out of the way."

"Okay, dude. Chill. No prob here." He leaned in close to Cheryl and whispered, "There's a bad rut just before number four. Go tight left." He winked.

Cheryl had no idea what he meant.

"Okay, dudes, you ready?"

Cheryl nodded.

Reed snarled, "Just do it."

Cheryl turned the right pedal up and put pressure on it ...

"Three ..."

... tensed her body ...

"... two ..."

... rose up off the seat ...

"... one!"

... and cast her heart down the mountainside.

"Yeah!"

The bandanna fluttered downward through her peripheral vision and Cheryl roared, pushing off with a power and anger that shot her out of the box. Marshall Reed rode tight beside her, his first push twisting him in close to her left side, the next pushing him away.

She cursed under her breath, then threw herself forward into the first gate, adrenaline, gravity, and a big ring taking her there faster than she had ever thought possible.

THE CROWD LINED THE LOWER THIRD OF THE COURSE, WITH MORE STREAMING in all the time.

The cross-country course was still busy, but that didn't seem to matter. The officials remained to watch the amateur riders, while the crowd flowed here, to the grudge match, telegraphed on the drums of a small community. Hootie Bosco smiled. It was working out better than he had ever imagined it.

He rose up on his toes and saw two television videographers running up the course, trying to get into position for a few gates, a little action, some great shots.

The race promoter pointed and smiled, knowing that any publicity this weekend was good publicity and that if this worked out, ESPN might come calling, and, if ESPN came calling, his job was secure for another six months.

Such was the world.

Will kept rising up on his toes but couldn't see over the first ridge.

She was flying and he was blind. He turned, frantically, looking for some way, any way, he could get a sense of what was going on. But there was no coverage, no vantage point, no....

"Here they come!" the small voice sang out.

Will looked to the top of a small storage building at the little girl with the bright red telescope pointed toward the top of the mountain. She was seriously intent on what she saw.

Will desperately wanted to shout out for information, but he instinctively turned back toward the mountain, rising up, peering ahead, forcing his eyes to see what they could not see at the moment.

He needed to know.

❋

SHE WENT WIDE ON THE THIRD GATE, THROWN OFF STRIDE, FOR A SPLIT second, by the speed with which it had appeared. These were too tight, too close. It couldn't be done.

"How does anyone," she thought, "how does anyone...."

Her break on the ridge was over. The next gate was already upon her. She cut back in, mentally counting the gates. Number 4. He had said something about number four.

Out of the corner of her eye she could see that Marshall Reed was close behind her. Not much, if at all, very close.

Very close.

Without even seeing the rut, she suddenly remembered the starter's tip and cut in, very close, to the gate, the lower half of her eyes watching in amazement as the edge of her tire danced along the lip of the gash in the mountainside. She cut in, brushed the flag and cut back out, the washboard surface of the course shaking her hands, her arms, her teeth, and any and all internal organs.

She fought for control, hit a smooth stretch and flew on. Her heart. Her heart was down there, somewhere. The gates were still as tight as before, but somehow she was finding a feel and a rhythm to the course.

There was madness in their method.

The mountain seemed to drop straight away and she could feel the sweat of effort, the sweat of outright fear, burst through the Spandex of her uniform and darken the colors. She shifted her weight again, instinctively, and pulled back through the next gate.

Beside and just slightly behind her, she heard Marshall Reed curse, and the curse recede in the distance. He had fallen off the pace. She dug down, determined to keep it clean, to not make any mistakes.

She slowed a bit too much for the next gate, which dropped her into a gully on a small turn then back onto the main slope. She was still heading south like a bat outta hell.

She slid cleanly into gate seven, shifting her weight, feeling the bike, the mountain, the course, through her hands, her feet, and her ass, hit eight and nine cleanly, then sat up with a start.

Marshall Reed.

Reed was right beside her.

Whatever she had gained, whatever he had lost, had been erased in three gates. She was outclassed and suddenly, like hitting a brick wall, Cheryl realized it.

She had no right being here. She had no right riding. She had no right challenging anyone on this course. Or any other. She had no right.

She felt the power begin to drain away from her. The desire. The fire. The hunger.

"Shut up!" she screamed aloud, as the two bikes roared over the lip leading to the final three gates and the run out to the finish.

"Shut up and ride-your-biiiiiiikkkke!"

Marshall Reed threw a quick glance over his shoulder, then turned back to the course, slipping in very tight on the next gate.

Cheryl used the fury of her cry to dig in again.

She rose up and over the final ridge, cleanly caught gates ten and eleven neck and neck with Reed, then put the bike in the biggest gear she could find, shot through the final gate and tore down the mountainside, crouched tight, streamlined into a bullet.

She dug hard, her heart banging out a roll, her lungs on fire, her legs, divorced from her mind, pumping madly away at the cranks. She flew over the final rise, caught big air, hit the ground, hard, carped to the right a bit, straightened, focused, and drove for the line.

She heard nothing until she hit the banner, when the screams and cheers broke through the pinpoint focus of her mind.

Marshall Reed had won.

By half-a-wheel.

She closed her eyes, grabbed her brakes and slid the rear wheel to the side, carving her way to a stop. She opened her eyes and stared at the crowd, only inches away behind the orange plastic barricade.

There were looks of sympathy and there were cheers and applause.

She followed the looks of the crowd over to Marshall Reed, off the bike and dancing before them—pointing at Cheryl, pointing in the air, pointing at his bike, pointing at Cheryl—the winner.

The winner and champion.

Winner take all.

WILL WAS THE FIRST TO HEAR HER.

A small voice, behind him and above, almost the sound of an angel giving moral advice, repeated, again and again, "No ... No ... No!"

Will turned and looked up at the little girl on top of the hut. She was shaking her head furiously and shouting at the top of her lungs, "No! No!"

In the tumult of Marshall Reed's victory dance, no one heard her.

Will looked at Reed, then back at the girl, tapped Hootie on the shoulder and pointed. Hootie mouthed a "What?" then followed Will toward the hut.

As they approached, Will waved at the girl, finally breaking her focus from the crowd she was trying to turn.

"What are you saying?" he shouted, a bit too loud for the circumstances.

"No," the girl shouted back, her thin voice fighting to be heard over the crowd, "he didn't win! He didn't win!"

"What? What do you mean?" Hootie shouted.

"I mean he didn't win!" she shouted back, the frustration of being small and being quiet and being ignored beginning to build behind her eyes.

"Well, Jesus, then. Don't tell me—" Hootie shouted "tell them!" He turned and pointed to the crowd, cupping his hands around his mouth in order to shout for quiet.

The little girl beat him to it.

"Scccrrrrrrrrrrrreeeeeeeeeeeeeeeeeeeek!"

The high pitched squeal instantly brought Will's hands to his ears and took Hootie's hands to his crotch.

Both were protecting something important from the explosive, 115-decibel sound.

The crowd cringed, then turned, as one, toward the hut, slowly rising back to full height, all ready to crouch again for protection if the little girl hurled another lightning bolt.

They were all, suddenly, silent.

The girl smiled and stood tall, finally holding the attention of the crowd in the palm of her hand.

"He didn't win!," she shouted, pointing at Marshall Reed.

"What? The hell I didn't."

"He-didn't-win!" she said again, pointedly, the fear of facing the volatile rider clearly showing in her eyes.

"Bullshit!"

She lowered her hand. The fear of confrontation with an adult getting the better of what she knew to be true.

Her father looked up at her and smiled.

"Dev—are you sure?"

"Daddy, I'm sure."

"Then say it. I'm here. He can't hurt you."

Will smiled at the man beside him and looked up at the little girl.

"So am I. You tell 'em. I'll back you."

Hootie Bosco nodded.

"Me, too."

She looked at Hootie and couldn't help but smile at his head. The purple welt above his eye was only partially masked by a droopy dreadlock.

He noticed her look and smiled.

"My hair's behind you, too, kid."

She laughed and nodded, then looked up at the crowd of teens and adults. A TV camera was pointed at her.

She took a deep breath and began.

"You need to go through all the sticks to win. Right? Right?"

Some people in the crowd nodded unconsciously toward her.

"But he missed two of them. I saw it. Just over that hill before they went down and I lost them."

"Oh, screw this," Marshall Reed shouted. "You can't see shit…."

"Shut up!" a woman in the crowd yelled. "Let the kid talk!"

"He hit a bump and his front wheel wiggled and he missed the gate and Cheryl went through two of them and was ahead but he skipped the next one and rode straight on and caught up with her. Just before they went into … that … that…."

She couldn't find the word.

"That gully," Hootie Bosco shouted, matching the girl's description to the course description in the race bible. "Just before the gully. Just when," he shouted, accusingly, at Marshall Reed, "a rider would think that nobody in the world could see him. From the top or from the bottom of the course."

"Bullshit. I hit those. That little bitch knows shit. She can't see from there. I win. You're gone," he pointed at Cheryl. "Winner take all. Your rules. You're gone."

"No," the girl shouted, insistently.

"I win."

"No!" a voice wheezed from behind them.

The crowd turned as one to see a young man, with a blue and red bandanna for a cap, panting and wheezing, leaning heavily on the finish line post for support.

"No. He missed … I followed. He missed two. Just before that dip thing.

As soon as I … launched … them I ran after, ran down the mountain. Just to watch. Can't see after that first ridge. I saw her make number four, but … woof … he missed five and then jumped six just to catch her. He missed. He-missed-two!"

"Like-I-said!" the little girl shouted from the top of the hut.

"Like she said!" Hootie shouted.

"Like she said!" Will shouted.

"Like she said," her father shouted.

The crowd picked up the chant, and the girl stood on the hut, one hand on her telescope, the other on her hip, a smile of pride on her lips. The man who had run the course from the top of the mountain sagged to the ground, wondering why no one cheered for him.

Cheryl Crane looked up at Devon, smiled, then touched her fingers to her lips and pushed a kiss of thanks toward the girl. She turned and faced Marshall Reed.

"Winner take all," she said.

And smiled.

He casually flipped her the finger.

The immediate drama over, the crowd began to break up, slowly, moving back toward the cross-country course.

Hootie watched them go.

"I shoulda had a guitar case here for donations. You don't get a show like that very often."

Cheryl nodded and then stepped over to the hut where the small girl still stood above everyone else.

"Thanks for watching. Thanks for speaking up."

"No one would listen."

"So you just have to say it louder."

"I did."

"And I thank you. Stop by the Haven truck later, Devon. We'll make sure you get outfitted with about everything we've got."

"You remembered my name," the girl said with a happy laugh.

"How could I forget?" Cheryl answered.

"I'll even give you my wrench," Hootie said with a grin.

The girl laughed, which made Cheryl smile. This was a good kid. This was a great kid. Nice to know they still existed. She turned to retrieve her bike and came full face with Marshall Reed.

"It's all bullshit, you know that, don't you? I kicked your ass from here to Cleveland."

"Odd, isn't it? My ass seems to be here."

"I beat you."

Will stepped up from behind him, causing Reed to jump.

"Two witness say you didn't. The crowd now says you didn't. Your face, Reed, your face even says you didn't. Give it up, pal."

Cheryl looked at her watch.

"You know, I've still got an hour before the start of my race. You want to go up to the top of the hill and try it again, then, by god, I'll do it. Right here, right now. I'll blow off the cross-country in a heartbeat to take you on again. And again. And again. Until you get it through your thick skull. Until you accept that I won."

"I...."

"Jesus," Hootie cried, "give it up, Marshall. She's got you on the ropes. She caught you in a lie. Accept it and get on. Get on, man."

Marshall Reed stood silently for a moment, swept up the Colnago and began to walk back toward the truck.

"Leave the bike," Hootie said. "I'll take it from here."

"Ease up," Cheryl said, quietly.

She reached out and took Reed's shoulder, turning him toward her.

"Look, the deal was: Winner take all."

"Yeah. Okay," he answered, his ego bruised and angry. "So, I'm leaving."

"Well, since I won, I'm still in charge of this team. And since I'm in charge of the team, I make the call on who stays and who goes."

"What's your point?"

"After this weekend, nobody in the world will touch you if I let you go. You're breaking a contract. People—right or wrong—thought you tried to cheat here. You haven't made any friends. You don't have a stellar riding record. You're poison, pal. So—with that in mind—why don't you stay?"

"What?"

"Why don't you stay and ride? We've only got a few more weeks in the season. Ride for us. See how it goes. Decide in November if you want to come back. Let all this …" she swept her hand around her "… die out a bit."

Marshall Reed paused, wanting desperately to bolt, stared at Cheryl, behind her to Will, then Hootie, then back to her.

He nodded.

"Okay. This time. Yeah. Thanks."

"You've got a race to prepare for," Cheryl said. "Go do it."

Marshall Reed turned and began to walk back to the van, the bike still slung over his shoulder. This time, Hootie didn't ask him to leave it.

About ten steps on and he turned again.

"You had me beat," he said, quietly. "You beat me, Cheryl Crane. You beat me fair and square. You saw the rut. I didn't. You played it right. I didn't. You had me beat, and I couldn't let that happen." He paused for a long moment. "Sorry."

"Thanks for telling me."

"Yeah." He nodded slowly and turned toward the village. "Yeah."

"Kick some ass and take some names this afternoon, Marshall," Cheryl called after him.

Reed nodded and waved his fingers, locked around the top tube of the Colnago.

Will turned to Cheryl and nodded.

"Nicely done."

"Thanks," she smiled at the compliment. Casually, she turned her watch up and froze. "Shit on a shingle. Fifty minutes until the start."

"Don't worry, don't worry," Hootie muttered, sounding amazingly like an overprotective mother. "I'll spin you twice, and you'll be on your way. Eat and hydrate and you'll be golden."

"I'll have to pee."

"That, too, shall pass." He grinned at his small joke. "You're okay, Cheryl Crane." He took the bike from her and began to roll it back toward the van. "You're okay."

"I agree, wholeheartedly." Will smiled. "You're okay, Cheryl Crane."

"Thanks."

She stared at the mountain for a long moment, a light breeze catching errant strands of her hair and carrying them up behind her, where the sun kept changing the color in subtle, beautiful ways. Even standing rock still, Will thought, she always looked like she was in motion, as if she were flying.

"Could you do me a favor?"

"Yeah, shoot," he said, immediately regretting his choice of words.

"Do you think you could get used to calling me Cangliosi again?"

"Yeah. I suppose I could."

"Thanks."

"But I'd rather call you Ross."

She blushed, but did not dismiss the idea.

"Promises, promises," she whispered.

"One I intend to keep."

He wrapped his arm in hers and they began the walk back through a beautiful world of green and brown and gold and blue and stark white toward the truck, sitting at the end of a long and brutal weekend. As they walked, Will caught their reflection in a shop window: two young people, athletes, lovers, walking arm-in-arm toward yet another starting line, a new starting line.

He stared intently at the face of the man who stared back at him.

"You okay?" she asked, quietly concerned.

"Yeah," he said, moving his eyes from the face of the one to the faces of the two. "Yeah. I'm great."

He smiled and nodded.

"I'm great."

EPILOGUE

"YOU'RE SHORT."

"Excuse me?"

"You're short," the short man with the fat fingers and bad haircut said, matter-of-factly.

Drawing himself to his full height, Stanley answered, brusquely, "I'm taller than you."

"Don't get personal," the smaller man said, looking to Ollie for help and finding none. The other short man in the room simply stared at the piles of money going into the heavy, lined packing box and didn't say a word.

"You're short," Tommy Wells said, casually checking a letter he pulled from his back pocket, "according to this, anyway, let's see, 3,965,470 dollars. No cents. You're short some 534, 530 dollars. No cents. "

"No sense is right," Stanley said, turning away from the greasy little man and stepping over to the curtained, second-floor window of the small, ancient warehouse. He pulled it aside and looked at the rear of the Denver City and County building some three-and-a-half blocks away. Idly, he watched a workman in the distance hang a thin wire across the back of the cupola of the municipal building, stop, look at his watch, and disappear within the building.

Stanley looked at his watch, 4:45. Quitting time.

"We're short what the mark decided to ditch," Ollie said, in explanation.

"And use for traveling money."

"What they doing there, stringing lights?"

"That's a lot of traveling money," Tommy Wells muttered, trying to answer them both at the same time, "Yeah, stringing lights."

"I can't help that," Ollie said, with a shrug. "Angelo took his own sweet time calling us in, and Leonard had expensive tastes."

"Christmas lights?"

"Yeah, Christmas lights," Wells snapped, his head going between the two like he was watching a ping-pong game. "It's the city's big damned display, it bleeds in here for a month-and-a-half and makes me look green. You know, you're going to have to explain this to Mr. Genna. He's not going to be happy he lost five-hundred grand."

"I'll take that chance."

"Are they nice?"

"The lights? Yeah, they, like, overwhelm your eyeballs, but people come from everywhere to see it. Take photos. You know, whole damned Christmas thing. I'm not taking the rap on this shortfall."

Ollie spread his hands in a gesture of surrender and nodded.

"We're thinking that Leonard was generous—spread a lot around. But, whatever he did, it's gone now. Just give us a receipt for what you've got there and don't worry about it. Mr. Genna knows where to find us if he has a problem with it."

"He will have a problem with it," Wells said, scratching out an unnamed receipt on a flimsy carbon pad. "He has problems with losing money, if I recall."

"Don't we all?" Ollie shrugged, eyeballing the receipt as Wells signed it.

Stanley stared out the window at the building and sighed. "Starting awfully early."

"Yeah, must be a big one this year," Wells said, speaking out of the corner of his mouth while keeping his eyes on Ollie, "they usually don't start stringing the things until October."

"Wish the lights were on, I'd like to see the lights."

Tommy Wells nodded.

"First week of December they turn 'em on," he flipped the lid over on the heavy-gauge box prior to sealing it, "it is something to see."

"Here, before you seal that, throw these in," Ollie said, tossing a wrinkled paper bag at Tommy Wells's head.

Wells caught the bag off balance, dropped it, bent, picked it up and, while rising, peeled back the top and looked in.

"Shirts?"

"Shirts. Gift for Angelo."

Stanley snickered at the window and continued staring out through the closed curtains.

"I don't get it."

"He will. He'll also understand that he shouldn't give us any grief about the missing stash. That was Leonard's doing. And if we have a problem …"

"Any problem at all …" Stanley added.

"We'll drive to Jersey, find him, and use those shirts to clean the back of his throat."

Stanley turned from the window and said, simply, "The truck is here."

Wells stood silently, holding the shirts above the box, unsure if he wanted to become a part of the joke. Still, he was two-thousand miles away from Angelo Genna and three feet away from "Old Cans" Cangliosi. A decision had to be made, and the decision was a simple one. Without a word, he dropped the two, well-worn, Hawaiian shirts into the box, fitted the foam lining carefully into the opening, and closed the heavy-gauge cardboard lid. He then fit the tongue-and-groove closures together and wrapped the finished product with wide strapping tape. He checked the airbill, stepped to the door, opened it, and shouted down.

"Larry, the truck's here. Grab a dolly and come up for this thing, would you?"

"How do you ship this sort of … package?" Stanley asked, watching the driver of the van step out, readjust his cap on a nearly bald, whitish grey head, and open the rear door with a "boom."

"Standard air freight. Mr. Genna will have it tomorrow afternoon."

"Don't you worry about it, well, disappearing?" Stanley asked, turning away from the window.

"Not really. The cargo manifest says it's legal documents. Which it is. I'm legit, a bail bondsman, I deal in such things. Which is true. It fits. It's safe. Which, unless the plane goes down, it is. Been doing it for years. Besides, I'm not the one who lost five-hundred grand."

"Well, neither am I. Like I said, Mr. Genna has a problem, he knows how to find me." He stared at the box for a long moment. "I'm glad you're comfortable with this system, Tommy," Ollie murmured. "This kind of cash I'd like to hand deliver."

"I can give it back to you and tear up the receipt."

"Nope. No thanks. Time to get home. You handle it your way. Give me your receipt book."

Wells handed it over.

Ollie took it, looked at the receipt, nodded that it all seemed correct, and made an inconspicuous mark next to Tommy Wells's chicken-scratch signature.

God, he thought to himself, don't they teach penmanship anymore? Or is that as much for his safety as my mark is for me?

He tore off the top copy, made out for $3,965,470, pulled up the carbon to check underneath it, tore the carbon plus several more receipts off as well, then handed the book back to Wells, slipping the folded receipts and carbon into the pocket of his new white shirt.

"Hey, that was a new book."

"You're breaking my heart."

There was a tap on the door, and Wells opened it. A man stepped in pushing a two-wheeled dolly, his mouth going from the moment the door opened.

"Jesus, you guys watching the news at all?" Wells shook his head as he twisted the box on the floor to bring it square to the dolly. "Man, they are having some day up near Vail, that's for sure." Wells stared at Larry and lifted one edge of the box, then glanced up at Ollie. Old Cans had no reaction at all. "Five bodies, can you believe it? Five bodies. One shot. One stabbed. One strangled. One big ass car wreck in Georgetown on Sunday morning, and some lady found half-eaten in the woods. Damn."

"Eaten?" Ollie said with surprise. He turned to Stanley, who gave him a quick look of sympathy that Wells noticed, but the workman did not.

"Eaten. Mountain lion. Bad shit. Can you believe that shit?"

The workman slid the lip of the dolly under the box. "Eaten. Oh man, I hate the thought of that shit, that's for sure, man." Wells nodded and pushed the box up and back, tipping the dolly to a 45-degree angle. Larry balanced it out and rolled the case toward the door, chattering all the way.

"God, I bet the small town cops are going nuts on this one," he caught an edge on the door, "they haven't had any shit like this since that celebrity dame kacked her skier boyfriend." He backed the box into the room, then rolled it out cleanly. The door fell shut behind him of its own accord.

"That was Aspen," Ollie said, under his breath, correcting the departed worker.

"Your handiwork?" The words were out before Wells could stop them. He cringed, waiting for a reaction that never came. The tall man continued to stare out the window, while the short, round one, the one who seemed truly dangerous, stared across the room and sank backward against a table, obviously lost in thought. His eyes seemed to be moist, as if filling with tears.

Jesus. They must have had some weekend.

Olverio made a deep sigh, shook his head and stood up.

The quicker rid of them, the better, Wells concluded.

"When are you gentlemen out of here?"

Stanley looked at his watch. "We've got an 8:30 flight. How far's the airport?"

Ollie looked at his partner with a hard stare. You never tell anyone your plans or schedule.

Wells didn't notice it. He said, simply, "About half-hour, forty-five minutes from downtown. I usually figure an hour-and-fifteen to the gate. Shouldn't be crowded on a Monday. What airline you flying?"

Stanley caught the look from Ollie and simply turned back to the curtain, pulling it to the side.

Wells didn't pursue the question.

Stanley watched, but did not see, the man named Larry roll the dolly onto the back of the truck, then sign four sheets of foolscap on the skinhead delivery man's clipboard. He did not see it because his mind was working overtime dealing with how Ollie would berate him at dinner for his slip.

He watched, blindly, as the driver closed the truck door with a sharp "bang," just as Larry closed the loading dock door with an equal amount of noise. It was as if they were competing with each other. Both snapped heavy-gauge locks on the bottom latches of the doors. Then, Larry waved as the truck pulled smoothly away from the single-door loading dock, before turning and reentering the building by the lighted door to one side of the dock. It made Stanley feel a bit more comfortable about the transfer. It seemed like they did this sort of thing all the time.

Stanley turned back to the room as Ollie said, "Thank you, Tommy, for everything," extending his hand.

Tommy Wells reached out and took it, carefully, never knowing what to expect. He had worked with these sorts of men for years without problems, but this entire job had been messy from start to finish.

It had been quick. It had been messy, obviously, given the news reports, and they had only brought back one of the guns. The MPK5. The Walther was still kicking around somewhere in Vail. Nasty little loose end, there.

No tie to him, at least directly, but he hated having loose ends.

Wells turned and extended his hand to Stanley.

Stanley ignored him, focusing on Ollie, obviously upset by the recent news, leaving the fishy palm of the bondsman floating in mid-air for a moment until Wells dropped it, uncomfortably, to his side.

"Come on, pal," Stanley said, quietly, "we have a plane to catch."

Ollie nodded and turned toward the door. The two stepped out, Wells following at a short distance, then stopping in his office door and leaning on the jamb. He watched the two as they walked down the concrete steps to the landing at the loading dock, then stepped over quietly to the door beside it.

As they stepped through and into the night, Wells felt a great weight lift off him. Five bodies. The gunshot, the strangulation and the stabbing victims for sure. The car wreck wasn't them. Probably not the lion, either. But who knew? These guys had a rep for creativity.

He ran his hands down the sides of his pants.

They were both wet enough to leave a streak.

※

STANDING OUTSIDE IN THE DARKNESS OF A COOL SEPTEMBER EVENING, STANLEY looked at Ollie and said, quietly, "I'm sorry, pal. I'm sorry about her."

"I know. So am I, Stan. In this whole goddamned mess, so am I. Shouldn't be. But I am."

Ollie stepped around to the passenger side of the rental car, unlocked the door and tossed Stanley the keys.

"You drive."

"Don't know how to get there."

"One block up to Colfax, west to I-25 North, then follow the signs."

"Okay, you've got it." Stanley opened the door, slid in, and started the car.

Ollie stood silently beside the open door and stared at the line of mountains to the west, the setting sun outlining them in red and gold and a deep blue, turning to black. He smiled as he stared, his heart filled with the beauty of it all.

"To you, my dear," he whispered. "What might have been. What could have been. I wish we could have learned."

He nodded toward the mountains, almost a bow, certainly a sign of respect, then slid into the passenger's seat of the small rental car.

It pulled out of the parking lot, pausing only a moment before it began the endless trip to Denver International Airport.

❋

POLICE CONTEND THAT THE GANG WAR THAT WAS TO FOLLOW OVER THE COURSE of the next six days, The Telephone Book War (so named, it's believed, because of the approximately four million dollars that had been replaced by some twenty copies of the U.S. West Direct Yellow Pages for the Metropolitan Denver area and delivered in a packing crate to Mr. Angelo Genna of Newark, New Jersey) was the shortest officially declared mob war since the Laundry Soap War of 1947. Within twelve hours of declaring it, the man who had declared it, the aforementioned Mr. Genna, reputed mob boss, was dead, having run screaming from his bedroom into the sights of the heavily armed and tightly wound bodyguards dozing in his suburban living room.

He was wearing nothing but a Hawaiian shirt.

Police have no theories as to who or what so frightened Mr. Genna, and don't particularly care.

Mr. Genna is dead.

The case is considered closed.

❋

SIX MONTHS AFTER THE END OF THE TELEPHONE BOOK WAR, IN DENVER, THE self-capitalized manufacturing firm of Bosco Bikes was incorporated with three-and-a-half million dollars in operating funds.

It took Hootie nearly two years to grow back his hair.

ABOUT THE AUTHOR

GREG MOODY IS A NOVELIST, AWARD WINNING TELEVISION REPORTER and newspaper columnist. His love of cycling began in the Midwest as a child on a cast-iron two-wheeler that he rode, much to his mother's dismay, miles from his home. He now lives in Littleton, Colorado, with his wife and two daughters. He dreams of owning a bicycle so wonderful he's afraid to ride it. His other novels include *Two Wheels* and *Perfect Circles*.